THE EMERGENCE
OF LATIN AMERICAN
SCIENCE FICTION

THE EMERGENCE OF LATIN AMERICAN SCIENCE FICTION

RACHEL HAYWOOD FERREIRA

WESLEYAN UNIVERSITY PRESS *Middletown, Connecticut*

WESLEYAN UNIVERSITY PRESS
Middletown CT 06459
www.wesleyan.edu/wespress
© 2011 Rachel Haywood Ferreira
All rights reserved
Manufactured in the United States of America

Wesleyan University Press is a member of
the Green Press Initiative. The paper used in
this book meets their minimum requirement
for recycled paper.

Library of Congress Cataloging-in-Publication Data
Haywood Ferreira, Rachel
The emergence of Latin Amercian science fiction /
Rachel Haywood Ferreira.
    p. cm.—(Early classics of science fiction)
Includes bibliographical references and index.
ISBN 978-0-8195-7081-9 (cloth : alk. paper)—
ISBN 978-0-8195-7082-6 (pbk. : alk paper)
 1. Science fiction, Latin American—History and
criticism.   2. Science fiction, Brazilian—History
and criticism.   4. Science fiction, Mexican—History
and criticism.   I. Title.
PQ7082.S34H39 2011
863'.087620998—dc22   2010034595

5 4 3 2 1

CONTENTS

List of Illustrations / *vii*
Acknowledgments / *ix*

Introduction: Latin American Science Fiction Discovers Its Roots / *1*

CHAPTER 1. Displacement in Space and Time:
The Latin American Utopia and Dystopia / *15*
    Fósforos-Cerillos, "Mexico in the Year 1970" / Joaquim Felício dos Santos, *Pages from the History of Brazil Written in the Year 2000* / Eduardo Ladislao Holmberg, *The Marvelous Journey of Mr. Nic-Nac . . .* / Eduardo de Ezcurra, *In the Thirtieth Century* / Godofredo Barnsley, *São Paulo in the Year 2000 . . .* / Eduardo Urzaiz, *Eugenia*

CHAPTER 2. The Impact of Darwinism:
Civilization and Barbarism Meet Evolution and Devolution / *80*
    Augusto Emílio Zaluar, *Doctor Benignus* / Eduardo Ladislao Holmberg, *Two Factions Struggle for Life* / Leopoldo Lugones, "Essay on a Cosmogony in Ten Lessons," "The Origin of the Flood," "Yzur" / Joaquim Manuel de Macedo, "The End of the World" / Aluísio Azevedo, "Demons" / Amado Nervo, "The Last War" / Martín Luis Guzmán, "How the War Ended in 1917"

CHAPTER 3. Strange Forces: Exploring the Limits of Science / *130*
    Eduardo Ladislao Holmberg, *Two Factions Struggle for Life* [coda] / Carlos Olivera, "Death at a Fixed Hour" / Leopoldo Lugones, "The Omega Force," "Psychon," "An Inexplicable Phenomenon," "Viola Acherontia," "Metamusic" / Miguel Cané, "The Harmonies of Light" / Juana Manuela Gorriti, "He Who Listens May Hear—To His Regret: Confidence of a Confidence" / Pedro Castera, "A Celestial Journey," *Querens* / Amado Nervo, *The Soul-Giver*, "The Sixth Sense"

CHAPTER 4. The Double: From Science to Technology / *172*
   Eduardo Ladislao Holmberg, "Horacio Kalibang or The Automatons" / Alejandro Cuevas, "The Apparatus of Doctor Tolimán" / Horacio Quiroga, *The Artificial Man*, "The Portrait," "The Vampire"

Conclusion: A Global Genre in the Periphery / *217*

Chronology: Latin American Science Fiction through 1920 / *225*
Notes / *231*
Bibliography
   Primary Texts / *257*
   Secondary Sources / *266*
Index / *283*

ILLUSTRATIONS

Figure I.1
The Arts in This Century by Aurelio Giménez, *Caras y Caretas*, 1901 / 2

Figure I.2
Housework in the New Century by Urtubey, *Caras y Caretas*, 1901 / 4

Figure I.3
Locomotion in the 20th Century by Francisco Fortuny, *Caras y Caretas*, 1901 / 7

Figure 1.1
Chart on the Evils of the Corset, *São Paulo in the Year 2000*, 1909 / 62

Figure 1.2
Celiana on the cover of *Eugenia*, 1919 / 71

Figure 1.3
The male gestators of the twenty-third century, *Eugenia*, 1919 / 73

Figure 1.4
Eugenic couple, Ernesto and Eugenia, *Eugenia*, 1919 / 75

Figure 1.5
The end of war, *Eugenia*, 1919 / 77

Figure 2.1
Journey of Doctor Benignus (map) / 89

Figure 2.2
Arachnids by Eduardo Ladislao Holmberg, 1881 / 94

Figure 3.1
Prolonging Life, advertisement for Magneteopathy, *Caras y Caretas*, 1910 / 134

Figure 4.1
Donissoff, Sivel, and Ortiz create a rat, *The Artificial Man*, 1910 / 196

Figure 4.2
The three scientists and the subject to be tortured, *The Artificial Man*, 1910 / 201

Figure 4.3
Biógeno, *The Artificial Man*, 1910 / 203

Figure 4.4
Deaths of Donissoff and Biógeno, *The Artificial Man*, 1910 / 205

ACKNOWLEDGMENTS

This book has been over ten years in the making, and writing it would have been impossible without an especially broad network of people. I owe many debts of gratitude for the materials, information, enthusiasm, and intellectual and moral support of more people and institutions than can be listed here.

I would like to thank Iowa State University and Yale University for supporting this project from the research through the publication stage. An Iowa State University Publication Subvention Grant has been immensely helpful, along with an ISU Center for Excellence in the Arts and Humanities Fellowship for Scholarship and Creativity and five College of Liberal Arts and Sciences Small Grants. Support from Yale included a Cleanth Brooks Fellowship in the Humanities, a John Perry Miller Award, a C. Malcolm Batchelor Award in Memory of Adalenie Morales, and a Hewlett Award.

I owe special debts to the following librarians and libraries: César Rodríguez, Curator of the Latin American Collection, and Jeffry Larson, Librarian for Romance Languages and Literatures, Linguistics, and Classics at Sterling Memorial Library, Yale University; Marta Palchevich and Luis Pestarini at the Biblioteca del Congreso, Buenos Aires, Argentina; the Academia Argentina de Letras; the Biblioteca Nacional do Brasil, in particular the Divisão de Informação Documental, directed by Eliane Perez, as well as the Secção de Periódicos and the division of Obras Raras; Regina Porto and the Casa de Rui Barbosa in Rio de Janeiro, Brazil. In the Interlibrary Loan unit of Parks Library at Iowa State, the efforts of Dr. Wayne Pedersen and his staff in obtaining rare primary source materials have been nothing short of heroic.

A number of texts consulted in writing this book are available only in private collections. Much information about Latin American science fiction is archived only in the memories of individuals. In all my research in Latin America and the United States, no one has ever refused an interview (or two, or three), and I am overwhelmed by people's generosity with their time and their materials. Particular thanks are due to Eduardo Carletti, Braulio Tavares, and Roberto de Sousa Causo, without whom the remainder of this list would be much shorter.

ACKNOWLEDGMENTS

In Argentina, special thanks to Eduardo Carletti and the members of the Taller de ciencia ficción argentina. Many thanks as well to Pablo Capanna, Gastón Gallo of Simurg, Elvio Gandolfo, Guillermo García, Carlos Gardini, Sergio Gaut vel Hartman, José Antonio López Cancelo, Marcelo Montserrat, Horacio Moreno, and Francisco Solano López. In Brazil, additional thanks to Gerson Lodi-Ribeiro, Gumercindo Rocha Dórea, R. C. Nascimento, Marcelo Simão Branco, Ataide Tartari, Humberto Fimiani, and Alfredo Keppler. In Mexico, Mauricio-José Schwarz provided key contacts and Miguel Ángel Fernández-Delgado was instrumental in identifying and locating texts. In Latin America and the United States, I am grateful to the community of scholars of international science fiction for their pioneering work in the field and for their support of my own scholarship; their names can be found throughout the text and bibliography of this book. Special thanks to Andrea Bell, Pablo Brescia, Luis C. Cano, M. Elizabeth Ginway, Dale Knickerbocker, and Yolanda Molina-Gavilán.

I would like to express my appreciation to the faculty of the Department of Spanish and Portuguese at Yale University. In particular, Professor Josefina Ludmer was and continues to be all that one could wish for in a mentor. Her advice, the clarity of her critical vision, and her friendship and encouragement I will value always. The support of my colleagues at Iowa State University has also been invaluable. Especial thanks for discussions both theoretical and practical go to Kevin Amidon, John Warne Monroe, Mark Rectanus, and Madeleine Henry. Thank you to Dawn Bratsch-Prince for encouragement, advice, and most importantly for her time.

Thanks to the external reviewers of my articles and book manuscript for their valuable input. Thanks also to Arthur Evans, Suzanna Tamminen, Parker Smathers, and everyone at Wesleyan University Press for their professional expertise and for their unstinting support of this project throughout the writing, revision, and publication process. I am especially grateful to Art Evans for working with me on this manuscript; his insight and his kindness have been truly inestimable. My thanks as well to all at the University Press of New England who shepherded this manuscript through the copyediting and production process.

Finally, I thank my mother for copyediting every early draft of my work. The grace of her punctuation and the accuracy of her whiches and thats are beyond compare, but I am most grateful for her company on the lonelier parts of the road. My parents Carl and Janis Haywood, my sister Kalé Haywood, my mother-in-law Maria Elisabete Roberto, my sister-in-law Tânia Ferreira, my husband Nuno Ferreira Haywood, and our son Lucas continue to teach me the meaning of family. This book is for them.

Portions of the introduction, chapter 1, and the conclusion first appeared in the article, "The First Wave: Latin American Science Fiction Discovers Its Roots," in *Science Fiction Studies* 34.3 (2007). A portion of chapter 2 was published as "By Burro and by *Beagle*: Geographical Journeys through Time in Latin American Science Fiction," in *Journal of the Fantastic in the Arts* 18.2 (2007). My thanks to both journals for permission to reprint the articles.

THE EMERGENCE
OF LATIN AMERICAN
SCIENCE FICTION

INTRODUCTION
LATIN AMERICAN SCIENCE FICTION DISCOVERS ITS ROOTS

RETROLABELING THE EARLY WORKS OF LATIN AMERICAN SCIENCE FICTION

If Hugo Gernsback's first act in the inaugural issue of *Amazing Stories* was to choose the term that would eventually become "science fiction" to designate the type of works that his magazine published, his second act was to use that term retroactively to label—or retrolabel—a body of existing texts that he felt belonged to the same tradition. "By 'scientifiction,'" he states, "I mean the Jules Verne, H. G. Wells, and Edgar Allan Poe type of story—a charming romance intermingled with scientific fact and prophetic vision" (3).[1] Although the genealogy of science fiction has been actively traced in its countries of origin since the moment Gernsback formally baptized the genre,[2] in Latin America this process did not get underway until the late 1960s and continues today. Like all such bibliographical processes, the effort to retrolabel Latin American sf has in part been the result of a desire for the stature and legitimacy that identifiable ancestors bestow upon their descendants. While Latin Americans can point to Northern Hemisphere antecedents for their science fiction and claim that established pedigree as their own, their late twentieth- and early twenty-first-century search for a more direct national or continental sf family tree represents a desire for evidence that science fiction has been a global genre from its earliest days and that Latin America has participated in this genre using local appropriations and local adaptations. This participation is one way in which Latin America has demonstrated a continuing connection with literary, cultural, and scientific debates

1

FIGURE I.1. The Arts in This Century [Las bellas artes en el siglo presente] *by Aurelio Giménez*. Caras y Caretas *118 (5 January 1901), Buenos Aires, Argentina.*

in the international arena. But the addition of pre-space-age works to the genealogical tree of Latin American sf does more than provide its writers and readers with local roots: it broadens our understanding of the genre in Latin America and in other areas of the periphery;[3] it extends our perception of the role of science in Latin American literature and culture; and, together with later Latin American sf, it contributes new perspectives and new narrative possibilities to the genre as a whole.

From the nineteenth century to the present day, science fiction has consistently proved to be an ideal vehicle for registering tensions related to the defining of national identity and the modernization process. These tensions have long been exacerbated in Latin America by the challenge of constructing and/or maintaining a national identity in the face of significant influence from the North and by the uneven assimilation of technology in Latin American countries, which has resulted in a situation that García Canclini has termed "multitemporal heterogeneity" (47). When characterizing Latin American science fiction, however, it is important to bear in mind the differences between the nineteenth century and the twentieth and twenty-first in terms of the production and readership of the genre, the perception of the relationship with the North, and the role of science in the national imaginations.

Association with the genre carried relatively little cost for nineteenth-century authors. Having their work carry the sf label has often been a double-edged sword for Latin American writers in more recent years. If the name recognition of science fiction brings them an easily identifiable genre home and a ready-made reader base, that reader base is still relatively small.[4] Texts carrying the sf label are frequently assumed to be second- or third-string works of pulp fiction, and they often draw charges of being a party to cultural imperialism and of failing to reflect local realities.[5] (It should be said that with the recent boom in the writing and criticism of Latin American sf, and with a shifting of genre tides away from the predominance of shiny, rocket-launched visions of the future, writers and promoters of the genre in Latin America are now better able to defend themselves against such charges.[6]) Prior to the heyday of the pulp era, however, sf was not so thoroughly perceived as an external genre that was unrelated to Latin American realities, nor had such strong links yet been forged between sf and popular culture.

FIGURE I.2. Housework in the New Century [El trabajo doméstico en la nueva centuria] by Urtubey. Caras y Caretas 118 (5 January 1901), Buenos Aires, Argentina.

Contrary to their more recent association with mass culture, science-fictional texts in the nineteenth century were read almost exclusively by the literate upper classes in Latin America. While many writers in the young nations sought to establish and make contributions to their countries' national literatures, it was more acceptable then to have works of Northern writers as literary influences. This was a time in Latin America when the political, economic, cultural, scientific, and even racial characteristics of northern European nations such as Britain, France, and Germany were often touted as models for bringing progress to, or "civilizing," the "barbarous" Latin American nations. The United States was largely viewed as an example of a nation that had successfully incorporated these models. Thus an association with literary genres of Northern origin such as the utopia, the fantastic voyage, the scientific romance—genres that were fast coalescing into the sf tradition—was more likely to increase than to decrease the cachet of a text.

The nineteenth century was also the time in Latin America in which scientific discourse was the supreme guarantor of truth. In *Myth and Archive*, his landmark study of Latin American narrative, Roberto González Echevarría describes what he has termed the "hegemonic discourse of science" as "the authoritative language of knowledge, self-knowledge, and legitimation" in Latin America (103).[7] This legitimating power of scientific discourse would imbue texts written in the nascent science-fictional genre with an additional authority originating outside the texts themselves. As in the twenty-first century, nineteenth-century Latin American nations were rarely producers of original scientific research, so the source of this authority would necessarily carry some association with the North. While Northern influence in science as well as literature is sometimes seen as doubly damning in Latin American sf today, this was much less the case a century ago. In addition, we must be mindful that what is sometimes conceived of as the external component of hybrid/*mestizo*/post-colonial Latin American cultures is not really so alien to Latin American reality. As González Echevarría states:

> It does not escape me that the hegemonic discourse described here comes from "outside" Latin America; therefore Latin America appears to be constantly explaining itself in "foreign" terms, to be the helpless victim of a colonialist's language and image-making.

5

There is a level at which this is true and deplorable. However, in Latin America, in every realm, from the economic to the intellectual, the outside is also always inside.... Latin America is part of the Western world, not a colonized other, except in founding fictions and constitutive idealizations. (41–42)

This is to say, political independence from European colonial powers did not completely divorce Latin Americans, especially Latin American elites, from their European roots.

Latin American scientific, economic, and cultural dependence was also expected to be short-lived. The mid to late nineteenth and early twentieth centuries were times of nation building in Latin America, in terms of institutions and infrastructure, and also of great real and/or perceived national potential. A number of Latin American nations prospered economically from booms in the markets for their natural resources. The dawn of the twentieth century also saw the birth of Spanish American modernism, the first of the Latin American literary movements to resonate beyond Latin American shores. In the sciences, as Nancy Stepan has said, "Latin Americans were still small contributors to science by world standards" (*Hour* 40), but she describes Latin American scientists as "attuned" to European scientific advances, and cites the history of eugenics in Latin America as an example of the region's "generalized endorsement of science, as a sign of cultural modernity, and as a means by which the various countries of Latin America could emerge as powerful actors on the world stage" (*Hour* 36, 40). Texts written in the sf tradition in nineteenth-century Latin America, then, would not have been perceived as pale imitations of imperialistic literary models portraying extrapolated societies based on unattainable technologies, but as works that described the present with the authority of scientific discourse and reached for the brighter future that seemed destined to come.

A better understanding of Latin American science fiction, both early and later, can provide insights into an oft-neglected aspect of Latin American reality, and can also serve to broaden our understanding of sf in general. In the North, especially in the United States, we suffer from a certain myopia in our perception of the world and its literatures. The preeminent Argentine sf critic Pablo Capanna has described this phenomenon as "the incapacity, characteristic of all imperial centers

FIGURE I.3. Locomotion in the 20th Century [La locomoción en el siglo xx] *by Francisco Fortuny*. Caras y Caretas *118 (5 January 1901), Buenos Aires, Argentina.*

in history, to understand what occurs far from the center of power, or how those who live in the periphery think" ("Entrevista" 165). Latin American sf can provide some much-needed correction to our vision; as M. Elizabeth Ginway notes in her article, "A Working Model for Analyzing Third World Science Fiction," "The subaltern or outsider position provides new and varied perspectives on hegemonic cultural production" (488).[8] In his keynote address at the 2007 International Conference on the Fantastic in the Arts, Geoff Ryman speaks of science fiction as a "collective activity," a "continuity," a "mass dream"; he characterizes the science fiction of the center (my term) as suffering from an ethnocentric view of the world, from gender bias, and from a limited view of the role of the "other" (we either shoot it or assimilate it).[9] Ryman then speaks of the potential for science fiction written in the periphery to help the genre break away from its stereotypes and contribute to the construction of a new mass dream. The retrolabeling of early Latin American science fiction is part of a process by which we are recognizing what the work of Latin American writers contributes both to the genre and to that dream.

SCIENCE FICTION, MAGIC REALISM, AND THE FANTASTIC: THE MISLABELING, UNLABELING, AND DUAL LABELING OF LATIN AMERICAN SCIENCE FICTION

While the labeling and retrolabeling of texts as science fiction have been proceeding apace in Latin America, there is simultaneously an inverse phenomenon of mislabeling and even unlabeling. Magic realism and the fantastic are the most common alternative genre labels for Latin American science fiction. Such categorizations sometimes occur for theoretical reasons, which vary in nature from misunderstanding to valid uncertainty regarding the degree of a text's affinity to multiple genres, or for sociocultural reasons, related in diverse ways to the stigma or prestige of a genre label.

Science fiction is a genre with notoriously nebulous borders, and Latin American science fiction has a particularly strong propensity to form hybrids with neighboring genres. The latter is due in part to influences from national literatures, including a number of strong traditions of the fantastic. Hybridity is also fostered by the nature of local reception for science-fictional works. As Molina-Gavilán et al. explain, "Historically, in the absence of sustained attention from the literary establishment, Latin American writers have been free to disregard the more stringent genre boundaries that shaped early sf production in the U.S." ("Chronology" 369). In light of these considerations, some latitude—up to and including dual categorization—clearly must be allowed when discussing genre and Latin American science fiction.

Those who would assert with James Gunn that "Latin America's greatest contribution to science fiction and fantasy (and literature itself) has been 'magic realism,'" however, go beyond acceptable limits of genre flexibility (480).[10] Most Latin Americans and Latin Americanists with an interest in science fiction do not discuss magic realism as a part of the genre or even as a particularly close relative. But more than the theoretical issues of genre delimitation, it is the underlying sociocultural implications of mislabeling science fiction as magic realism and magic realism as science fiction that concern us here.

When Northerners label science-fictional texts as works of magic realism, it is often due to the status of magic realism as the prime export genre from Latin America to the North. This phenomenon can lead to what David William Foster has described as "the often quite seriously distorting image of Latin American literature provided by what gets translated into English (i.e., what satisfies the English-reading public's tastes) and what gets studied by foreign scholars" (v). From a Latin American perspective, Capanna writes of a desire to escape these limiting stereotypes, to show, as it were, the other side of the coin: "The alternative (to magic realism) is what many of us want: . . . to adopt an attitude of critical reflection that permits a less passionate analysis of a reality that, 'magical' as it may be, has its own rationality and its own profound strengths" (in "Coloquio a Distancia" 16). Science fiction is not written as a counterbalance to magic realism—it has far too long a history in Latin America for such a theory to hold any water—but it does provide an alternative angle on Latin American literature and culture. To have an understanding of Latin American science fiction, then, is to have a more complex and complete picture of Latin American reality.

There is also a more deliberate way in which Northerners and Latin Americans alike mislabel science fiction, and this may take the form of denying a text's kinship with the genre. This mislabeling and unlabeling reflect a desire to disassociate a text from the mass or pop culture stigma that can be attached to science fiction. As Ursula Le Guin has put it, "At the moment, most literary critics carefully use terms such as 'magical realism' for fantasies they approve of, and take no notice whatever of the popular and commercial forms of fantasy" (29).

Magic realism is not the only alternative label here. In the United States, writers and publishers of science-fictional texts may seek to locate their works in the "Fiction/Literature" section in the bookstore rather than on the "Science Fiction/Fantasy/Horror" shelves out of a desire to be taken more seriously in certain intellectual circles and to reach a potentially broader cross section of the reading public. This instinct is all the stronger in Latin America, in light of the lesser degree of academic acceptance of science fiction and of the reduced possibilities for genre texts to achieve mainstream crossover. Even in Brazil, where magic realism—and the fantastic—holds far less sway than in Spanish America (Ginway, *Brazilian* 29), both publishers and authors of sf have been attracted to magic realism as a genre label because of the marketing power it has attained since the 1970s and because "'science fiction' had strong North American connotations, whereas 'magical realism' suggested the possibility of a literature more closely identified with Latin American cultural roots" (Tavares, *Fantastic* 6).

The more firmly established tradition of the fantastic as a genre in many Latin American countries, as well as its more canonical literary pedigree, has made it a particularly attractive alternative option to science fiction. We must first clarify that, when used in reference to Hispanic American literature, the term "literatura fantástica" usually indicates a narrower corpus of works than by the Northern use of "fantastic" as a blanket term for sf, fantasy, and "all forms of human expression that are not realistic" (Westfahl 335). Works of the Spanish American fantastic tend to be in the vein of the Todorovian fantastic and its adjacent genres, though the origins of the tradition in Latin America are found much earlier in the gothic and in the powerful influence exerted by Poe and others on Latin American fiction. The fantastic generally flows well within or quite near to mainstream fiction in Latin America, and it is with this in mind that Sergio Gaut vel Hartman asks his fellow Latin American writers of science fiction: "Why don't we huddle under the generous wing of 'the fantastic,' obtaining the favor of the 'general public' and avoiding being catalogued as suspects of lese-literature?" (11). Greater prestige and wider acceptance may also be sought by emphasizing links with the work of more canonical authors. Although Borges is often the author of first recourse in these cases in Latin America, it should not be forgotten that Borges did not despise genre fiction or hesitate to champion "the pleasure of adventures" to be found in "works of reasoned imagination" [obras de imaginación razonada] such as Bioy Casares's classic work of Argentine science fiction, *The Invention of Morel* [*La invención de Morel*] (Borges, "Prólogo" to *Invención* 9, 12).

The dual labeling of works as both science fiction and fantastic is perfectly valid and not infrequently necessary. One must, however, be cautious and not overhasty in the unlabeling of works as science fiction in favor of these other genres. Eduardo Ortiz is not wrong, for example, to discuss Holmberg's *The Marvelous Journey of Mr. Nic-Nac to the Planet Mars* (1875–76) as a fantastic text. Ortiz's arguments to deny that the text is also an early work of science fiction, however, depend on a narrowly defined characterization of sf that does not take into account the permeable boundaries of the genre, especially during a time before it had been more rigidly codified by publishers, writers, critics, and tradition ("Transition" 63).[11] When science fiction is excluded from the genealogy of such Latin American texts, valuable tools for understanding and analysis are lost. Examining works through a lens of science fiction underscores the authoritative role of scientific discourse in nineteenth-century Latin America. Without such a perspective, direct literary influences from the sf tradition may be removed from the picture, and the writer's knowledge and intentional deployment or adaptation of the emerging themes, icons, and conventions of science fiction may be missed or misinterpreted. Further, reading a Latin American text within the framework of the genre can shed light on the ongoing exploration of issues of influence, imitation, and originality in Latin American literature and culture. With these thoughts in mind, broad selection criteria were employed for the "Chronology of Latin American Science Fiction through 1920" at the end of this book. The objective is not to parse genre delimitations but to build upon the valuable bibliographical work and retrolabeling processes begun by others and to serve as a reference for those wishing to explore the field further.

THE SCOPE AND PLAN OF THE BOOK

This book examines the early science fiction of Argentina, Brazil, and Mexico from c. 1850 to 1920. The dangers of working as a generalist and a comparativist on this broad topic are outweighed by the dangers of not doing so. Scholars and others interested in early science fiction will find a discussion of new primary sources from this time period. Students of Northern science fiction will find new approaches to the genre and new perspectives on the "first" world and its cultural production. Those with an interest in Latin America will find both a discussion of little-known Latin American texts and a new approach to canonical Latin American texts and authors examined through the lens of science fiction. In deference to the diverse backgrounds of potential readers, I provide explanations of a number of terms, concepts, and events—from "fanzines" to the unique character of the Brazilian monarchy—that may fall more within the realm of expertise of one readership than another.

The geographical and chronological parameters of this monograph have been established to represent patterns of theme and variation in what I have called Latin America's "first wave" of science fiction.[12] Argentina, Brazil, and Mexico are home to three of the strongest sf traditions in Latin America. They hold several elements in common, such as Iberian colonial pasts, heterogeneous populations, unequal modernities, and the challenges of consolidating national identity and unity in the face of direct and indirect Northern influence. All are located on the periphery of political influence and scientific research, yet all have potential for advancement in both arenas. Despite these commonalities, the three nations also illustrate the geographical, linguistic, political, racial, economic, and sociocultural diversity of the region.

The term "nineteenth century" is understood here as an extended period that ends with World War I. The time span under discussion in this monograph—1850 to 1920—falls before the formal recognition of science fiction as a genre in the 1920s and '30s. It encompasses the emergence of early Latin American science-fictional texts in the industrial era, and also the previously mentioned era of the hegemony of scientific discourse—a hegemony that changes in the 1920s (González Echevarría 12). This period can be thought of as including approximately the first hundred years after the abolition of colonial rule in each nation, as well as the first century following the publication of Mary Shelley's *Frankenstein; or, the Modern Prometheus* (1819).

The chapters in this book are organized by subgenre and theme: displacement in space and time, evolution and devolution, the noncanonical sciences and the fantastic, and the figure of the double. There is also a chronological progression, both within each chapter and in the book as a whole. Over the many decades that comprise this extended nineteenth-century cluster of Latin American sf texts, there is a gradual transition from a climate of optimism to one of pessimism: science may not be the guarantor of truth it had long been thought to be, the impact of technology on individuals and society may not be positive, political stability and national potential may be difficult to achieve. Science fiction in Latin America during these years also passes from an elite tradition to a more popular one. Other issues persist throughout the era: the importance of defining and consolidating national identity; tensions between science and religion, city and countryside, and the canonical and the pseudosciences; and finally the production of literary hybrids formed by an endless variety of combinations of science-fictional and fantastic elements from national as well as Northern sf literary traditions.

Chapter 1 examines three generations of texts which employ strategies of cognitive estrangement in order to comment upon modernization, national identity, and political and sociocultural issues of the day. Building on the theoretical groundwork on displacement, the fantastic journey, futuristic fiction, and utopia/dystopia established by critics of

Northern science fiction, these works are examined both in the context of national literary traditions and as part of a more global science-fictional continuum. The chapter begins with a discussion of three foundational works written by authors who were nation builders; these men viewed their texts as agents of change in times when Argentina, Brazil, and Mexico appeared to have the potential to join the nations of the first world. This hopefulness contrasts with the greater pessimism that emerges in the novels from subsequent generations. Eugenic-type discourse surfaced as writers sought new routes toward their visions of national progress and unity. The length of this chapter reflects the relative importance of the utopia in early Latin American science fiction as well as the length of the works discussed.

Chapter 2 explores the frequent attempts to amend, challenge, or reverse the tenets of Darwin's theory of evolution by proponents of Lamarckian evolution and Spencerian Social Darwinism. The tensions between these competing conceptualizations of the world were particularly acute in Latin America, where discussions on evolution were often displaced reenactments of the eternal debate on civilization versus barbarism. The first section of the chapter examines two widely differing interpretations of evolutionary theory from 1875, in which each writer seeks to establish the location of the world's modern/progressive/evolved future in his own nation. Portrayals of evolution give way to portrayals of devolution in the works of the modernist, Leopoldo Lugones. Poe's *Eureka* and a belief in Theosophy were the motivating forces behind Lugones's "Essay on a Cosmogony in Ten Lessons" and its literary companion piece "The Origin of the Flood." Lugones's famous ape tale "Yzur" is discussed as his most nuanced exploration of evolutionary and devolutionary themes. The chapter concludes with an examination of four Latin American visions of the end of the world—or at least of society as we know it—of what will become of us and of what we will become.

Chapter 3 examines the limits of the science fiction genre in Latin America through a study of those early texts in which the border between the science fictional and the fantastic is most blurred. The fingerprints of Shelley, Poe, and particularly Flammarion are discernible throughout these works. Their writers question the ability of the canonical sciences either to provide an adequate substitute for religious beliefs or to bring modernization to Latin America. Their disillusionment with the empirical sciences leads them to suggest practices such as Magnetism, Spiritism, Theosophy, and the use of sundry "strange forces" as viable alternatives for attaining and extending knowledge. The relative credibility enjoyed by the less canonical sciences in the nineteenth century, and the degree to which their proponents employed and promoted the scientific method, draw these texts closer to the realm of science fiction and, at the same time, expand the genre's borders in Latin America.

Chapter 4 traces the passage of science fiction in Latin America from an elite to a more popular genre. This process is exemplified by a series of texts that deal with the creation of a double. The critical framework for this chapter is Beatriz Sarlo's discussion of Argentina's transition from a university-based science accessible to few to a technology that finds its way into the home workshops of the masses. In this progression, the more erudite and theoretical science of a Holmberg or a Lugones becomes the more popularized and practical technology of a Quiroga. Holmberg's 1879 "Horacio Kalibang" is a Hoffmann-influenced tale in which a mechanically constructed secret army of automata gradually overtake the world, replacing both stranger and friend. By 1910 Horacio Quiroga is writing of a biologically constructed double in *The Artificial Man*, his modernization and Latin Americanization of Shelley's *Frankenstein*. But the success of Quiroga's builders of men soon turns to ashes, as does that of Cuevas's Dr. Tolimán, in a Mexican tale of an apparatus that can bring the dead back to life. In a coda to the chapter, two other tales of the double by Quiroga reflect trends and traditions in technology and in Latin American science fiction at the close of the extended nineteenth century.

DISPLACEMENT IN SPACE AND TIME THE LATIN AMERICAN UTOPIA AND DYSTOPIA

FOUNDATIONAL UTOPIAS

Three of the earliest works of Latin American science fiction are "Mexico in the Year 1970" [México en el año 1970], hereafter "Mexico 1970" (Mexico, 1844), by the pseudonymous author Fósforos-Cerillos; *Pages from the History of Brazil Written in the Year 2000* [*Páginas da história do Brasil escripta no anno de 2000*], hereafter *Brazil 2000* (Brazil, 1868–72), by Joaquim Felício dos Santos (1828–95); and *The Marvelous Journey of Mr. Nic-Nac to the Planet Mars* (complete title: *The Marvelous Journey of Mr. Nic-Nac in Which Are Recounted the Prodigious Adventures of This Gentleman and Are Made Known the Institutions, Customs and Preoccupations of an Unknown World: A Spiritist Fantasy* [*Viaje maravilloso del Señor Nic-Nac en el que se refieren las prodijiosas aventuras de este señor y se dan á conocer las instituciones, costumbres y preocupaciones de un mundo desconocido: Fantasía espiritista*]), hereafter *Nic-Nac* (Argentina, 1875–76), by Eduardo Ladislao Holmberg (1852–1937). When they were originally published, readers would certainly have recognized the "loose bonds of kinship" between these texts and those written by the founding fathers and mothers of Northern sf (Stableford, *Scientific Romance* 4). The clearest indications of these kinships are the use of the tropes of time and space displacement, direct citations of the works and ideas of Northerners in the texts themselves, and the advertisement published by the newspaper *El Nacional* promoting the forthcoming book version of *Nic-Nac* as a narrative that would awaken "the same interest as any of the best novels of this genre coming from the pen of the popular Jules Verne"

(Mar. 13, 1876). Only in the last fifteen years, however—after over a century of being lost and found and re-lost and re-found—have "Mexico 1970," *Brazil 2000*, and *Nic-Nac* come to be definitively and universally recognized and retrolabeled as some of the first examples of the genre in Latin America.[1] In recent years the three have frequently been cited as such; the individual texts have often been referred to in prefaces and articles—and occasionally been analyzed in greater detail—but they have never been considered in conjunction. Before continuing to a detailed examination of the uniqueness of each text, it might be useful to outline some of the parallels among these three works.[2]

Northrop Frye has said, "The utopia form flourishes best when anarchy seems most a social threat" (27). These three utopian texts all emerged during conditions of national unrest (with at least two of them published in specific response to political events) although, as has been discussed, a more ideal society seemed to lie just over the horizon. All of the tales set their utopian societies in locations remote either in time or in space, using these devices of displacement to achieve Suvin's effect of cognitive estrangement of the writer's own reality. All are, to use Lyman Tower Sargent's terminology, satirical utopias, depicting "a non-existent society described in considerable detail and normally located in time and space that the author intended a contemporaneous reader to view as a criticism of that contemporary society" ("Three Faces" 9). As Suvin puts it, a utopia's "pointings reflect back upon the reader's 'topia'" (51).[3]

These texts, then, sought to pinpoint areas that required improvement in order for their nations to join the forefront of world progress and take what their writers felt to be their rightful places near the center of the international stage. Thus, the oft-cited function of the science-fictional text as an agent to bring about change would have been especially attractive to our three writers, as all were active participants in the processes of nation building and consolidation in their home countries.[4] All three writers were also abreast of the scientific and technological advances of the day, and they viewed these advances as one of the principal means to national progress. Lastly, all were writers for national or regional newspapers and magazines, and at least two of the three were also editors. All three were originally published in these rather ephemeral media and—even as utopias, futuristic fictions, or serial publications of fiction go—they are particularly localized both temporally and geographically. The works were in fact so narrowly time-stamped and place-stamped that they were less about showing the world a broad vision of utopia that happens to be set in or related to Latin America than about bringing Latin American nations forward, catching them up to Northern nations. Once this was accomplished, our writers appear to be saying, Latin Americans would be able to describe (or be described by) more general visions of what was to come.

As is often the case in utopian tales, all three texts are, to varying degrees, framed narratives. The nineteenth-century or Earth-based outer frames work together with other metafictional, realistic, and fantastic narrative devices—such as footnotes, epigraphs, sessions of Spiritism, and the inclusion of real, extrapolated, and fabricated texts, events, and figures—to emphasize their own fictionality while at the same time claiming the authority lent by their use of historical fact and scientific discourse.[5] The narrative frames also create what Alkon has described as "a twofold narration that proceeds simultaneously along [two different] time tracks": a "double temporal perspective" in the case of our two futuristic fictions, a double spatial perspective in the case of the planet-hopping *Nic-Nac* (*Origins* 125).[6] It is no coincidence that *Don Quijote* is mentioned directly in two of the texts, not for the science-fictional episode of the cosmic voyage aboard the horse Clavileño described by Marjorie Hope Nicolson in her *Voyages to the Moon* (18–19), but rather for Cervantes's magisterial use of the framed narrative and for the episode of the marvelous journey into the Cave of Montesinos.

The sociocultural, political, and literary influences of Europe and the United States are central to the form and content of these works. All of the authors portray the estranged, utopian versions of their own nations as strong, politically independent, culturally rich, and globally important,[7] yet each text betrays in some way the legacy of the deeply ingrained culture of dependency: either the Latin American nation in question maintains this high level of "civilization" with some sort of European and/or North American support, or the authority or approval of the North is symbolically required to legitimize and seal the Latin American success. While the influence of Latin American writers is surely important in our three texts, that of Northern writers is at least as strong, particularly that of Northern writers of proto- and early science fiction. Flammarion is mentioned by name in *Nic-Nac*, and the works of Kepler, Mercier, Poe, and Verne, among others, likely influenced our writers in terms of their use of the fantastic voyage, of a specific future setting for utopia, of travel through time and space via medium or spiritist, of scientific detail and didacticism, of extrapolation from the present, and of the combination of real and fictitious characters and events. Other themes that appear in most or all of our texts reflect each writer's vision of progress for his Latin American nation: individual merit to be valued more highly than one's inherited title or class or race; the involvement or integration of different races and immigrant groups into national life; the importance of education and literacy; the political as well as the economic and cultural benefits of new technologies of transportation and communication; and the necessity of a free press.

But it is time to let each text speak for itself.

Fósforos-Cerillos, "Mexico in the Year 1970"

"Mexico 1970" was originally published in *El Liceo Mexicano* [*The Mexican Lyceum*]. Although the magazine stopped publication after only two issues (January and May of 1844), *El Liceo Mexicano* was part of a significant publishing phenomenon of the time: the literary magazine. Advances in the technology of typography and economies of scale contributed to the new look, content, and popularity of the "revista literaria" in 1840s Mexico. According to a study of publishing trends in Mexico during this time period, this type of magazine generally "reproduced the latest in letters, the sciences, and the arts from Europe and the United States," and eventually works by national writers as well; the contents were "miscellaneous, instructive, and entertaining" (Suárez de la Torre 584). In the introduction to their first issue, the editors of *El Liceo Mexicano* declared their *raison d'être* to be nothing less than "to make the multitude ... well acquainted with useful discoveries, with progress in the sciences, and with the steps being taken on the path that must lead to the perfection of man's knowledge" ("Introducción" 3).

The two pages of "Mexico 1970" appeared amidst four-hundred-plus pages of other "perfecting" articles on topics ranging from railroads, the daguerreotype, aviation, and electricity to hygiene and education, to Mexican history, literature, and figures of note, to poetry, fashion plates, and musical scores. The editors of *El Liceo Mexicano* stated their intentions to emphasize Mexican topics and include "very few translations" (4). Because they wanted the magazine to be accessible to all and "a source of varied and very useful instruction" to their compatriots, they promised that the articles on scientific progress would be "written in a colloquial style ... avoid[ing] the use of technical terms" (3). The ultimate proof that they give of the worthiness of their enterprise, however, was that Europeans recognized the value of this type of publication; the opening lines of the introduction are: "The utility of publications such as this one is universally recognized today. It is sufficient to peruse the voluminous list of publications of this type that are being produced in Europe in order to be convinced of the degree of acceptance which they have merited" (3). As has been noted, Fósforos-Cerillos can be credibly linked with the mission of *El Liceo Mexicano*, as he wrote a number of articles for both issues, varying in nature from the sociocultural to the scientific to the literary. In the opening paragraph of "Mexico 1970" itself, his protagonist don Próspero [Mr. Prosperous] criticizes the majority of literary periodicals from the past (nineteenth) century for lacking just those elements that *El Liceo Mexicano* prided itself for including: articles on scientific and historical themes.

"Mexico 1970" was published during particularly violent times. Between 1833 and 1855, Mexico's presidency changed hands thirty-seven times, with Antonio López de Santa Anna of Alamo fame holding that office on eleven different occasions; this period in Mexican history can be summed up as "constantly teeter[ing] between simple chaos and unmitigated anarchy" (Meyer et al. 312). The text of "Mexico 1970" does not mention the political intricacies of 1844 directly. It takes the form of a dialogue between don Próspero, a man of ninety, and his nephew, Ruperto. They touch on a variety of topics in their short conversation: the importance of specialization in fields of study and work, the death of the governor of the Californias (with no implications that "the Californias" would soon be lost to the United States), a twentieth-century elopement via balloon in a well-lit neighborhood, the punishment of a corrupt politician, and the theater scene in Mexico City with its French acting troupes and Italian opera companies that pop over from Europe several nights a week to perform. The common thread running through this hodgepodge of themes is the writer's desire to reveal the progressive national future that has replaced the retrograde national past. Mexico has left behind the superficial "encyclopedic spirit" of the nineteenth century (Fósforos-Cerillos 347). Sophisticated and efficient transportation and communication networks make it possible for the nation to hear of the death of a far-off governor and have governors of other states gather for his funeral on the same day. Advanced daguerreotype technology allows for life-sized images of the events to be viewed in other cities. Balloons—never mind trains or cars—are the principal means of private as well as public transportation. Corruption in the Mexican political system is now extremely rare, and perpetrators are given the death penalty. National institutions provide a wide range of cultural and educational opportunities as well as social services to the citizenry.

"Mexico 1970" is not a framed narrative per se. There is no actual journey through time, as in many utopias or futuristic fictions, and the dialogue format provides no room for a third-person narrator who might address comments to the contemporary nineteenth-century reader. And yet that "double temporal perspective" is clearly present: the text is, as the Mexican critic Gabriel Trujillo Muñoz points out, "more an X-ray of the Mexico of 1844 than a premonitory fiction about the Mexico of 1970" ("El futuro en llamas" 13). The creation of a de facto narrative frame is carried out via the character of don Próspero and by metafictional means.

Don Próspero's first words lay the groundwork for the constant connection of past and present (or present and future) narrative threads throughout the story: "It is necessary to confess, my dear nephew, that the advances of the 20th century are gigantic in all areas" (347). Fósforos sets 1880 as the year of don Próspero's birth and makes him an eyewitness to the reforms that have brought his nation out of its troubled past and into the mainstream of global progress. This potential great-grandchild to Mexicans of Fósforos's generation is thus the ideal authority to contrast the utopian Mexican society of the twentieth century with the problems of the nineteenth and so to serve as mouthpiece both for Fósforos's criticisms of his present and for his ideas about the correct path to a better national future. Don Próspero continually refers to the past during the conversation: to those inferior literary periodicals, to the bad old days when corrupt politicians were the norm, to the value of a coin collection a century earlier. His final pronouncement closes the frame he opened with his first lines. Here he describes the Mexico City of 1970 as seen through the eyes of a typical nineteenth-century Mexican leader, and he makes it clear that this utopian future is not due to the efforts of such men:

> If one of our *pseudo-great men* from the past century were to come back to life and see in Mexico City 22 theaters, 43 libraries, 164 literary institutes, 32 hospitals; in short, if he were to see 800,000 inhabitants enjoying liberty, salubrity, and inalterable peace in the

most beautiful city in America, he would ask to be returned to his tomb immediately for fear of finding himself confronted on all sides by the curses of men. (348)

Si uno de nuestros *seudo hombres grandes* del siglo pasado, resucitara y viera en México 22 teatros, 43 bibliotecas, 164 institutos literarios, 32 hospitales; en fin, si viera 800.000 habitantes disfrutar de libertad, de salubridad y de una paz inalterable en la ciudad más hermosa de la América, pediria se le volviese inmediatamente al sepulcro por temor de encontrarse por todas partes con la maldicion de los hombres.

The text of "Mexico 1970" also carries out temporal doubling on a metafictional level, in the epigraph and the footnote appended to the tale. The epigraph is attributed to J. J. Mora, one of the possibilities suggested for Fósforos's true identity.

> How many times our great-grandchildren will cross themselves
> When they take the annals of this century
> Into their hands! They will say: "Our grandparents
> "Were discreet, cultured, theatrical:
> "In conversing and writing, they were accomplished men;
> "In self-praise, without equal;
> "But in the midst of so many perfections
> "They were great scoundrels." (347)

> ¡Cuántas cruces se harán nuestros biznietos,
> Cuando en la mano tomen los anales
> De este siglo! Dirán: "Fueron discretos
> "Nuestros abuelos, cultos, teatrales:
> "En charlar y escribir, hombres completos;
> "En alabanza propia, sin iguales;
> "Pero en medio de tantas perfecciones
> "Fueron unos grandísimos bribones."

This sarcastic ditty is, then, a perfect gloss of the story itself, as it pokes fun at Mora's contemporaries by referring to their great-grandchildren's future poor opinion of them. It also foreshadows don Próspero's concluding praise of the accomplishments of 1970 that have come about in spite of his predecessors. The other metanarrative connection to 1844 is a single but lengthy didactic footnote that Fósforos cannot resist including. He adds the note to explain that his portrayal of Mexico City in 1970 as illuminated at night is not so farfetched, as it was extrapolated from experiments with flammable hydrogen bicarbonate being carried out in Paris. Fósforos recounts the details and progress of the experiment, and completely abandons his technologically advanced fictional future to directly address his readers of 1844. "It seems ridiculous to say," he begins, then acknowledges, "The project seems harebrained at first glance"—that is to say, ridiculous and harebrained to someone in 1844. Fósforos ends by assuring the unnamed French scientist that if he imitates the work ethic of Daguerre, his labors are sure to bear fruit.

If Fósforos's primary purpose is to satirize the Mexico of 1844, his intent does not negate the fact that his vision of the national future is fairly optimistic. Although Mexico lacked the infrastructure and the political stability of Northern nations in his own time, a writer in Fósforos's position could envision a leap in development driven by rapid advances in science and technology. Like many nineteenth-century Northern writers of science-fictional texts, Fósforos was up-to-date on new advances in contemporary science. All of the technology that appears in this story was extrapolated from the latest in nineteenth-century inventions: the daguerreotype process had been perfected in 1839, the telegraph was not put into use until the spring of 1844, and balloons would not serve as steerable methods of transportation until the early twentieth century (see also the articles by "F.C." in *El Liceo Mexicano* on electricity [30] and the construction and use of the thermometer [61]). It should also be noted that despite his portrayal of Mexico's tremendous progress in the text, there is a certain shortfall in the daring of Fósforos's vision. As might be expected, not all groups are represented as participating equally in the utopian "liberty, salubrity, and inalterable peace" of Fósforos's future: no mention is made of members of any but the governing class; the issues of race and racial minorities are not addressed; and the only woman in the story elopes to escape a forced marriage with a cousin interested in her dowry. What is somewhat more surprising is that Fósforos has been unable to free himself from the concept of—and possibly the belief in—European ascendancy. In the episode of the governor's funeral, Fósforos shows that revolutions in transportation and communication have served to unite Mexico, but he gives just as much importance to the fact that these technologies also link Mexico more closely with Europe. Although at first glance it seems that the future Mexico is on a par with Europe, the only artists and scientists mentioned in the text are French or Italian, privileging Europeans as the purveyors of culture and science even in this imagined utopia. Perhaps Fósforos believed that national scientific and artistic contributions would come once Mexico had caught up with the North in terms of access to the products of scientists and artists. Don Próspero does speak early on of his hopes that the next Mexican generation "will cause a brilliant revolution in the sciences and arts," now that specialization is the accepted method of study (347), but apparently Fósforos did not believe that 126 years would be enough time to complete that revolution.

Joaquim Felício dos Santos, *Pages from the History of Brazil Written in the Year 2000*

Joaquim Felício dos Santos was a member of a prominent family from the state of Minas Gerais. A lawyer by training, he also worked as an educator, a businessman, a politician, and a newspaperman. He wrote in multiple genres, but he is best known for his historical text, *Memoirs of the Diamantino District* [*Memórias do Distrito Diamantino*], and for the Indianist fiction *Acayaca*; he himself considered his greatest work to be his multivolume project rewriting the Brazilian civil code. Felício dos Santos was the writer, editor, and "the principal person responsible" for *O Jequitinhonha* (pronounced "Zhe-kee-chee-NYO-nya," named for a mesoregion in Minas Gerais), a four-page weekly newspaper based in the city of Diamantina and serving the northern part of the province of Minas Gerais (Teixeira Neves 21). Here he published *Brazil 2000* in almost weekly installments between 1868 and 1872. An ardent Liberal-cum-Republican, Felício dos Santos wrote *Brazil 2000* in direct response to specific political events of the day. It was a biting satire against the Brazilian emperor and his regime, a sort of fictional complement to or "gloss" of the contents of the newspaper's front and editorial pages (Eulálio, "Páginas" 104).

Some historical background is necessary to understand the driving force behind the work of this early writer of Brazilian science fiction. Brazil's path to independence, and the resulting political situation, are unique among Latin American nations. When Napoleon's forces invaded Portugal, King João VI and the Portuguese royal court fled with sixteen thousand of their closest friends to Rio de Janeiro, a move that was, as Skidmore points out, "unprecedented not only in the history of the Americas but in the whole history of colonial exploration" (35). From 1815 to 1822, the state of Brazil enjoyed equal status to Portugal in a united kingdom. In 1821 Dom João returned to Portugal, leaving his son Pedro as prince regent of Brazil; in 1822, with his father's blessing, Pedro declared Brazilian independence and was crowned Emperor Pedro I of Brazil. After his father's death in 1831, Pedro I returned to Portugal to assume the Portuguese throne, leaving his five-year-old son, the Brazilian-born Pedro II, to rule Brazil. The reign of Pedro II, referred to as the Second Reign, lasted for most of the nineteenth century, and is often compared to that of Queen Victoria for its length and stability. The violent rebellions against the colonizer and the internal upheaval that preceded independence and national consolidation in Hispanic America had virtually no counterpart in Brazil.

Brazilian development during the Second Reign looked good on paper: factories were built at an increasing rate, railroad tracks and telegraph lines expanded rapidly, and the steamship reduced what had been a two- to three-month trip up the Amazon to a mere nine days.[8] A look beyond the numbers, however, reveals that this economic growth benefited only a wealthy few; independent Brazil continued the colonial pattern of dependency both within its borders and in its relationship with Europe. Land ownership remained in the hands of an elite minority and the expanding railroads, instead of serving to unify the far-flung provinces of the vast Brazilian empire, "generally ran between plantation and port. Thus, they helped to speed exports to market rather than . . . to create an internal economic infrastructure" (Burns, *History* 160–61). Brazil extended telegraph lines to Europe (1874) before sending lines to its nearest neighbors (Montevideo in 1879, Buenos Aires in 1883) or to many of its own provinces. This process of quantitative growth without real qualitative development contributed to the phenomenon of unequal modernity that persists in Brazil today. The Second Reign lasted until 1889, when Pedro, much weakened physically and politically, ceded power to junior military officers who rose up in a nearly bloodless coup.

Felício dos Santos had halted publication of *O Jequitinhonha* in order to attempt to change the Brazilian political situation from within. He was elected to a term in the legislature of the Empire of Brazil for 1864–66, but left government in frustration after only a few months, as his attempts at political reform were virtually ignored. By the late 1860s the first cracks in the national political situation were already becoming visible. Brazil was embroiled in a costly war with Paraguay (1865–70) for which Dom Pedro II took much of the blame at home. When Pedro II invited the Conservative rather than the Liberal Party to form a government in July of 1868—in order to consolidate support for a less conciliatory Paraguayan policy than that supported by the Liberal majority in the Chamber of Deputies—Felício dos Santos resumed publication of his newspaper with a vengeance. On August 23, 1868, the first installment of *Brazil 2000* appeared in its pages.

Despite the independence enjoyed by the press at that time, the degree to which Felício dos Santos felt free to attack Brazil's political system and the figure of her monarch in *Brazil 2000* seems surprising. The text has, in fact, been called "the best critique of the monarchy in our country" (Magalhães 252). Some of Felício dos Santos's favorite targets were the alleged nonconstitutional intentions of the constitutional monarch; the institution of the lifelong senate term; the lack of any real difference between the Conservative and Liberal parties; corruption among legislators; the centralization of political power and economic infrastructure to the detriment of outlying provinces such as his own; the war with Paraguay; and the prevailing custom of determining a person's worth based on social class, economic means, royal favor, or race rather than on individual merit. This list is quite particular to the Brazilian milieu, yet has marked similarities to Fósforos's targets in "Mexico 1970." The mordancy of Felício dos Santos's satire can be attributed to his belief that he was publishing in the relative "anonymity" of *O Jequitinhonha*, and consequently that *Brazil 2000* would not reach farther than the newspaper's regional *mineiro* audience (Eulálio, "Páginas" 104). The work was "ephemeral" by design, which perhaps explains why he never republished it in other newspapers or in book form, as he did several of his other serialized works (Eulálio, "Páginas 103). By all accounts, however, this impassioned literary editorial did not go unnoticed at court, and it is likely that his attacks on the monarchy in *O Jequitinhonha*, and particularly in *Brazil 2000*, were the deciding factor in Pedro II's rejection of Felício dos Santos's projected revision of the legal code (Teixeira Neves 26; Eulálio, "Páginas" 107–8).

Brazil 2000 eventually sank into relative oblivion. A few historians and literary critics have revealed knowledge of the text, but only Alexandre Eulálio has written about it in depth. The fragility of the medium on which the text was printed meant that not even Eulálio had access to the complete work ("Páginas" 106n5); for the purposes of this study I have been able to read the majority of the text and Eulálio's summaries of most of the remainder.[9] Although we do not have either the beginning or a true ending to the text of *Brazil 2000*—Eulálio tells us that the text peters out in late 1872, rather than ending definitively ("Páginas" 103)—we do have something almost as good. On November 22, 1862, Felício dos Santos published a short story in *O Jequitinhonha* entitled "A History of Brazil Written by Dr. Jeremias in the Year 2862" [A História do Brasil escrita pelo Dr. Jeremias no Ano de 2862], which I have examined in greater detail elsewhere ("Emergence" 155–63). According to Eulálio and to my own reading of the text, "Dr. Jeremias 2862" is the seed of what eventually became *Brazil 2000* ("Páginas" 106). Both "Dr. Jeremias 2862" and *Brazil 2000* are futuristic utopias, and the narrative premise of each involves a nineteenth-century re-(pre-)edition of a history of Brazil brought back in time from the twenty-ninth or twenty-first century (with notes, excisions, and commentary by sundry historians, narrators, translators, and historical or fictional authorities from the two time streams). Eulálio goes as far as to call Felício dos Santos a "Jules Verne from the Brazilian *sertão* region" [Júlio Verne sertanejo] ("Páginas" 103), but he does not analyze either of these texts as science fiction. *Brazil 2000* was only definitively reclaimed for the genre by Braulio Tavares in the early 1990s, most visibly in the second edition of *The Encyclopedia of Science Fiction*.

The text can be divided into two clearly defined parts or, to use Eulálio's term, "phases" ("Páginas" 105–6). Phase one runs from August 23, 1868, through December 5, 1869, and phase two from December 12, 1869, through late 1872. The second phase of the text is referred to far more often by both historians and literary critics for several reasons: it is "more action oriented" (Eulálio, "Páginas" 105); it contains the actual time-travel journey to the year 2000; it is the more utopian half of the tale; and it contains Felício dos Santos's often accurate or "prophetic" predictions about the Brazil of the future (Magalhães 252). The installments of the first phase of *Brazil 2000* do not devote a great deal of space to life in the future, but they do not have to in order to be considered sf since they are purportedly *from* the future. These time-traveling pages do not proclaim the progress and scientific advances of the coming years so much as they describe the anti-scientific forces working against progress in nineteenth-century Brazil. We are not shown the wonders of the future republic, but rather the evils of empire which hold Republican forces in check.

Phase one of *Brazil 2000* is an unofficial, nonestablishment version of the events of 1868–69, a version written from the periphery of national power—though not, it should be remembered, from a position of complete powerlessness—and revelatory of the darker side of the empire. What Felício dos Santos's science-fictional history of Brazil's present is able to do (which his historical text, *Memoirs of the Diamantino District*, cannot) is to claim for itself the authority of the ultimate victors, to say that this will be the official history, this will be how today's people and events are remembered in the future. Despite the literary realism of phase one, with its heavy emphasis on dialogues and diatribes, there is also a great sense of metanarrative play. As Alkon has observed, "Where fantasy is avoided, various metafictional devices often play an equivalent role in moving futuristic fiction away from unselfconscious realism" (*Origins* 193). Figures such as a nineteenth-century editor and a translator of the history book from the year 2000 leave clear and deliberate editorial scissor marks and opinions scattered throughout the text. Their interjections provide constant connection with the future-time perspective of the text from 2000 by reminding readers that this is not simply a nineteenth-century history book narrated in an omniscient style, but rather a mediated, retrospective view of nineteenth-century history whose writer and mediators *know* which facts and information have become most pertinent and which opinions and attitudes have proven to be the correct ones. Yet Felício dos Santos is so blatant about his narrative manipulation in *Brazil 2000* that the reader never forgets that this is a *projected* history written with an overt nineteenth-century agenda. Felício dos Santos's satire—as well as his sense of humor—extends to the very notion that an unmediated, ultimate, and true history is possible, and to his own endeavor to persuade the reader that this text is just such a work.

Phase one of *Brazil 2000* is a dystopia in which Felício dos Santos portrays the evils of Brazil's political system, the Paraguayan war, and the usurpers in the new Conservative cabinet. He focuses on the figure of Pedro II as the personification of corrupt, nonprogressive forces that arrogate all power to the central government. To support his criticism, he links Dom Pedro with the outmoded past in a number of ways, using both metanarrative and plot.

First, the writer makes it known that Brazil's monarchical system of government has fallen before the year 2000, and has the emperor himself betray his "true" motivations and character. This is done both in the outer framework of the year 2000 history—in a footnote, one Dr. Sckwthrencoff cites a tradition that "was preserved until the fall of the Brazilian monarchy" (Dec. 5, 1869)—and within the text itself. At one point, the fictional monarch recognizes that the Brazilian people will inevitably unite against him—"Wretches, who one day will decide to rise up and contest the divine prerogatives of royalty!" (Feb. 28, 1869)—although it is never made clear how the year 2000 historian gained this fly-on-the-wall perspective. At other points in the narrative, Felício dos Santos prefers to place this type of insider's view within a citation of a text written by someone else. Most but not all of the writers of these intercalated texts share names with real people. Conversely, most but not all of the texts are completely or partially fictional. On several occasions, for example, Felício dos Santos "cites" from a play, *The Ceará Elections* [*Eleições do Ceará*], supposedly by the well-known writer and newly minted Conservative José de Alencar (1829–77); in scene thirty-seven of this one-act play, Pedro II admits his tendency toward the accumulation of power to one of his ministers:

In monarchies the nation is a great head on a rickety body, all the vitality of the extremities should flow to a single point, the capital. . . . Paris is France; London, England; Saint Petersburg, Russia; Rio de Janeiro, Brazil. Washington goes unnoticed on the world map: it is the capital of a savage, degenerate people, the scourge of nations, who disdain the supreme happiness of government by a crowned brow! (Dec. 5, 1869)

Nas monarchias o paiz é uma grande cabeça em um corpo rachitico, toda a vitalidade dos extremos deve affluir para um ponto unico, a capital. . . . Pariz é a França, Londres a Inglaterra, S Petersburgo a Russia, Rio de Janeiro o Brasil. Washington passa desappercebido no mappa-mundo: é a capital de um povo selvagem, degenerado, a escoria das nações, que desdenhára a suprema felicidade do governo de um testa coroado!

The passage is of further interest for its association of Dom Pedro with Europe (the Old World) rather than the United States (the New World); Pedro II is repeatedly shown seeking approval and recognition from Europe and speaking against the decentralization of power in the United States, a political model that is the bane of his existence.[10] This inversion of Felício dos Santos's own ideas is another example of how he uses the king's view of the world as a foil for his own.

Felício dos Santos also relegates Pedro II and his monarchy to the past by portraying Dom Pedro as anti-scientific and therefore anti-progress, unable to function in the modern world. Felício dos Santos makes this accusation in spite of the fact that Pedro II was a patron of the sciences and something of an amateur scientist in his own right.[11] In *Brazil 2000* Pedro II is represented as a presumptuous dabbler who uses science as an instrument of imperial control, a vain man who believes that a scientific veneer will grant him status and respect from the European monarchs he longs to impress. One of many examples of the king's complete ignorance of all things scientific is given in a (fictional) passage cited from a (fictional) scientific text by a (nominally real) writer. Here Dom Pedro favors a new technique he has read about in a pamphlet claiming it is possible to produce detonators from roasted coffee beans (Feb. 21, 1869). Thus, instead of bringing Brazil to the higher level of technological sophistication required to produce detonators from the usual fulminate of mercury, the king invests national resources in low-tech quackery.

Phase two of *Brazil 2000* functions as an antidote to phase one; it is as much an anti-dystopia as a utopia. Here Felício dos Santos draws an even tighter connection between the two temporal threads of his narrative. In addition to bringing a text back in time, he sends a person traveling into the future. But he does not take the more usual course of choosing someone sympathetic to his own vision; rather than sending a person to admire, learn about, and bring ideas back from his ideal future, Felício dos Santos sends his fictionalized Pedro II.[12] This rather abrupt turn of events begins in the episode of December 12, 1869, which opens with these words from the nineteenth-century editor:

> We owe the reader an explanation of our title—*Pages from the History of Brazil Written in the Year 2000*. How, in the year of our Lord 1869, can you publish fragments of a history book that will not be written for another 131 years?
>
> Devemos ao leitor uma explicação do nosso titulo—*Paginas da Historia do Brasil escripta no anno de* MM. Como no anno de graça de 1869 publicais fragmentos de uma historia, que ainda hade [sic] ser escripta um seculo e trinta e um annos depois?

The editor insists that a text that travels through time should not seem absurd in a world of instantaneous communication through space between America and Europe. He then makes a connection that would resonate with contemporary Brazilian readers: the text of *Brazil 2000* has been brought from the future by a medium. Spiritism had arrived in Brazil via France in the 1850s, and by the 1870s it was enjoying wide popularity among the Brazilian elite (see Machado 68, 92). It is important that Felício dos Santos's choice of Spiritism as a method of time travel be viewed in this context and in the context of typical science-fictional methods of travel through time and space prior to Wells's *Time Machine* (see, for example, Nicolson and the entries on "Time Travel" by Edwards and Stableford and "Sleeper Awakes" by Clute in the Clute/Nicholls *Encyclopedia of Science Fiction*). Felício dos Santos was clearly not a believer in Spiritism himself, and his inclusion of Spiritism in the text should not be construed as a third-world, low-tech alternative to travel via technological means nor as evidence for the common and only partially correct characterization of Latin American sf as tending toward the "soft" sciences and the fantastic.

In a somewhat confused plot twist, the editor's promised explanation of how he obtained the year 2000 history morphs into an account of Pedro II's trip to the future. The monarch's journey through time in *Brazil 2000* is immediately preceded by a (meta)literary experience:

> It was 14 minutes and 23 seconds after 11 o'clock at night. Profound silence reigned in the palace of St. Christopher, everyone slept; only H.R.M. the emperor remained awake. Reclining near a table, H.R.M. was attentively devouring the marvelous adventures of Don Quijote of la Mancha . . . the reading of which is permitted only to great monarchs.
>
> "Oh! If only a prince were allowed to read about the history of his reign in the future!" His majesty broke off. Through the shadows of his thoughts he discerned the pallid figure of a man. It was not an illusion. The man advanced, bowed, and kissed the imperial hand.
>
> "Who are you? Where did you come from? What do you want?" the emperor asked.
>
> "Dr. Tsherepanoff, your majesty's most humble servant. A native of Russia, I have just come from France; I have traveled 9,645 leagues today."

"A madman!"
"No, Sir, I am not a madman. I am a *medium*." (Dec. 12, 1869)

Erão 11 horas, 14 minutos e 23 segundos da noite. Reinava profundo silencio no palacio de S. Christovão, tudo dormia; só velava s.m. o imperador. Recostado junto a uma meza, s.m. devorava attento as portentosas aventuras de D. Quichote de la Mancha, . . . cuja leitura é só dada aos grandes monarchas.

Oh! fosse dado á um principe ler no futuro a historia do seu reinado!

s.m. interrompeu-se. Através das sombras de seus pensamentos enxergou a figura palida de um homem. Não era uma illusão. Este avançou, curvou-se, e beijou a mão imperial.

—Quem és? Donde vieste? O que queres? Perguntou o imperador.

—O Dr. Tsherepanoff, humillissimo servo de v.m., natural da Russia; venho da França, percorri hoje nove mil seiscentas e quarenta e cinco legoas.

—Um louco!

—Não, Senhor, não sou louco. Sou um *médium*.

After Dr. Tsherepanoff gives further evidence of his credentials as medium-to-the-monarchs, he puts the emperor into a hypnotic sleep.

Dom Pedro awakens on January 1, 2000. Instead of discovering the greatness of his legacy, he finds that a Republican government has decentralized Brazil and made it a federation. In the "confederation of the United-States of Brazil," transportation by "aerostatic packet" [paquete aeróstatico] and communication via "electrical telegraphy" [telegraphia electrica] allow for power and influence to be shared equally among all Brazilian cities, towns, and villages, uniting the entire country rather than concentrating power in the capital (Dec. 12, 19, and 26, 1869). In the text of this author from the provinces, Rio is reduced to a virtual ruin, and a statue of Pedro I has been replaced with one of Tiradentes, a Republican hero. Pedro II learns that he was deposed at some point, and that his body lies in a modest tomb in Italy, where most of his descendants are now hard-working farmers. When Pedro II happens to meet a Brazilian descendant, the man knows nothing of the former glories of his line and barely remembers that Brazil had ever been an empire.

Despite a few errors and exaggerations, Felício dos Santos was surprisingly successful in a number of his predictions for the year 2000. Brazil would indeed become a republic in his own lifetime. He also predicted the relocation of the national capital to the geographic center, an end to slavery in Brazil (1888), the population of Brazil in 2000 (within 20 million people), and the creation of a United Nations. But, as Fredric Jameson has noted, "the most characteristic SF does not seriously attempt to imagine the 'real' future of our social system. Rather, its multiple mock futures serve the quite different function of transforming our own present into the determinate past of something yet to come" ("Progress" 152). Felício dos Santos's device of a history of the nineteenth century written in the year 2000 is a literalization of this transformative process. He was far less invested in representing an idyllic future in his text than in using that text to plant seeds of change in his own time. With another of his predictions, for example, he sought to prepare his countrymen for a change he believed to be inevitable. Although he was unable to predict the presidency of Lula, Felício dos Santos did imagine a president of mixed Indian and African ancestry, which was for his time and place an extremely unlikely possibility. Anticipating his readers' rejection of the idea of such a president, he has his fictional nineteenth-century editor argue his case:

> Peace, friend reader; our poor imagination does not come into this at all; it is reality. . . . Other times, other customs. Peoples are like individuals: their ideas, their principles, their tastes, their character change with the eras. The nineteenth century in which we live is not the same as the twenty-first. We say with Voltaire, "what things, what marvels our children will see!" In the twenty-first century color and birth are purely accidental qualities; people consider things from a rational point of view, they heed only the personal qualities of the individual. (*Brazil 2000* 139–40)

> —Paz, amigo leitor; aqui não entra em nada a nossa pobre imaginação; é a realidade. . . . Outros tempos, outros costumes. Os povos são como os indivíduos; suas idéias, seus princípios, seus gostos, seu caráter mudam-se com as épocas. O século *XIX* em que vivemos não é o mesmo que o século XXI. Diremos com Voltaire—que coisas, que maravilhas verão os nossos filhos! No século XXI, a côr, o nascimento, são qualidades puramente acidentais, consideram

as coisas debaixo de um ponto de vista racional; só atendem-se as qualidades pessoais do indivíduo.

Felício dos Santos uses his chosen science-fictional narrative technique to particular advantage here: this is not supposition or invention, it is reality; this is not literary imagination (claims the author's literary invention, the nineteenth-century editor), but historical fact. This is one of the beauties of the time-travel narrative; as Scott McLemee has pointed out in his analysis of Bellamy's *Looking Backward*, the future may be radically different from the time traveler's present, but "there is also the evidence of [the time traveler's] senses: you can't argue with success" (23).

In comparison with Fósforos's vision of a twentieth-century Mexico, Felício dos Santos projects a Brazil that is far more secure in its sense of national identity and far less dependent on the North. Once the Brazilian republic has recovered from the backward conditions Felício dos Santos blames on the monarchy, it finds itself "rivaling the cultured nations of old Europe" (*Brazil 2000* 137). Brazil and other nations of the nineteenth-century periphery are now producers of science and of culture: the mechanism for steering dirigibles has been discovered by an African engineer from Timbuktu (Dec. 26, 1869); Pedro II reads a scientific treatise by Dr. Japoti, a celebrated chemist from the Macuné Indian tribe (139); more newspapers in African languages than European languages are available in the future Brazilian capital (Dec. 26, 1869); and European and North American students come to study at superior Brazilian universities (Mar. 19, 1871). But even though Brazil has become the future and Europe the past, Felício dos Santos cannot quite rid himself of the last vestiges of the mindset of dependency. In what is perhaps an unconscious slip into nineteenth-century rhetoric, a transportation engineer in the year 2000 explains the benefits of connecting Brazil's interior with the coast with the phrase, "Duty-free passage down the river was promoted, opening it [the republic] to the sea, to foreign commerce, to light and civilization" [promoveu-se a navegação franca do rio, abrindo-a (república) para o mar, para o comércio estrangeiro, para as luzes e civilização] (143). Felício dos Santos can see Brazil helping European and other central nations financially, politically, and even educationally, but he still refers to "light and civilization" as coming from without rather than from within.

Felício dos Santos's decision to transform a future history into a time-travel narrative reflects his increasing optimism about the future of Brazil. He himself went from Liberal to full-fledged Republican during his years of writing for *O Jequitinhonha*, whereas Pedro II went from an evenhanded user of his moderating power to a conservatively biased monarch at the head of a long and costly armed conflict. Still, the author of *Brazil 2000* had to live through nearly twenty more years of monarchy, waiting for his country to take what he firmly believed was the key first step along the way to realizing its true potential. Felício dos Santos was a nation builder, but as he began to run out of time to build as he saw fit, he created his own time in which to do so:

> A patriot in a nation that was taking its first steps, surrounded by difficulties of every order, having its aspirations to become a great power curbed by the naturally inferior situation that we [Brazil] occupied in international politics, he turned to the blank page of the future where he would draft his dreams of greatness. In this way he sublimated his disenchantment and his dissatisfaction with contemporary reality at the same time as he spiritedly served his political faction. (Eulálio, "Páginas" 107)[13]

Amid his musings on the wonders of his utopian future, Felício dos Santos writes rather wistfully, "Oh! if only some fairy, medium, or spiritist could prolong our lives until then!" (140). Before Joaquim Felício dos Santos died in 1895, he participated in the industrialization of Brazil, witnessed the abolition of slavery (1888) and the fall of the monarchy (1889), and was elected to a term in the Republican senate (1890).

Eduardo Ladislao Holmberg, *The Marvelous Journey of Mr. Nic-Nac*

Our third text, *Nic-Nac*, was published by Eduardo Ladislao Holmberg in weekly installments in the Serials [Folletín] section of the Buenos Aires newspaper *El Nacional* between November 29, 1875, and March 13, 1876. At this time, Argentina was just emerging from a period of national unrest. The domination of national politics by the caudillos of the mid-nineteenth century had been broken, and the aftershocks of the rebellion of Bartolomé Mitre, the losing presidential candidate in the elections of 1874, were almost over. National institutions were being founded left and right, and the watershed year of 1880, commonly cited as the point at which Argentina achieved national consolidation, was almost in sight. This was a time of great optimism about Argentina's potential for development. "Compared to other Latin American countries," Julia Rodríguez writes in *Civilizing Argentina: Science, Medicine, and the Modern State*, "Argentina was surging ahead. It appeared that the nation had a chance to reach the levels of prosperity and development of its northern neighbor, the United States" (2). The hegemony of scientific discourse was at its height and—as science was perceived as one of the keys to national progress—was accompanied by a pragmatic drive to improve scientific education. Argentina's greatest educational reformer was Domingo Faustino Sarmiento, the republic's second president (1868–74). As part of his efforts, Sarmiento brought foreign scientists to Argentina. These scientists, however, usually published their findings in Europe, in languages other than Spanish, and did not generally devote significant time or energy to training students. It fell to the Argentine Generation of 1880 to improve national scientific literacy and to build the foundation of an Argentine scientific establishment.

Holmberg was a prominent member of the Generation of 1880, although he was also well known in the modernist circles of the subsequent generation. This "shining star of early Argentine natural science" was a licensed medical doctor (Rodríguez 29), an Argentine Linnaeus who worked to catalogue the national flora and fauna, an educator who taught in most branches of the sciences from anatomy to zoology, and the director of the national zoo. He was also a poet, a prolific writer of fiction short and long, and the person often credited with introducing three genres in Argentina and/or Latin America: the fantastic tale, detective fiction, and science fiction.[14] He was instrumental in importing scientific and literary ideas and trends from the North through his professional work and his translations of documents from English, French, and German. He was also a key figure in the movement for scientific and literary autonomy, a founder of the first scientific periodical written and published in Argentina by Argentines (*The Argentine Naturalist* [*El Naturalista Argentino*]), a contributor to a project on national variants of the Spanish language (the *Dictionary of the Argentine Language* [*Diccionario del lenguaje argentino*]), and the author of *Lin-Calél*, an epic poem in the Indianist tradition. Holmberg was not merely interested in introducing the rest of the world to Argentina, but in introducing Argentina to itself. Perhaps Holmberg's "transitional/

border character" [carácter de frontera] (Ludmer, *Cuerpo* 173, translation mine), his location "in between"—between generations, between intellectual disciplines, between national traditions—was what made him such an important national literary innovator and popularizer of science.

For Holmberg and his generation, national development was inextricably linked to the creation of a scientifically informed population. As he wrote in the "Note to the Reader" [Advertencia] of the first issue of *The Argentine Naturalist* in 1878, "The natural sciences, the sciences of observation, should be considered the foundation of modern progress" (qtd. in Pagés Larraya 18). Holmberg saw literature and science as natural partners in this process. "In order to awaken a love for Natural History in the Argentine public," he said in 1876, "it is indispensable to use fairly literary language to present the material, to love science, and above all to always combine the useful with the pleasant" (qtd. in Luis Holmberg 76). It is therefore no surprise that when Holmberg became the one to present Darwin's theories to the Argentine reading public, he chose to do so in a work of fiction, *Two Factions Struggle for Life: A Scientific Fantasy* [*Dos partidos en lucha: Fantasía científica*] (1875; discussed in chapter 2). In addition to defending Darwinism in *Two Factions*, Holmberg also recognizes a number of Northern writers for making science more accessible and more palatable. He cites scientists such as Flammarion and Figuier for their contributions toward putting science "within reach of all levels of intelligence" (70). He also cites writers of adventure and science-fictional tales such as Jules Verne and Mayne Reyd (or Reid) for making science seem more attractive and appealing (70).

The influence of all of these writers is also clear in *Nic-Nac*, which Holmberg wrote during the same period as *Two Factions*. In the tale, Nic-Nac, a doctor, and a supposedly German medium called Friedrich Seele travel together to Mars. Not unlike the Europeans arriving in the New World, two of Nic-Nac's first actions on Mars are to name geographic features after familiar places and to worry that the inhabitants might be cannibals. Nic-Nac and the doctor soon become acquainted with the landscape, beings, customs, and institutions of the red planet. Before Seele—who turns out to be a Martian[15]—leaves the other two to their own devices, he endows each with a phosphorescent aura that will function as a protective shield against any aggression by the natives as well as overcome any language barriers, a sort of nineteenth-century version of the universal translator in *Star Trek* or the babel fish in *The Hitchhiker's Guide to the Galaxy*. A series of adventures follow, including an interspecies love affair between the doctor and a Martian girl, Nic-Nac's visit with the local Martian leaders, and a flight via some unnamed means to the capital city. At many points in the tale the Martians appear to be an advanced, utopian civilization; at others they seem to possess flaws with marked similarities to those of their terrestrial counterparts. The text ends with Nic-Nac's return to Earth, where his efforts to share the lessons of his journey result in his being treated like a modern version of the proverbial prophet in his own country: he is confined to an insane asylum.

The tale of Nic-Nac's fantastic journey has two distinct narrative frames. The outer narrative takes place in Buenos Aires on November 19, 1875, a week before Holmberg's *Nic-Nac* began to appear in *El Nacional*. In this frame we hear the voices of the inhabitants of Buenos Aires reacting to the news that Nic-Nac claims to have returned from a trip to Mars, and we read the latest news bulletins on the matter. Some citizens believe Nic-Nac, calling him "the daring Livingstone of outer space" (3); others refer to his supposed journey as "his harebrained and fantastic excursion" (4). The authorities are in agreement with the latter group,[16] and Nic-Nac is declared mad. Over the next three days Nic-Nac writes the tale of his adventures in order to defend their veracity and his own sanity; his book, *The Marvelous Journey of Mr. Nic-Nac to the Planet Mars* [*Viaje maravilloso del Sr. Nic-Nac al planeta Marte*], is published on November 22. As this frame closes, the third-person narrator turns to address the reader directly, employing language similar to that which Holmberg had used to laud Verne's talents as a popularizer of complex scientific ideas. "In our times," the narrator says, "serious ideas do not fulfill their destiny except when they are wrapped in the mantle of fantasy . . . let us then read Mr. Nic-Nac's book; it may resolve some important matter" [En nuestros tiempos las ideas sérias no cumplen su destino sino envueltas en el manto de la fantasía . . . vamos pues á leer el libro del Sr. Nic-Nac,—quizá resuelva alguna cuestion importante] (7).

The narrator's injunction is followed by the text of Nic-Nac's account, which is a framed narrative in its own right. The frame to Nic-Nac's tale is his own explanation of the mechanism he used for the first known space trip from Earth. Like Felício dos Santos's Pedro II, Nic-Nac achieves his displacement, or "transplanetation" [transplanetacion]

(122), with the help of a foreign medium. Also, as with *Brazil 2000*, this method of transportation in *Nic-Nac* should not be read as an avoidance of technology in Latin American sf. Rocket ships were not *de rigueur* for space travel in early science fiction, and Holmberg undoubtedly modeled the voyage in *Nic-Nac* after that in Flammarion's *Lumen* (1872).[17] Under the guidance of the medium, Seele, Nic-Nac decides to induce the separation of his "spirit-image" [espíritu-imagen] from his material body by depriving himself of "all that might debilitate the spirit by strengthening the material being," that is to say, by starving himself (*Nic-Nac* 18). His declared purpose is to gain a new perspective on the great questions of this life and the next: "It is necessary . . . to liberate the spirit from the weight of the material being and to elevate it essentially to those regions that may serve to resolve the most difficult issues of the Universe" [Es necesario . . . libertar el espíritu del peso de la materia y elevarlo sustancialmente á aquellas rejiones que puedan servir quizá para resolver los puntos mas difíciles del Universo] (10).

The invitation by the narrator to look below the surface of Nic-Nac's fantastic journey for a more serious subtext also has a literary echo in Nic-Nac's choice of reading material during his initial preparation for his trip. Immediately after making the decision to starve the body to feed the soul, he sits down with the same book that Felício dos Santos's Dom Pedro was reading prior to his displacement: "As proof of my determination," Nic-Nac tells the reader, "I spent the rest of the day reading the description of the wedding of Camacho" (18). In the second volume of *Don Quijote*, this wedding is immediately followed by the famous episode of the Cave of Montesinos. Upon being lowered into the cave, don Quijote says, "I was, all of a sudden, overpowered by a most profound sleep" (Cervantes 485). Don Quijote goes on to describe awakening in front of Montesinos's castle and the many marvelous things he witnessed in the company of Montesinos over the next three days, although Sancho Panza informs him he was gone only an hour and that a number of the events his master has described could not have happened. When Sancho doubts don Quijote's sanity aloud, the good knight rejoins: "As thou art not experienced in the events of this world, every thing that is uncommon, to thee seems impossible" (491). In addition to the comedic value of a starving man reading about a feast and to an interest (also seen in *Brazil 2000*) in Cervantes's use of narrative frames, Holmberg includes this reference to the *Quijote* as a second injunction to the reader to look beyond Nic-Nac's apparent insanity to the sense that lies beneath. Holmberg directs our attention from Mars to Earth, from fictional situations to real ones, from utopia to "topia."

Holmberg's Mars fluctuates between a direct analogy for Earth and a representation of a more advanced, utopian society that Terrans would do well to emulate. Chapter 7 of *Nic-Nac*, the first chapter that takes place on Mars, ends with a direct statement that each continent of Mars has an equivalent on Earth (31). Chapter 8 then commences with a declaration of Martian superiority: "Their advances, superior to those of the Earth, have been conquered by means of numerous sacrifices that today place them at the first level among planetary civilizations" (31–32). Nic-Nac again implies that Martian society is the more advanced when he later uses the nebular hypothesis (as H. G. Wells also did over twenty years later in *War of the Worlds*) to state that because Mars is an older planet than Earth, Martian life evolved earlier (61). On the next page, however, he brings the Martians back to the level of Terrans, saying that Martians have evolved at a slower pace (62). The utopian Mars continues to reappear throughout the narrative. There is no illness on Mars; love on the red planet is "more elevated, more sublime" than on Earth (120); Martians are more generous (126). Indeed, at one point Nic-Nac laments the need ever to return to his inferior home planet:

> Ah! What a shame! . . . to arrive at the pedestal of glory and of hopes on the rosiest of the planets, and to return to Earth to contemplate the same storms, the same valleys, the same faces . . . . . . What a shame! To rise so high only to sink so low! (84)

> Ah! qué desgracia! . . . llegar al pedestal de la gloria y de las ilusiones en el mas rosado de los planetas, y volver á la Tierra á contemplar las mismas tormentas, los mismos valles, los mismos rostros. . . . . . ¡qué desgracia! subir tan alto para hundirse tanto!

When Nic-Nac arrives at the twinned Martian cities of Theosophopolis (city of God and of the wise; 48), his visit to the Sophopolis section seems to confirm the utopian characteristics of the planet's inhabitants. Sophopolis is the embodiment of Frye's characterization of utopias as "elite societies in which a small group is entrusted with essential responsibilities, and this elite is usually some analogy of a priesthood.

... The utopias of science fiction are generally controlled by scientists, who of course are another form of priestly elite" (35). In Sophopolis, the Academy of Sciences functions as the seat of government. It is also a substitute for a religious institution; weddings are held there rather than at a church because, Nic-Nac tells his readers, the academy is "a more worthy temple, a more sacred building" (128). At the same time as he elevates the sciences, however, Holmberg turns a critical eye on scientists. He portrays the scientists in *Nic-Nac* as myopically focusing on their special fields of interest and as tending toward interdisciplinary squabbling. Upon witnessing an astronomer and a zoologist bickering, Nic-Nac exclaims, "Poor wise men! . . . They are the same everywhere; always ill-humored, and not infrequently irrelevant!" (82). Eduardo Ortiz has persuasively compared the Sophopolitan scientists in *Nic-Nac* with Burmeister and the younger generation of German scientists that Sarmiento had brought to Argentina, whom Ortiz terms the "Córdoba Six." If Holmberg was indeed a "keen supporter of the German scientists" in their disagreements with Burmeister (Ortiz 60), he was also critical of them for staying inside their ivory towers and failing to spread scientific knowledge throughout their host country.[18] Holmberg was more overt elsewhere in his criticism of Argentina's scientific dependency on the North and in his advocacy of his country's becoming a producer of science (*Two Factions* 90, 113, 133; Luis Holmberg 4). In *Nic-Nac* he limits his commentary on the matter to the above-mentioned rather negative characterization of scientists and to the fact that, in the narrative, all scientists—canonical and occult, fictional and actual, identified and implied—are associated with the North: Seele, Gould, Flammarion, Burmeister, and the "Córdoba Six."

But if Nic-Nac describes Sophopolis, the semi-utopian "city of the wise," as a place where "the light is of a white or rosy cast, and a pleasant yet at the same time rigorous majesty seems to have traced the lines of the buildings" (49), he does not characterize Theopolis, "the city of God," as such a model: "The doors of the houses almost never open; a profound silence reigns during the day, interrupted only by the creaking, or rather the lamentations of some instruments that the inhabitants of Earth would call bells . . . and by the sacred choirs that no one understands, because if they were understood they would lose their eminently mystical character" (48). To the Argentine reader of Holmberg's time, as well as to the alert reader of today, Theosophopolis clearly represents the Argentine city of Córdoba, famous as the seat of the Jesuits in Argentina and home of the Academy of Sciences of Córdoba, founded in 1874. In his personal life Holmberg was a skeptic; publicly he attacked religious hypocrisy and intolerance rather than religion itself. In *Nic-Nac* he is not interested in placing science above religion, but rather in mutual respect between the two, a respect he saw as one-sided in Argentina at that time: "The Sophopolitans viewed the inhabitants of Theopolis as their equals, but the latter, in their heart of hearts, saw an inferior in each Sophopolitan" (75). Holmberg's criticisms of religion in *Nic-Nac* are limited to the ostentatious, opaque, intolerant brand of Christianity practiced by the Theopolitans; unlike other Martian Christians, Seele explains to Nic-Nac,

> the characteristic feature of their life is the exaltation of an abominable quality: hypocrisy; and this quality, converted by them into dogma, has brought more evils to Mars than all of the Martial/Martian wars and abuses. (73)

> el rasgo característico de su vida es la exaltacion de una cualidad abominable: la hipocresía; y esta cualidad, convertida por ellos en dogma, ha derramado mas males sobre Marte que todas las guerras y abusos Marciales.

As for his own beliefs, Nic-Nac sums them up with the words, "I am a Christian, but in my own way" [Soy cristiano, pero á mi modo] (97).

From Theosophopolis, Nic-Nac and Seele cross an unpopulated plain bearing a strong resemblance to the Argentine *pampa* in order to reach the capital city of the country of Aureliana (*argentum* becomes *aurum*) on the coast. They find the unnamed capital city, much like the Buenos Aires of the time, divided by the factional squabbling that is, Seele tells Nic-Nac, "so common in countries that have not yet consolidated their internal organization" (145). Nic-Nac claims to have the most impartial view of the situation due to his outsider's perspective; the critical distance of "an extranatural being like myself, yes, I, Nic-Nac . . . who is ruled by the single desire to learn and to judge" (165). Nic-Nac tries to convince the two major factions to value peace and national unity as a route to progress, explaining, "The progress of nations is the favorite son of Peace" (146). He tries to make the factions realize that they are not two groups (on Mars they are given names other than "Nationalists" and "Autonomists") but one (never quite called

"Argentines"). Although this situation is not resolved in the narrative, there is a sense of optimism at the end of the episode. As Nic-Nac and Seele leave the capital to return to Theosophopolis, Seele promises positive changes to come: "Later, when all is calm, we'll return, and you will see such a metamorphosis!" (173).

Once he has read Nic-Nac's account, the narrator, who now refers to himself as the "publisher," declares that he is disillusioned and concludes that Nic-Nac suffers from "planetary mania" [Mania planetaria] (186). The publisher does, however, explicitly and implicitly rescue some of Holmberg's "serious ideas" from underneath the "mantle of fantasy" of Nic-Nac's Martian odyssey in this closing frame of the text. Rather tongue-in-cheek, the publisher rejects the veracity of Nic-Nac's means of transportation, but insists that Nic-Nac is to be believed on the existence of life on other planets. Further, he cites the testimony of "brilliant spirits like that of Flammarion" to support Nic-Nac's story (184), and declares in his own right: "The plurality of inhabited worlds is not a fantasy born of a fevered brain, it is a necessity, a conquest of the human spirit, an homage to the greatness of the Universe" (184–85). The publisher also indicates that he sees the Argentines reflected in the Aurelians and understands Nic-Nac's criticisms of them. But why, he asks, must Nic-Nac insist upon presenting his story using "that indefinable vagueness of the concepts, those luminous forms, those indecisive glows" (185–86)? The same could be asked with regard to Holmberg's choice of using a science-fictional "mantle of fantasy" to speak to his audience. The publisher provides answers to both questions when he admits that "all of those elements that constitute the whole tale could not, perhaps, have been expressed in any other way" [todos aquellos elementos que constituyen el conjunto, no habrían podido expresarse, talvez, de otra manera] (186).

THE NEXT GENERATION(S): WHEN IS UTOPIA NOW?

The heading "The Next Generation(s)" reflects both the period in which the three texts considered in this section were written (1891–1919) and also one of the key themes of their authors: the composition, nurture, and education of the next generation of Argentines, Brazilians, or Mexicans. The three texts in question are *In the Thirtieth Century* [*En el siglo XXX*] (Argentina, 1891) by Eduardo de Ezcurra (1840–1902), *São Paulo in the Year 2000 or National Regeneration (A Chronicle of Future*

Brazilian Society) [*São Paulo no Anno 2000 ou Regeneração Nacional (Chronica da Sociedade Brasileira Futura)*] (Brazil, 1909) by Godofredo Emerson Barnsley (1874–1935), and *Eugenia (A Fictional Sketch of Future Customs)* [*Eugenia (Esbozo novelesco de costumbres futuras)*] (Mexico, 1919) by Eduardo Urzaiz (variously Urzais, Urzáiz, and Urzaiz Rodríguez, 1876–1955). Each text is the only known work of long fiction that its author produced. The optimism of the three utopian texts discussed earlier in this chapter contrasts with the notes of uncertainty that begin to creep into these turn-of-the-century novels. During the period in which Ezcurra, Barnsley, and Urzaiz were writing, projects of national consolidation had begun to reveal weaknesses, and the modernization process seemed less inevitable or purely beneficial. All three writers consciously engage in the global science fiction tradition, with direct literary influences such as Poe, Hoffmann, and Verne being joined by more recent Northern writers such as Edward Bellamy and H. G. Wells. Scientific discourse continues to hold sway as an indicator of authority in these science-fictional texts. All three works also demonstrate attitudes of technophilia, although science and technology are often portrayed as not being used to their best potential. Each text utilizes the cognitive estrangement of displacement in time to extrapolate present tendencies or to posit the benefits of change. The authors use the didactic options of utopia and dystopia to educate readers while at the same time expressly seeking to attract the interest of a wider public by writing in a fictional mode.[19]

Despite emerging from national realities that differed in terms of politics, economic situation, racial or ethnic composition, and class distribution, these next generations of futuristic fiction are permeated by the discourse and concerns of eugenics. None of our authors were known eugenicists, and I do not consider that these works' primary motivation was the promotion of the movement. It is important to note, however, that many topics of concern to the field of eugenics were of eminent importance in Latin American nations during these years. Those concerns—particularly as they relate to national progress and national identity—are reflected to some degree in each text; thus, the topics and discourse of eugenics can be useful tools for analyzing each work's roadmap to utopia.

In her groundbreaking study of eugenics in Latin America, *The Hour of Eugenics: Race, Gender, and Nation in Latin America*, Nancy Stepan provides a useful overview of the science of eugenics in the Anglo-Saxon world as well as a detailed comparison of its selective adaptation in Latin American nations. Stepan provides the following definition(s) of eugenics:

> As a science, eugenics was based on supposedly new understanding of the laws of human heredity. As a social movement, it involved proposals that society encourage the constant improvement of its hereditary makeup by encouraging "fit" individuals and groups to reproduce themselves and, perhaps more important, by discouraging or preventing the "unfit" from contributing their unfitness to future generations. (1–2)

Anglo-Saxon eugenics was based on the Mendelian, or "hard," tradition of genetics, in which "human ability was a function of heredity and not of education," but in Latin America, ideas regarding eugenics were by and large based on "an alternative stream of Lamarckian hereditary notions," a "softer" brand of eugenics in which "there was a place for traditional, environmental approaches to the reform of human heredity" (23, 8, 34). Stepan emphasizes that this basis for Latin American genetics was not due to deficient scientific knowledge—indeed, she says, it "was often hidden, even from themselves" (65, 83).[20] Rather, this neo-Lamarckian outlook arrived in Latin America via France, the traditional source for Latin American scientific ideas (72), and perhaps more importantly, this approach to genetics was attractive to Latin Americans because it posited that there were acceptable scientific solutions to their problems. As Stepan explains:

> Politically, neo-Lamarckism also often came tinged with an optimistic expectation that reforms of the social milieu would result in permanent improvement, an idea in keeping with the environmentalist-sanitary tradition that had become fashionable in the area . . . [and it] justified the belief that human effort had meaning, that improvements acquired in an individual's lifetime could be handed on genetically, that progress could occur. (73–74)

This apparent route to "civilization" would have been particularly welcome in a world in which "Latin Americans were, to most eugenists situated outside the region, regarded as 'tropical,' 'backward,' and racially 'degenerate.' Not eugenic, in short" (8).

The three principal Latin American issues addressed by neo-Lamarckian-based eugenics that are of interest here were "racial poisons," population, and national identity. Examples of racial poisons believed to affect the heredity of the next generation were alcohol, drugs, venereal disease, and tuberculosis. Latin Americans widely accepted that social welfare legislation and programs to improve public hygiene would result in the leeching of such poisons from the national genetic makeup.[21] The primary population-related concern in Latin America during this period was underpopulation, stemming both from the historical notion encapsulated by Alberdi as "to govern is to populate" [gobernar es poblar] and also, in the case of our Mexican text, from the huge loss of life suffered in the Mexican Revolution (1910–20).[22] Of secondary importance, a Malthusian concern for overpopulation also appeared to affect several of our future-oriented writers.

The definition of national identity continued to be an issue in Latin American nations during these years, with writers often urging greater national unity or national sentiment. National identity seemed threatened by political and class divisions, by waves of immigration (Argentina and Brazil), or by national minorities (Brazil and Mexico). What seemed lacking was, in the words of Stepan, "a common purpose, a shared language and culture, and a homogeneous population" (105). Several solutions to these woes were proposed, ranging from racial hybridization to a Latin American version of negative eugenics. Racial hybridization was particularly popular in Brazil and Mexico. In Brazil it was expressed as *mestiçagem*, a concept that reached its full development in the work of the sociologist Gilberto Freyre in the 1930s. In Mexico it culminated in José Vasconcelos's concept of a superior *mestizo* race, or "cosmic race" [raza cósmica]. Underlying the melting-pot ideals of these times, however, lurked the desire to "whiten" the national population, a concept expressed as *branqueamento* in Portuguese and *blanqueamiento* in Spanish. As Stepan summarizes the Mexican case: "Equality with diversity was far from being the eugenic goal. . . . the aim was rather to create one racial type" and in the process "a satisfactory myth of nationhood" (151, 147). Negative reproductive eugenics—the aforementioned "discouraging or preventing the 'unfit' from contributing their unfitness to future generations"—rarely took the more extreme forms of sterilization, abortion, birth control, or euthanasia in Latin America as it did in a number of Northern nations (most notably in Nazi Germany but also in the United States); rather it consisted of proposals such as prenuptial tests or certificates for marriage that were designed to prevent unions between—and thus reproduction by—those judged to be less fit (102–7, 122–24, 133–34).

All three of our science-fictional texts contain laundry lists of various racial poisons that must be eliminated to improve future generations. All address problems of underpopulation or uneven population density. All express concern about the composition of the population and about who would marry whom. It is no accident that all three novels end in weddings or unions either celebrated or negated, thus securing a superior genetic heritage and progress for the next generation.

Eduardo de Ezcurra, *In the Thirtieth Century*

Eduardo de Ezcurra was a lawyer by profession, specializing in customs law, and his treatise *Customs Legislation: Concordances, Jurisprudence and Commentaries* [*Legislación aduanera; concordancias, jurisprudencia y comentarios*] went through two editions (1896, 1900). Little information is readily available about Ezcurra's literary production. He is known to have been within the literary circle of Rubén Darío in Buenos Aires; he wrote for the newspaper *La Lira Argentina* [*The Argentine Lyre*], subtitled "Periodical of Literature, the Sciences, and Fashions" [Periódico de literatura, ciencias y modas]; and he dedicated *In the Thirtieth Century* (hereafter *Century XXX*) to Lucio V. López, calling him "my old teacher and friend."[23] Like Holmberg, Ezcurra belonged to the Argentine Generation of 1880, but his *Century XXX* belongs to a later moment in national history. *Century XXX* portrays a generally dystopic Argentine future that reflects the increasingly dire national economic and political situation. President Miguel Juárez Celman's economic policies had led to the crisis of 1890, which was exacerbated by the financial crisis in Britain.[24] Related political unrest had begun to ferment in 1889 with the formation of the Civic Union [Unión Cívica], and this culminated in the Revolution of 1890 in July of that year and in Juárez Celman's resignation.

In response to this national climate Ezcurra composed *Century XXX*, moved, he says in his preface, by "a spirit of true sadness in the presence of the evils that still rule us and the profound discouragement of desperation that weighs upon the morale of men of good judgment" (xi).[25] In his preface and throughout the novel Ezcurra repeatedly speaks of the irony that this terrible situation in Argentina should be occurring "amid the tumult of progress of truth and of analysis of the end of this astonishing century, which has excited universal public spirit" (xiii). He is motivated to write his self-described "essay of criticism and social philosophy" by the very real fear of Argentina's falling further behind, of not participating fully in global progress after the promise of the previous decade (xi).

Ezcurra declares that he is writing in an established—though unlabeled—literary form that suits his purposes, which he lists as: "truth that is allegorical, harsh, raw, naked, but sincere and with patriotic intention" (xiii). Both these purposes and this literary form are repeated in something of an inverted mirror image within the text itself. The apparent frame of *Century XXX* contains the formulation and development of the plan of the protagonist, Andros Cosmos, and his good friend, Filos Sofos, to write their own work of criticism of their nation and society. These erudite and therefore unusual inhabitants of the city of Fisiocrata [Physiocrat] (formerly Buenos Aires) in the thirtieth century had originally intended to write a work of ancient history, but they modified their plan, realizing that such a book would attract only the handful of readers who possess the thirst for learning. Andros begins the following discussion of the parameters of the work:

—Let us consider the material or plot.
—The spirit that rules, of the present thirtieth century, in our country.
—I understand. And the means of conveying this?
—The nineteenth century.
—As discussed. Our century transported to that one. And the observations?
—Criticism.
—And the commentaries or reflections?
—To say that in those times everything was going backward, indirectly referring to our times, which, relatively speaking, are not going any better. (17–18)

—Veamos la materia ó argumento.
—El espíritu que domina, del actual siglo XXX, en nuestro país.
—Comprendo. ¿Y el medio de desarrollo?
—El siglo XIX.
—Lo dicho. El nuestro transportado á aquél. ¿Y las observaciones?
—La crítica.

47

—Y los comentarios ó reflexiones?
—Decir que en aquellos tiempos todo andaba al revés, indirectamente refiriéndose á los nuestros, que relativamente no andan mejor.

Rather than being presented with a true inner frame consisting of the text of this work, entitled *In the Nineteenth Century* [*En el siglo XIX*], we read of Filos and Andros's thirtieth-century fieldwork and witness their discussions about the displacements to the nineteenth century they will carry out in their project. We travel with the two friends from the mysterious, museum-like building where they reside with Andros's wife Parelia and their two children Adamiro and Evalinda to various representative points and events of interest in the city of Fisiocrata. We begin at the theater, where they attend a new comic opera version of *Hamlet*, now titled *Hamlet or the Crazy Prince of Damselmark* [*Hamlet ó el Príncipe loco de Doñamarka*], by the playwright Worse N. Worse [Wors I. Wors]. Next they go to a conference series at the Academy for Mutual Admiration, where they comment on papers given on themes such as journalism in the nineteenth century, women in the nineteenth century and today, and current fashions from the political to the artistic.[26] Other destinations are a public park where they are the only family group with children, a charity ball so lavish that it pushes the charity into the red, and a salon [peluquería] that at first appears to be just another hub of gossip, typical for such locales. In the end this salon yields up don Pedro, the owner, who has been forced into this ignoble profession by political factionalism, and his lovely daughter, Angélica. *Century XXX* ends with the completion of *In the Nineteenth Century*, the retirement of don Pedro, and the wedding of Filos and Angélica.

Ezcurra employs the tools of his "established literary form" throughout the novel. He sets his dystopian society over a thousand years in the future in order to show the consequences of present actions extrapolated to their fullest extent, or as Carlos Abraham puts it, "A recurring idea in Ezcurra is that current problems . . . if not solved, will hypertrophy in the future" ("Género utópico" sec. 4). Filos and Andros reiterate this mission as they discuss the text of *In the Nineteenth Century*, hoping that by indicating the "latent symptoms of disorganization and degeneration" in the past, they will alert their compatriots to the need for change in the present (247). The immediate target of their finger pointing will not, of course, be their contemporaries, as they show themselves to be fully cognizant of one of the principal uses of cognitive estrangement: "No one complains or quarrels because of seeing his vices and his evils attributed to someone else" (247). The two, like Ezcurra, are aware that they are following in the literary footsteps of others, though they note the original structural twist they are contributing; as Andros declares: "I understand, Filos, that something similar was done or written in that remote century, although in place of looking backward, they advanced to our times . . . imaginatively" [Tengo entendido, Filos, que algo parecido se hizo ó se escribió en aquel remoto siglo, aunque en lugar de retroceder, avanzaron á nuestros tiempos . . . imaginativamente] (16, ellipsis in original). Although it is not so clear in the original as in my translation, the allusion here is almost certainly to the enormously influential and widely translated *Looking Backward from 2000 to 1887* (1888) by Edward Bellamy. Ezcurra refers to Northern writers of proto- and early science fiction by name throughout the novel, among them Rabelais, Voltaire, Hoffmann, and, most frequently, Poe. Although he paints a largely negative picture of the future, Ezcurra does not cite technology as a contributing cause. He speaks favorably of factories as "monsters of progress" (278). He shows a technophiliac's delight at inventing advances in transportation and communication such as the "automatic car" [autómata], the "aerial train" [ferro-carril aéreo], the "electric trolley" [tramvía de tracción eléctrica], and the "telephonograph" [telefonógrafo]. He illuminates the streets of the future Buenos Aires with "luminescent asphalt" [asfalto luciente] and gives his characters time-saving gadgets such as the "automatic pen" [pluma automática]. His only technology-related criticism is that its Argentine beneficiaries do not use these conveniences or this extra time to elevate themselves or their nation. In thirtieth-century Fisiocrata, a fire does major damage because of the lack of individual and institutional organization necessary to put it out, and socialites use the twenty-lane avenues to parade their trappings of material wealth in their automatic cars and to pass the time in shallow gossip. Ezcurra was eminently aware of the opportunities that the science-fictional/dystopian genre placed at his disposal, as he displaced, extrapolated, satirized, and technologized, courting readers' attention by casting a Holmbergian "mantle of fantasy" over contemporary events.

The primary targets of Ezcurra's satire were those national characteristics he believed had led to the economic and political crises of his day, or could potentially impede future progress. In the economic sphere his criticism carries religious overtones: he condemns his society's "moral decadence," as evinced by, for example, the prevalence of a philosophy of "you are what you own" and by the national government's bad credit (8, 7). In politics Ezcurra laments factionalism, the disregard for republican ideals, and the concentration of power, saying "The tunic of the republic . . . had remained in the power of a few, when it belonged to all" (9). He denounces electoral fraud and corrupt rulers living off graft while "the Sovereign Populace slept the sleep of hunger in the tubing of the telephonograph wires or in some water main" (167–68). Despite Ezcurra's ardent defense of the rights of the people here and elsewhere in *Century XXX*, his aim—typical of the Generation of 1880—was not the reform of national class structure. Abraham explains that in *Century XXX*, "The questioning of the upper classes does not have the objective of opening its ranks to the popular sectors, but rather it constitutes only a self-critique leading toward a better consolidation of the prevailing system" ("Género utópico" sec. 4). To correct Argentina's course away from dystopia, Ezcurra advocates rule by a reunited Argentine elite—meaning the old money "patricios," or founding families. Andros and Filos are provided as good examples of those fit to lead. They are educated, independently wealthy, maintain a large home with servants, and are "uniters not dividers," as evidenced by Filos's wedding to Angélica, through which they are rejoined to representatives of an elite faction that had fallen out of favor.

Ezcurra saw Argentina's lack of national identity—also described as national sentiment, spirit, or unity—as the chief cause of its current political and economic woes, with additional potential for bringing future disaster. From the perspective of the thirtieth century, Andros and Filos observe "the beginning of a race in decline [literally "decadence"] . . . that has no fixed notion or feeling of nationality" [el principio de una raza en decadencia . . . que no tiene una noción, ni un sentimiento de la nacionalidad fijos] (117). At many points in *Century XXX*, the term "degeneration" [degeneración] is used interchangeably with "decadence," i.e., "the degeneration in individuals today" [la degeneración en los individuos de ahora] (106). At the time, the concept of degeneration had close ties to eugenic concerns such as racial poisons and population size and content. In the late nineteenth century, as Nancy Stepan tells us, "'Degeneration' replaced evolution as the major metaphor of the day, with vice, crime, immigration, women's work, and the urban environment variously blamed as its cause" (*Hour*

24). Virtually all of these sources of degeneration concerned Ezcurra to differing degrees, and *Century xxx* provides clear evidence of the discourse of eugenics beginning to creep into nineteenth-century texts.[27] "Vice" or racial poisons are specifically mentioned by Ezcurra only in passing, as he contrasts the factory worker who "brings the races closer to the future of their always longed for perfection . . . moving the complicated machinery of progress" [acerca las razas al porvenir de su siempre anhelado perfeccionamiento . . . moviendo la complicada maquinaria del progreso] (278) with people who do not work, whom he characterizes as "sickly beings" and drunkards (278–79). Of greater concern to Ezcurra was the heterogeneity of the national population; many residents of Argentina "had barely a notion of their own nationality: newcomers some, foreigners others, indifferent the rest" (35). The "newcomers" [advenedizos] he referred to were those Argentines who migrated from country to city and also to the nouveau riche among the elite ("advenedizos" can also be translated as "upstarts," and Ezcurra also uses the word in this context). By "foreigners" he clearly meant the huge numbers of immigrants who were pouring into Argentina at an ever-accelerating rate.[28] Immigrants are described at multiple points in *Century xxx* as uneducated, materialistic, degenerate, and corrupt, and they are associated with antirepublican values as false pretenders to European titles of nobility. Finally, the "indifferent" were those who should have felt the national sentiment most keenly but did not—those involved in political factionalism or those too superficial to think beyond the materialism of the times to the greater good. Racial heterogeneity is not directly addressed in *Century xxx*, as it was less an issue in Argentina than in Brazil or Mexico. When Ezcurra uses the term "race" [raza], he is referring to the symbolic idea of an Argentine national race.[29]

In truth, *Century xxx* does not have a strong dystopian flavor but functions more as a satire of the present, a science-fictional extrapolation of present-day tendencies, and as a roadmap to utopia. The protagonist Andros is described as a "dreamer of utopias" in the early pages of the novel (8), and rather than the nightmare future of the dystopia, Ezcurra presents the reader with a satirized exaggeration of a nightmarish present and indicates, if not a complete recipe, at least the main ingredients necessary for progressing toward perfection.[30] Some of the solutions Ezcurra proposes for the national problems he identifies are "time, experience, schooling, and morality" (139). Time and experience were needed to allow for a greater degree of national consolidation, morality would combat rampant materialism, and education meant academic study for the upper class and work for the populace.[31] Furthermore, he instructs, the immigrant must acculturate, and all Argentines must stop being "imitators of evils from abroad and indifferent to what was good that belonged to them" (244). French-inspired laws permitting civil marriage and divorce, for example, were foreign ideas that Argentine society did not need. Ezcurra characterizes America as the "most modern" of the continents, and as promising "a newer, purer, more tranquil life and a future . . . more in harmony with one's hopes" (14). "The good elements had not disappeared completely," Ezcurra tells the reader, and Andros's utopian dream might just come about if Argentines can only unite and rediscover the strength of their "noble, great, active, and creative [race], as the Argentine has always been" (9).

A final hope for the nation's future lies in the important contributions women can make to the development of national spirit. In *Century XXX* the focus is on the woman as the foundation of the national family (in our next two texts, the woman's role is discussed at greater length and in more eugenic terms). Ezcurra takes what he views as pernicious tendencies in the typical nineteenth-century woman and extrapolates them into a thirtieth-century female devoid of charm, maternal feeling, and patriotism. In Fisiocrata most women dress and wear their hair in masculine styles much decried by Andros and Filos; such women see motherhood as "disguised slavery" and turn their children over to "nursemaid establishments" [establecimientos de amas] to be raised (201, 150). When women like these stray from what Ezcurra views to be their prescribed role, they do not flourish as intellects or in the professions but degenerate into shallow, materialistic socialites—doing irreparable harm to subsequent generations in the process. For Ezcurra, preparation for citizenship begins at the mother's knee: "After the mother, who educated the soul of the child, came the school, which fortified his faculties, and then the man came to the gigantic idea of the motherland, which he honored and dignified" [Después de la madre que educaba el alma del niño, estaba la escuela que fortificaba sus facultades, y luego aperecía (*sic*) el hombre ante la idea gigante de la patria, que honraba y dignificaba] (107). Parelia, the epitome of femininity who raises and educates her own children, is touted by Ezcurra as "that woman who should serve as a model to many mothers" (197).

When the family of Andros and Parelia (whose progeny, after all, are *Adam*iro and *Eva*linda) is joined by that of Filos and Angélica, the little utopian oasis in degenerate Fisiocrata has been expanded, and the foundation for "the future national family" has been strengthened (320). The wedding with which the novel closes produces "the new family, formed with the precious elements of truth, love, and law [that] would take charge of carrying out, making flesh, the ideals of the moral man and the pure and beneficent principles of the philosopher" [la nueva familia, formada con los preciosos elementos de la verdad, del amor y del derecho (que) se encargaría de realizar, de hacer carne, los ideales del hombre moral, y los principios puros y benefactores del filósofo] (320). Thus the novel ends with hope for the future: for correcting the national path, unifying Argentines as a people, and rejoining the progress "of the end of this astonishing century" (xiii).

Godofredo Barnsley, *São Paulo in the Year 2000*

Godofredo (né Godfrey) Emerson Barnsley was born in Quartis, Brazil, in 1874, the third child of George Scarbrough Barnsley and Mary Lamira Emerson.[32] George Barnsley was originally from Georgia, a second-generation member of the cotton aristocracy of the North American South. He had been a surgeon in the Confederate Army during the U.S. Civil War, and in 1867, after refusing to sign the oath of allegiance to the Union, he was one of a number of Confederate veterans to emigrate to Brazil. There he married the daughter of another such veteran from Mississippi. In addition to practicing medicine in Brazil, George invested heavily in a gold mining venture. When that venture failed, he returned with his family, including fourteen-year-old Godofredo, to Woodlands, the family's estate in northwest Georgia, now the site of Barnsley Gardens (see "Godfrey Barnsley and Barnsley Gardens"). At sixteen Godofredo left Woodlands and rode the boxcars to Philadelphia, where he put himself through dental school by working as a dishwasher and at sundry other jobs. Upon completing his education he returned to Brazil to set up practice. Godofredo Barnsley married Alzira Montfort, daughter of a well-known doctor in Campinas, and he became a very successful dentist and professor of dentistry at the Universidade de São Paulo. He died of yellow fever in 1935.

Barnsley remained, to some extent, a man between two countries. Although he spent less than a decade of his life in the United States, his personal and familial ties with that nation were never completely severed. His grandson, Godfrey Barnsley, notes that his grandfather spoke English with a strong Southern accent and that his spoken Portuguese always betrayed his North American roots. He took his wife to visit Woodlands in the year before his death, and the family maintains connections to the United States to this day. When Barnsley wrote *São Paulo 2000* he wrote in Portuguese, published the book in São Paulo, and focused on Brazil and Brazilian topics. The city that he portrays is a Brazilian utopia, but Barnsley constructs significant aspects of this future society in specific comparison to the United States and to a North American work of science fiction, Bellamy's *Looking Backward from 2000 to 1887* (1888).

Barnsley wrote *São Paulo 2000* two decades after the founding of the First Republic (1889–1930), at a time when Brazil faced "the first seriously contested presidential election of the Republic" and when the national economy was threatened by a crisis in the all-important coffee market (Skidmore 88). Despite radical changes—the elimination of slavery, the abdication of the monarch, the establishment of the Republic, the increase in the number of immigrants—Brazil was still far from becoming the progressive world power envisioned by Felício dos Santos. Stepan summarizes some of the continuities from the days of the empire:

> Brazil entered the twentieth century a highly stratified society, socially and racially—a society that, though formally a liberal republic, was governed informally by a small, largely white elite and in which less than 2 percent of the population voted in national elections; a society in which the majority of the people were black or mulatto and could not read or write; in which, though there was technical separation of church and state, Catholicism had considerable cultural influence; and in which democratic liberalism was seen by many intellectuals as irrelevant or harmful to Brazil's future. (*Hour* 37)

At the same time, Brazil continued to enjoy a greater degree of political stability than did many of its Spanish American neighbors. The beginning of the twentieth century also saw important strides taken in the development and application of Brazilian science, through the establishment of research and teaching institutions such as the Butantã

Institute and the Oswaldo Cruz Institute and through increasing importance given to public health programs (see Stepan, *Beginnings of Brazilian Science*; Barnsley 353).

São Paulo 2000 is a product of these times. Barnsley's immediate reasons for writing the novel were Brazil's economic and political situations—principally the latter, as attested to by fervent passages in favor of the candidacy of Ruy (modernized spelling "Rui") Barbosa for president. The process of writing, editing, and publishing the novel was rushed, Barnsley tells the reader in the errata pages. These corrections to the text are dated October 22, 1909 (394), and Barnsley had been working on the manuscript as late as August 22 of that same year, the date upon which Barbosa was officially nominated to run for the presidency and which is specifically mentioned in the text (366). Other issues that motivated Barnsley to put pen to paper were national agricultural practices, poor public health, immigration policy, and improving the composition and education of the Brazilian population. *São Paulo 2000* is the only work of fiction or nonfiction that Barnsley is known to have written, and he financed the publication himself. Family history has it that the book was not a commercial success and that critics advised Barnsley to stick to dentistry. Whatever its critical reception may have been, *São Paulo 2000* provides an important gauge of the status of Brazilian politics, society, and literature of its day.

São Paulo 2000 is a tale of "adventures so singular and extravagant that they would be worthy of the plume of a Jules Verne or a Baron Münchhausen," a first-person narrator tells the reader at the outset (1). He then introduces himself as Jeremias Serapião Pacifico de Santa Cruz Barbuda, a young *paulista* [person from the province of São Paulo] just coming of age in the first decade of the twentieth century. "It matters little to you to know if I descend from princes, bootblacks, warriors, or from peaceful burghers" [Pouco te importa saber si descendo de principes, engraxates, guerreiros ou de pacificos burguezes], he begins his self-introduction,

> Physiologically, the knowledge of one's genealogy is of great importance due to the transmission of the ascendents' physical and moral qualities through heredity; socially, nevertheless, it does not deserve great interest in a republic in which an individual's value is assayed based on merit, on personal attributes, and not on *fleurs de lis* and noble robes. (1–2)

> Physiologicamente, o conhecimento da genealogia é de grande importancia na transmissão pela hereditariedade das qualidades physicas e moraes dos ascendentes; socialmente, porém, não merece grande interesse numa Republica em que o valor individual se aquilata pelo merito, pelos atributos pessoaes e não pelas flores de liz e mantos fidalgos.

With this statement Serapião reveals an Ezcurra-like disdain for archaic European notions of nobility as well as a belief in Lamarckian heredity. He soon discloses that he comes from elite stock, as his father is a recently bankrupted coffee plantation owner (rather like an economic version of Ezcurra's don Pedro, a member of the elite who has temporarily come upon hard times). Luckily Serapião has also acquired a fine education, which he believes will both support him economically and improve the genetic qualities he will pass on to his descendants.

While sitting in one of São Paulo's gardens, pondering the downturn of his fortunes, Serapião picks up a newspaper and reads about the other national crisis, "the political crisis brought on by the question of the presidential candidacies" (3). He is clearly a supporter of Senator Rui Barbosa, since he compares Barbosa's opponent, Marshall [Marechal] Hermes da Fonseca, to Napoleon and speculates that any government under a military man would involve "coups d'état, gaucho justice [*justiça á gaúcha*], that is, throat cutting, falls into the Paraná River, and other heinous things characteristic of military presidencies" and would keep Brazil down at the level "of a Nicaragua or an Honduras" (7, 6). Turning away from such negative topics, Serapião consoles himself with thoughts of his future bride, the "dear little cousin" [querida priminha] who is "the supreme hope of my life" (8), and begins to relax:

> The purity, the benevolence, the tranquility of those places produced an easy lethargy in me, and, as I closed my eyes to the world of realities, another, entirely imaginary world populated with marvelous visions presented itself to me. Little by little, imperceptibly, the scene, the trees, the objects were transformed, as in cinematographic films. (9)

> A candura, a benignidade, o socego daquelles sitios produziu em mim um suave torpor e, fechando-me os olhos ao mundo das

realidades, apresentou-me um outro mundo inteiramente imaginario, povoado de visões maravilhosas. Pouco a pouco, insensivelmente, o scenario, as arvores, as cousas, foram-se transfigurando, como nas fitas cynematographicas.

Serapião awakens on the same park bench, but the trees seem larger and he spies several gracious pavilions he does not recall seeing before. Several young women of splendid but, to him, singular *toilette* pass by, and he says to them "I am experiencing the sensations of one who awakens from an extraordinary dream. I even find this place strange which I thought I knew so well! . . . Can I be dreaming?!" (10). The young women present him to their grandfather, Dr. Orecnis Ocitirc, from whom Serapião learns that he is still in São Paulo, but in the São Paulo of the year 2000.

Dr. Orecnis is the ideal cicerone to guide a young man from 1909 through the intricacies of the future. At age 110, he is an "eyewitness and vast repository of so many events of national history" as well as a widely traveled person who has worked and studied in many places in the United States, Europe, and Brazil (330). The thinly disguised "Sincere Critic" [Crítico Sincero] has received this name not for his descriptions of Brazilian society in the year 2000, but for his explanations of what changes have been necessary in the intervening years in order to create this twenty-first century utopia. The nineteenth-century customs indicated as hindering Brazil's progress vary from ladies' fashions and health regimens, to marriage between near relations, to a tendency to be overly influenced by ideas and objects from abroad and its corollary "disdain for anything that was national" (42). Through the course of the three-hundred-page day, which we eventually learn is none other than September 7—Brazilian Independence Day—the conversations between Dr. Orecnis and Serapião also cover progressive changes on the national scene: Rui Barbosa's victory in the 1910 election, the Revolution of 1920, and Brazil's subsequent rise to the forefront of world politics, commerce, and culture.

In the evening, Serapião accompanies the whole Ocitirc family in their airplane ("Airplanes are as common today as automobiles were in the past," thanks to their invention by the Brazilian Santos Dumont, Serapião is told)[33] to an Independence Day celebration at Ipiranga, where Pedro I had declared Brazilian independence with his famous "I will remain!" [Fico!] on September 7, 1822 (267). From the airplane they watch a reenactment of Dom Pedro's declaration. The confluence of the three 7 Septembers—that of 1909, of 2000, and of 1822—is too much for Serapião; he is so moved that his echoing cry of *"Independence or death!"* causes the airplane's propeller to crack (390). As the plane begins to plunge downward, Serapião describes what happens next:

> Overcome by vertigo, immobilized by terror, I saw the ground rushing upward with incredible rapidity to meet the vehicle. I closed my eyes and was waiting for death, when I felt a collision, and, readers, I had . . . fallen from the bench where I had been dreaming in the Forest Garden! . . .
> All a dream, illusion! I did not find myself in the year 2000, but, like the poor mortals, my contemporaries, in the middle of the night of September 7, 1909. (390, first ellipsis in the original)[34]
>
> Tomado de vertigem, immobilizado pelo terror, via o solo subir com incrivel rapidez para se encontrar com o vehiculo; fechei os olhos, esperei a morte, senti um choque e, leitores, tinha . . . cahido do banco onde estivéra a sonhar no Jardim da Floresta! . . .
> Tudo sonho, illusão! Não me achava no anno 2.000, mas, como os pobres mortaes, meus contemporaneos, em plena noite de 7 de Setembro de 1909.

Regardless of whether Serapião has experienced actual time travel or merely a dream, he will never be the same. In seeming compensation for the realization that he must call off the biologically unwise marriage to his cousin, Serapião is imbued with a renewed faith in Brazil's future possibilities: "Such are the consequences of the wanderings of my ambitious spirit among other worlds" (391).

To make the year 2000 the setting of one's national utopia or dystopia was to write a near- (rather than far-) future narrative, and the symbolic meaning of this chosen year changed as the millenium approached. As we have seen, Eduardo de Ezcurra set *Century XXX* in the more distant year 3000 to allow for the hypertrophy of national problems. Bellamy too had originally set *Looking Backward from 2000 to 1887* in the year 3000, as he explained in an invited essay the year after the book was published:

In undertaking to write *Looking Backward* I had, at the outset, no idea of attempting a serious contribution to the movement of social reform. The idea was of a mere literary fantasy, a fairy tale of social felicity. There was no thought of contriving a house which practical men might live in, but merely of hanging in mid-air, far out of reach of the sordid and material world of the present, a cloud-palace for an ideal humanity. ("How I Came" sec. 2)

Once Bellamy hit upon the military as the prototype for his projected world-altering national industrial service, he changed the temporal venue from the year 3000 to the year 2000. Once that imagined future became for him a possible and even inevitable one, "Instead of a mere fairy tale of social perfection, [*Looking Backward*] became the vehicle of a definite scheme of industrial reorganization" (sec. 6). Both *Brazil 2000* and *São Paulo 2000* were envisioned by their authors as vehicles with comparable—if not so wide-ranging—purposes.[35] Despite similarities in the titles, motivations, and predictions of their texts, Felício dos Santos and Barnsley had different attitudes toward the republic, and there is a shift in the quality of optimism with which each regarded the future of Brazil. For Felício dos Santos, writing during the Second Reign, the republic was a goal, an ideal in itself, and he constructed his utopia in strict opposition to his present reality. Barnsley, on the other hand, was writing twenty years after the fall of the monarchy, amid growing national disillusionment with the republic. It was becoming clear that "the ambitious republican promises of the late 1880s had not been fulfilled" and that "Brazil had fallen behind in the struggle for modernity" (Skidmore 102–3). As Dr. Orecnis explains it, "The republican form of government is the best of all of the political regimes; but . . . there is an abyss between theory and practice, and never was there a more stupendous, more impressive demonstration of this than in Brazil" (286). In addition to the differences in their temporal perspectives on the Brazilian republic, Felício dos Santos's and Barnsley's attitudes toward the future destination of their time-traveling characters were affected by their relative proximity to the date of their projected utopia, the year 2000. As the second millenium drew closer, there was "a shift in the focus [from one of fascination with the year 2000] to one with a more 'real' sense about it. Works . . . began to examine the coming landmark date in a more concrete fashion" (Kopp sec. 5). When Pedro

II visits the year 2000, his descendants are so far removed from his time that they have forgotten key points of family history, and it is necessary for him to speak with engineers, lawyers, politicians, and a variety of "men on the street," in addition to his principal cicerone, Dr. Tsherepanoff, in order for him to begin to understand and accept this future. Kopp cites "an increasing number of studies that began to forecast with a focus on the year 2000" in the years after World War I. "Clearly," he writes, "the year 2000, which was now within the life span of those being born, was becoming more of a reality" (sec. 5). By stretching the limits of longevity Barnsley manages to provide Serapião with a cicerone in the year 2000 whose life spans the entirety of the republic. Dr. Orecnis, at 110, would have been born in 1889 or 1890, around the same time as Serapião himself. Thus, just as the utopian republic of the year 2000 represents the maturity of the young republic of 1909, Dr. Orecnis represents the man our narrator could grow up to be.

The route to "national regeneration," the alternate title given for *São Paulo 2000*, might begin with the voters' choice in the next elections, Barnsley suggests, but also necessary are continuing efforts at reforming public health, bolstering traditional family values, and fostering a biological and cultural melting pot. Other, overarching contributors to solving Brazil's problems are scientific and technological advances and education. As Stepan tells us, regeneration was seen as the answer to degeneration in Latin America (*Hour* 91), and Barnsley wastes no time in identifying "the five greatest factors causing national degeneration": "syphilis, tuberculosis, alcoholism, marriage between blood relations, and the corset" (93–94). Dr. Orecnis tells Serapião that these national evils had been defeated in much the same way that yellow fever had been eradicated by Brazilian scientists in the first decade of the twentieth century, through national health campaigns (95).[36]

The elements of national health upon which Barnsley dwells at greatest length are those that most immediately impacted the next generations of Brazilians. In one chapter he preaches the genetic evils of "consanguineous marriage" which, according to Dr. Orecnis (M.D.), is "a violation of biological laws . . . an attempt against the progress of society" (56). This chapter is followed by extended treatment of issues related to women's health and what Stepan has termed "reproductive poisons" (*Hour* 81). In the chapter titled "Physical Education for the Young Woman" [Educação physica da moça], Barnsley recommends that Brazilian women take up "European and American gymnastics" (even providing a photo of a group of women performing such exercises) in order to be "physically up to their elevated purpose in the propagation of the species" (69, 80). A later chapter contains a diatribe against the corset, along with a chart detailing the evils the corset produces in a woman's body—such as asthma, weakened intelligence, and an inability to produce milk to nurse infants—and in her children, including hereditary rickets and various monstrous deformities (102; see figure 1.1). Like Ezcurra, Barnsley believes a mother is responsible for "the private education of children, from a physical, intellectual, and moral standpoint" (47). He also connects that education to national progress, explaining that "the preservation and progress of societies" depends upon a mother's successful completion of this "extremely important social function" (47). The pernicious idea of women pursuing advanced degrees and working outside the home is eliminated from the advanced Brazilian society in Barnsley's future utopia; as a female character in the novel tells Serapião: "It is an absurdity here in Brazil and is only justified in miserable Europe, where the struggle for life is more intense than among us and demands that a woman aid her husband. This story of women pretending to exercise the same professions as men only contributes to the disorganization of the family" (74).

Dr. Orecnis tells Serapião that, by the year 2000, a single Brazilian national identity and unity of national spirit have been forged through the gradual emergence of a racially and culturally homogeneous population:

> Here we are not like the United States or Europe: we no longer have races. The majority of the families that you see here are composed of the national element, descended in part from foreigners; but, if they appear to be of different racial origins, origins which the years and crossbreeding are gradually abolishing and rendering unnatural, they are brothers of the same family because they were born in the same land and they live under the same sky, under one flag, and are governed by identical customs and by a single constitution. (54)

> Aqui não é Estados Unidos nem Europa: não temos hoje mais castas. A maioria das familias que aqui vês, compõe-se do elemento nacional, descendente em parte de estrangeiros; mas, si se mostram differentes pela origem de raças, origem que os annos e o cruzamento vão apagando e desnaturando aos poucos, são irmãos de

Espartilho (ou mutilação physica do corpo) produz o atrophiamento dos orgams:	Pulmão — estados pathologicos	o enfraquecimento cellular	predispondo para a:	thysica pneumonia bronchites asthma etc.
		e a sub-oxydação do sangue	occasionando:	palpitações do coração, arthritismo, anemia, enfraquecimento da vista, da intelligencia, da memoria etc.
	Estomago — estados pathologicos	dyspepsia: demora da digestão, fermentação dos alimentos etc.		
	Figado — estados pathologicos	funcções anormaes, incapacidade physiologica de purificação sanguinea, diabetes		
	Seios — estados pathologicos	Nevralgias dos seios. Concorre, nas pessoas predispostas por hereditariedade, para os tumores e cancros, para o estancamento do leite; leite anormal com pouca força nutritiva, causa do rachitismo constitucional adquirido pelos filhos por nutrição imperfeita, e causa das mortes por inanição.		
Espartilho (ou mutilação physica do corpo) e a falta de cultivo physico da moça, produzem o atrophiamento dos orgams e os seguintes estados pathologicos:	Incapacidade maternal ou deformação da bacia pelvica		que gera:	o rachitismo hereditario, os máos *ossos e dentes*, as irregularidades da bocca, seres monstros, os cretinos, etc. Predisposição para thysica nos filhos etc.
	Deslocamento dos rins		que produz:	as doenças renaes

FIGURE 1.1. *Chart on the Evils of the Corset*, São Paulo in the Year 2000, *p. 102*. "The corset (or physical mutilation of the body) and the young woman's lack of physical fitness produce atrophy of the organs and the following pathological conditions . . ."

uma mesma familia, porque nasceram numa terra commum e vivem sob um mesmo céo, debaixo de uma mesma bandeira e governados por identicos costumes e por uma mesma constituição.

Over the course of Serapião's day in the future, it becomes increasingly apparent that the ultimate goal of Barnsley's melting pot is a eugenic whitening of the Brazilian population.[37] Barnsley virtually ignores the large Afro-Brazilian segment of the population in the novel, but passing comments make it clear that their genetic contributions are among those that require improving. Barnsley's views on race are more evident in his representation of indigenous groups. Dr. Orecnis denounces the extermination and enslavement of the Indians by the Europeans in former times in no uncertain terms, but the Indians are also depicted as saying to Brazilians of European origin, "We know that we are condemned to disappear, because you are infinitely stronger, and this law is very old" (117). The law of the survival of the fittest does not operate in the short term, however; in the meantime—circa 1960 according to Dr. Orecnis—it is acceptable and desirable for Brazilians from São Paulo and Rio ("Portuguese people" [portuguezes], the Indians call them) to hop in their aeroplanes, fly to the rich but previously inaccessible interior of Brazil, and carry out the "colonization" and acculturation of tribes such as the Chavante and the Canoeiro (271). As in Ezcurra's Argentina, Barnsley's Brazil experienced massive waves of immigration dominated by arrivals from Italy; by 1907 Italians outnumbered Brazilians in the city of São Paulo by two to one (Stepan, *Hour* 38). Unlike Ezcurra, however, Barnsley welcomes this union of the "sons of the land of the sublime Dante" and the "descendants of the land of the ingenious Camões" (254), calling the Italians "the greatest factor in our progress" (248). These immigrants could help to populate the *sertão*, fill shortages in qualified labor, and contribute both a strong work ethic and the practice of polyculture (rather than monoculture) in farming. Dr. Orecnis encourages Serapião—and all Brazilians—to marry foreigners (61, 66), and lauds the Italians' willingness to intermarry with Brazilians "for the even greater purification of our race" [para mais ainda apurar a nossa raça] (252). His praise for the "Latin race" [raça latina] that would result from these unions anticipates Latin American eugenicists' use of this term by more than two decades (254).[38]

Barnsley summarizes the key to national progress under the heading "education," following the tradition identified by Frye, "Nearly all [utopia-writers] make their utopias depend on education for their permanent establishment" (37). Addressing his visitor from 1909, Dr. Orecnis exclaims, "The lack of NATIONAL EDUCATION! This, Jeremias Serapião, was the supreme source of all of our misfortunes, of the weakness of our development" (292). On the most basic level, improved access to education had removed the epithet "Illiteracyland" [Analphabetolandia] from the Brazil of the year 2000 (291). A shift in emphasis from the theoretical to the practical in higher education had improved Brazilian competitiveness in agriculture, manufacturing, business, and industry (301). Every potential educational venue—from newspaper to pulpit to cinema—had been used to inform the twentieth-century public of the applications of science to their daily lives in the areas of personal and public hygiene (105–6). Finally, Dr. Orecnis tells Serapião, the presidency of Rui Barbosa had turned out to be a springboard for the Regenerative/Reform Party [Partido Regenerador], whose national education platform was the "precursor of our political regeneration and economic renaissance" (304).

The United States generally functions as the model for Barnsley's construction of the future; in the novel's final pages, he refers to his extrapolated Brazil as "a new United States of South America" (391). Throughout the book he expresses admiration for the Yankee work ethic, commercial operations, and educational system, though he criticizes the United States for its acceptance of divorce, its high crime rate, and its sensationalistic press. The clearest indication of how Barnsley views not only the United States but also Brazil can be seen by comparing *São Paulo 2000* to Bellamy's *Looking Backward*. Although Barnsley never mentions the U.S. writer or his utopian work by name, he frequently uses Bellamy's text as a specific point of departure for his own.

The deliberate alterations that Barnsley makes to elements from the Northern work reveal his views as to how Brazilian reality did and should differ from that of the United States. These alterations also serve as an example of how Brazilian writers were already adapting—rather than adopting—elements of the Northern science fiction tradition to suit their own needs. Whereas Bellamy integrates women into his "industrial army" (with allowances made for relative physical strength and childbearing), Barnsley values the maintenance of a more traditional family structure. While there is virtually no race question in *Looking*

Backward, Barnsley makes multiple references to race, reflecting its relative importance in the construction of Brazilian national identity. In the political arena, Barnsley is happy to stop Brazil's leftward trajectory at republicanism, rather than continuing on to Bellamy's more Marxist vision, and he connects his political stance to these very un-Bellamian views on class structure, as Dr. Orecnis expounds to Serapião:

> Let it not be inferred from this that I approve of Communism, because that would be to negate the work, the effort, the aptitude of some to the benefit of others who are less active, diligent, and competent. If nature has made men unequally intelligent and competent, if their education has given them diverse qualifications and different inclinations, it is natural that they do not enjoy the same happiness and well-being. (33)

> Não se infira dahi que approvo o communismo, porque seria negar o trabalho, o esforço, a aptidão de uns em proveito de outros, menos activos, diligentes e capazes; si a natureza fez os homens desigualmente intelligentes e capazes, si a sua educação lhes deu habilitações diversas e inclinações differentes, é natural que elles não gozem da mesma felicidade e bem estar.

Later in *São Paulo 2000*, Barnsley describes Brazil's social classes by modernizing Bellamy's metaphor of society as a coach. "By way of attempting to give the reader some general impression of the way people lived together in those days, and especially of the relations of the rich and poor to one another," Julian West remarks in *Looking Backward*, "perhaps I cannot do better than to compare society as it then was to a prodigious coach which the masses of humanity were harnessed to and dragged toilsomely along a very hilly and sandy road" (3). The "prodigious coach" of nineteenth-century society was pulled by the masses; the coachman was hunger, and the wealthy rode in the comfortable seats on top, doing their utmost to remain there. It is necessary for West to explain these things to his readers because, in the twenty-first century, everyone is equal. In a chapter entitled "The Social Automobile" [O Automovel Social], Barnsley's Dr. Orecnis describes a "gigantic vehicle . . . which carries in its belly almost all of the social classes": Brazil's independently wealthy elite ride in first class, the educated professionals in second, and the middle class in third (155). The masses, which he refers to as "the dregs of society" [o Rebotalho social], are left to run after the social automobile, but only rarely, by herculean effort, does a member of this group manage to get into the third-class section (161). Where this vehicle's motor formerly produced only 1,909 horsepower, it now churns out 2,000, and where it previously used steam power, it now runs on electricity. There are many such vehicles, Dr. Orecnis explains to Serapião, and each country has its own: "They advance, at different velocities, but in a progressive gear that is always increasing" (155). Rather than mimicking Bellamy's use of a vehicle as a metaphor for outdated past inequalities, Barnsley's vehicle continues to move forward with class divisions intact. In his Brazilian utopia, the goal is not equality for all but the elevation (increased horsepower) of the whole social structure.

In the final chapter of *Looking Backward*, West appears to reawaken in the nineteenth century, which he now sees as a backward, wretched reality. To his great relief, that reawakening turns out to be only a nightmare; he remains in the future and marries the granddaughter of his former fiancée, a thoroughly modern version of the same woman. Because Bellamy saw his utopia as virtually inevitable, West does not need to share his knowledge of the future with the present. As the author noted in the conclusion to his retrospective essay: "The more advanced nations, ours surely first of all, will reach the summit earliest and, reaching strong brotherly hands downward, help up the laggards" (sec. 7). As a member of one such "laggard" nation, Barnsley must needs end his tale on a different note. As Del Fiorentino describes the message of *São Paulo 2000*, "the future society glimpsed through the utopia is revealed to be the result of a project requiring immediate attention" (149). Serapião's experiences in the year 2000 have been only a dream. He needs to awaken in his own time in order to help the Brazil of 1909 to become the future that he has seen so clearly. His decision not to marry his cousin will be the first contribution to the construction of that future.

Eduardo Urzaiz, *Eugenia*

The first discussion of Urzaiz's *Eugenia (A Fictional Sketch of Future Customs)* as science fiction appeared in Ross Larson's *Fantasy and Imagination in the Mexican Narrative* (1977; 55). Since then this work has often been described as a utopia that gradually descends into a dystopia, anticipating Huxley's *Brave New World* (1932). To the modern reader, this seems a fairly accurate description. A purportedly near-perfect future society has been achieved at the expense of turning control of human reproduction over to the state, which employs practices such as forced sterilization and euthanasia, while a distinctly unheroic hero abandons a strong female character for the rather insipid Eugenia. When we consider the author's intentions or the work's reception at the time, however, it is less clear that this characterization of the novel is accurate. "Some texts intended (and internally marked) as utopian or dystopian (or perhaps not written within a utopian/dystopian strategy at all) can be received by readers as utopian or dystopian according to their own aesthetic and political judgments," writes Moylan (155). And since such value judgments often reflect individual beliefs, as well as a specific time and place, one person's dystopia may be another's utopia. An exploration of authorial intent in *Eugenia*, along with initial reader reception, can reveal much about Latin American reactions to eugenic ideas. An examination of the novel itself further demonstrates how texts in the science fiction tradition—no matter how distant the future setting or different the society portrayed—are uniquely suited to reflecting the realities from which they emerged.

Eugenia appears to have been perceived as a completely dystopian work by Urzaiz's contemporaries. As Peniche Vallado writes in his preface to the third edition:

> In its time, *Eugenia* upset the critics and the public and was, perhaps, the work by Dr. Urzaiz that most contributed to people viewing him as having an undesirable reputation and regarding him with the precautionary distrust reserved for eccentrics and the unbalanced. He anticipated popular consensus when he announced in the prologue: "I am certain that many individuals . . . will exclaim, scandalized, upon reading my book: 'But this is the work of a madman!'" (22)

Urzaiz's son and biographer, the obstetrician Carlos Urzaiz Jiménez, writes in a milder vein that, with the publication of *Eugenia*, "without a doubt his fame as an eccentric grew" (42). The strong negative reaction to the book in 1919 was undoubtedly related to the drastic alterations Urzaiz portrayed in traditional family structure, social customs, and religious values, and to the more Mendelian-driven aspects of his approach to eugenics.

It is less evident how Urzaiz himself judged his projected society. Urzaiz Jiménez calls *Eugenia* "the most candid reflection of his uneasiness of spirit" (42). In his own prologue to the novel, Urzaiz states that it is intended to represent a positive reality: "a vision—even if pale and imprecise—of that future humanity of my dreams and hopes" (3). The author's selected path to humanity's perfection was clearly influenced by his own professional background.

Eduardo Urzaiz Rodríguez was born in 1876 in Guanabacoa, Cuba, and emigrated with his family to the Yucatán at the age of fourteen. His son summarizes his fields of interest as "medicine . . ., teaching, art, and politics" (37). After earning degrees in pedagogy (1894) and medicine (1902) in Mexico, Urzaiz continued his studies in psychiatry and obstetrics in New York (1905–6). Early in his medical career, he did a great deal of work as an obstetrician, specializing in performing Cesarean surgeries. From the beginning of the twentieth century he taught pedagogy and literature, and at different times he also taught English, French, sociology, history of religions, psychology, and biology (López Cortes 32). In the years before or immediately following the publication of *Eugenia*, he held positions as founding director of a psychiatric hospital, the Ayala Asylum [Asilo Ayala] (1906–30); head of the Yucatán Department of Public Education (at several points in the 1920s); head of the State Board of Health (beginning in 1926); and first president of the National University of the Southeast [Universidad Nacional del Sureste], later the Autonomous University of the Yucatan [Universidad Autónoma de Yucatán] (1922–26, 1946–55).[39] In addition to scientific papers on psychiatry and biology (including a paper on reproductive hormones), Urzaiz wrote on a wide variety of topics from Cervantes to Mexican and Cuban history to religious history. He also translated Longfellow's poem *Evangeline* and was locally well known as an artist (he illustrated his translation of *Evangeline*, and the illustrations for *Eugenia* are thought likely to be his). In a prologue to the second edition of the novel, Menéndez Díaz connects certain aspects of Urzaiz's imagined advances in reproductive engineering, specifically the possibility of male gestation, to his research on hormones (14–16). In the prologue to the third edition, Peniche Vallado refuses to confirm or deny this assertion, but joins Menéndez Díaz in comparing Urzaiz to H. G. Wells, genetic manipulator extraordinaire in *The Island of Dr. Moreau* (1896). It seems evident that Urzaiz's work in obstetrics also had a significant impact on the medical aspects of the work. *Eugenia* is Urzaiz's only novel.

When Urzaiz published *Eugenia* in 1919, the world was trying to recover from the devastating losses of the Great War, and Mexico was enduring the final months of the first of the major twentieth-century revolutions. During the long and bloody Mexican Revolution, it is estimated that one in eight Mexicans died (about 1.5 to 2 million people in a population of 15 million), including hundreds of thousands of civilians, and there was large-scale destruction of property and infrastructure (Meyer et al. 532). Stepan traces these connections between the revolution and the form that eugenics took in Mexico:

> The deaths and dislocations caused by the war and the staggering problems of poverty and sickness, combined with the growing nationalism of the revolutionary state, provided the setting for the appeal to eugenics. Ideologically, the revolution's socialism, anticlericism, and materialism made Mexico receptive to new developments in science and social thought. (*Hour* 55)[40]

As we will see, Urzaiz was less motivated by nationalism than by an opposition to religious fanaticism and a concern for replacing and regenerating a diminished Mexican population. As with most writings that stem from the utopian tradition, the fictional plot merely serves as the underpinnings for the writer's thesis. Urzaiz tells the reader in his preface that the "simple love story plot" provides a "pretext" for evoking a vision of the future of his dreams (3). He uses *Eugenia* as a literary platform to show how Mexico and the world might emerge from the violence of his times and (re)construct a superior society.

Urzaiz's tale takes place in the year 2218 in Villautopía [Utopiaville], Subconfederation of Central America. By setting his novel three hundred years from his own time, Urzaiz effectively places his projected society in a fairly near future but beyond the reach of the present population or their immediate descendants. It is a reality that can be accomplished with extrapolated versions of existing scientific tools and methodologies, yet it is distant enough in time to be very unlike Urzaiz's present. The novel begins with the arrival of an official letter for Ernesto from the Bureau of Eugenics [Bureau de Eugenética],[41] calling him up for a year's reproductive service as an "Official Breeder of the

Species" [Reproductor Oficial de la Especie] (9).⁴² He has been selected by the government to propagate the species due, as the letter says, to "the robustness, health, beauty and other qualities that are combined in you" (9). Until receiving this call-up, Ernesto had not been gainfully employed. He had won athletic competitions piloting his "aerocycle with a colloidal nitroglycerin engine" [aerocicleta de motor de nitroglicerina coloidal] (36), but has been essentially a playboy, maintained by his lover, Celiana, and the other members of their *grupo* [group], Miguel, Consuelo, and Federico. In 2218 the nuclear family has been replaced by the *grupo*, a communal arrangement in which adults choose to live together based on complementary goals, tastes, and "affinities of character" (23–24). The figure of Celiana—with her "disturbing and original beauty" [belleza inquietante y original], from her "Greek nose" and "high and spacious" forehead to the "porcelain transparencies" of the skin of her feet—graces the cover of the novel (see figure 1.2). She had been Ernesto's teacher, but once they became lovers she had left teaching and achieved international success giving conferences on sociology and history. Due to her "insatiable and almost morbid thirst for acquiring knowledge," or "excessive cerebrality," Celiana had been judged in her youth to be "incapable of engendering perfectly sound and balanced products" and had been sterilized, as had Miguel (24–25). "Through such procedures, at that time common practice in all the civilized world," the omniscient narrator concludes, "they had managed to build a secure dike against the progress of degeneration" (25).

Ernesto visits the Bureau of Eugenics to learn about his new duties from the director, Dr. Serrato. Because Ernesto's arrival coincides with that of two African doctors, who have come to learn about eugenics in hopes of reversing the degeneration of their own country, he ends up touring the whole bureau along with these men, who are described as having "formidable sets of cannibal teeth" and resembling "a tame chimpanzee" (54, 55). The practice of government-controlled artificial selection in humans had begun in more advanced nations when the wars of men and the growing tocophobia (excessive fear of childbirth) in women threatened to depopulate the world (23, 148). Advances in the hormonal sciences have made it possible for artificially "feminized" men to act as "gestators" [gestadores], or "selfless incubators of future Humanity" (70, 71). In a Lamarckian genetic extrapolation, the female uterus has adapted to this situation, and women in these "civilized" countries can no longer carry a child to term (88). Dr. Serrato

FIGURE 1.2. *Celiana with her customary cannabis cigarette. Cover of* Eugenia. *Used with permission of the Universidad Nacional Autónoma de Yucatán*

tells the group that "those of the purely muscular type" are preferred breeders over the "cerebrals/intellectuals" [cerebrales], who make poor reproducers (62). Inherent or recidivist criminals, the mentally ill, and people who suffer from other racial poisons (such incurables as epilepsy or tuberculosis) are sterilized. Those who suffer terribly or are unconscious due to terminal illness are euthanized. Such harsh measures are required less and less every year, he tells them, concrete proof of the regeneration of the population. Once children are born, they are raised in state-run "Farm-nurseries" [Granjas-almácigas], then schools, until they leave to form *grupos* (12, 75–77).

As Ernesto commences his task of engendering twenty genetically superior children in one year, he and Celiana begin to grow apart. She seeks solace in her work and in debates with an old teacher and his circle. Topics for discussion include the changes in the family over the last three hundred years, archaic nationalisms and war, the likelihood of attaining complete economic equality, and the vestiges of organized religion that remain in 2218. Ernesto's behavior becomes increasingly insensitive and brutish as a result of his new lifestyle. Though she cannot stop loving him, even Celiana realizes "the low moral value of the man whom she had placed so high in her esteem and her affection" (133). Her deteriorating relationship with Ernesto causes Celiana to retreat from reality through increasing abuse of cannabis cigarettes.

More than three-fourths of the way through the novel, Ernesto meets Eugenia, another chosen reproducer and, as her name might suggest, "an admirable example of the human species, the prototype of feminine beauty" (180). The attraction between them is instantaneous, and their "first, absolute, integral love" is described in biological terms: "already all the cells of their organisms, feeling themselves complementary, were inclined to join together with a force superior to all reason and to all conscious volition" (181, 182–83). Neither the intellectual and spiritual (but physiologically sterile) relationship Ernesto had with Celiana, nor the physical and biological (but emotionally sterile) unions with prior eugenic collaborators [colaboradoras], appears to provide the basis of a lasting and happy relationship: the ideal pairing must combine both of these elements. As Celiana's mental and physical health continues to decline, Ernesto and Eugenia establish their own love nest on the outskirts of Villautopía. Within twenty days, the eugenically gifted pair have conceived a child, and Ernesto lovingly describes to his mate the "manner of incubating a child, by the scientific

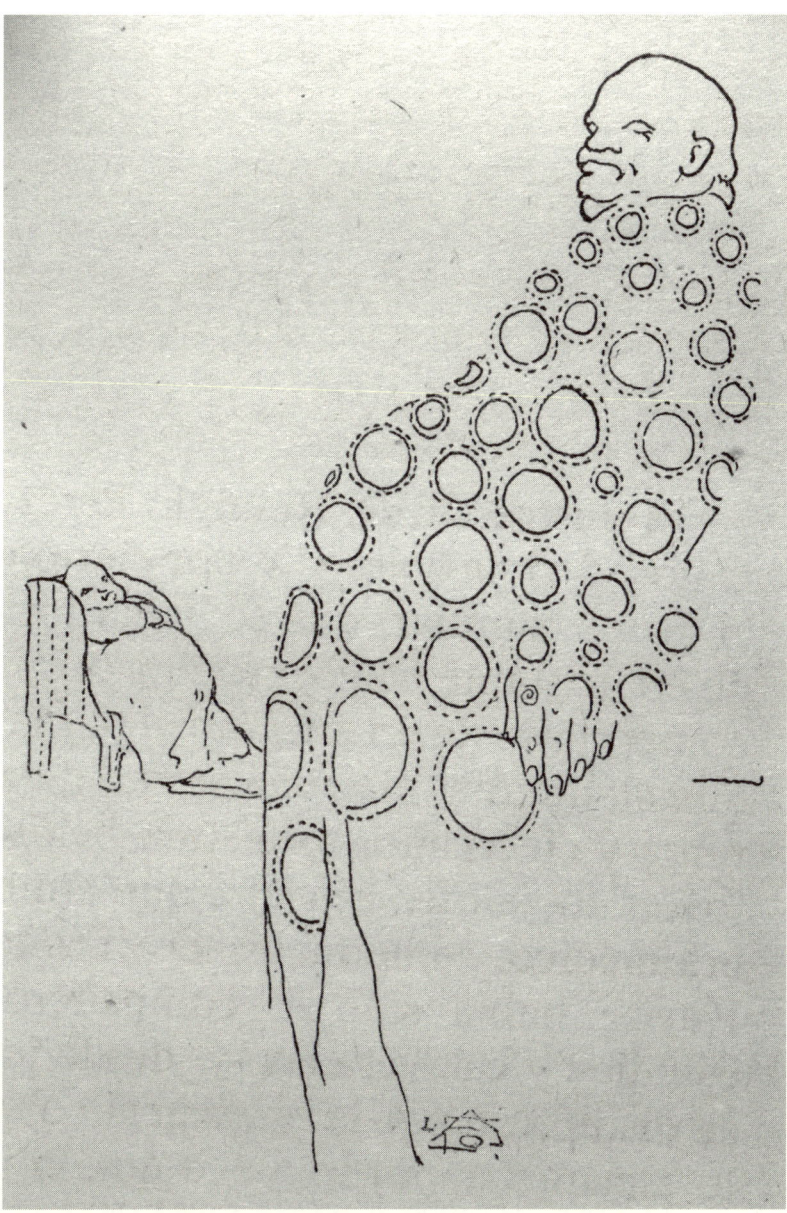

FIGURE 1.3. *The male gestators of the twenty-third century.* Eugenia, *p. 79.*
Used with permission of the Universidad Nacional Autónoma de Yucatán

method in use at that time" (193). The proud parents of the future look forward to the "removal of the ovule," the "implantation in the peritoneum of the gestator," and the "final solemn surgical delivery": "With what anxiety and anticipation they would await each of those steps; how intense their emotions would be as they witnessed them, clasped in each other's arms!" (193).

The text does not close with this "happy" prospect, however. The last chapter of *Eugenia* belongs to Celiana. The once brilliant thinker and orator reads the "cruel and heartless" farewell letter that Miguel has forced Ernesto to write in an attempt to help her start anew (203). But Celiana continues to fall more deeply under the influence of degenerating drugs. In the novel's final lines, Miguel mourns this loss, "one of the spoils that, on their triumphal march, Love and Life toss to the side of the road" (206).

"In my dreams, friend reader," Urzaiz writes in his prologue to *Eugenia*, "I contemplate an almost happy humanity; free, at least, of the fetters and prejudices with which at present it voluntarily complicates and embitters life" (3). Some of the "fetters and prejudices" he addresses in the novel include social customs, religious values, war, and nationalism. While the extremity of his suggested remedies often provoked negative reactions among his compatriots, these remedies were products of Urzaiz's own milieu.

Urzaiz found early twentieth-century morality impracticable and unprogressive. Once the gradual process of overcoming the "religious prejudices" and simplifying the "legal procedures" of his own times was completed, unrealistic demands for romantic fidelity would be replaced by the practice of free love and the traditional family unit by the *grupo* (22–23). Women, freed from the burdens of childbearing and child rearing, would attain equal status with men.[43]

Writing in the immediate aftermath of international war abroad and in times of great unrest at home, Urzaiz is less concerned than Ezcurra or Barnsley with the construction of a specifically Mexican national identity. Although he places his utopia in a recognizably Mexican setting—Villautopía is Mérida, according to Peniche Vallado (27), and the architecture is described as "in the neo-Mayan style" (Urzaiz 20)—the inhabitants of his twenty-third century disparage patriotism, national honor, and the flag. During one of the informal debates with Celiana's old teacher, Matías Urrea—a character believed to represent Urzaiz himself (Peniche Vallado 27–28)—pronounces these three things

FIGURE 1.4. *Eugenic couple, Ernesto and Eugenia, with aerocycles and other futuristic modes of transportation in the background.* Eugenia, *p. 184. Used with permission of the Universidad Nacional Autónoma de Yucatán*

to be "our great-grandparents' convenient props, . . . the pretexts with which they covered up their collective crimes" (115). Urzaiz has little confidence that World War I has improved the global order; as Celiana says, "that triumph was very transitory and more apparent than real" (121). In the novel, World War I has led to a series of international wars in the twentieth and twenty-first centuries, and these wars finally result in "universal disarmament and the disappearance of nationalities" (41). The Mexican Revolution is never directly mentioned, but it seems to permeate the narrative alongside the Great War. The series of world wars projected by Urzaiz are said to have ended not so much due to the fighting itself, but to "misery, hunger, epidemics, the lack of commerce, and the paralysis of industry" and to the ensuing "weariness and exhaustion of the warring peoples" (126–27, 147; see figure 1.5).

The Mexican Revolution also would appear to be a prime motivation behind the repeatedly expressed anxiety in *Eugenia* regarding depopulation, an anxiety that is far stronger than might be predicted by the notion that "to govern is to populate."[44] Compared with *Century XXX* or *São Paulo 2000*, the creation of a single national identity is of less importance in *Eugenia*. The desire for homogeneity remains, but is subsumed under the dual emphases of increasing the population and combating degeneration. As we have seen in *Eugenia's* title, rhetoric, and plot, the application of eugenics is both more overt and more extreme in this novel. We can observe the persistence of Lamarckian hereditary thought, as improvement in the environment is expected to improve the population's health and genetic makeup.[45] Racial poisons are blamed for degeneration, Ernesto is prohibited from smoking or drinking alcohol while working as an official breeder, and the sterile Celiana's downfall is symbolized by her increasing drug use. Urzaiz's proposal to select the best human breeders, such as Ernesto and Eugenia, would have been acceptable within the tenets of the Lamarckian tradition of eugenics popular in Latin America at the time. On the other hand, his plans to "de-select" the unfit—sterilization for some, euthanasia for others—was undoubtedly a major cause of negative reaction to the novel in Mexico. Such actions targeted heredity rather than environment, incorporating methods more popular in Anglo-Saxon countries with their Mendelian-based eugenics.[46]

The novel does not directly address Mexico's racial heterogeneity. In fact, the indigenous population is conspicuous by its absence (barring the passing reference to neo-Mayan architecture). The word *mestizo* is

FIGURE 1.5. *The end of war. The global wars of the twentieth and twenty-first centuries lead to global peace. Broken spears, remnants of the U.S. flag, and a crowned skull can be discerned on the pyre.* Eugenia, *p. 129. Used with permission of the Universidad Nacional Autónoma de Yucatán*

never used, as the "cosmic race" has not yet become the predominant paradigm. Ideas of superior/inferior races and of crossbreeding between races to combat degeneration do appear, however. The African doctors that visit the Bureau of Eugenics tell the director: "In order to escape the evolutionary stagnation in which our people lie, we have tried to crossbreed with superior races," but they have been unable to attract either white immigrants or those from more advanced African nations to mix with them because economic conditions in the home countries of these "superior" races are too good (89). Their only recourse, they believe, is to imitate the techniques of artificial selection in use in the Subconfederation of Central America and other civilized regions. Not coincidentally, in addition to sharing similar immigration issues, Africa is directly linked to the Mexico of Urzaiz's time, as the doctors admit that, in comparison with the Subconfederation, their nation "is at least three centuries behind" (88–89).[47]

"We must not forget, sirs, that the progress of Humanity is unlimited," Urrea/Urzaiz tells his intellectual circle in Villautopía, and we must also remember that Urzaiz was writing about "an *almost* happy humanity" (146; 3, emphasis mine). Some imperfections remain in 2218, such as vestiges of social and economic inequality. As in a number of other early Latin American utopias, conditions for all have improved to the point that no one wants for any material necessities and the "poor" are those who, "due to laziness, lack of ambition, or lack of ability," must go without nonessential luxuries (143). Once the practice of artificial selection has eliminated differences of "aptitude and merit" in humans, Urzaiz's characters posit, a state of absolute social and economic equality may be attained (146).

Utopia or dystopia? Unless we can determine how Urzaiz viewed *Eugenia*, we are left with irresolvable inconsistencies in the narrative. Urzaiz says that the novel is a representation of his hopes and dreams, calls his city Villautopía, and closes the story with the union of an ideal pair that is soon to produce a still more perfect child. However, it remains difficult to call the novel utopian when considering the extreme degree of state control over private life—and indeed over a citizen's right to live. To play the devil's advocate, Urzaiz gives us two responses to these objections. First, the state alone did not control reproduction. "The reproduction of the species," as Celiana writes in an article on the evolution of the twenty-third-century family, "was supervised by the State and regulated by science" (23)—science, that impartial, truth-bearing guarantor of progress. Second, as a scientist who had worked with the mentally ill, researched reproductive hormones, and studied in the United States, Urzaiz appears to believe that the ends justify the means. As the group touring the Bureau of Eugenics contemplates the robustly healthy infants produced there, Urzaiz's narrator makes the following Machiavellian observation:

> That splendid flowering of life and health was enough in itself to justify whatever violent or immoral aspects there might be in the methods to which Humanity had been forced to resort to halt its degeneration and disappearance and continue steadily on its evolutionary march toward an ideal of perfection. (77)

> Aquel espléndido florecimiento de vida y salud bastaba por sí solo para justificar cuanto de violento o inmoral pudiese haber en las medidas a que la Humanidad se había visto obligada a recurrir para detener su degeneración y acabamiento y seguir con paso firme su marcha evolutiva hacia un ideal de perfección.

Another possibility—one that always suggests itself when a scholar of Cervantes is involved—is that *Eugenia* is meant to be satire. But satirical passages are thin on the ground in the novel, and 1919 is historically too early in the trajectory of eugenics in Latin America (or anywhere else in the world) for either satire or dystopia based on fear of eugenics to be likely. Perhaps the most perplexing aspect of *Eugenia* in this debate is the degree to which the supposedly secondary love story undermines the novel's utopian society. A reader cannot be entirely comfortable with the fact that all of the principal theses of Urzaiz's utopia are expressed via the sterilized, genetically "unfit" characters, or that these characters are far more sympathetically portrayed than the insensitive Ernesto and the vapid Eugenia. Although the novel is named after Eugenia, readers begin with Celiana on the cover and leave with Miguel's parting words ringing in our ears. Urzaiz may have thought he had envisioned a perfect world, but he could envision no perfect way to reach it.

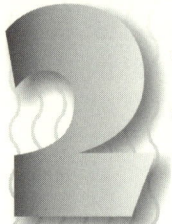

THE IMPACT OF DARWINISM
CIVILIZATION AND BARBARISM MEET EVOLUTION AND DEVOLUTION

In contrast to British writers of scientific romances and French writers of early science fiction, Stableford tells us, "American writers after the turn of the century were much less disposed to adopt premises from evolutionary theory, and early American speculative fiction was mostly content to steer clear of this particular war of ideas" (*Scientific Romance* 6). Unlike the U.S. writers to whom Stableford is referring, Latin American writers regularly included evolutionary themes in their science-fictional texts, though they often espoused theories of evolution alternative to that of Darwin. Latin American ties to France and to French scientific thought have been discussed in chapter 1 with regard to eugenics; the same affinity for Lamarck's ideas can be found in Latin America in the broader context of evolution. In nations seeking to progress, to become more "civilized," to "evolve," the appeal of concepts such as the inheritance of acquired characteristics and the perfectibility principle is readily apparent.[1] These ideas would also prove to be particularly attractive to adherents of Spiritism, Theosophy, or other alternative belief systems—including a number of prominent Spanish American modernists—who sought to extend the scope of evolution beyond the earthly or physical plane. Writers of early Latin American science fiction explored evolutionary themes using settings that ranged from the distant past to the far future, envisioning Latin America as the locus for realities that varied from Edenic utopia to apocalypse.

The impact of evolution on conceptions of time is especially notable in Latin America and in early Latin

American sf. Typical tensions between cyclical and linear visions of timeflow, between evolution and its counterpart devolution, between progress and degeneration or decadence are exacerbated in a context in which, as we have stated in the introduction, discussions on these themes were often displaced reenactments of the eternal Latin American debate on civilization versus barbarism. Latin Americans sought scientific solutions for promoting the civilization/evolution of their societies and for ameliorating the barbarism/degeneration they found in them. Scientific Darwinism was not long in arriving in Latin America, but Social Darwinism, with its scientific veneer, also proved to be particularly persistent and insidious there. Cyclical theories of history such as that proposed by Nicolai Danilevsky in his *Russia and Europe* (1869) were also popular in Latin America well in advance of Spengler's *The Decline of the West* (1918), as they allowed non-first-world regions such as Russia and Latin America to push influential Europe toward the past and claim the future as their own.

As the century turned, trends in non-utopian Latin American science fiction included a general movement away from optimism toward pessimism, and from technophilia to technophobia. With utopias as well as some tales of artificial humans (see chapter 4) among the notable exceptions, science fiction tended to be based less on the canonical sciences. A broader definition of science was gaining acceptance among many Latin American writers, as the academic sciences failed to unravel all of life's mysteries. The nation-building, overtly political nature of much of Latin American sf of the late nineteenth century also began to change in the first decades of the twentieth. Issues of national identity, influence, and politics were woven more subtly into geographies of setting, into characters' nationality or social class, and into choices to pursue noncanonical alternatives to traditional sources of authority.

BY BURRO AND BY *BEAGLE*: GEOGRAPHICAL JOURNEYS THROUGH TIME IN LATIN AMERICAN SCIENCE FICTION

In his discussion of Twain's *A Connecticut Yankee in King Arthur's Court*, Bud Foote makes a provocative connection between travel through geographical space and travel through time in North American culture, stating, "Americans have a peculiar tendency to identify past, present, and future time with location; as one travels to the past in space, one can generate the idea of doing so in time" (65). Foote goes on to trace the multiple geographic-temporal currents present in the United States, with the Western frontier representing the future and the East the past, the past of the agricultural South playing against the future of the industrial North and, somewhat more problematically, the nation as a whole symbolizing the future versus Europe as the past. He describes the U.S. position toward Europe as "contradictory and ambiguous," with images of Europe as the sentimental motherland competing with those that assign it to a past beyond which we have progressed. Foote argues that such time-place associations cannot exist in the same way for Europe, where past, present, and future must coexist in the same geographical space.[2] Foote further differentiates North America from South America in this regard, stating that, "in South America, since the Spanish tended to colonize from the west, the Portuguese from the east, the future never got to lie in any particular direction" (65). It is with this statement that I want to take issue. With the help of two early writers of Latin American science fiction and their texts, we will see not only that there is a Latin American variation to this geographic-temporal theme, but that Latin America's science-fictional representations demonstrate an even more problematic relationship with Europe while exemplifying the efforts of Latin American countries to consolidate their own histories and national identities as they struggle to locate—or relocate—the geography of the future.

While specifying the location of the future vis-à-vis Latin America is a somewhat thorny issue, the past is not quite so elusive, though as in North America it is associated with more than one geographic location. A glance at any map of colonial Latin America shows the great majority of early Spanish and Portuguese settlements established on the coasts. Current population-density maps reveal that, in much of Latin America, the coastal cities retain their importance. The heavy concentrations of commerce, industry, and political and cultural institutions in the coastal centers pinpoint them as the general location of the geographic present, if not the future. In contrast, the past has generally been located in the interior of Latin American nations, or beyond other frontiers that separated "civilized" regions from those that were more sparsely settled and less known. To this day, the Amazonian interior is internationally known for harboring remnants of primeval forest as well as some of the last blank spaces in terrestrial cartography.

With his seminal *Civilization and Barbarism or The Life of Juan Facundo Quiroga* [*Civilización y barbarie o vida de Juan Facundo Quiroga*] of

1845, Sarmiento canonized the popular perception of the Argentine *pampa* as linked with the barbarous gaucho-caudillo-rural-backward past in contrast with the civilized-populous-urban-modern capital, the port of Buenos Aires. Other representations of Argentine national pasts can be found in the Misiones province of the short stories of Horacio Quiroga, in the *pampa* of José Hernández's *Martín Fierro*, and in the South of Borges's "The South" [El Sur]. In Brazil, Euclides da Cunha's *Rebellion in the Backlands* [*Os Sertões*] of 1902 represents the relationship between a (then) coastal national government and a group of *sertanejos* from one of Brazil's interiors. Alongside these typical nineteenth-century associations of Latin American interiors and frontier regions with a retrograde past, however, we often find a "rebranding" of that relationship. These regions are also portrayed as areas of untrammeled natural beauty and bountiful natural resources, as wellsprings of national history and identity, and as potentially containing the keys to the most significant scientific puzzles of the day.

As we have seen, a relatively large proportion of the earliest texts of Latin American science fiction depict fantastic voyages to outer space or to the future. Concurrently, however, some of these same writers were publishing tales of marvelous overland journeys set in contemporary Latin America—journeys to a nation's natural, historical, and cultural pasts. The Brazilian Augusto Emílio Zaluar (1825–82) and the Argentine Eduardo Ladislao Holmberg each produced one such work in 1875. Both Zaluar's *Doctor Benignus* [*O Doutor Benignus*] and Holmberg's *Two Factions Struggle for Life: A Scientific Fantasy* [*Dos partidos en lucha: Fantasía científica*] were based on the travel narratives of European naturalists and Latin American expeditionaries, including the authors themselves. Zaluar had published *Peregrination through the Province of São Paulo (1860–1861)* [*Peregrinação pela Província de S. Paulo*] in 1862 and, among other such accounts, Holmberg published *Travels through Patagonia* [*Viajes por la Patagonia*] in 1872. Despite marked dissimilarities between the backgrounds and world views of their authors, the two works in question share a number of common elements. Both *Doctor Benignus* and *Two Factions* were influenced by the works of Jules Verne, Camille Flammarion, Darwin, and Sarmiento, and among the central themes of both are scientific and pseudoscientific uses of evolutionary theories, national progress through the spread of scientific knowledge, and the representation of South America as the locus for a utopian future.

Augusto Emílio Zaluar, *Doctor Benignus*

Born in Portugal in 1825, Zaluar arrived in Brazil in 1849 and became a naturalized Brazilian citizen in 1856. He spent a portion of his professional career as a professor of pedagogy at the Teacher Training College; he was also a journalist. Zaluar produced texts in a variety of literary forms and genres: poems, short stories, at least one play and one novel, plus the aforementioned travel narrative, for which he is best known. In politics he was a staunch supporter of the status quo, a conservative monarchist who upheld Dom Pedro II's policies and his claim to the throne of the Brazilian Empire. He was a member of the Auxiliary Society for National Industry [Sociedade Auxiliadora da Indústria Nacional], the closest thing to a scientific society in Brazil and, though not a scientist himself, he has been described as "reasonably informed about the scarce scientific activities of the time" (Carvalho 9). Zaluar's writings reveal a belief in the alliance of scientific and religious principles and in an undifferentiated evolutionism with aspects reminiscent of the arguments of Lamarck, Spencer, Darwin, Haeckel, Huxley, and Wallace.

Although several Brazilian texts of a science-fictional nature were already in existence in 1875, the editors of the first edition of *Doctor Benignus* called it Brazil's "first exercise in writing a scientific or instructive novel" (qtd. in Zaluar 27). The publishing company's assertion is evidence that early Latin American works of science fiction did not constitute a coherent local tradition, and that writers' connections with the genre tended to be either exclusively or primarily with Northern European and North American authors and works. Zaluar himself affirms his scientifically enriched novel to be "the simple presentiment of the new phase that contemporary literature must necessarily enter," part of a trend which he claimed was already in evidence in "the most advanced societies" (he mentions England, Germany, and the United States specifically; 28).

The eponymous protagonist of *Doctor Benignus* is a Brazilian scientist and a "true wise man" (33). So devoted is he to the pursuit of knowledge that he vows in the first chapter to leave the bustling and worldly capital city of Rio de Janeiro for the relative isolation and tranquility of a country estate in the neighboring province of Minas Gerais. Upon the eve of his departure, the good doctor describes himself as a Brazilian version of one of the contemporary science-fictional heroes of Jules Verne:

I do not know if you have read a clever book by Jules Verne, which has for its title *From the Earth to the Moon?* Well, I am the Michel Ardan of that daring expedition, with the difference that, instead of going to the Moon, I am going to the interior of Brazil; instead of being transported by a cannon ball, I will be transported by a burro, an animal less dangerous than a projectile, and which has biblical tradition—so highly recommended by the orthodox church—in its favor. (Zaluar 43)

Não sei se já lestes um espirituoso livro de Júlio Verne, que tem por título *Da Terra à Lua?* Pois eu sou o Miguel Ardan dessa arrojadíssima expedição, com a diferença que, em lugar de ir para a Lua, vou para o sertão; em lugar de ser transportado por uma bala, sê-lo-ei por um burro, animal menos perigoso que um projetil, e que tem a seu favor a tradição bíblica, tão recomendada pela igreja ortodoxa.

The value of exploring the Brazilian interior is placed on a par with exploring the great Vernian unknowns. Despite the overt analogy between Ardan and himself, however, Benignus links the European hero with the latest of futuristic technologies while, in contrast, his own method of transportation belongs to the past.

Benignus soon establishes another connection with Europe, writing a letter to the French scientist, writer, and popularizer of science, Camille Flammarion. The two of them are, Benignus ventures, "two souls that understand one another" (55). He expresses particular interest in Flammarion's works, from his *The Plurality of Inhabited Worlds* [*La pluralité des mondes habités*] (1862) to his *Stories of Infinity* [*Récits de l'infini*] (1873) because, he reasons, if Flammarion's theory that there is life on other worlds is correct, it would then follow that "there will be beings on other worlds that are more perfect than we, and, in consequence, closer to absolute unity, to the originary principle" [haverá em outros mundos entes mais perfeitos do que nós, e, por conseqüência, mais próximos da unidade absoluta, do princípio originário] (49–50). This allows a transitional evolutionist to claim the existence of evidence of the perfectibility of the human species, a religious man to believe that his striving to become more like God may yield tangible results on Earth as well as in heaven, and a Brazilian Social Darwinist to hope that his own nation might aspire to "evolve" industrially, scientifically, culturally, and racially and to reach the heights already attained by European civilization.

Indeed, in his letter Benignus proposes to "extend the hand of America to Europe," but he does not see the relationship as one in which America merely imports scientific knowledge and other civilizing influences from Europe (56). Brazil, Benignus emphasizes in various ways, does not come to the table empty-handed. Throughout the letter he extols the fecundity and the diversity of Brazilian flora and fauna and the optimal conditions of the unspoiled, crystalline Brazilian skies for astronomical observation. He invites Flammarion to come to Brazil in search of "new and more fertile inspiration from these favored regions of sun and of liberty" (53). González Echevarría has written that in the nineteenth century, "To travel to Latin America meant to find history in the evolution of plants and animals, and to find the beginning of history preserved—a contemporary, living origin" (110). Benignus repeatedly links Brazil's natural riches not with the backward, uncivilized past, but with the past of antiquity and the roots of humanity: the Brazilian sky is "like the mythological sky of the ancients," the forests are composed of "trees coetaneous to those of the first centuries of creation" (54, 51). He portrays Brazilian nature not as a barbarous opponent but as a "fecund laboratory" of unspoiled beauty and untapped potential (69). In making these connections Benignus seeks to establish Brazil's bona fides as a locus of cultural and historical significance in its own right, as an active participant in the creation of its own national identity. Europe is thus not the only source of humanity's—and Brazil's—past, and it is not the only arena in which scientific progress can be made. Zaluar represents the Brazil of the 1870s as less evolved than Europe, but he also emphasizes his adopted nation's associations with a privileged past that owed nothing to the Old World, and he stresses Brazil's potential as a contributing partner in the construction of the future.

On the naturalist's first sally into the Brazilian countryside, Dr. Benignus and his chef, Katini, a Peruvian Indian, "descendant of the Incas," discover a crude Indian mortuary urn containing a piece of papyrus that bears the legend "À pora" underneath an image of the sun (62). Upon discovering that "À pora" is Tupi for "ECCE INCOLAE: *here there are people, this place is populated, here there are inhabitants!*" (91), the good doctor interprets the inscription to be a sign of the merit of Flammarion's theory on life on other worlds. He decides to mount another, larger scientific expedition that will take advantage of the superior celestial viewing conditions of the Brazilian interior in order to prove that there is more advanced life on the sun. Secondary reasons for the expedition are provided by the other two men who join Benignus as its leaders: Fronville, a Frenchman, will study the riches of Brazilian nature, while a young British man, Jaime River, will try to rescue his anthropologist father, William, from the clutches of the savage Carajá Indians of Tocatins. Two other Northerners will be incorporated into this group during the course of the expedition. Frei Custódio, an Italian priest, embodies Zaluar's desired link between science and religion: "Blessed be your name, Lord," elucidates the priest, "for making science one of the greatest instruments of your power!" (334). James Wathon, an engineer and iron-foundry millionaire from Philadelphia who had once been cured of a near-fatal illness by Dr. Benignus, also joins the expedition in the interior after a record-breaking balloon journey of several thousand kilometers. In *Doctor Benignus*, Europe and the United States represent examples of possible futures for Brazil; Europe is the model for culture, religion, and science, while the United States sets an example of industrialization, the Protestant work ethic, and practical Yankee applications of technology in transportation and communication. But other, higher futures for all of humanity are possible—beyond Earth, on other planets and stars—and Benignus intends to claim first contact with representatives from these more distant futures for Brazil and Brazilian science.

The joint Brazilian-European venture departs from Benignus's estate in southeastern Minas Gerais. From there, the expedition proceeds in a northwesterly direction across Minas, through Goiás, culminating in a visit to the Ilha do Bananal [Banana Grove Island] in the region of Tocatins on the western border of Goiás (see figure 2.1). The journey's trajectory is summarized by the Frenchman, Fronville, in terms that illustrate our extension of Foote's theory, linking geographical and temporal travel in the Southern hemisphere:

> We are traveling, to put it one way, in the inverse direction of the evolutionary march of civilization. First we depart from the frontiers of the inhabited world, which are actively engaged in its intellectual and moral emancipation; we then move into the vast province of Minas Gerais, which marks, in a certain way, the transition between social activity and the primitive indolence

of less advanced peoples; and finally, we are going to enter the wilderness which is still inhabited by the savage but picturesque types belonging to the families of the first humans! Our excursion could not be more singular or more instructive. (271)

Vamos seguindo, por assim me exprimir, em sentido inverso à marcha evolutiva da civilização. Partimos primeiramente das fronteiras do mundo habitado e ativo na obra de sua emancipação intelectual e moral, penetramos depois na vasta província de Minas Gerais, que marca de um certo modo a transição entre a atividade social e a primitiva indolência dos povos menos adiantados, e vamos entrar finalmente nos desertos ainda habitados pelos tipos selvagens, mas pitorescos das primeiras famílias humanas! A nossa digressão não pode ser nem mais curiosa nem mais instrutiva.

The population-dense Brazilian coast from which Benignus has come, then, forms the last bastion of the inhabited/emancipated/advanced world connected to Europe and the future. Again, the city has historically been associated with civilization and progress in Latin America, and the Brazilian frontier, unlike that of the nineteenth-century United States, did not tempt the average inhabitant to "Go West, young man" and create a future in the freedom of open spaces.

The semi-civilized longitudes of Minas Gerais and Goiás have been held back, Benignus and Fronville lament, by the very mineral riches that first brought them to prominence. "Gold," they say, "is the origin of ostentation and debauchery"; its presence discourages the development of renewable sources of wealth such as agriculture and cattle ranching (156). Iron, they tell each other, would historically have been much better for these provinces because its properties make it "the safeguard of civilization . . . the grave and holy instrument of work, the generator of the economy and the counselor of morality!" (155–56). Fortunately for the future of Brazil, Benignus tells of recent discoveries of iron in these areas, and Fronville discovers a new deposit during the expedition. According to these two men of science, it is precisely such "conquests of science over the natural riches of the soil" which, together with industrial development, will bring "happiness and civilization" to cure the "decadence" of Brazil's interior (276).

Zaluar depicts the far interior using contradictory terms and images in a continuing effort to locate a silver lining in the region his character

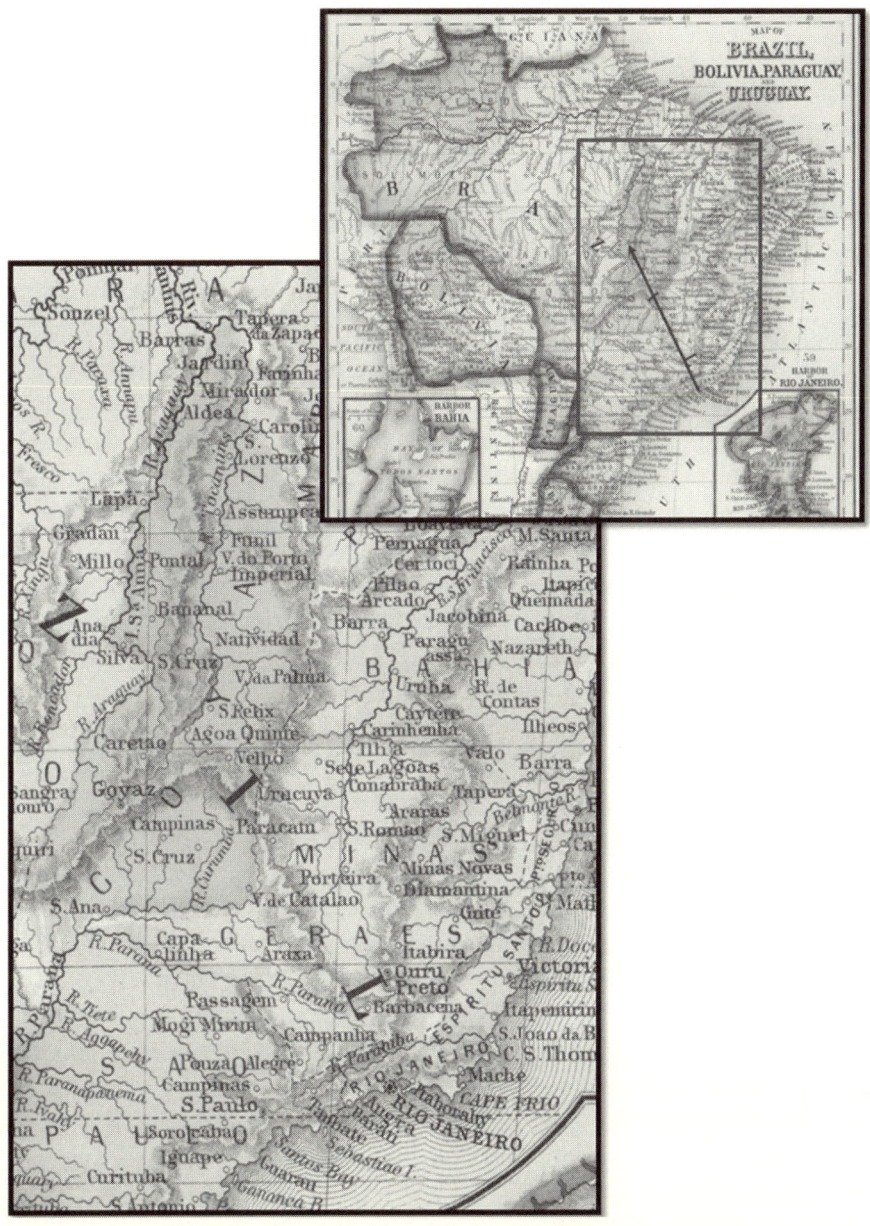

FIGURE 2.1. *Journey of Doctor Benignus from Rio de Janeiro, through Minas Gerais and Goiás, to the Ilha do Bananal in the interior of Brazil. Details of the "Map of Brazil, Bolivia, Paraguay, and Uruguay."* Mitchell's New General Atlas. *Philadelphia: S. Augustus Mitchell, Jr., 1865. Courtesy of the University of Florida George A. Smathers Libraries, Map & Imagery Collection*

describes as most distant from the "march of civilization" (271). Fronville characterizes the inhabitants of the *sertão* as "savage but picturesque types," describing them as "primitive" and "less advanced," while claiming that they belong to the "first human families," thus usurping the distinction of "cradle of humanity" from Africa.[3] At one point during the expedition, the scientists think they have located the missing evolutionary link, but it proves to be a false alarm. Zaluar appears to be far more interested in the implications of Social Darwinism than in the work of Darwin or his disciples. He subscribes to the view that sentient beings fall along a linear evolutionary continuum and—despite his expressions of interest in elevating the status of indigenous peoples—he clearly believes that, at present, they belong at the lower end of what his narrator describes as the "unequal series of the human family" (310). Reconstructed from clear assertions and assumptions throughout *Doctor Benignus*, Zaluar's racial hierarchy lists, in ascending order: apes, the fabled "missing link," black slaves,[4] Brazilian Indians, members of the great indigenous civilizations such as the Inca, free men of Brazil, Northern Europeans/North Americans/enlightened Brazilian elites, scientists, and finally, beings on other orbs who have evolved beyond humanity and beyond material form.

Zaluar does believe in the possibility of moving up in this hierarchy, through education and the subsequent passing on of acquired traits to one's descendants. Fronville's location of the evolutionary past in Brazil's interior, therefore, complements as well as contrasts with Benignus's search for the evolutionary future. After carrying out his observations of sunspots and reviewing the supporting scientific authorities, Benignus is more convinced than ever that there is life on the sun. When a meteorite lands near the camp during their travels in Goiás, Benignus falls asleep atop it and a luminous being appears to him. This Sun Being tells Benignus that he has deigned to visit such an insignificant world as Earth due to Benignus's "thirst for knowledge, so rare among your fellows" (293), and he lauds and encourages Benignus's efforts to make this knowledge accessible to others, declaring:

> Among the efficacious means of elevating man, your fellow creature, to his spiritual perfection, which is also morally his objective goal, lies the principle of the fruitful and noble mission that you have taken upon yourself, that is, to popularize scientific issues and by that means to raise the intellectual level of the people. (295)

> Entre os meios eficazes de elevar o homem teu semelhante ao seu aperfeiçoamento espiritual, que é também moralmente o seu ponto objectivo, consiste o principal na fecunda e nobre missão de que te encarregaste, isto é, vulgarizar os resultados da ciência e fazer subir por esse meio o nível intelectual do povo.

The Sun Being further recognizes Benignus as "the symbol of the alliance and the fraternization of the civilized nations on this part of the American continent" (295). Although the ultimate objective is the evolution of the entire human race, Benignus's immediate mission is to raise the evolutionary level of Brazil by spreading the gospel of science and serving as a link between a multitemporal Brazil and the more future-oriented, evolved, and "civilized" (Europeanized, westernized, modernized) nations of the world.

Zaluar reaffirms Benignus's mission at the lower end of his evolutionary scale as well. When the expedition reaches the Ilha do Bananal to rescue the British anthropologist, William River, Chief Koinaman of the Carajá tribe tells Benignus that they have kept River a prisoner in order to learn from him, declaring: "I am the first to recognize his superiority over us" (317). Here, in the heart of the Brazilian darkness, Benignus decides to establish a utopian settlement to be led by the Brazilian, French, British, and North American expedition members and their families. The island's original inhabitants, the Carajá Indians, will be elevated from wild savages to workers on the new estates and in the new factories of this agricultural and industrial colony. The emissaries from the civilized Northern hemisphere and Brazilian coast will bring concrete advances in iron-working, industry, and agriculture, "attracting the races still immersed in indolence and barbarism to civilization through the holy communion of labor" (346). Transportation and communication with the North will be improved as well, with the steamships that had formerly run between New York and Rio now supplanted by the Wathon-improved balloons.[5]

Less tangible civilizing benefits include a work ethic, Christianity, peace with near neighbors and distant coastal authorities, and education in subjects from languages to the sciences. By strong implication, the higher evolutionary status of the newcomers will also benefit the natives by example, by association, and, perhaps, by miscegenation or *branqueamento* [racial whitening]. Those Latin Americans who thought of race in terms of Social Darwinism were avid proponents of "improving" the indigenous races by intermarriage; as Doris Sommer has written, "Miscegenation was the road to racial perdition in Europe, but it was the way of redemption in Latin America, a way of annihilating difference and constructing a deeply horizontal, fraternal dream of national identity. It was a way of imagining the nation through a future history" (39). It is noteworthy in Zaluar's case that he does not specifically discuss racial mixing. The only marriage that takes place at the end of *Doctor Benignus* is between two Europeans residing in Brazil: the Frenchman, Fronville, and the British daughter of William River. This is most atypical for a text that purports to be a foundational fiction for Latin America, but it is likely explained by Zaluar's belief in the possibility of intellectual and moral evolution, his Portuguese roots, and/or his support for the Brazilian but Eurocentric monarchy of Pedro II. As a conservative monarchist, Zaluar could not envision an ideal future that entailed any changes in the national political or economic power structure.

González Echevarría writes that "scientific exploration brought about the second European discovery of America, and the traveling naturalists were the new chroniclers" (11); he further discusses the ways in which "scientific discourse presumably establishes a distance between naturalists and the world they study" (107). If we reframe these concepts in science-fictional terms, these scientific expeditions in the New World were no longer "first contact" situations, but situations of second contact and beyond. In our text, Benignus, a Europeanized member of the Brazilian upper class, brings about a second or final subduing of the indigenous population that is less violent than the first but just as colonial. Benignus uses the distancing—or estranging—lens of science to analyze his own nation; this perspective allows him to envision a solution for pulling the backward Brazilian interior out of the past and into the future. Although Zaluar may locate the future in Brazil, he does not represent it as belonging to Brazil alone. His vision must be achieved in partnership with North America and Northern Europe, and can only be accomplished once the barbaric aspects of the Brazilian past have completed their transformation.

Eduardo Ladislao Holmberg, *Two Factions Struggle for Life*

The Argentine Eduardo Ladislao Holmberg was a medical doctor by training, a naturalist by vocation, and an educator by primary profession. A member of the third generation of one of Argentina's leading families, he was also a translator, the writer or editor of countless scientific and literary works, and an explorer of his country's remotest provinces. His grandfather Eduardo Kannitz, Baron of Holmberg, had left Europe in 1812 to fight alongside San Martín in Argentina's wars for independence; his father, don Eduardo Holmberg y Abalbastro, fought with Lavalle's armies and subsequently accompanied Sarmiento into temporary exile in Chile. Our Eduardo Holmberg followed the family tradition of taking part in national life by working at the "noble civilizing projects that the country would undertake once the difficulties of its own organization were surmounted" (Pagés Larraya 10).

These "civilizing projects" took several forms. In politics Holmberg supported a democratic system, a "Republic governed by knowledge" ruled by an educated but permeable "select minority" (Luis Holmberg 104). As a naturalist Holmberg was responsible for collecting and categorizing samples of Argentine flora and fauna as part of the scientific inventory of the fledgling Republic of Argentina. These activities also formed part of Argentina's nineteenth-century transition from "source of raw scientific data" (as it was of raw materials), sent to Europe for analysis and processing, to "producer of knowledge" (Rodríguez 29). As Rodríguez elaborates:

> The first science in Argentina had been colonial in its methods and purposes. Specimens gathered had been sent to Europe for inspection and classification. Diseases were fought with the goal of protecting the European colonists. But now, decades later, the flow of information was in the other direction: scientists focused on the needs of the nascent nation, though they were still dependent largely on European theories and models. (30)

In his own life, then, Holmberg was an active participant in a process that seemed destined to reverse or at least alter the polarity of these European-Argentine associations (Europe-science-future and Argentina-raw data-past).

In his capacity as a scientist and professor of science, Holmberg founded scientific journals, participated in Argentina's first scientific societies, produced scientific textbooks, and taught virtually every known branch of science to the nation's future teachers. Holmberg's strong desire to popularize the sciences was founded in a belief, similar to that of Zaluar, in the connection between scientific knowledge

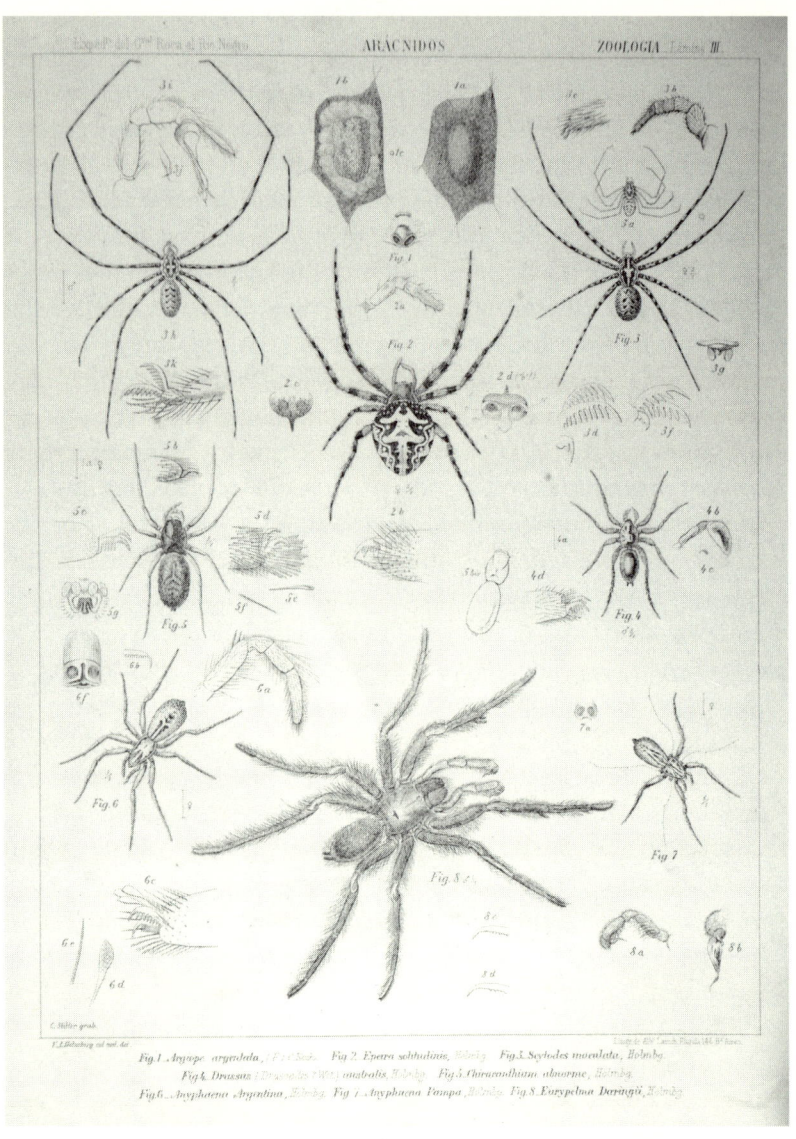

FIGURE 2.2. Arachnids [Arácnidos] *by Eduardo Ladislao Holmberg. Drawings accompany Holmberg's article in the report of a national scientific expedition, published in* Informe oficial de la comisión científica agregada al estado mayor general de la expedicion al Río Negro (Patagonia) realizada en los meses de Abril, Mayo y Junio de 1879, bajo las órdenes del general d. Julio A. Roca. *By Julio Argentino Roca, Adolf Döring, Carlos Berg, Eduardo Ladislao Holmberg, P. G. Lorentz, and Gustavo Niederlein. Vol. 1. Buenos Aires: Imprenta de Ostwald y Martinez, 1881. Zoology, Plate 3.*

and national progress, and in the use of education to move from the past into the future. Like Zaluar, Holmberg is voluble in his praise for Jules Verne. Holmberg particularly appreciates the Frenchman's gift for contributing to the scientific education of his readers by making science more understandable and more palatable: "[Verne,] with his powerful imagination, has sheathed the mysteries of science with a vaporous mantle that is full of attractions" (*Two Factions* 70). It should be noted that Holmberg's oft-expressed admiration was not necessarily due to Verne's specific interpretations of contemporary scientific theories. Where Verne was an opponent of Darwinian evolution, Holmberg was one of its staunchest defenders.

Although he was a pioneering writer of fantastic literature and maintained a lively interest in the alternative sciences, Holmberg's worldview and belief system were most heavily informed by the empirical sciences. He was a strong proponent of Darwin's theory of evolution, never giving credence to the tenets of Social Darwinism (Ortiz, "Transmission" 113). Holmberg was not the first Argentine to show interest in Darwin's ideas. In 1868 Sarmiento wrote: "Darwin's theory is Argentine, and I propose to nationalize it via Burmeister" (qtd. in Marún, "Introducción" 13).[6] As mentioned in chapter 1, Sarmiento brought a number of European scientists to Argentina during his presidency (1868–74), as part of his campaign to improve the national education system and to raise the nation's level of scientific knowledge and production. At the head of this group was Karl Hermann Burmeister, a respected German scientist. Unfortunately for Sarmiento's plans, Burmeister was an ardent creationist at the time.[7] It thus fell to homegrown scientists such as Holmberg to propagate Darwin's revolutionary theories among the general public. As a professor of the history of science, Marcelo Montserrat, tells us: "It is not strange for Darwinism to knock on the doors of a Republic avid for the latest novelties at that time; what is unusual is for the first public profession of the Darwinist credo to be expressed through a work of fiction written by a twenty-two-year-old medical student" (25). That work of fiction was Holmberg's novel, *Two Factions Struggle for Life*.

In the outer frame of *Two Factions*, dated December 1874, a narrator named Eduardo Ladislao Holmberg explains that the "true author of the literary diversion"—that is, the manuscript of *Two Factions*—is his friend Ladislao Kaillitz, a Darwinist.[8] The narrator claims that Kaillitz entrusted him with the pages of *Two Factions* before setting out across the Atlantic, for parts unknown, in September of that same year. Kaillitz's first-person tale contains two main geographical-temporal journeys, the first within Argentina itself, the second from Europe to Argentina.

In the first journey, which takes place in 1872, a young Kaillitz travels south from Buenos Aires to Río Negro, a region associated at the time with the "barbaric" and backward past. This trip echoes a southern journey made by Holmberg in the same year.[9] More significantly, it is a re-creation of the young Charles Darwin's original journey to Latin America aboard the *Beagle* in the 1830s. In the narrative, Kaillitz and his party come across the vestiges of one of Darwin's camps. The ship's captain, who served on the *Beagle* while Darwin was aboard, is inspired to teach Kaillitz the basic principles of evolution. By this device, Holmberg enables Kaillitz to retrace the English scientist's discoveries of forty years earlier, while taking his first steps toward becoming a leading Argentine Darwinist.

The central events of the narrative are two fictional debates between evolutionists and creationists, set in Buenos Aires in 1874.[10] The Argentine Darwinist faction is led by Kaillitz's new mentor, Pascasio Griffritz. Like Kaillitz, Griffritz is a semiautobiographical character, but one with ten more years of seniority and credentials than our young author.[11] The local creationists are represented by Francisco P. Paleolitez and Juan Estaca. Although Paleolitez's evocative name consigns him to the prehistoric strata of scientific thought, his name is also likely an allusion to the scientist Francisco Pascasio Moreno, a disciple of Burmeister and an adversary respected by Holmberg (Montserrat 27n18). Burmeister himself is not a principal actor in the story, but his name is invoked as the major authority behind the creationists. Estaca [literally, a stake, post, or cudgel] exemplifies the brand of creationist that Holmberg does not respect; the superficial nature of Estaca's scientific understanding is evidenced by his recitation, at every opportunity, of a memorized list of 323 Latin names of botanical species in lieu of a reasoned argument.

The novel's second journey is set up by the real political subtext behind the fictional debates.[12] Nicolás Avellaneda defeated Bartolomé Mitre in the Argentine presidential elections of February 1874, but he was not inaugurated until October of that year. During the intervening months, which encompass both of Holmberg's debates, Mitre led a revolt; the ensuing national unrest did not subside completely until December. Holmberg's "dos partidos" [two parties, or two factions] are political as well as scientific. While Holmberg hoped to bring the creationists among his reading public over to the Darwinist camp, he also used the text as a vehicle for the condemnation of political violence and an affirmation of the recently restored national unity, saying: "The colors of the political parties had merged in the blue and white of national unity after the electoral battles had been resolved with the almost-naming of the new president of the Republic" (11).

The capacity both to achieve political stability and to debate the latest scientific issues is touted in *Two Factions* as evidence that Argentina was prepared to take a more prominent place on the world stage, to be a locus for the future. As a debate organizer tells a crowd gathered in the Plaza Victoria: "The moment, long awaited by all of us, has finally arrived for us to show Europe and the world that we know how to maintain universal equilibrium with the peace that we enjoy and with the enlightenment that our ancestors bequeathed us" (14). This same quotation is also evidence, however, that Holmberg's Argentina has not completely broken free of its colonial relationship with Europe. Simply declaring the end of Argentine dependency is not enough; Argentina must prove her worth in the eyes of Europe, and the legitimacy of her new status requires recognition by the other nineteenth-century powers. The continuing primacy of European scientific theories in nineteenth-century Argentina is embodied both in Holmberg's characters and in the authorities he cites: all of the novel's acknowledged scientific—and literary—models are European, and all of its scientists (except for the false one, Estaca) possess European ancestry and surnames.

The ambiguity of the future's location in the text reaches its height in the second scientific debate. Although the Darwinists do fairly well in the first debate in Buenos Aires, they fail to convince the creationists of the superiority of their way of thinking. Holmberg then imagines a second journey to Argentina by an aging Darwin. Since Darwin had already landed once on Argentine shores, as part of the voyage on the HMS *Beagle*, why should he not then return—this time aboard the HMS *Hound*—to defend his theory? If Holmberg feels the need for Darwin's authority to bolster his case for Argentina's recognition as a progressive scientific nation, he refuses to acknowledge the debt; his narrator declares: "Not only do we owe [the English] nothing, we do not want to owe them anything" (90). This brash assertion is undermined, however, when Holmberg proceeds to make full use of his purloined Englishman to vouch for Argentine scientific legitimacy.

This second voyage does provide some evidence that the temporal currents have been reversed, however. Upon his arrival in Buenos Aires, the fictionalized Darwin proceeds to give his blessing to the Argentine Republic in the person of its president-elect, saying: "Permit me to take advantage of this glorious opportunity to wish you all the blessings to which an old man can aspire for the next government of the young President-elect of the Argentine Republic" [Permitidme aprovechar esta gloriosa oportunidad para desearos todas las bendiciones que un anciano puede anhelar para el próximo gobierno del jóven Presidente electo de la República Argentina] (113). With this benediction, Holmberg presents the passing of the torch from Europe to the New World—and specifically to Argentina, under this stable and progressive political leadership—as the new locus for cutting-edge scientific research, discovery, and debate.

During the second debate, Holmberg's Darwin completes the relocation of the future to Argentina and the relegation of Old World Europe to the past. He defers to an Argentine scientist, saying, "Mr. Griffritz will make known his opinions, which are more advanced and daring than my own" (133). Toward the end of the debate, Griffritz declares the transfer to be part of a Hegelian natural progression:

> The evolution of human society followed its progressive course from the Orient to the Occident . . . . And if it is true that for many centuries the Enlightenment has been linked to Europe, the dawn of the world Empire is already being divined in none other than America. (136)
>
> La evolucion de la sociedad humana siguió su curso progresivo de Oriente á Occidente . . . . Y si es verdad que durante muchos siglos la ilustracion ha estado encadenada á la Europa, no lo es menos que en la América se presienten ya los albores del Imperio del mundo.

In a further extrapolation by Holmberg, *Two Factions* culminates with new evidence of Argentina's scientific primacy, with Argentine scientists providing physiological proof—to the creationists and the world—that the Akka (an African pygmy tribe) represent the elusive missing link, a definitive verification of Darwin's theory of evolution.[13]

At the end of Kaillitz's account, the Holmberg-narrator returns to contribute an appendix to *Two Factions*, entitled "The Akkas: A Pygmy

Race of Central Africa" [Los Akkas: Raza pigmea del Africa central]. This appendix is a real translation (by Holmberg) of a real article (by respected French anthropologist Paul Broca) about a real scientific issue of the day: the place of the pygmy, or Akka, in human evolution.[14] In an introductory epigraph to the appendix, the narrator declares that "This article . . . more than eloquently explains the suppositions of Mr. Kaillitz," adding, however, that "It does not need to be read as an integral part of *Two Factions Struggle for Life*, but rather only by those who desire to illuminate themselves somewhat about one of the most important anthropological events of the nineteenth century, if not of the modern age" (140).[15] Because the article reveals that the Akkas have not yet been proven to be Darwin's missing link, the appendix seems to cloud Holmberg's vision of the new Argentina. This interplay of the real, the fictionalized, and the imaginary in the frame of the appendix, however, mirrors that in the body of the novel. Although the real article partially undermines the extrapolated fictional finale, by showing that real scientists were making the same suppositions as his fictional characters, the author supports their defense of Darwinism and, by association, their dreams for Argentina's future. Holmberg's journey toward a geographical relocation of the future is complete.

For these two nineteenth-century Latin American writers, the geography of the past—whether it is represented as lying in a "barbaric" interior or in national scientific backwardness—was not invulnerable to change. While Zaluar manages a science-fictional relocation of a utopian future to Brazil, this relocation is only possible—or desirable—in open partnership with Europe and the United States. Holmberg attempts to wrest ownership of the location of the future from Northern hands, yet he too requires European aid (through a fictional Darwin) to do so. By burro or by *Beagle*, these tales represent some of the early steps by Latin American science fiction writers to stake a claim on the geography of the future.

FROM HOLMBERG TO LUGONES:
THE INVERSION OF THE DARWINIAN LADDER

The relationship between Eduardo Ladislao Holmberg and Leopoldo Lugones (1874–1938) provides a rare example of direct literary influence in early Latin American science fiction.[16] Holmberg was "friend and mentor" to Lugones (Alter-Gilbert 17), and Lugones's admiration for Holmberg and his work is clear from his review of *Nelly* in *El Tiempo* on September 18, 1896. He refers to Holmberg as "one of the most complete intellectuals in Argentina" and notes that "*Nelly* constitutes a true novel in our meager literary world, . . . it has real value for its plot, for its style, for its originality" (qtd. in Pagés Larraya 87). Unlike Holmberg, whose work is only recently being exhumed from near oblivion, Lugones enjoys a firm place in the pantheon of Argentine authors; the national Day of the Writer is celebrated on the date of his birth. As Borges wrote in a biographical essay: "Leopoldo Lugones was and continues to be the greatest Argentine writer," and "American literature still gains nourishment from the work of this great writer; to write well is, for many, to write in the style of Lugones" (*Leopoldo Lugones* 95, 10). Beyond the disparity in their literary reputations, the commonalities and divergences in the lives and works of Holmberg and Lugones are generally illustrative of the changes that Argentine sf was undergoing at the turn of the twentieth century.

Education and science played an important role in the careers of both men. Holmberg was a secondary school inspector, the author of textbooks, and a teacher; Lugones also held a school inspector's post, wrote about education, and was the director of the Library of the National Education Council. Although Holmberg undoubtedly had superior scientific training, Lugones was, as Ortiz describes it, "warmly received in the *tertulias* [gatherings, circles] of the scientists" ("Transmission" 113). He wrote on scientific themes as a young journalist, represented Argentina at the Latin American Scientific Congress in Montevideo in 1904, and was instrumental in bringing Albert Einstein to Argentina in 1925 (Ortiz, "Transmission" 113–16; Scari 169–70). Both men had a tendency to be scientifically didactic in their literary works, though Lugones based more of his arguments on the noncanonical sciences, which he embraced more wholeheartedly than did Holmberg. Both wrote on a diverse range of topics in a wide variety of genres, although each had his own areas of expertise.

Whereas the older Holmberg perched on the fence between romanticism and modernism, Lugones belonged far more to the modernist movement. As Borges wrote, "The story of Leopoldo Lugones is inseparable from the story of modernism, although his work, as a whole, exceeds the limits of this school" (*Leopoldo Lugones* 13). Modernism was a global movement, and it marked the first instance in which literary influences moved from the Hispanic New World to the Old World. For Lugones, as for many of his contemporaries, it meant "an effort to incorporate Hispanic American literature in the western tradition with its own voice, without a loss of identity" (García Ramos 35). At the turn of the century, modernists were attempting to recover from, as Cathy Jrade expresses it, "the anxiety of their age as generated by fragmentation: individuals were out of touch with themselves, with their companions, and with Nature." She explains further: "They longed for a sense of wholeness, for innocence, for the paradise from which they had been exiled by the positivist and bourgeois emphasis on utility, materialism, and progress" (12). Modernists sought either to evade or to fill the void left by the crisis of belief that had resulted in Nietzsche's declaration of the death of God. Although they sought to express this new totality for which they searched in the language of science, the modernists found traditional science to be lacking as a substitute for religion:

> They maintained a respect for science, its breakthroughs, and its contributions to progress; they rejected it, however, as the ultimate measure of all things. Despite the promises made, it became clear that, far from becoming more understandable, life appeared more enigmatic, and the great inventions and discoveries had not provided answers to the fundamental questions of existence. (Jrade 11)

While Holmberg managed to be both scientist and "a Christian, but in my own way" (*Nic-Nac* 97), Lugones was profoundly anti-Christian. He turned to Theosophy as an extension of the scientific spectrum from the canonical sciences into the regions of the occult, in order to allow both his belief in a spiritual existence and his respect for modern science to coexist—in order, as Moore puts it, to "make religion rational" (7). Lugones was a member and sometime secretary general of the Theosophical Society in Buenos Aires. In an article in its official journal, *Philadelphia*, he delineates his position clearly:

> Science encompasses a much vaster concept than is attributed to it today. Today it is defined as the *aspiration* to truth; he who only knows facts is not a wise man; he is, if you will, an erudite man. In order to be wise it is necessary to know the laws of the universe, to feel beauty and to practice moral principles, to know, in a word, the

whole, and to proceed in light of it. This means the possession of the Truth. . . . if something is still needed in order to justify [the Theosophical doctrine], the scientific movement which it has originated would be the most brilliant proof. Theosophy aspires to synthesis, demonstrating in moral principles, the common origin of all religions; in science, the single law that comprehends all knowledge; in sociology, the solidarity that will be the definitive triumph of peace. (qtd. in Marini Palmieri 39–40)

Not all of the twelve stories in Lugones's *Strange Forces* [*Las fuerzas extrañas*] (1906; revised 1926) can be considered science fiction, and the claims that science fiction stakes on the works discussed in this book are not uncontested.[17] Cano has described three significant science-fictional aspects of the tales in *Strange Forces*: "the appropriation of the rhetoric of scientific discourse, the narrativization of the figure of the researcher and his methodology, and the deconstruction of the two prior concepts that Lugones carries out using alternative scientific principles" (116). Lugones's deconstructions include a wide range of targets, from scientific objectivity to the laws of planetary attraction and molecular cohesion. In the texts discussed in this chapter, Lugones focuses on Darwinian evolution, with its sequential conception of time. Lugones views time as cyclical, and he paints the ape-faced threat of devolution lurking behind the mask of progress and civilization. In the absence of tangible, universally acceptable, or corroborated evidence to support the theories expounded in *Strange Forces*, ultimately it is not science but literature—science *fiction*—that is presented as the route to truth.[18]

Leopoldo Lugones, "Essay on a Cosmogony in Ten Lessons" and "The Origin of the Flood"

With his "Essay on a Cosmogony in Ten Lessons" [Ensayo de una cosmogonía en diez lecciones, hereafter "Cosmogony"] (1906) Lugones places himself between the known and the unknown, the provable and the unexplainable, "an intermediate position, if only in terms of distance, between materialism and supernaturalism" ("Cosmogony" 274).[19] "Cosmogony" rounds out the collection of stories in *Strange Forces*, and provides the basic themes of which the stories are variations. "The Origin of the Flood: Narration of a Spirit" [El origen del diluvio: Narración de un espíritu] (1906) is the story with the closest ties to "Cosmogony," functioning as a partial, more literary, restatement of it.[20]

Both texts contain detailed descriptions of chemical reactions during Earth's formation, side by side with accounts of lunar beings that travel to Earth via a "cone of shadow." Both texts reveal Lugones's view of Earth's formation as a cyclical process ("When the matter of the planet has reached its *maximum* stability, the process of disintegration of this matter begins"), rather than as a linear process such as evolution ("The Darwinian ladder is thus totally inverted. Man is, then, the progenitor of the animal kingdom . . . thus if man was no more than a step, there was no reason for him to be the superior and the top one, but rather one of many"; "Cosmogony" 262, 276). Lugones justifies his anti-Darwinian stance by citing Adam's naming of the animals in Genesis as proof that man preceded the other species. Although man is not the result of an evolved perfection, Lugones tells us, as Earth is presently in the process of rounding the bend from integration into disintegration, the point of maximum stability for our planet seems to coincide with the age of modern man ("Cosmogony" 276, 263).[21]

Lugones's conception of the universe uses the language of science to demystify the Bible, myths, and natural phenomena alike. God's activities in the biblical first six days are analyzed in terms of chemistry, physics, and biology, although the theosophical lens through which Lugones views these processes leads to conclusions unacceptable to academic scientists both of our times and his.[22] The flood, or "the catastrophe which men afterwards called the flood," he explains as a consequence of Earth's increasing attraction for the moon's atmosphere and the subsequent evaporation of the lunar seas, which then recondensed on Earth ("Origin" 82; 175).[23] Huge, gelatinous beings that Lugones posits as an early form of organized life which later disappeared "were the giants of which the legends speak" ("Origin" 81; 174). The "fish with human faces" of the "Cosmogony" (279) are elaborated in "Origin of the Flood" into "beautiful monsters, half fish, half women, later called sirens in mythology" [monstruos hermosos, mitad pez, mitad mujer, llamados después sirenas en las mitologías] (85; 178).[24] These sirens (or mermaids) were, we are told, the first human beings after life arrived on Earth from the moon, and they knew certain moon secrets that modern humans have lost: "They possessed the secret of the original harmony, and they brought to the planet melodies of the moon which contained the secret of death" [Ellos dominaban el secreto de la armonía original, y trajeron al planeta las melodías de la luna que encerraban el secreto de la muerte] ("Origin" 178).

"Cosmogony" is the only text in *Strange Forces* to include numerous footnotes supplementing an already dense quotient of scientific content. These footnotes, as well as the ten lessons that form the body of the text, are addressed to the reader in the first person by the same narrator who appears in the framing preface and epilogue. This narrator purports to be transmitting the words of a mysterious "wise man" [sabio]—not, he makes clear, a mere "scholarly man" [erudito], whose training is limited to the canonical sciences—whom he meets in the Andes (282). The first-person narrator of the scientific core of "Origin of the Flood," however, claims to be a witness to the events described, though not a human or an earthly witness:

> And thus have you called forth my memories, across millions of years, evoking human sentiment, summoning me here to speak from the dimension where I dwell—the earth's cone of shadow. For there I am condemned to abide, throughout the ages, so long as the planet endures. (85)[25]

> He aquí lo que mi memoria, millonaria de años, evoca con un sentido humano, y he aquí lo que he venido a deciros descendiendo de mi región—el cono de sombra de la tierra. Os añadiré que estoy condenado a permanecer en él durante toda la edad del planeta. (178)

Upon hearing this revelation by the moon being, one Mr. Skinner gives this reaction: "Outlandish fakery, charlatanism," he says (85; 179). Eventually we learn that the moon being has come to Earth and conversed with eight people, including Skinner, who are attending a medium's séance. Although the séance scene appears rather abruptly at the very end of the story, it has been prefigured by the story's subtitle, "Narration of a Spirit."

The lunar spirit proceeds to demonstrate where its own interests lie. Upon concluding its account, it begins to escape from the body of the medium who had been serving as its mouthpiece. Skinner and the rest of the company freeze in fear. A new first-person narrator, another of the eight observers, describes the being in monstrous terms, as a gigantic tentacled spider, and compares the effect it created to that of an enveloping glue: "It didn't have definite form in the darkness made more dense by its presence," he says, adding "but if horror can be objectified in some fashion, this was horror" (86, modified; 179). The medium manages to call for light, and when the narrator reaches the switch, the ensuing rays cause the "shadowy mass" to explode, covering the company with something resembling a freezing mud (86; 179). As the narrator and Skinner engage in the mundane activity of washing the mud off themselves in the medium's washbasin, the situation seems to be returning to a state of normalcy. But they are soon presented with a final piece of evidence designed to convince doubters like Skinner (and any reader not yet overwhelmed by the logic of Lugones's narrators): when they look into the bottom of the basin, they find a small, dead mermaid. Perhaps this miniature of the story's earliest form of human is but proof that the moon being's tale was not a figment of their séance-primed imaginations. Or perhaps she is a remnant, the original essence of what had become the shadowy moon being. And perhaps mermaids had eventually been confined to the cone of shadow because they knew the secrets of original harmony that humans are no longer meant to possess.

Leopoldo Lugones, "Yzur"

Swift's *Gulliver's Travels* (1726), Edgar Rice Burroughs's Tarzan books (1914+), and the *Planet of the Apes* movies (1968+) are only a few of the many examples of ape stories in proto-, early, and recent science fiction. A veritable flurry was published in Argentina in the first decade of the twentieth century. Howard Fraser has identified Poe's "The Murders in the Rue Morgue" (1841) and Robert Louis Stevenson's *Strange Case of Dr Jekyll and Mr Hyde* (1886) as key literary influences on these works ("Apocalyptic Vision" 14), but he also cites frequent fictional and nonfictional accounts involving apes published in the popular magazine *Caras y Caretas* [*Faces and Masks*] at the turn of the century as contributing factors to this phenomenon ("Apes and Ape Lore," particularly 69–71, 73–75; "Apocalyptic Vision" 13).[26]

"Yzur" (1906) is perhaps the best realized of all of Lugones's science-fictional tales; not only does the story showcase his basic scientific premises, but it does so by showing rather than telling the reader what they are. Unlike the narrators in many of his science-fictional works (see chapter 3), the narrator in this tale is not the "*initiate* confidant" to whom the scientist reveals his discoveries, but the scientist himself

(Barcia 31).²⁷ He is an independently wealthy amateur who reads about a Javanese belief that monkeys are silent not because they cannot speak but because they will not, so that no one can force them to work. He converts this belief into an "anthropological theory" that monkeys are humans who for some reason stopped speaking and eventually devolved into animals who are virtually unable to speak (111; 199).²⁸

The scientist then describes how he acquired a trained chimpanzee, Yzur, from a disbanded circus, and how—through the strict observance of the scientific method—he set about teaching the ape to speak again. It is important to note that this narrator, unlike most of his brethren in *Strange Forces*, refrains from the exaggerated employment of what would later become known as technobabble. He is methodical and even didactic in his explanations, but does not descend into the technical minutiae of chemical compounds or the wavelengths of various light and sound waves, nor does his narrative become mired in the constant citation of corroborating scientific authorities. Carefully and objectively, he outlines the steps he has taken toward proving his postulate. After five years spent in exhausting the pertinent bibliography, he concludes "that *there is no scientific explanation for the fact that apes do not speak*" (112; 200). He then proceeds to work on developing Yzur's phonic apparatus, a prelude to getting the ape to produce words, and finally attempts to elicit meaningful speech. Lugones's use of the clinical tones of the scientist to describe the physical brutality of his methods marks an early example of the story's "subversion of scientific discourse" (Fraser, "Apocalyptic Vision" 14). After a further three years of effort, Yzur is able to produce only isolated vowel sounds and a limited number of consonants.

The reader gradually becomes aware that, despite our narrator's appropriation of scientific method and scientific discourse, his pretensions to objectivity are undermined by evidence of his partiality in interpreting his subject's development. Initially there are numerous and fairly understandable (in that era) comparisons of Yzur to humans: his walk is like that of a drunken sailor, his brain like that of a human idiot; his attention span compares—favorably—to that of a child, and his youthful capacity for learning to that of the negro.²⁹ Eventually, we witness the narrator completely cross the line into subjectivity in the space of a single paragraph:

> For all the slowness of his progress, a great change had come over him [Yzur]. His face was less mobile, his expression more serious,

his attitudes were those of a creature deep in thought. He had acquired, for instance, the habit of gazing at the stars . . . . And at the same time his sensibilities had developed: I noticed that he was easily moved to tears. (107, ellipsis in the translation only)

Por despacio que fuera, se había operado un gran cambio en su carácter [de Yzur]. Tenía menos movilidad en las facciones, la mirada más profunda, y adoptaba posturas meditabundas. Había adquirido, por ejemplo, la costumbre de contemplar las estrellas. Su sensibilidad se desarrollaba igualmente; íbasele notando una gran facilidad de lágrimas. (205)

It becomes more and more apparent that the narrator's increasing attribution of human reactions and emotions to his subject is the result of his own paranoid inability to handle his frustrations. Like the narrator of Poe's "The Tell-Tale Heart," his sanity appears more and more in question as the tale proceeds.[30] Based on his cook's terrified, incoherent, and far from reliable assertion that he has heard Yzur speaking complete words, the narrator begins to claim that Yzur is giving him "hypocritical winks" and sees irony in the ape's facial expressions as it stubbornly refuses to speak for him (115; 206).

At the same time he describes the humanizing of Yzur on the ape's path to re-evolution, however, the narrator's words betray a certain devolution or animalization on his own part. He describes his fruitless efforts to get Yzur to speak as a "painful obsession," revealing that, "As time went on I felt inclined to resort to force. The failure was embittering my disposition, filling me with unconscious resentment against Yzur" [Poco a poco sentíame inclinado a emplear la fuerza. Mi carácter iba agriándose con el fracaso, hasta asumir una sorda animosidad contra Yzur] (115; 205–6). Eventually he whips the chimpanzee, who responds with complete silence. Yzur's supposedly civilized master interprets this silence as a form of passive resistance in the face of "despotism of darkest barbarity" [despotismo de sombría barbarie] (208). The narrator speaks of such despotic behavior in terms of ancient history, linked to the apes' original enslavement, but it is clear that his beating of Yzur—an episode he now refers to as his "exasperation" [exasperación] (207)—is just such a case of "barbarous injustice" [bárbara injusticia] (208).

As Yzur lies on his deathbed—due, we are told, to mental as well as physical suffering—his master humanizes him to an ever greater degree, eventually conceding, to a certain extent, his own partiality: "In my great solitude, he [Yzur] was rapidly assuming the importance of a person" (116; 207). In spite of this realization, the narrator's self-acknowledged "perversity" leads him not to a more friendly relationship with the ape, but to a resumption of his attempts to get Yzur to speak (116; 207).[31] He uses language to re-impose the same superior-inferior relationship he posits as the cause of simian devolution millenia ago, as he tries to get Yzur to respond to the phrases with which he has begun every lesson: "I am your master" [Yo soy tu amo] and "You are my ape" [Tú eres mi mono] (116; 207). His efforts are to no avail until, with an expression that is "so human that I was seized with horror," the dying Yzur speaks: "Water, master. Master, my master" [AMO, AGUA. AMO, MI AMO] (117; 209).[32]

With these final sentences, Lugones gives us an ending that follows a familiar pattern in his stories: a researcher fails in his attempt to share his access to higher planes of knowledge with the world (in this case, with even a single witness). The narrators of the other scientific tales in *Strange Forces* (discussed in chapter 3) are observers who have managed to achieve some sort of closure following the events they recount, and thus have some pretensions to objectivity. But the narrator of "Yzur" lacks this perspective. Ultimately he is unable to prove his postulate to the scientific world or even to himself. Rather than administering large doses of supporting evidence and steamrolling the reader into agreement, Lugones leaves the ending open to interpretation, and this greater degree of ambiguity magnifies the story's power. Indeed, did Yzur produce words at all? The narrator's account reveals his own doubts as he protests too much: "He murmured—I am sure—he murmured . . . these words" [Brotaron—estoy seguro—brotaron en un murmullo . . . estas palabras] (209). Were Yzur's "words" merely the rote reproduction of sounds? Perhaps the narrator's desire to hear what he has longed to hear supplies the links that now connect Yzur's previously isolated vowels and consonants, as all of the sounds used in the deathbed utterance (in the original Spanish) do fall within the ape's stated range. Even if Yzur has somehow advanced to the production of linked sounds or entire words, any meaning in the phrases is at least partially imparted by the narrator's choice of punctuation. Could Yzur's speech be more than a tacit admission of the truth of the narrator's postulate, and also carry an acknowledgement of the narrator as his "master" and superior? This is certainly the narrator's hope, as he designates Yzur's murmurs as "these words, whose humanity reconciled our two species" (117; 209).

Or, as the narrator suspected, has Yzur been able to speak all along, providing evidence only when his "master" could no longer use a speaking ape to his own advantage? Herein lies the genius of Lugones's multiplicity of possibilities: the interpretation that poetic justice tempts even the staunchest of evolutionists to choose is also the one which upholds the narrator's theory of devolution. This version allows Yzur the dignity of the passive resister and the ultimate revenge against his oppressor. According to the narrator, Yzur's final words "at once crowned and blasted all my hopes," proving him correct and then denying the scientific validation of a corroborating witness (117; 209). For the narrator, as for all who stress the "science" in "occult sciences," success can come only with recognition by the scientific community. He knows that the testimonies of his cook and himself are insufficient evidence without a walking, talking Yzur. Because Yzur's death removes the source of scientific proof, our narrator turns to writing as a last resort: "And the last afternoon, the afternoon he died, the extraordinary thing occurred that decided me to write this account" (117; 209).

THE END OF THE WORLD AS WE KNOW IT

Fraser has described the stories in Lugones's *Strange Forces* as "eschatological texts which document the decadent phase of the cosmos, the millennial Apocalypse" ("Apocalyptic Vision" 18). A small but varied group of early works of Latin American science fiction goes one step beyond documenting decadence to documenting the final days of human life on Earth. Catastrophes that bring about the end of the world generally fall into two categories: natural and man-made. A natural catastrophe might originate on the planet itself (Noachian flood, earthquake, volcano, ice age, plague) or come from the heavens (solar flare, comet, death of the sun). Agents of apocalypse created by humans include war, overpopulation, machines/technology, and ecological devastation. Prior to World War I, natural catastrophes are more prevalent but, after the war that brought the nineteenth century to a close, man-made catastrophes predominate (Wagar, "Rebellion" 141). The means of destruction reflect the present-day concerns of the writer or, as Eric Rabkin expresses it, "the agency of the end of the world as we know it, the mechanism employed, indicates what we are to think of our own imaginings" (ix). At the same time, the end of the world is rarely definitive: "When the world ends, what really ends is not all of creation but—only—the world as we know it" (Rabkin viii).

The apocalyptic corpus of early Latin American sf includes tales that take place in the present, the far future, and the recent past. Dreams and madness are prevalent. In each case the narrative is transmitted by the last man alive, after the rest of the population has been eliminated by a passing comet, a global war, or an undefined disaster that may or may not have been caused by humans. In these texts a fresh start for life on Earth seems doubtful . . . but not entirely impossible. Contrary to what often happens in end-of-the-world narratives, no utopias emerge from the ruins of these razed societies (Wolfe, "Remaking of Zero" 3–4), nor are any future utopias specifically projected. (Indeed, none of the utopias discussed in chapter 1 come about as a result of catastrophe; Latin Americans had experienced too much violence first-hand for this to be an attractive option.)

Of our four disaster narratives, only "Demons" [Demônios] (Brazil, 1893) by Aluísio Azevedo (1857–1913) and "The Last War" [La última guerra] (Mexico, c. 1898)[33] by Amado Nervo (1870–1919) deal directly with the themes of this chapter: civilization and barbarism, evolution and devolution. Like Lugones in "Yzur"—but unlike our 1875 texts— both of these works represent civilization as but a veneer masking an inherent barbarism. In both there is some (d)evolution toward perfection and/or an ultimate understanding of the universe, though with atypical consequences. The other two apocalyptic narratives are "The End of the World" [O fim do mundo] (Brazil, 1857) by Joaquim Manuel de Macedo (1820–82) and "How the War Ended in 1917" [Cómo acabó la guerra en 1917] (Mexico, 1917) by Martín Luis Guzmán (1887–1976). Though not strictly evolutionary texts, they form chronological bookends for this section. They also can help us trace other trends in Latin American science fiction, such as the progression toward technophobia during the extended nineteenth century; the use of science fiction for social, economic, and political satire; and the trope of the alternate or future history.

Joaquim Manuel de Macedo, "The End of the World"

In 1857, two years before the publication of Darwin's *On the Origin of Species*, a German astrologer predicted that a comet would strike the earth on June 13, causing widespread if not total destruction. "This disturbing news was published in an almanac and the bogus prediction spread rapidly throughout Europe, particularly Paris," Donald Yeomans explains in *Comets: A Chronological History of Observation, Science, Myth, and Folklore* (187). Word of the imminent threat also arrived in Brazil, occasioning no small degree of panic among the population. It also inspired Joaquim Manuel de Macedo to publish a tale entitled "The End of the World" in the *Jornal do Commercio* [Business Journal] on the appointed day.[34]

Macedo was a prolific, best-selling writer who epitomized his times. His work, *The Little Dark-Complexioned Girl* [*A moreninha*] (1844), is regarded as "the first major Brazilian novel" (Stern 187). If Macedo's writing is considered superficial and reductionist today, it remains appreciated for its documentary value, and Macedo is recognized for his pioneering work in portraying both the customs and the inhabitants of Rio de Janeiro (Cândido 145). He obtained a degree in medicine—one of the few fields of study offered in Brazilian higher education in the nineteenth century—but never practiced. He taught Brazilian history at the Colégio Pedro II, served as tutor to the emperor's grandchildren, and occasionally held political office as a member of the conservative wing of the Liberal party, though he had no great political ambitions. Although Cândido's description of Macedo as "conformist and discreet" is undoubtedly apt (143), the satirical vein running through works like "The End of the World" left few egos unpricked. This earliest of the retrolabeled works of Brazilian science fiction pokes fun at the local response to the comet scare, but its primary goal is economic and political satire.

The events of June 12–13, 1857, are recounted by a first-person narrator who shares the name of a famous Brazilian actor (and acquaintance of Macedo): Martinho Corrêa Vasques (modernized as "Correia"; 1822–90). The narrator describes himself as "the new Noah who survived the new flood" (51). He lives through the passing of the comet by building "a staircase that would take me a short distance from the moon" out of a pile of the recently created Brazilian banks, with the Bank of Brazil as the first step ("with its high interest rates, that bank alone was worth a thousand steps"; 60, 61). The comet passes rather quickly, so Martinho discards his original plan of proceeding to the moon and other planets via balloon. He returns to Earth, almost colliding with the ground at the end of his descent because the banks have "broken."[35] Back in Rio de Janeiro, Martinho finds that the comet's heat has apparently killed every living being. Despite the previous hysteria, the inhabitants are portrayed not in a tableau of mass panic but as engaged in fairly typical daily activities. In keeping with the satirical tone, the narrator comes across Macedo himself dead in the offices of the *Jornal do Commercio*, with a smile of satisfaction on his face, because he will not have to write his column for the next day's paper. Martinho also stops by theater rehearsals, his club and favorite café, a police station, city hall, and the national senate—allowing the author to direct barbs at the self-interest and poor qualifications of a wide range of public officials, from local politicians to ministers of state, and to poke fun at the cooperation among Liberal and Conservative senators during this final year of the Period of Conciliation in Brazilian national politics.[36]

Martinho begins to appreciate the magnitude of his desolation, describing himself as "a sort of Adam without an Eve, and on top of that an Adam who, instead of living in Paradise, must live in an enormous cemetery!" (78). He enters another theater, where he finds a chorus girl still alive, and rejoices: "She was the Eve that I, poor Adam, ardently desired for the good of humanity, that it might not be extinguished" (82). At first the chorus girl is less than excited at the prospect of spending eternity with Martinho (they have been lovers in the past), but she apparently reconsiders, running from him with a "flirtatious giggle" (85). He sets off in pursuit but soon finds himself on the ground groaning in pain: he has fallen out of bed. "In spite of the pain," Martinho concludes, "I give thanks to God; because today is June 13, and the world is not coming to an end" [Apezar da dôr . . . dou graças a Deos; porque hoje é o dia 13 de Junho, e não ha de acabar-se o mundo] (86). As would prove to be the case in the real world, the comet in the story is a false alarm. Everything we have read has been a dream.

The story's narrative frame complicates the typical conclusion to the end-of-the-world tale, in which the end leads to a new beginning. A fresh start is possible in Macedo's "The End of the World" only insofar as his fellow citizens profit from seeing their customs, institutions, and fears satirized. Still, the story does include many of the elements commonly found in narrations of catastrophe and apocalypse: a comet as agent of doom, a study of people's reactions when the end is nigh, the narration by a "last and first man" (a Noah, an Adam), and even the present-day setting. Many of these elements will appear in later Latin American narratives of the end, though the repercussions of the theories of evolution and devolution will echo throughout each of them.

Aluísio Azevedo, "Demons"

Aluísio Azevedo enjoyed the rare distinction of being able to live on the proceeds of his writing for a significant period of time in late nineteenth-century Brazil. He was best known for naturalist novels such as *The Mulatto* [*O mulato*] (1881) and *The Brazilian Tenement* [*O cortiço*] (1890), for his anticlericalism, and for his denunciation of racial prejudice. In his science-fictional work "Demons," Azevedo combines a naturalist's eye for detail with a romantic's penchant for the macabre.[37] The tale opens in the chambers of a writer in Rio de Janeiro. The young man tells us that he has awakened to utter darkness and silence, after an apparent long night's sleep. Thinking that dawn is about to break, he sits at his desk and begins to write page after page, "and the ideas came boiling toward me like a band of demons, devouring one another in a delirious rush to arrive first" (21). When the frenzy subsides, he finds he does not remember anything he has written. Ten hours have passed, yet the world is still dark. He seeks out the other boarders in his *pensione* and discovers them dead in their beds, "as if those lives had been extinguished in a single breath; or as if the earth, suddenly overcome by a great hunger, had gone mad and devoured all of her children at once" (29).

An unknown but apparently natural—not man-made—catastrophe has left our narrator alone. Like Martinho in "The End of the World," his city has become a giant cemetery. He expresses the faint hope that Laura, his betrothed, might have survived too, becoming the Eve to his Adam, living with him "in an eternal self-centered paradise, helping to recommence the creation . . . to form the world anew, to bring forth life anew" (31). He sets out for Laura's home, but only his familiarity with the route keeps him from losing his way. No light can penetrate the primeval darkness, and thick layers of mold and mud are starting to cover buildings and streets. He finds Laura's family dead, but hesitates before entering her bedroom saying, "I had never dared penetrate that chaste maiden's chamber . . . such a pure and religious asylum of modesty" [Nunca houvera ousado penetrar naquella casta alcova de donzella . . . tão puro e religioso asylo do pudor] (44). Valor overcomes discretion. Although Laura appears to be dead, she revives in the young writer's embrace.

Just as the mysterious darkness has negated all light, the enveloping silence has negated all sound. The couple is unable to speak aloud and must communicate via some form of telepathy. The mud and mold begin to engulf the city. Amid these worsening conditions, the writer and Laura resolve to seek death in the waters of the sea. Strangely, however, the mud begins to repel them less, and they find themselves losing not only the ability to use language, that benchmark of humanity, but also the ability to think coherently. "Our brains began to become beast-like" [Nossos cerebros principiavam a bestialisar-se], the narrator says (63). Soon it is not only their minds but their bodies that transform. They grow some sort of hair or fur, snouts emerge, teeth lengthen, and they become quadrupeds. As they gain strength, they are overcome by the need to fight, to establish physical dominance. They lose their human memories and with them their inhibitions:

> Laura threw herself at me in a savage and plethoric caress, seizing my mouth with the strong lips of an irrational woman. She clasped me to her sensually, biting my shoulders and arms as if wanting to awaken in me the desires of the flesh. (66)

> Laura atirava-se contra mim, n'uma caricia selvagem e pletorica, apanhando-me a bocca com os seus labios fortes de mulher irracional, e estreitava-se commigo sensualmente, mordendo-me os hombros e os braços, como se me quizesse acordar os desejos da carne.

The narrator is unable to say how long they lived this animal existence, but they awaken one day, still in the darkness, to find that their claws have softened and their feet feel "numb, heavy, and as if they were inclined to bore deep into the earth" (74). They undergo a second metamorphosis, becoming two giant trees, "tranquil and entwined in our silent happiness" (78). After another unspecified length of time, they transform again, a further step down the developmental scale, into a single rock.

Centuries pass, and the ever-present mud dissolves them into a liquid, which then evaporates into a gas. The narrator compares this "general gasification" to the one at Earth's beginning, when "the first two molecules . . . found one another and were joined and became fruitful, only to begin the interminable chain of life, from atmospheric air to mineral, from Eozoon to biped" (80). Rather than begin the process of rebuilding that chain of life on Earth, the writer and his lover, now literally reduced to the most elemental state, find their gaseous selves dispersing and rising into the vacuum of space: "We began to traverse the firmament, revolving around one another like a pair of errant and loving stars that goes through space in search of the ideal" (80–81). This sentence ends the narration of events that followed the catastrophic darkness, but it does not quite end our tale. A final sentence reads:

> Here in these dozen silly chapters, patient reader, lies what I wrote on that cursed night of insomnia in my bachelor's quarters while waiting for His Highness the Sun to deign to open his morning audience with the birds and the flowers. (81)

> Ora ahi fica, leitor paciente, n'essa duzia de capitulos desenxabidos, o que eu, n'aquella maldicta noite de insomnia, escrevi no meu quarto de rapaz solteiro, esperando que Sua Alteza o Sol se dignasse de abrir a sua audiencia matutina com os passaros e com as flôres.

With this explanation of the text as words that had come "boiling toward me like a band of demons," the narrator establishes that the cycle of devolution has been metaphorical rather than literal, despite the extensive details provided and scientific terms employed.[38]

Although this narrative frame might initially appear to undercut the interior text by openly denouncing it as fiction (and a "silly" trifle produced on little sleep at that), it serves several useful purposes. First, it provides Azevedo with a means of exploring the (d)evolutionary process from within the mind and body of a character, as a firsthand account. At the same time, he uses this not-quite-the-end-of-the-world mechanism to juxtapose his characters' reactions to impossibly different social settings: civilization and barbarism. This dichotomy is typically used in Latin American fiction to examine national composition, national politics, or technological or educational progress. Azevedo, by contrast, uses it to show that the "civilized" but strictly codified expressions of romantic love between a respectful young suitor and a chaste young maiden mask an elemental imperative to express more "barbaric" physical, emotional, and intellectual desires and needs. Only the extremity of an end-of-the-world scenario could allow a young couple to completely escape the rigid morality of their own culture—in this case by providing a setting in which the larger society that maintains laws, rules, and customs has disappeared.

Like Macedo's story, "Demons" contains many elements common to more completely apocalyptic narratives. Within the framed text, several possibilities arise for new beginnings for life on Earth. First the narrator and Laura are proposed as a second Adam and Eve, but this option is ruled out by subsequent events. After the devolution of their humanity down to the molecular building-blocks of life, it is suggested that the couple might come full circle and regenerate life on Earth beginning at the first stages of an evolutionary cycle. But this, too, proves to be a false lead. The ultimate implication within the framed text is that—as with Flammarion's Lumen, Holmberg's Nic-Nac, or Zaluar's Sun Being—these virtually noncorporeal spirits have (d)evolved into something more advanced than "civilized" humanity, something that has come closer to attaining the ideal.

Amado Nervo, "The Last War"

Amado Nervo was born in Tepic in western Mexico. After abandoning early intentions to join the priesthood, he worked as a journalist in his hometown and in Mazatlán before moving to Mexico City in 1894. In 1900 the newspaper *El Imparcial* sent him to Paris, where Nervo completed a modernist's ideal apprenticeship, living a bohemian lifestyle, getting to know the French literary scene, and becoming friends with Rubén Darío, that ultimate exponent of Spanish American modernism. By the time he returned to Mexico in 1904, Nervo had published several collections of poetry and a work of prose and was gaining literary renown at home and abroad. After joining the Mexican diplomatic corps in 1905, Nervo was sent to Spain, where he would be posted until 1918. Although, as Manuel Durán tells us, "His diplomatic position would sharpen his political and sociological sensibility even more," Nervo intervened very little in matters political throughout his life (84, 108). Because he lived abroad during virtually the entire span of the Mexican Revolution, for Nervo "the Revolution was not an active ingredient in his experience or in his development" (Durán 24). In 1918 Carranza's government sent him to Argentina and Uruguay as its special envoy and plenipotentiary minister. He received great acclaim as a poet in New York, en route to the River Plate, and upon his arrival. Because of worsening chronic health problems, Nervo died less than a year after assuming his post. His funeral celebrations were the stuff of a García Márquez tale, taking place over a period of six months and including a convoy of warships from multiple nations to escort his body, international homages along the route home, 300,000 attendees at his burial, and numerous re-editions of his works. Notwithstanding Nervo's undeniable qualities as a person and as a writer, Durán attributes the scale and scope of these events to the times, to the public's regret at not having sufficiently celebrated other modernists at their passings, and to the fact that Nervo was—of all of the modernist poets—"perhaps the most 'presentable,' the most socially acceptable," due to his political neutrality, the fine figure he cut, and the nicety of his manners (107–8).

Like Lugones, whose work he admired, Nervo was a member of the second generation of Spanish American modernists and one of the most important national literary figures of his time. Again like Lugones, he was known more for his poetry than his prose, even though his professional earnings as a writer derived largely from his work as a journalist. Nervo also shared with Lugones what Fraser has termed the modernist's "apocalyptic vision of the future as revealed in the movement's ambivalent attitude toward scientific discourse" ("Apocalyptic Vision" 9), seeking answers both within and beyond the canonical sciences, and exploring a "wide variety of unorthodox belief systems" (Jrade 50). In Nervo's case this exploration was especially extensive, including "pantheism, mysticism, theosophy, spiritualism, Bergsonian Vitalism, Buddhism, and Hinduism" (Jrade 50). Blanco-Fombona has aptly described this former aspirant to the priesthood as a man who "lacks faith and does whatever he can to find it" (264). Finally, Lugones and Nervo both examined their beliefs and their realities through the vehicle of the nascent science fiction genre, producing texts that ranged from the more scientifically oriented to the fantastic.

The aforementioned Spanish American modernist's ambivalence about scientific discourse manifests itself in Nervo's life and work in the form of concurrent impulses toward technophilia and technophobia. On the technophiliac side, Nervo was an avid amateur astronomer who belonged to the Astronomical Society of Mexico. In a pair of lectures he presented to the society in 1904, entitled "Lunar Literature and the Habitability of the Satellites" [La literatura lunar y la habitabilidad de los satélites], he dissertates upon the eight known planets and their satellites, talks of the possibility of extraterrestrial life (citing the theories of "our beloved teacher Camille Flammarion" and others to support his arguments), and discusses Wells's *The War of the Worlds* (1898) and *The First Men in the Moon* (1901) in detail (506). Nervo also demonstrates a lively interest in technologies of the future with chronicles like "Airplanes: These Will Kill That—The Automobile Will Not Survive Long" [Los aeroplanos: Esto matará a aquello.—el automóvil vivirá poco]. Both here and in his science-fictional poem, "The Great Journey" [El gran viaje], he anticipates the time when technology will—literally—provide the vehicle to broaden the scope of humanity's search for truth by making space travel possible. In other works Nervo shows marked leanings toward technophobia; Larson has indicated "One Hundred Years of Sleep" [Cien años de sueño] and "The Frozen Ones" [Los congelados] in particular (59). In the former, technology is incapable of solving a man's true problems; in the latter, Nervo portrays a scientist's abuse of the power he has acquired over life and death.

Still, as Nervo told the Astronomical Society, "My supreme aspiration would be to become the poet worthy of singing this celestial miracle, the cosmic poet" ("Lunar Literature" 512). He discusses the role that science might play in the literature of such a poet in a later essay, "Marvelous Literature" [La literatura maravillosa]. Here Nervo affirms that science was not, as many had feared, taking the mystery out of life but rather the opposite, it was opening up new avenues of the unknown: "We have wanted to kill mystery," he writes, "but every day mystery envelops us, saturates us, penetrates us more . . . . We thought that science would destroy it, and yet science brings it by the hand and places it in front of us" (707, ellipsis in the original). Nervo's list of writers of this "marvelous literature" reads like a *Who's Who* of proto- and early science fiction: Lucian of Samosata, Ariosto, Rabelais, Kepler, Godwin, Wilkins, Cyrano de Bergerac, Kirchen, Holberg, Voltaire, Swedenborg, Alqueberg, Poe, Egrand, Corelli, Verne, Conan Doyle, and Wells (706–7). The most important influences on his own science-fictional works were Poe, Flammarion, and Wells.

Upon more than one occasion Nervo speculated about the end of the world and life in the distant future. In "The Last Goddess (A Tale of the Absurd)" [La última diosa (cuento absurdo)] a great cataclysm terminates much of sentient life on earth. The brief "Clouds" [Las nubes] is a far future reflection about living on Earth once the sun has cooled and the water supply diminished. Nervo's best-known apocalyptic narrative and the one that concerns us here, "The Last War" (c. 1898), is also a far future tale. Whereas in a tale of the *near* future, the world "exists only imaginatively and hypothetically, but . . . is nevertheless a world in which (or something like it) we may one day have to live, and towards which our present plans and ambitions must be directed," in a tale of the far future, "the far future tends to be associated with notions of ultimate destiny . . . its images display a world irrevocably transfigured" (Stableford, "Near Future" 856). The main events of "The Last War" take place in the year 5532, and against the norm outlined by W. Warren Wagar, the story is a pre–World War I account of the end of the world (as we know it) brought about by human rather than natural agency.[39]

"The Last War" begins with a recounting of the three great revolutions of humanity: the Christian Revolution, the French Revolution, and the Socialist (also called "Social") Revolution of 2030. With each revolution greater progress, freedom, and equality are attained. The French Revolution is described as having paved the way for the Socialist Revolution. We learn that in 1916 Europe becomes the United States of Europe, modeled after the U.S.A. ("whose memory in the annals of humanity has been so brilliant"); the world's last monarch dies in 1950 (240). Before the third revolution there remain "certain very visible signs that physically distinguished the then-called privileged classes from the proletariat" (240). The long, delicate fingers of the elite contrast with the six-fingered (and calloused) right hands of the workers. The lower limbs of those workers who drive vehicles such as the "aeroplanes, airships, aerocycles, automobiles, magnetic expresses, ultradirect transetherealunars" [aeroplanos, aeronaves, aerociclos, automóviles, expresos magnéticos, directísimos transetéreolunares] have atrophied to the extent that, away from the workplace, they need "small electric space cars" [pequeños carros eléctricos espaciales] to get about (240). With the Social Revolution these differences begin to disappear. Humans finally become equal to one another, reaching a high level of peace and stability "both in the sciences, thanks to the definitive nature of the principles conquered, and in the social sphere, thanks to the marvelous wisdom of laws and the high moral level of customs" (241). In addition to their physical evolution, humans evolve mentally. They now dedicate themselves to intellectual and spiritual pursuits, leaving any remaining tasks requiring physical force or action of any kind to the likewise evolving lower animals. A summary of human progress is provided:

The natives of Europe disappeared before the Latin force; the Latin force before the Saxon force, which took over the world . . . and the Saxon force disappeared before the Slavic invasion; the latter, before the yellow invasion, which in turn was swept away by the black invasion, and so, from race to race, from hegemony to hegemony, from preeminence to preeminence, from domination to domination, man arrived perfect and august at the limits of history . . . (244, ellipses in the original)

Los autóctonos de Europa desaparecieron ante el vigor latino; desapareció el vigor latino ante el vigor sajón, que se enseñoreó del mundo . . . y el vigor sajón desapareció ante la invasión eslava; esta, ante la invasión amarilla, que a su vez fue arrollada por la invasión negra, y así, de raza en raza, de hegemonía en hegemonía, de preeminencia en preeminencia, de dominación en dominación, el hombre llegó perfecto y augusto a los límites de la historia . . .

Despite all of this perfection, humans forget the lessons of their own past and lose, we are told, "even the notion of what vigilance and caution were" (241). In 5532 the fourth of the great revolutions, the animals' revolution, begins (Yzur's passive resistance become active).

The causes of this fourth and last revolution are not new, we are told, but rather "the same that have caused, it can be said, all the revolutions: old hungers, old hereditary hatreds, the tendency toward equality of prerogatives and rights, and the aspiration, latent in the soul of all beings, to that which is better" (241). The rebels are the horses, dogs, monkeys, and elephants who carry out all nonintellectual tasks, who run the machinery, who still have not forgiven the interloping "species of blond monkeys" for usurping their ancient role as the rulers of the earth by using the spear to dominate them (243). As one revolutionary organizer, the dog Can Canis, puts it: "Man had invented the machine, and that pointed stick was his scepter, the king's scepter that nature gave him" (243). There is no doubt that progress has been made, that in 5532 better people treat animals better. Humans are paternal(istic) toward animals, "much more paternal than the nobles were to the proletariat after the French Revolution" [muy más paternal de lo que lo fueron para el proletario los grandes señores después de la Revolución francesa] (241). Humans no longer use animals as food; they clothe and house them well and treat them with kindness. But animals still occupy an inferior position in society. They still perform the meanest tasks, and their rights are determined for them by humans. Can Canis summarizes the animals' reasons for rebelling: "We are not free, we are not masters, and we want to be masters and free" (243).

Progress is the condition of all beings that breathe, Can Canis tells his co-conspirators via a secure form of global uplink. He reviews the "gradual emergence of humanity" within his brethren, saying, "Something divine that existed in our rudimentary spirits, a luminous germ of intellect, of future humanity . . . was developing in the most intimate recesses of our being" (243). Animals eventually acquired an understanding of human language and developed a language of their own. Perfected humanity considered the animals' language primitive and refused to learn it. In 5532 the role of the animal language changes from an inferior workerspeak, to the secret code of the rebellion, to the *lingua franca* of power. Can Canis ends his speech, declaring: "The last revolution of the planet, the animals' cry of rebellion against man, will explode, filling the universe with fear and defining the equality of all of the mammals that inhabit the earth" (243–44). And here, with the word "mammals," is evidence that, like the first three revolutions, the fourth carries the seeds of its own downfall. Equality is attained by those next in line on the evolutionary scale but, in order to be "masters" as well as "free," they exclude those on the rungs below.

Although the mammals' revolution is global, Can Canis's speech is transmitted from Mexico, one of the "great control centers" of the revolution "due to its geographic position in the middle of America and between the two great oceans, in the center of the world" (241–42). The mammals attack humans using the technology only they know how to use. Next to these "terrible machines," the weapons that humans had used in the previous revolution—"the electric projectiles, the grenades filled with gasses, the horrifying effects of radium used to cause death in a thousand ways, the formidable blasts of air, the microbe-injecting darts, the telepathic shocks" [los proyectiles eléctricos, las granadas henchidas de gases, los espantosos efectos del radium utilizado de mil maneras para dar muerte, las corrientes formidables de aire, los dardos inyectores de microbios, los choques telepáticos]—were as nothing (244).

At this point in the story, the narrator's identity is revealed: "Despite the cleverness of men, *we* were surprised in all areas of the globe" [Los hombres, a pesar de su astucia, *fuimos* sorprendidos en todos los ámbitos del orbe] (244, emphasis mine). Writing in 5542 as the fourth revolution comes to a close, he is "one of the few remaining men in the world" (244). The narrator suggests no hope that the last humans will become new Adams and Eves, however, appearing resigned to extinction. Despite—or because of—their highly evolved state, "Their mission came to be to disappear since, due to the absoluteness of their perfection, they were no longer capable of perfecting themselves further" [Su misión se cifraba en desaparecer, puesto que ya no era susceptible, por lo absoluto de su perfección, de perfeccionarse más] (244). Humanity will be eliminated to make way for the "humanized ones of the future" [humanizados del porvenir] (244). And despite his earlier intimations that the fourth revolution will be the war to end all wars, he now cites the cycle in which preeminence among humans has moved "from race to race" (244) and goes on to extrapolate that the mammalian animals "in their turn, perfected and serene, will die to make way for new races" (245). Once all of these levels of "inferior animality" have advanced in turn to occupy the top rung, this cycle will continue on younger worlds with new humanities, "so that," as the narrative ends, "all can begin again!" (245).

We are not told the identity of the narrator's intended audience, but we do learn something about the recording process. Early in the story, the narrator remarks that he must cut short his description of the first three revolutions, since he has already used "more than three phonoteleradiograph cylinders to think these reminiscences" [más de tres cilindros de fonotelerradiógrafo en pensar estas reminiscencias] (240). We also know something of the narrator's reasons for making this recording, as he tells us of his hope that others will learn from his account, which "perhaps tomorrow will constitute an extremely useful piece of history" (244). The only evidence we have as to the identity of his first readers, the preparers of this manuscript/transmission, are their two brief editorial comments. The first is a footnote to the narrator's mention of the "phonoteleradiograph." In the note, the editors explain how the mechanism works before stating, "Today this apparatus has been completely reformulated" (240). They intervene again immediately after the description of the technology by which Can Canis's speech is transmitted, clarifying that these special emitters were "now obsolete because they were not very practical" (242). We do not know if these editors are mammals, other classes of animals, or extraterrestrial beings, nor do we know if they have reissued this document as a historical oddity or as a valuable lesson, but we can make an educated guess.

The ultimate message of "The Last War" is ciphered in its representation of time. In his essay on cyclical time in eschatological fiction, "Round Trips to Doomsday," Wagar discusses "ends that lead to fresh beginnings and further ends," but he also finds that this circular pattern is often subjected to the competing force of chronological time (73). He calls the resulting pattern "spiraliform" (80), and he explains it thusly:

> When science-fiction writers adopt cyclical conceptions of history, their strategy is often to combine elements of cyclicism with the dominant world view of modern industrial man, a positivist faith in science, technology, and human effort, culminating in an affirmation of progress. The paradigms of the cycle and linear progress are thus joined together, sometimes awkwardly and unconvincingly, with linear progress enjoying the last word. (74)

Nervo's temporal strategy differs slightly from this norm. The technological advances he describes are linear. Nervo generally describes new forms of transportation and communication with a technophiliac's joy in gadgetry, though technophobia eventually predominates in this tale of revolutions, as war machines advance in destructive capability from spear to telepathic shock and beyond. Humanity, too, has progressed—to utter perfection, the narrator affirms repeatedly—but little comes of this perfection. There are no intimations of higher planes of noncorporeal existence, leading ever closer to God or to some ideal form, as in "Demons," *Doctor Benignus*, and several texts discussed in chapter 3. This is a predominantly cyclical tale in which there is apparently no degeneration, devolution, or barbarization—once humanity is perfected, we are told, "their mission came to be to disappear." Yet at the same time there is an inherent barbarity in each dominant race, a blindness to the inequalities perpetuated by its "equalizing" revolution.[40] Each new "humanity" is no better than the last, containing the same tragic flaw and repeating the same mistakes, but with bigger guns. The tale verges on the pure cyclicism that Wagar calls "an index to cultural fatigue and despair" ("Round Trips" 93). As a "race" ends, it does not leave a phoenix (or Adam and Eve) to rise from its own ashes. Each new revolution is represented as doomed from the start. No race has learned the lessons of the first three great revolutions, and it seems likely that this fourth revolution is not "the last war" but simply the last in which humans will participate. The only small note of hope lies in the text itself. At least someone in the future has read it. And passed it on.

Martín Luis Guzmán, "How the War Ended in 1917"

Like Amado Nervo, Martín Luis Guzmán was a major literary figure in the Mexico of his time. He did important work in journalism, including founding the periodicals *El Mundo* (1922–24) and *Tiempo, Semanario de la Vida y la Verdad* [*Time: Weekly Periodical of Life and Truth*] (1942–98). For over fifteen years he lived abroad, chiefly in Spain and France. Guzmán belonged to a later generation than Nervo, however. He was not a modernist but a member of the Young People's Literary Circle [Ateneo de la Juventud] and, as Guzmán scholar Emmanuel Carballo puts it, was a writer of the twentieth century "from head to foot" ("Dos textos" 5). Also in contrast to Nervo, Guzmán was deeply involved in politics throughout his life. He was elected to the national legislature, served as Mexico's ambassador to the United Nations, and campaigned for several victorious presidential candidates. Guzmán is remembered most, however, for his work in and on the Mexican Revolution. During the war he attained the rank of colonel and worked closely with a number of commanders, most famously with General Francisco "Pancho" Villa. To escape Villa's inner circle, Guzmán went into voluntary exile in Spain and the United States for the second half of the revolution (1915–20). While living in the United States, he worked as a professor of literature at the University of Minnesota and as a journalist. He wrote in many genres, but his best-known works are *The Eagle and the Serpent* [*El águila y la serpiente*] (1928) and *The Shadow of the Tyrant* [*La sombra del caudillo*] (1929), which recount his experiences of the revolution.

The only short story that Guzmán wrote, and his only work of science fiction, is "How the War Ended in 1917."[41] Guzmán published the story in the December 1917 issue of the Spanish-language *Revista Universal* while he was living in New York. According to Larson, Guzmán was "greatly impressed by contemporary technological achievements" and these impressions had an important influence on the story's composition (59). This may well be the case, though the way in which technology is represented in the text smacks much more of technophobia than technophilia. Guzmán also was undoubtedly affected by the flood of violence around the world: the Russian Revolution, the U.S. declaration of war on Germany in the ongoing Great War, and continuing national upheaval in Mexico.

This tale of war and technology is narrated by a self-declared "last man alive." He recounts the events leading up to Earth's destruction, with no expectation of an audience. His dedication reads: "To the memory of the earth and her daughter the moon, beautiful heavenly bodies that have disappeared through the fault of human weakness, the last of men dedicates this singular work, which is condemned to remain unread" (191).

In the story, the world ends at 3:00 A.M. on November 22, 1917 (for Guzmán's original readers, the subscribers of *Revista Universal*, this would have been in the previous month). We do not immediately learn the exact date and time; for several pages we know only from the title that the war has ended this year. First we are introduced to our narrator and to the machine. The narrator is a physical scientist, a former university professor, now a supervisor of the censorship machine at the Central Censorship Offices, Department of Romance Languages. All of the nation's letters are fed through one of these great machines (though machines that process other languages are never mentioned directly). The machine collates the information in each letter with all previous input and spits out cards containing its "infallible conclusions" (192). For the government, the most valuable conclusions are those regarding the war: "trenches, troop movements, provisioning, personal valor" (192). For example, one war-related conclusion reads: "William Bechstein. Shameful germanophile. Author of secret project to militarize Mexico" (193). The name of the war and the country in which the narrator and censorship office are located are never specified. However, details such as "trenches," "germanophile" (Germans are also referred to as the "enemy camp"), and "Mexico" (the narrator also later mentions "a certain Mexican poet . . . a friend of mine, to be sure") imply that we are in the middle of something like World War I, in some sort of alternative Mexico in which a Big Brother–type government uses technology to monitor the lives of its citizens (193, 195). Guzmán does not differentiate Mexico economically, industrially, or politically from the rest of the world; rather, Mexico appears to be just another node for housing Central Censorship Offices in a non-combatant sector of the Allied bloc.

Our narrator owes his prestigious position to his invention of the "distribution center with alternating parallel perforations" [foco de distribución alternada por perforaciones paralelas] (192). This discovery has greatly improved the machine's efficiency, an important contribution to the war effort. For the machine's operators, however, its conclusions about the war are its least interesting output. The narrator's colleagues live for tidbits of juicy gossip: "Don Juan de Armas, Count. He dyes his hair and claims ancient lineage. Parents unknown" (193). The narrator himself is most interested in what he terms "the great, important news"—rectifications in historical data, geographic locations of unexplored places, lacunae in bibliographies, astronomical observations, forgotten or unknown canonizations—that fills in the gaps in human knowledge and helps to inquire into the "ultimate human and cosmic destiny" (194, 191).

The narrator's belief in the machine is complete, perhaps a last vestige of the nineteenth-century trust in the hegemony of scientific discourse, but more likely an anticipation of the "modern times" to come.[42] "Who spoke of the submission of man to the machine, of the universal modern tyranny wherein the machine is the daughter of her own slaves, and they glorify her as the oppressed have always glorified their oppressors?" he asks in the first paragraph of his account (191). And he responds to his own question:

> It does not matter. I was the slave of my machine: its grip seemed like glory to me, and I never rebelled against it because it never caused me pain. (Changing one's point of view was the sole origin of rebellions on Earth: we believed a thing to be good and we enjoyed it until the moment we thought it bad. The thing remained the same.) (191)

> No importa. Yo era esclavo de mi máquina: su garra me sabía a gloria, y nunca me rebelé contra ella porque nunca llegó a causarme tortura. (Cambiar el punto de vista fue en la Tierra el solo origen de las rebeliones: creíamos buena una cosa y la gozamos hasta el momento de creerla mala. La cosa permanecía idéntica.)

No one questions the machine's authority or purpose, but others do not share the narrator's utter submission to or faith in it. Thus it is he alone who understands when the machine warns of an impending "horrible catastrophe" of global proportions (194).

One day the machine begins to produce "unintelligible and strange cards" that others ignore but that contain, the narrator tells us, "an internal coherence so evident to eyes accustomed to reading those messages" (194). The first of the peculiar cards reads: "Lat. 41° 50', Long. 87° 38' W. Cat that flies. November 22, 3 A.M. The souls will die before the bodies" (194). He locates the geographic reference as the city of Chicago. The flying cat reminds him of a poem by his Mexican friend. The rest of the message he identifies as some sort of "terrible final sentence/judgment" [terrible sentencia final] (195). The machine produces more such cards. It seems to be achieving sentience: "The machine struggled to express something . . . guided by its acquired consciousness, it strove to exceed its creator's designs, as men did, no more no less" (195). In addition to repeating the date and hour given in the first of the odd cards, subsequent cards announce enormous velocities, extremely high temperatures, inconceivable densities, extraordinarily complicated vibrations and waves (195). It becomes ever clearer that the narrator believes the machine is forecasting a great natural catastrophe (perhaps a comet striking Chicago?) that will destroy the world.

How, the narrator wonders, can simple letters written by men lead to a prediction of "immense supraterrestrial phenomena" and "impending interplanetary cataclysms" (195)? He pauses a moment to ask himself if men themselves might not be causing the disaster, with their letters carrying "destructive passion" throughout the world, especially to the warfronts (195). "Useless to try to investigate it," he concludes, and instead reorganizes his department and adds workers in an effort to help the machine to reveal the "complete truth" (196).

"The machine appeared to reach maximum knowledge/consciousness" [La máquina pareció alcanzar el sumo conocimiento] in the final days before November 22 (196). On the twenty-first, the narrator warns his coworkers of the terrible fate that awaits them. They confuse him with their laughter and murmurs of "madman," but do not report him to the authorities, allowing him to continue to monitor the machine. "Today I evoke the anxiety of those final moments in a confusing mixture with the changing and inexorable face of the clock," the narrator confesses (197). Even in the wee hours of the twenty-second, the narrator never doubts the machine's veracity, only wanting to be sure that nothing impedes the arrival of a "message of salvation" (197). He checks the machine's contacts. He disassembles its master cylinders. When he is "almost in the entrails of the machine," somehow parts get loose and begin to spill out onto the floor (198). With cries of "Betrayal!" his coworkers pry him out, still clasping "a handful of twisted and broken little pieces" (198). In the middle of the struggle, the clock begins to strike 3:00 A.M.

> I tried to go toward the door; the clock struck a second time; suddenly a bright flash blinded me and I felt, as though inseparable from an internal explosion, a great pain in my forehead. (198)

> Traté de ir hacia la puerta; dio el reloj la segunda campanada; bruscamente un vivísimo resplandor me cegó y sentí, cual si hubiese sido inseparable de un estallido interno, un enorme dolor en la frente.

Although this concludes the story of the events of November 22, the narrator appends a final framing paragraph, which opens, "How was this portion of the world in which I find myself spared? I do not know" (198). He seems to sense the passing of days and nights, but is convinced that this cannot be so because the machine could not have been wrong. He describes the place in which he now finds himself as a building filled with "distant but familiar noises" (198). One "being" who attends to his needs wears white; another dresses "like a woman" (198). He has dreams that leave him "painfully tired, with less desire to think about why I am here and why the light that shines on me seems so much like that of the sun" (199). He closes in confusion, wondering why the kind beings do not allow him into the garden.

To the readers of December 1917 and beyond, the world might appear to have ended in the mind of only one man. The narrator is not merely a solitary madman, however; he represents a world gone mad. The war (or wars) is not simply something being fought "over there" but is a pervasive violence that touches the lives of all. In Guzmán's story, the world is not destroyed by technology; instead, humanity is destroyed by its relationship with technology. By accepting the authority of the censorship machines, people lose both their freedom and their souls, although their bodies have not yet died.

Stableford reminds us that "stories of disasters which come about because of new inventions usually stress that the real root cause of the disaster is the element in human nature which drives us to seek advantage over our fellow men" ("Man-Made" 118). At the beginning of the story, the narrator admits that humans had not built the censorship machine for the purest of motives, noting that the machine had been "created by base passion for evil ends" (191). But if the narrator consciously chooses to believe that a natural catastrophe, predicted by the machine, has destroyed his world, his unconscious betrays inklings that the "destructive passions" of men—the "human weakness" that has led to the disappearance of the earth and the moon—have been the ultimate cause (195, 191).

What hope, then, for a new beginning after this particular ending? In the story, society shows little inclination to talk of peace or to throw off the yoke of the machine ("Betrayal!" the workers cry as they defend the machine that the narrator has unintentionally/unconsciously slain). And the protagonist shows little sign of returning to any semblance of his former life, or of building a vigorous new life with these familiar yet alien "beings" who will not give him access to the garden, never mind providing him with an Eve. The war ends for the narrator in November of 1917, but the rest of the world fights on. As for the end of the world, Guzmán tells his readers, it has already happened. Do you know where your souls are?

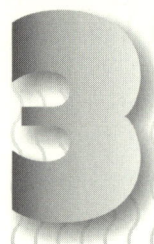

STRANGE FORCES
EXPLORING THE LIMITS
OF SCIENCE

BETWEEN SCIENCE FICTION AND THE FANTASTIC

Holmberg's primary aims in *Two Factions Struggle for Life* [*Dos partidos en lucha*] were to spread the Darwinist message and contribute to the popularization of science in Argentina.[1] Still, it would not do to forget that Holmberg also authored a fair number of works in which a supernatural explanation prevails. Although the novel has strong ties to the emerging science fiction continuum, its author judiciously employs notes of the fantastic, not only to add moments of drama and suspense to his at times didactic treatise, but also to bolster his scientific arguments when Todorovian hesitation is resolved via proof of natural causation.

"I have never believed in witches, nor in demons, nor in kobolds, nor in anything of the sort," so Ladislao Kaillitz begins his description of his first visit to Griffritz's private museum of natural history (*Two Factions* 28). The suggestion of witchcraft, the occult, and the magical is soon forgotten amid the descriptions of the copious exhibits of flora and fauna and the detailed scientific discussions between Kaillitz and Griffritz that follow, until a scene in which Griffritz revives a dried *sensitiva* plant [*Mimosa pudica*] harks back to the more fantastic tone of Kaillitz's initial words. The pedigreed plant in Griffritz's possession had been cut and dried by the French botanist Aimé Bonpland and sent to Alexander von Humboldt over fifty years earlier. Throughout the revivification process, Griffritz provides the young Kaillitz with extensive scientific explanations involving the relation between the diameter of the plant's vessels and the ambient temperature at the time it had been cut, and Holmberg's narrator supplies a supporting footnote in which he reviews and confirms the science involved. On a less empirically verifiable note, however, Kaillitz recounts that Griffritz places the plant in water to which he adds "some drops of a liquid that was not known to me," and a short time later the *sensitiva* returns to life (39). Kaillitz, now referring to Griffritz's liquid as "magical," compares Griffritz both to Christ raising a "vegetable Lazarus" from the dead and to a "necromancer" (45). The as yet untutored Kaillitz admits, "My science was not developed to the point that I could explain the causes that had brought about that strange phenomenon" (45). Despite Holmberg's obvious delight in giving the initial impression that Griffritz is putting mysterious or supernatural forces to work in his museum laboratory, the ultimate lesson of the *sensitiva* episode is to provide Kaillitz (and the reading public) with ammunition against irrational interpretations of events and to encourage Kaillitz to pursue further scientific training and become a full-fledged Darwinist. As Griffritz explains:

> For those who believe in miracles easily, the resuscitation of a *sensitiva* plant—or even of a man—is nothing special; but, for those who only seek in natural phenomena the natural cause which produces them, seeing a thing which departs completely from the regular order is something which quickly incites their intelligence to investigate that cause. For the former group, everything is explained by the power or the will of God; for the latter by the simultaneous action of several physical forces. (44-45)

> Para los que créen facilmente en milagros, nada tiene de particular que se resucite una sensitiva, ni aún que se resucite un hombre; pero, para los que solo buscan en los fenómenos naturales la causa natural que los produce, ver una cosa que se aparta completamente del órden regular, es algo que incita vivamente su inteligencia á la investigacion de esa causa. Para aquellos, todo se explica por el poder ó la voluntad de Dios; para estos por la accion simultanea de varias fuerzas físicas.

In Griffritz's declaration, then, we find yet another precursor to Arthur C. Clarke's famous statement that "any sufficiently advanced technology is indistinguishable from magic."[2] Griffritz, the positivist par excellence, worships not at the altar of any orthodox or occult religion but at that of science—"I serve a scientific doctrine: *Darwinism*," he testifies (45).

Two Factions was reviewed by the Argentine writer and critic Miguel Cané soon after it was published. Cané first laments what he views as the unfortunate element of political allegory in the text and then praises Holmberg's intelligence and talent as a writer, particularly his ability to combine literature and science, "to base the fantasies of his spirit on scientific axioms" ("*Dos partidos*" 177). The only scene from the novel that Cané singles out for discussion in any detail is that of the *sensitiva*. He lauds the episode as "poetic" and wishes that a plant could really return from the dead "at the magical evocation of a naturalist" (177). If only such a thing were possible, he adds, "I would sacrifice my dignity as a human being and accept Darwin's distasteful theory on the transformation of the species" (177–78). This is not to say that Cané misread *Two Factions* as a work of the fantastic rather than of science fiction or even that he misread the *sensitiva* episode. But he did discuss that episode selectively, mentioning the novel's central Darwinian premise only for the purpose of disagreeing with it, and valuing the more "poetic" and "magical" aspects of the *sensitiva* scene in isolation from its Darwinist message. Cané's worldview is manifestly more in line with Lamarckism, according to which "evolution was the result not of blind material forces but of changes brought about by will and choice" (Stepan, *Hour* 74).[3]

The *sensitiva* episode in *Two Factions* and Cané's subsequent commentary on it illustrate the many possible hybrid permutations and perceptions of early science fiction and the fantastic, as well as the tensions between competing interpretations of scientific truth in late nineteenth- and early twentieth-century Latin America. The debate between differing though equally "scientific" worldviews grew more intense in Latin America as ever more radical alternatives emerged to challenge the hegemony of the canonical sciences. The liminal nature of this chapter, which discusses texts located in the limbo between science fiction and the fantastic, necessitates a description of the selection criteria. Rather than requiring that works ultimately support natural or rational interpretations of events, I have included works in which the writer places a high value on employing or popularizing the scientific method, uses theories and methodologies which s/he believes may attain acceptance in the wider community, or attempts to achieve a viable synthesis between an alternative belief system and orthodox science. When exploring the limits of science in order to explore the limits of science fiction, two areas of potential territorial overlap require clarification: the sometimes nebulous borders between the canonical and the alternative sciences and those between science and religion.

BETWEEN ORTHODOXY AND HETERODOXY: OFFICIAL SCIENCE, RELIGION, AND ALTERNATIVE BELIEF SYSTEMS

The account of the emperor's time travel in Joaquim Felício dos Santos's *Brazil 2000* is introduced with the following statement:

> I do not know if the reader believes in magic, in Mesmerism, in Magnetism, in Spiritism, in hypnotism, in electro-biologism, in mediums, in *tables tournantes* and *parlantes*, in the spirit rappings of the Americans; in Mirville, Gougenot, E. Levi, V. Hennequin, R. Houdin, H. Carion, Guldenstubbe, A. Kardec, Home, and a thousand others who have written about supernaturalism. I am a firm believer: I am a Spiritist. (Dec. 12, 1869)

> Não sabemos se o leitor crê na magia, no mesmerismo, no magnetismo, no espiritismo, no hypnotismo, no electro-biologismo, nos *mediums*, nas mesas rodantes e fallantes, nos *spirits rappings* dos americanos; em Mirville, Gougenot, E. Levi, V. Annequim, R. Houdin, H. Carion, Guldenstubbe, A. Kardec, Home, e mil outros que escreverão a respeito do supernaturalismo. Nós cremos firmemente: somos spiritista.

As discussed in chapter 1, Felício dos Santos uses Spiritism merely as a literary device; however, the catalogue of noncanonical sciences and its practitioners in this passage is indicative of the range of alternatives available in Latin America in the second half of the nineteenth century. Of these alternatives, Magnetism, Spiritism, and Theosophy are especially notable in our corpus of texts, as well as individual syncretisms of one or more of these belief systems with varying degrees of faith in the empirical sciences or orthodox religions. While remaining mindful that these alternative belief systems varied widely in tenets and adherence, and that they met with diverse receptions in different Latin American nations, a few broad generalizations can help us to better understand the cultural milieu of Latin American writers of early science fiction.

FIGURE 3.1. Prolonging Life [Prolongación de la vida]. *Advertisement in* Caras y Caretas *590 (22 January 1910), Buenos Aires, Argentina. The subtitle reads: "A surprised humanity prostrates itself before Magneteopathy, the marvelous discovery of Professor Berecochea." The caption proclaims that the doctor has at his command "the unfathomable mysteries of occult science" and informs that "no illness has resisted the powerful influence of his treatment" at the Institute of Magneteopathy in Buenos Aires.*

During the nineteenth century and the first decades of the twentieth, alternative sciences enjoyed a far greater degree of mainstream acceptance than they later would. The French *Académie de médicine* commissioned several studies of Magnetism between 1825 and 1842, and the roots of hypnosis are often located in Puységur's work on "magnetic sleep" (Monroe 68–70).[4] The Cambridge-based Society for Psychical Research (SPR) was founded in 1882 to investigate what it termed "supernormal" phenomena in an academic setting; an American Society for Psychical Research (ASPR) was founded three years later.[5] During the last decade of the nineteenth century, the infant field of psychology also was open to conducting psychical research.[6] While these alternative sciences had been generally discredited by the late 1920s and early 1930s—psychical research had "drifted further and further toward the margins of the scientific world" and the associations between Spiritism and science had dissolved (Monroe 254, 221)—within our time parameters they still generated widespread interest and retained a fair degree of respectability. The successes of the alternative sciences were due in no small part to their efforts to gain recognition and respect in the scientific community. As Moore writes of North American Spiritualism:[7]

> Any interpretation of spiritualism's impact must begin with what has appeared to many as an anomaly.... For most of the nineteenth century, leading spiritualists held a childlike faith in empirical science as the only approach to knowledge. They tried to emulate the scientific method; more important, they copied and helped popularize scientific language. Certainly no others tried so hard to borrow science's prestige, and as a consequence, probably no one else benefited as much as they did from the great interest in science awakened in that century. (7)

An essential component of this endeavor to attain scientific legitimacy was Spiritualism's rejection of supernaturalism, a view also shared by Theosophists (Moore 19, 233).[8] Finally, one of the principal ways in which alternative sciences often attempted to gain a foothold in the mainstream was to frame their belief system not as replacement for the canonical sciences but rather as an expansion of them. Moore cites the efforts of North American Spiritualists to get scientists to accept Spiritualism as an enlargement of their fields of study from the physical to the nonphysical, or "to recognize an extension of the laws of physics and engineering into unseeable worlds" (22).

Because the alternative sciences generally came to Latin America from Europe, particularly France, this lent them a certain seal of legitimacy. Ubiratan Machado describes the "certain exotic halo of progressionism" that surrounded practitioners of Spiritism in the Brazilian royal court, many of whom came from the French colony residing there. "For Brazilians," Machado continues, "the doctrine of Kardec came consecrated by its European origin" (67). In Latin America, the alternative sciences—like most imports from the Old World—found their greatest reception among the elite, more so than was the case in Europe itself. Likewise, because of the central role played by France in the transmission of Spiritism to Latin America, we see a greater acceptance of reincarnation there than in Great Britain or the United States, as Anglo-American Spiritualism generally rejected multiple earthly incarnations (Monroe 111). Spanish American modernists were especially receptive to such alternative belief systems, as their combination of scientific and spiritual components dovetailed with the modernist search for a new totality.

Alternative belief systems often served as a middle ground in the nineteenth-century struggles for authority between religious and scientific worldviews, and the inroads made by heterodoxy are explained to a great degree by what was at stake in the debate. As Stableford explains it:

> The conflict between the world-view of religion and the world-view of science was not a battle between equals, nor was it a matter of like replacing like. It is perhaps too easy to see what was happening in Comtean terms, as an obsolete system of false beliefs being carefully devastated by the true belief of justified knowledge. There was more involved than truth; there was pride, and feeling, and morality. If the rationalists were to win the war of ideas, the losers would have to sacrifice far more than a few illusions: they would be thrust into an existential and psychological situation far more precarious and far less comfortable than the one they had previously enjoyed. (*Scientific Romance* 42)

Although the late nineteenth century saw a "growing skepticism of reason's power to encompass every aspect of human experience" (Monroe

205), a feeling that science alone was not an adequate replacement for religious faith, the return to a purely orthodox religious worldview was no longer possible for many in the modern world. In this climate, heterodoxy's promises of reconciliation between science and religion were particularly appealing. As we have already noted, alternative belief systems offered an expansion of science into the spiritual realm. At the same time, these belief systems also sought to expand the realm of religion beyond orthodox limits, as well as to verify its underpinnings with more tangible certainties; for example, to confirm the existence of life after death by communication with spirits and the continuing progress or evolution of the soul in the spiritual realm.[9] As one contemporary explanation read, "Spiritism has an advantage over Catholicism: Catholicism is founded on fixed principles the nature of which it leaves unknown or obscure: Spiritism explains those principles" (qtd. in Machado 108).[10] The decades around the turn of the century witnessed increasing interest in using heterodox philosophies to reconcile—or occasionally to replace—science and religion.

"There is a good deal of speculative fiction," Stableford tells us, "which deliberately aims at the reconciliation of traditional religious beliefs with scientific discovery," citing Flammarion's work as a prime example of this type of synthesis (*Scientific Romance* 39). Stableford identifies scientific romance and science fiction as genres of speculative fiction that lean more toward a scientific worldview, and heroic fantasy and supernatural fiction as genres that lean away from science. Despite the inherent tensions between the approaches taken by these genres, he emphasizes that "the two thriving halves of the tradition of fantastic fiction failed to disentangle themselves completely from one another" (39).[11] The same hybridization that was taking place in the Northern Hemisphere was also occurring in Latin America, but while Stableford's early scientific romancers "were on the side of reason against superstition" (42), in Latin America the more supernatural or "fantastic" literary tradition held equal or greater sway than the science fictional. This can be seen especially clearly in the hybrid texts examined in this chapter.

In Carlos Olivera's "Death at a Fixed Hour (Revelations of a Medical Doctor)" [Los muertos a hora fija (Revelaciones de un médico)] (Argentina, 1883), a young doctor asks his mentor if it is possible that a patient can know in advance the precise hour at which he will die of natural causes. The young doctor, who describes himself as "prepared by my studies not to believe in the least supernatural thing," is inclined to believe that the man cannot (147). The older doctor is less certain, replying: "You are still young, and you have more faith in science than I, who am much older and have been your teacher . . . . There is a multitude of phenomena in medicine for which we still do not have even the shadow of an explanation" (141, ellipsis in the original). He recounts a case he had witnessed in his own student days, in which a terminally ill patient with "something supernatural, from beyond the grave" in his tone had correctly predicted his own time of death, whereas the official medical prognosis had been off by several weeks (142). The two physicians make a bet: the younger man that his patient will not die at the predicted hour of eleven o'clock, the older man that he will. The patient is suffering from interstitial hepatitis. The older doctor examines the man himself, and while his medical knowledge suggests that the man should live at least another month, the older physician doubles his bet on the patient's perspicacity.

The younger doctor narrates that the bet is only of secondary importance to him; his primary motivations for prolonging the patient's life are self-respect, pride, and "the mad ambition to fight hand-to-hand with the Eternal Unknown and defeat it" (148). He tries every remedy at his disposal, including having the man drink a cup of hot wine with milk, port, and egg yolk, changing his clocks, injecting him with sulfuric ether, and applying electric current to his spinal column. To no avail. The man dies at 11:05.

Whereas the rational explanation prevails in Holmberg's *Two Factions*, the Eternal Unknown triumphs in "Death at a Fixed Hour." In Olivera's text, there are limits to what science can do or know, there are regions that belong, in the words of Rubén Darío, to "the unknown empire in which science is groping its way" [el imperio desconocido en que la ciencia anda a tientas] ("Cuento de Pascuas" 379). Throughout the corpus of Latin American science fiction, we see the tensions played out between a more canonically scientific worldview (described under headings such as materialism, rationalism, utilitarianism, and positivism) and a more spiritual worldview (encompassing both orthodox religious conviction and heterodox belief systems, an interest in nonphysical mysteries and acceptance of the supernatural). A literal debate between Darwinists and creationists rages in *Two Factions* (see chapter 2), and other oppositions can be found in texts such as *Querens* (between two colleagues), *The Soul-Giver* (between two friends), and

"Horacio Kalibang" (between two family members). Because of the pervasiveness of the debate between scientific purists and synthesists in early Latin American sf, because of the strength of the fantastic tradition in a number of Latin American countries, and because of the frequent tendency of Latin American science fiction to form hybrids with neighboring genres, there are a number of texts covered elsewhere in the book that could also quite easily be discussed here. (It is particularly important to observe that the absence of Brazilian texts in this chapter cannot be entirely explained by the relative weakness of the fantastic tradition in Brazil compared to Spanish America.[12])

HARNESSING THE STRANGE FORCES: LEOPOLDO LUGONES AND MIGUEL CANÉ

In chapter 2, we saw Lugones—a modernist and Theosophist—seeking to construct a coherent worldview that encompasses the realms of both science and the spirit. Beyond his (d)evolutionary tales and essay, Lugones's collection *Strange Forces* [*Las fuerzas extrañas*] contains five other science-fictional short stories: "The Omega Force" [La fuerza Omega], "Psychon" [El Psychon], "An Inexplicable Phenomenon" [Un fenómeno inexplicable], "Viola Acherontia," and "Metamusic" [La metamúsica].[13] Like the medium in "The Origin of the Flood," who evokes a being whose force she does not fully comprehend, the Lugonian protagonists in these tales attempt to wield powers beyond their ken. Like her they presume to go beyond the knowable to penetrate the essential mysteries of the universe, in search of power and knowledge that are either inappropriate for humans or that belong only in the hands of the initiated. In these tales, however, there are lasting consequences.

The mysterious forces that Lugones's characters attempt to harness run the gamut from the physical to the supernormal, but the functions of these forces in the narratives are quite similar: "These powers operate when a limit is crossed, when a scientist breaks an equilibrium or alters an order, freeing them. The act committed constitutes an error, a transgression that is punished with insanity, death, blindness, etc." (Barcia 14). At the same time, the strange forces in these tales are counterbalanced by what Cano has described as "extensive scientific reflections that explain the theoretical principles behind the experiment" (117). According to Cano, these passages serve to create the impression of reading a scientific essay rather than a work of fiction, and they have the ultimate effect of accentuating the authority of the protagonist's discourse (117). The scientists, both amateur and professional, attempt to master mysterious forces—molecular cohesion, human thought, clairvoyance, a reverse-Frankensteinian power to produce death rather than life, the translation of the senses—using the scientific method. If the scientific method is defined as "consisting in systematic observation, measurement, and experiment, and the formulation, testing, and modification of hypotheses" (OED), Lugones's scientists are largely successful in the initial stages of this process, but when they arrive at the final, practical stages, or when they try to wield their new knowledge for their own ends, the forces escape their control and destroy them. The five stories discussed here are all narrated in the first person, either by the scientist's assistant or an acquaintance who is sympathetic to the protagonist's alternative approach, but who has lived, or remained mentally stable enough, to tell the tale.

Leopoldo Lugones, "The Omega Force," "Psychon," "An Inexplicable Phenomenon," and "Viola Acherontia"

"The Omega Force" is representative of our Lugonian formula. Using knowledge gained from the occult as well as from the physical sciences, an inventor discovers the mechanical power of sound. He builds an apparatus to harness this force and use it to overcome the molecular cohesion of any object, thereby causing the object to disintegrate. He reveals his discovery to two close friends, a doctor-philosopher and our narrator, a freethinker who, while not a practitioner of the occult sciences like the inventor, does not share the general public's pious disdain for them. A true believer in the "science" in alternative science, the inventor compares his Omega force to Hertzian (radio) waves and X-rays, insisting that his discovery "has nothing to do with the supernatural," though even he does not understand exactly how the Omega force works (100).[14] The narrator and the doctor return to the inventor's house several days later to find their friend dead, the apparatus in front of him, his brain matter mysteriously atomized. No one else can make the apparatus function.

In these tales Lugones varies the specificity of identifiers as well as the ratio of canonical to alternative scientific elements and the fate of the protagonist. "The Omega Force" contains no mention of the characters' nationalities or of a particular national setting, though all scientific authorities referenced are Northern. In the next two instances identification is more overt. "Psychon" and "An Inexplicable Phenomenon" feature European experimenters and an Argentine narrator. Thus a colonial relationship continues to have a significant presence in this cluster of texts, though Lugones is meticulous about representing his own scientific bona fides along with those of his Argentine characters, who are capable of understanding, if not replicating, the experiments of the Northern scientific innovators. Citations of data from the hard sciences saturate "The Omega Force." Such data is certainly present in the other two works, but descriptions of procedures stray further from accepted norms. The scientist in "The Omega Force" is ultimately killed by his incompletely tamed strange force. The protagonists in "Psychon" and "An Inexplicable Phenomenon" escape with their lives, but in these two tales Lugones explores consequences that may be worse than death.

In "Psychon," Dr. Paulin, a European-educated scientist and "Spiritualist" of unspecified provenance, arrives in Buenos Aires.[15] Like virtually all of the scientist figures in Lugones's tales, he is "detached from official scientific doctrine, keen on the occult, withdrawn from the world, if only temporally" (García Ramos 97n2). With the aid of our *porteño* [native of Buenos Aires] narrator, Paulin engages in experiments ranging from the spectrographic analysis of the glowing haloes emanating from exposed scalps to the cutting-edge process of the liquefaction of gases. By combining these areas of research, Paulin eventually seeks to distill all of the thoughts floating around in what he terms the "psychosphere" [psicósfera], potentially leading to the development of the capability of preserving and storing thoughts and characteristics such as genius, poetry, audacity, and sadness. Paulin recognizes that his theory belongs in the territory just beyond the present limits of the canonical sciences and is intent on extending those limits, asking: "Might this not be a premonition of the phenomenon which science is on the road to discovering?" (124; 228). When the initial distillation is successful, Paulin and his assistant release the liquid thoughts so as not to cause any distress to the souls of their originators. But human thought proves to possess properties Paulin had not suspected. To the two men's surprise, the thoughts—laughter, crime, mathematical problems, and more—are absorbed by their own brains and even by the brain of a cat that happens to be in the room, causing all three to act briefly in accordance with each thought. Unique among these tales, this narrator experiences something of the power of the strange force first hand. The neighbors finally disperse the thoughts by opening the doors. Paulin disappears the following day and, when the narrator next hears of him, he has repeated the experiment and been committed to an asylum in Germany: "There could be no doubt that the pure thought we had absorbed was surely the elixir of madness" (126; 231).

In "An Inexplicable Phenomenon," clairvoyance is the strange force in question. The force is associated with India, that most favored of modernist/Theosophist sources of the mysterious. Frustratingly, temptingly, the force has been successfully harnessed by a select few, members of a group with extensive specialized training. The tale is narrated by a traveler through the Argentine provinces who, in order to escape the horrors of rural public-house cuisine, seeks lodging for a night at the home of a reclusive Englishman. The Englishman is a homeopath, and because the traveler has also studied and conducted experiments related to homeopathy, his host declares that, for the first time, he has found someone capable of understanding the strange and unhappy situation to which his interest in alternative sciences and practices has led him. Despite his longstanding distress, however, the Englishman waxes poetic about the wondrous potential at the limits of the canonical sciences: "Science is so beautiful—free science, that is, without chapel or academy! . . . The case you are about to hear will reveal to you how far one can reach" [¡Es tan hermosa la ciencia, la ciencia libre, sin capilla sin academia! . . . El caso que va usted a conocer, le revelará hasta dónde puede llegarse] (131). He explains that he is a veteran of the English campaigns in India and, while in His Majesty's service there, witnessed the yogis as they performed feats of clairvoyance by inducing their minds to venture forth from their bodies. There was no question of fraud, as photographs reproduced everything as he had seen it: "Hallucination? Impossible! Darkroom chemicals do not hallucinate!" he states (40; 131). The Englishman's subsequent actions reveal the same tragic flaw common to so many of Lugones's researchers: "I aspired to unravel these same powers. I had always been audacious, and had no way of knowing that I would later rue the consequences" (40; 131). Even without the benefit of the yogis' training or by following any prescribed method, the Englishman manages to reproduce what he has seen the yogis do, but then the power he has awakened begins to turn rebellious. A prolonged displacement outside his body leads to a division, an inability to reintegrate what has split off from him. When he seeks to see this double by reentering the autosomnambulistic state, what he beholds is a horrible monkey which, although separate from him, has followed him ever since, neither leaving him nor allowing him to be whole again—"I have lost the concept of unity," he tells his guest (41; 133). The narrator at first thinks his host insane, suffering from some form of extreme posthypnotic suggestion, but with his own eyes he observes that the man's shadow does not move with him. And when he traces his host's silhouette, his untutored hand reveals not the refined facial features he expects, but the bestial, simian outline of the double.

"Viola Acherontia" is something of an odd fish in this group of tales because of its open ending. It is the story of a gardener whose intense desire to create a flower of death leads him to stop at nothing, including, it is suggested, the murder of children, in order to reach his goal. The reader never learns what becomes of the gardener or his nefarious project, or if there is ultimately any punishment for his transgressions. The narrator ends his visit to the gardener once he suspects the lengths to which the man has gone, and he never returns.[16]

"Metamusic" and "The Harmonies of Light"

"Metamusic" contains remarkable similarities to "The Harmonies of Light" [Las armonías de la luz] (1877), a story written by Miguel Cané more than two decades earlier. The differences between the texts reflect some of the generational as well as the individual distinctions between these two Argentine writers of science-fictional works. In his narrative Cané respects virtually every traditional boundary of science, though he portrays science as a poor substitute for his inventor's lost religion. A generation later, Lugones's projected expansion of the limits of science into the unknown, reaching toward divine but forbidden knowledge, leads to the unleashing of uncontrollable forces.

In Lugones's story, a studious music lover adapts his piano to translate sound waves into light waves, a literal synesthesia. Cané's "The Harmonies of Light" involves a similar instrument, a "color organ" [órgano de colores] (247). Despite a number of commonalities in the impulses behind the two inventions, the theories employed in designing them, and the steps taken to construct them—and despite the tragic endings of both stories—Lugones and Cané make very different uses of their creations and of the forces harnessed by them.

Lugones's young inventor, Juan, is inspired to work on his audio-to-visual project by the inability of a close friend, our narrator, to appreciate music. For Juan, to understand music is to understand the universe: "The universe is music," he tells his friend, citing the work of thinkers from Pythagoras to Kepler (66; 169). He also invokes the "theory of unity" (160) and goes so far as to state that "music is the mathematical expression of the soul" (65; 167). The inventor does not formulate his theories based on the work of past authorities alone, he also incorporates the latest advances in modern science, including the discoveries in color photography of Gabriel Lippmann (winner of the 1908 Nobel prize in physics). During their detailed discussion, which Juan describes as "my little scientific party," he relates how he has adapted existing apparatuses, connecting his grand piano via a series of tubes to a vacuum chamber and employing a piece of black glass, a disk of mercury, a projection screen, and other laboratory equipment (160). Juan then sits down at his metamusical instrument to play . . .

Cané's "The Harmonies of Light" is the story of an Argentine tuberculosis patient who goes to Italy in search of a curative climate. The narrator describes the great lengths to which he must go to avoid any overexcitement that might bring on an attack: taking regular exercise, getting up early, reducing his consumption of opera ("music had a violent effect on my prodigiously overexcited sensibility"), avoiding heated discussions, and reading only books with hopeful messages (238). Eventually he meets an Italian man, Andrea Tanarotti, whose sixteen-year-old daughter, Magdalena (Lena), is deaf and also in delicate health. Tanarotti, a self-proclaimed man of science and religious skeptic, tells our narrator that when his wife died in childbirth, "I had the profound consolation in my soul of not believing in God: I would have cursed him!" (245). Because Tanarotti feels that Lena is "deprived of intellectual commerce" (246), he seeks distractions to keep up her spirits and therefore her health. To this end he has constructed a "color organ" which will bring the deaf girl "the celestial pleasures of music, that supreme consolation of sad and sick souls" (247). The purpose of the invention, then, is to compensate for an inequality, to give Lena something of what most mortals take for granted. Tanarotti builds the organ based on the theories of an eighteenth-century monk, Jehan de Castel, whom he describes as "one of those simple monks who . . . prepared the way for the advent of science" (248). "What for Father Castel was impossible," Tanarotti assures our narrator modestly, "has been easy for me with the aid of modern science" (251). Tanarotti cites the essential numbers (which Castel lacked) for the measurements of the vibrations of ether and of light waves and credits the superior expressive powers of the organ over Castel's clavichord for his success. (This part of the narrative also footnotes several scientific studies.) Although the greater rapidity and simultaneity with which we perceive light versus sound waves means that the organ must be played with great speed, Tanarotti assures the narrator that Lena has mastered this ability with little effort and promises him a concert the next day . . .

In both "Metamusic" and "Harmonies," then, the connection between music and emotion is valued. Music is seen as a conduit for things spiritual, for putting us in touch with something greater than ourselves. Both inventors build instruments based on existing devices and base their designs on older as well as recent scientific knowledge, though Lugones's inventor has consulted alternative as well as empirical scientific authorities. Likewise, both stories end in tragedy.

When Juan the metamusician begins to play, his tone-deaf friend feels the stirrings of an emotional reaction to music for the first time. Juan explains, "What you are hearing is a harmony composed of the specific notes of each planet in the system; and this simple combination ends with the sublime octave of the sun, which I have never dared to play, as I am afraid of producing excessively powerful influences" (170). The narrator describes what he is seeing as "a vague phosphorescence and something like sketchy figures," then he realizes that he is not getting the full effect of the metamusic because the room is too light (67; 170). He turns to switch off the lamp at the same moment that Juan dares to play the octave of the sun. The chord invokes even more powerful forces than anticipated. Under their impact, the projection screen bursts into flames so intense that they liquefy the musician's eyes. In the text's final lines, the narrator watches as Juan, "insensible to pain, radiant with madness, exclaimed, stretching his arms out toward me: 'The octave of the sun, old chap, the octave of the sun!'" [insensible al dolor, radiante de locura, exclamaba tendiéndome los brazos: '¡La octava del sol, muchacho, la octava del sol!'] (171).

The promised concert in "Harmonies" never takes place. Our hypersensitive narrator, whose long illness has caused his "moral organism" to become "out of tune, forgetful of the habit of emotions" (252–53), finds himself so overstimulated by the mere discussion of the color organ that he suffers a cerebral attack. During the month-long delirium that ensues, he writes, his consciousness is taken over by "all my dearest impressions, those which had filled my soul with adorable memories" (253). Visions of Faust and Hamlet pass through his fevered brain, along with wonderful dreams. He also speaks constantly of Andrea, Lena, and Father Castel. When he recovers, he learns that Tanarotti has nursed him through the first half of his illness, but that the inventor and his daughter are now gone. The narrator eventually recovers from his tuberculosis as well and, just before leaving Italy, receives a letter from Tanarotti; Lena has died of complications from her chronic health problems. Tanarotti describes his present state as one "confronting the tremendous solitude of doubt" (258). We never learn what becomes of his invention, but the narrator closes with thoughts of Lena "evoking on her marvelous organ the indescribable combinations of light, in its splendid harmonies" (258).

Where Lugones is the epitome of the Argentine modernist, Cané has been called the prototype of the Generation of 1880 (Castagnino 10), and "Harmonies" a mixture of the romanticism popular in Cané's youth and the fantastic of Hoffmann (Santiago González 42–43). Although the story implies that Tanarotti's belief in science rather than religion has led him to the existential loneliness of the materialist, his suffering is not the result of his invention. Neither is his daughter's death in any way connected with the playing of the organ. Wielding the harmonies of light brings her only joy. While the narrator's weakened health is broken by the mere thought of the organ, once physically sound he is able to contemplate its never-witnessed marvels with no detrimental effect. No limits have been transgressed because no limits have been posited. In contrast, Lugones conceives of an instrument capable of tapping into strange and potentially transgressive forces of immense power. These forces, unleashed through the mysterious "octave of the sun," seem to be related to the "music of the spheres" and the mathematical expression of the human soul, neither of which is meant for mere mortals. Like the other Lugonian inventors discussed here, Juan upsets the balance of the universe by pushing the limits of science too far, and he is punished for it.

SUBVERTING THE LIMITS: GORRITI'S EARLY FEMINIST SF

Juana Manuela Gorriti (1818–92) led a far from traditional life during which she crossed limits—national, social, and literary—time and again. Born into a wealthy family in the northern Argentine province of Salta, Gorriti refused to attend the local Catholic girls' school that custom dictated. According to Thomas Meehan, she was self-educated from the age of eight, and her reading led her to acquire "erroneous scientific notions and superstitions that she would take to the grave" as well as "a propensity for all that was strange, exotic, and supernatural" (5). With the rise to power of the Federalist caudillo Juan Manuel de Rosas, the Argentine political climate turned against Gorriti's Unitarist family and they emigrated to Bolivia. In 1833 Gorriti married a captain in the Bolivian army, Manuel Isidoro Belzú, who later became Bolivia's president (1848–55). The course of their married life ran less and less smoothly as time went on. In the same year that her husband assumed the presidency, Gorriti established her own household in Peru, where she lived for many years. She is known to have had at least two illegitimate children, in addition to her two daughters with Belzú. In Lima, Gorriti opened an unconventionally coeducational primary school. She hosted a literary salon attended by such luminaries as Ricardo Palma and Clorinda Matto de Turner. Meehan cites sessions of Spiritism among the bohemian activities that took place during these soirées (7); Francine Masiello notes that women's issues such as public education and legal emancipation were prominent topics of discussion (46). Rather surprisingly, considering her nontraditional lifestyle—we have not yet mentioned her younger admirers or the time she dressed as a man for a return visit to Salta—Gorriti was not the object of social censure, either in Peru or Argentina. This has been attributed in part to the high status of her family, which included a number of heroes of the Argentine independence; her own "persuasive personal charm" also seems to have been a factor (Lojo 12). During the last years of her life, Gorriti returned to Argentina, where she was celebrated in social and literary circles.

The dominant theme in Gorriti's writing is the need for change in the power structure of nineteenth-century Latin American society. Her two most frequent targets were *criollo* men [men of European descent], who occupied positions of power at all levels from the household to the state, and the Catholic Church, which dominated both religion and education. Gorriti often staged her challenges of the traditional power structure from the margins. She defended the rights of women, occasionally in a subaltern alliance with Latin American Indians. Gorriti's successes in questioning the social order—in her own life and in her writing—were due in large part to the fact that, as María Rosa Lojo puts it, "Juana Manuela . . . was such an astute transgressor that she avoided being disarmed or neutralized prematurely" (13). Gorriti's most subversive ideas are accessible only to the subtle reader, one who looks past the "'morals' that are tacked onto the fascinating narration like a safe-conduct" (Lojo 13).

Juana Manuela Gorriti's writing enjoyed widespread popularity throughout her lifetime, and she has been called one of the three most significant Latin American women writers of the nineteenth century, along with Gertrudis Gómez de Avellaneda and Clorinda Matto de Turner (Meehan 4). Her work fell into relative obscurity in the midtwentieth century, likely because of the fragmentary nature of her publications,[17] but in recent decades there has been a revival of interest in Gorriti and her oeuvre both in Latin America and abroad, as witnessed by recent critical studies, re-editions, and translations. The changing fortunes of Gorriti's literary fame are not related to her interest in the fantastic or the science fictional; her production is too varied and her literary reputation not confined to these genres. As a member of the literary generation prior to Holmberg's, however, she is becoming more often cited as the earliest Argentine—and perhaps earliest Latin American writer—to experiment with the fantastic in a significant way. Though they have usually been discussed in the context of the fantastic, two of Gorriti's texts, "Herbs and Pins" [Yerbas y alfileres] (1876) and "He Who Listens May Hear—To His Regret: Confidence of a Confidence" [Quien escucha, su mal oye: Confidencia de una confidencia] (1865), also can be considered science fictional, largely due to the centrality of Magnetism to both their plots. In "He Who Listens," Gorriti deploys this nontraditional science in a nontraditional way, while also making use of a marginal literary genre to define and to question the sociocultural "center" of her day. "Fantasy characteristically attempts to compensate for a lack resulting from cultural constraints," Rosemary Jackson has written, "it is a literature of desire, which seeks that which is experienced as absence and loss" (3). Jackson describes fantasy as a literary mode that, through its point of departure in the "real," its compensatory seeking, and its subsequent impulse toward transgression of the dominant cultural order, serves as "a telling index of the limits of that order" (4, 9). It seems fitting that the only female writer of early science fiction discussed in this study should seek to expose and to subvert the limits that society set for women, and that she should find the space to do so not only at the limits of traditional fiction but at the limits of traditional science.[18]

The story's title, "Quien escucha, su mal oye," is also a popular saying. A literal translation is "S/he who listens hears evil of her/himself"; a more epigrammatic translation would be "Listeners never hear good of themselves" (Del Mar 153). Gorriti affixes a subtitle—"Confidence of a Confidence"—to the axiom, and the text's original edition also carries the dedication, "To Miss Cristina Bustamante." Already we have indications of multiple levels of narration—Pablo Brescia has identified no fewer than eight narrative sequences and thirteen storylines in the tale (69)—but, though many narrative frames are opened, few are closed. Events take place in Peru at various points from the late colonial period to circa 1865, though not in chronological order. Gorriti clearly seeks to create a certain degree of confusion in the reader. The text requires a subtle reading, not only to understand her subversive ideas but also to unravel the plot(s) and to achieve a sense of closure.

In a brief outer frame to the story,[19] an unnamed female narrator tells of a male friend's offer to confess an error he has committed, if she will act as—he uses the masculine—"my confessor" [mi confesor] (77; 136). The woman accepts on the condition that she not be required to keep the secrecy of the confessional. The man ruefully laments, "Bah, women! Women! You cannot refrain from talking even when your life depends on it. Women, who in your idolatrous chatter profess to form a cult" (78; 136). The man then proceeds to declare himself guilty of the offense of curiosity, and of satisfying it.

In the untitled first section, the man tells of hiding from government agents who want him for conspiracy. He takes refuge in an outbuilding in the garden of a friend's home, occupying a richly appointed room that had once belonged to the friend's grandfather. Each night the man hears the beautiful voice of a woman, first speaking with men, and then alone, reading aloud or singing. Because the voice seems to be loudest in an area of the room near a large armoire, the man seeks the aid of an old black serving man, Juan, to move the heavy piece of furniture. The servant confesses that in days gone by he helped his old master, the friend's grandfather, to build a secret door at the back of the armoire, connecting the room to the chamber of the master's lover, a cloistered nun in the convent next door. The affair had not lasted long, Juan explained, as "his little caged dove . . . loved too passionately, and as that love could no longer breathe in the poisonous atmosphere of the cloister, it bore her soul off to a better place" (78; 139–40). Our narrator promises to keep Juan's secret; Juan shows him the hidden door and leaves. While still hesitating "between curiosity and discretion," the man hears the voice on the other side of the wall quite clearly (79; 140). The woman wonders aloud where her lover might be; he had left two months before without saying goodbye or where he was going. "But I shall learn," the woman vows, adding, "the science whose power men without faith deny—he among them—that science shall tell me" (79; 141). No longer able to resist his curiosity, the man waits until all is silent, then opens the door in the armoire and enters the woman's room.

The second section of the story, entitled "The bedchamber of an eccentric woman" [La alcoba de una excéntrica], begins with a description of what the man finds when he steps through the hidden door. His eyes are first drawn to a small library at the foot of the bed. Books by Andral, Huffeland, and Raspail sit next to anatomical drawings and skulls for study. "One would have been led to believe that this was the room of a man of science," the man explains, had it not been for the feminine fripperies scattered around the rest of the room (79; 142). He then notes paintings of the baby Jesus and of a young man who must be the missing lover and reflects: "So, then, I was at last in the former cell of the nun, the sanctuary of her love now the temple of one no less impassioned" (80; 143). He quickly uses the woman's sewing scissors to gouge a spyhole in the carved wood paneling, and returns to his own political sanctuary.

As he converses with his host that evening, our narrator's mind is on his as yet unseen neighbor, wondering, "What was the science she had spoken of, and what had its arcane secrets revealed to her?" (80; 144). The moment his friend leaves, he returns to his peephole. He sees a surprised-looking man seated in the center of the room; the woman enters a moment later, as beautiful as her voice has promised. The woman immediately regards the seated man with "a grave, fixed, profound look" [una mirada grave, fija y profunda]; the man's eyes appear "fascinated" [fascinados] by her gaze and are soon overcome by a "strange languor" [extraña languidez] that causes them to close (145).[20] The woman makes a series of passes with her hands around the man's head and upper body and then, "in a soft but imperious tone," she calls his name, "Samuel" (81; 146). She places her thumb and index finger on Samuel's forehead and orders him to look into her heart and search for an image. Samuel seems to sleep, then shudders convulsively and murmurs a name. The woman then orders him, "Turn your all-seeing gaze toward the boundless horizon . . . and seek the one whose name you have just spoken" (81; 146). Our narrator describes the scene:

> The hour, the place, the surroundings, all contributed to the truly fantastic character of the scene. Seeing how that fragile creature, through some mysterious influence, dominated the powerful man, watching her there in her sheer, flowing robes, her hand held above the head of the man subjected to the power of her gaze, one would have thought her a magus celebrating the rituals of some unknown cult. (82)

> La hora, el lugar y los objetos que alli se presentaban, todo contribuia para dar á esa escena un carácter verdaderamente fantástico; y al contemplar aquel sér débil dominando con una influencia misteriosa al sér fuerte; al mirar á esa mujer envuelta en los largos pliegues de su flotante y vaporosa túnica, de pié y la mano estendida sobre la cabeza de ese hombre sometido al poder de su mirada, habríasele creido una maga celebrando los misterios de un culto desconocido. (147)

Samuel then describes what his clairvoyant gaze has revealed: the scene of an elegant party. The woman's lover is there in the company of another. The woman asks Samuel to specify what he sees. "Do not ask . . . you should not know," Samuel begs, but the woman insists (148, ellipsis in the original). Samuel replies using "a strange/foreign tongue" [una lengua extranjera] (148). The woman demands further, "Read the heart of that man," and Samuel tells her that the man loves the other woman (82; 148). She covers her lover's portrait with a black cloth and guides the sleeping Samuel from the room. The narrator hears her command Samuel to awaken, then she returns to her room and hides her head in her hands.

Helpless to intervene in the intimate situation he has witnessed, the narrator realizes that he loves the woman, whose heart belongs to another, with an impossible and desperate love. "He who listens may hear—to his regret" [Quien escucha su mal oye], intones our original female narrator, interrupting the man's confession (83; 150). The man makes as if to continue his tale, but hears the whistle of the express train from the south. In hopes of obtaining "interesting news from Arquipa," the man makes a hasty departure, despite the woman's threats to deny him absolution (83; 150). She then lists a series of revolutions in which the man subsequently took part in Latin America and abroad (Peru, Chile, Sicily and Aspromonte with Garibaldi). This "incorrigible conspirator" is now wandering in parts unknown, and our female narrator concludes, in a belated apostrophe, "May Heaven watch over him so that one day he can complete his confession and we can learn, my beautiful Cristina, the end of his tale of culpable and severely punished espionage" (84; 151).

Behind Gorriti's title and its tacked-on moral ("listeners never hear good of themselves"), what transgressions are to be found in this tale full of loose ends? In a reading of the text that echoes Jackson's characterization of the mode of fantasy, Michèle Soriano describes "He Who Listens" as a work that pretends to reproduce the power structure of a traditional sociocultural reality, including "a masculine gaze and discourse on a feminine object," but that in fact subverts this reality, producing "the space necessary for the articulation of a contradictory discourse, inverting the poles of the processes of objectivization" (265). Soriano traces Gorriti's inversion of the established power dynamics through the generational changes represented in the stories within the story. Whereas, in colonial times, the master of the house had used the door in the armoire to seduce a cloistered nun, two generations later the male narrator "does not manage to maintain the relationship of domination . . . he no longer seduces, but rather 'is seduced'" (Soriano 249).[21] In both generations, the women on the other side of the armoire have their privacy violated and their hearts broken by men, but unlike the nun in years past, the "eccentric woman" rebels against patriarchal tradition on multiple levels: she is able to come and go from her room at will and even hosts men in her apartments (Samuel and others who are overheard but not seen); she studies the male-dominated canonical sciences using the resources in her small library, described as that of "a man of science"; and rather than being smothered by the "poisonous atmosphere of the cloister" like the previous occupant of the room, the woman uses the alternative science of Magnetism (the terms "Mesmerism" or "hypnotism" are also apt) to escape the limits of the chamber and to gaze upon the masculine object of her desire.[22]

Gorriti's description of the magnetization of Samuel—including the "truly fantastic character of the scene," the eccentric woman's "mysterious influence" over him, the comparison of the woman to a "magus celebrating the rituals of some unknown cult"—might seem to indicate a stronger affinity for the fantastic than the science fictional. However, as Cano explains, "Gorriti's tale presents, in an incipient way, one of the elements that a short time later would characterize the nascent sf in Spanish America: the inclusion of non-rationalized scientific procedures to justify the transgression of spatial and temporal categories" (76). As Cano also states and as we have noted regarding the translation of the text, Gorriti does not employ the typical rhetoric associated with Magnetism, does not "rationalize" the mysterious proceedings in the bedchamber of the eccentric woman. Nonetheless, she does follow the procedures of her alternative science quite faithfully, and the abilities of Samuel, her somnambulist, do fall within limits deemed acceptable in the field. The woman displays the "assertiveness," "prodigious willpower," and "general air of assured mastery" John Monroe cites as common personal attributes of prominent *magnétiseurs* (69). She also makes the classic magnetic passes around Samuel's body, and forces him to discover and reveal information against his will. For his part, Samuel is able to divine the thoughts of others both present and absent as well as to "see" people and events that are both distant from him and blocked from view; these capacities match those claimed for somnambulists by nonfictional Mesmerists (Monroe 68).

In truth, Gorriti must respect mesmeric procedures and laws in her tale in order for the full impact of her transgressions to become clear to the discerning reader. In "He Who Listens" Gorriti uses science as a category to perpetrate multiple subversions of dominant orders. Not only does her eccentric woman have access to male-dominated official science, but she also uses an alternative science—the "science whose power men without faith deny"—to gain knowledge that is physically and socially inaccessible to her. In addition, within the alternative science itself, the eccentric woman inverts the usual power dynamics by inverting traditional gender roles. Magnetizers, whose role was to serve as "manipulator of fluid, objective observer, poser of questions, and documenter of answers," were generally men, and somnambulists, "the instrument on which the *magnétiseur* acted," were usually women (Monroe 69). Although the male magnetizer was usually the dominant member of the duo, "in the trance state itself, the inequality between *magnétiseur* and *somnambule* seemed to disappear or even be reversed" (Monroe 69). Gorriti inverts this inverting tendency as well, as her female *magnétiseuse* controls her male somnambulist throughout the hypnotic process.

The loose ends and open endings of "He Who Listens" are themselves the ultimate structural subversion of literary tradition and of social mores. Although, as Jackson states, "nearly all literary fantasies eventually re-cover desire, neutralizing their own impulses towards transgression," Gorriti's science-fictional tale is not one of these (9). In "He Who Listens," our curiosity is left unsatisfied on a number of levels (what did Samuel murmur and what did he say in a strange/foreign tongue? what was the eccentric woman's next step after learning of her lover's infidelity? did the male narrator ever develop any real relationship with her? what was the man's political fate? who is Cristina and what will she do with the information revealed in this confidence of a confidence?). The "confession" outlined in the opening of the story is never completed and, as Soriano points out, it leads neither to absolution nor to any sort of moral lesson for the listener within the text or the reader without (260–62). Rather, the text itself leads the reader into transgression: "It forces the reader into vice by multiplying, mirroring, this position of *voyeur* in which desire grows because it is infinitely deferred" (Soriano 262). The reader is left a curious gossipmonger, with an eye pressed to peepholes in several armoires. At the limits of science and of science fiction—like Gorriti's characters and like Gorriti herself—we become unrepentant transgressors of the limits of her traditional society.

EXPANDING THE LIMITS:
CASTERA'S SEARCH FOR SYNTHESIS

"A Celestial Journey" [Un viaje celeste] (Mexico, 1872) opens with an epigraph by Flammarion: "We are all citizens of the heavens" [Nous sommes tous des citoyens du Ciel]. The narrator declares, "I could not tear my eyes away from this line, whose letters shone with magical light" (430). He continues to ponder Flammarion's thought, concluding, "The infinite is the veil with which God covers himself, and sooner or later the Supreme Ideal will have satisfied the constant yearning of our spirit" (430). The narrator's concentration is such that he falls into a state of "spontaneous somnambulism," and his soul begins to separate from his body (430). He thanks his Creator for the sweetness and ease of what he assumes has been his own death and, through his newly heightened senses, perceives that, much like Flammarion's unmentioned Lumen, he can travel immense distances with a thought. He launches himself into the heavens and realizes with awe that the planets of our solar system are all worlds inhabited by "humanities like our own, equal to us or more perfect" (431). Thanking God again for revealing His omnipotence in His works, the newly liberated spirit briefly explores his celestial neighborhood from the Eden that is Jupiter to the far reaches of Neptune. He is then caught up in a comet's tail and whisked through countless systems of worlds, filled with beings who worship God and with suns and planets whose song forms "the sublime, magnificent, divine concert of universal harmony" (431).

Humbled by his own insignificance amid such grandeur, the traveling soul comes to a stop. His home galaxy is a small silver ribbon in the distance, and he searches in vain for Earth. Realizing with terror that a beam of light would take fifteen thousand years to circle the Milky Way, that Earth is but a "paltry atom" in this immensity, the little lost soul cries out to God, "Return me to my atom and forgive me my mad pride" (431). His rapid course through the heavens begins again, he feels vertigo, and "at that moment Manuel de Olaguíbel gave my arm a strong shake; I found myself seated at my desk with my hair somewhat burned, my hands convulsed, a multitude of papers in disarray, and the above lines written" (432). His friend Olaguíbel tells him he has been gesturing and writing in a "veritable delirium" for some time (432). Olaguíbel has been reading the pages as they were finished and has finally awakened his friend out of fear he would end his "fantastic journey" in the madhouse (432). The disturbed and exalted traveler can only repeat, "The heavens, the heavens" (432). Olaguíbel remonstrates with him—somewhat unjustly—for devoting little space in his writing to how the heavens "manifest to us and teach us the Supreme Omnipotence of God" and much to "*scientific, axiomatic, irreducible truths* that form the patrimony that this impious century leaves to the future" (432). The fresh night breeze calms the narrator's thoughts, but he concludes that, no matter how hard he tries, "I cannot stop thinking that the Universe is the homeland of humanity and we the citizens of the heavens" (432).

"Celestial Journey" is a microcosm of the concerns that defined the thinking and writing of Pedro Castera throughout his life (1846–1906). Principal among these concerns were the tensions he felt between religious and scientific worldviews, spirit(ual)ism and materialism, romanticism and realism, the mysterious and the rational.[23] Castera's most complete biographer to date, Luis Mario Schneider, has characterized him as a "religious and at the same time analytical scientist [who] needed to rediscover the unity between matter and spirit that the advance of science had broken" (21). In his effort to achieve a coherent synthesis, Castera exhibited contradictory ideations of spirituality, at times describing a traditional, detached God, and at others a pantheistic conception of the universe (Schneider 21). The first two scientific columns that Castera wrote for the newspaper *El Domingo*—under the heading "A Word on Science" [Una palabra de la ciencia]—began with lengthy dissertations on the relationship between science and religion. In his first column, "Steam" [El vapor], Castera initially appears to take a firm stand on the primacy of spirituality, but in the next breath he manages to incorporate science as an essential ingredient in the perfecting of humanity:

> I am a partisan of those who believe that science can resolve all matters, except one: the great mystery that is dissolved and manifested in light, in love, and in life; that is, the Divinity.
>
> But more than this, I also believe that science has barely begun to speak, or rather, to lisp its first sentences: from time to time science pronounces a word that produces great cataclysms in humanity; philosophical sects reform their doctrines; religious ideas are transformed, improved; scientific and industrial schools modify and develop their methods; everything changes, everything varies, everything advances, and this arises from the fact that a word from science is equivalent, in its true sense, to our world progressing one step toward the unknown, from the shadow to the light, from ignorance to clarity; let us say it once and for all, one more step on the scale of infinite progress. (147)

In his second column, "Electricity" [La electricidad], Castera reiterates his own faith in Christ prior to recounting the history of the study of electricity. He then connects the dots, affirming that, according to major (Northern) authorities in the field, "Electricity, heat, and light are nothing more than *spiritual forces*" (235). He ends with the asseveration that, in order to progress, humanity needs both scientific advances to develop our intelligence and "the moral force of Christianity" to draw us closer to our Creator (237). Castera was almost inevitably drawn to the ideas of other synthesist thinkers such as Flammarion. Like the "illustrious astronomer," Castera also searched for meaning at the limits of official science, both in Flammarionian/Spiritist conceptions of life on other worlds and the continuous progress of humanity, and in the field of Magnetism, with its extrapolation of the laws of science from the physical into the nonphysical universe ("Celestial Journey" 430). As his friend Manuel de Olaguíbel concluded his article, "Magnetism" [El magnetismo] (published the year before "Celestial Journey" in the same newspaper): "Let us not reduce the spirit to the sphere of the known, and let us fix our eyes on all of those occult forces that draw us closer to the infinite" (39). Castera was the epitome of a man *between*, fraught with internal divisions and seeking unity—or at the least a path toward it—in alternative schools of thought, while never completely leaving orthodoxy behind.

Luis Mario Schneider has marveled at how little is known about the man who authored the popular novel *Carmen* (1882) and whose work once received critical acclaim from the likes of José Martí, Ignacio Altamirano, and Vicente Riva Palacio (7). We do know that Castera was a mining engineer and held posts as a scientific, political, and literary journalist, as well as serving as a representative to the Mexican national congress. Of further note is the fact that the fear he placed in the mouth of his fictionalized Olaguíbel eventually came true: Castera was interned in the asylum of San Hipólito from approximately 1883 to 1889, suffering most likely from bipolar disorder (Schneider 15–18). Castera resurfaced in public life for only a few years after that; nothing is known of his life from 1891 until his death in 1906 (Schneider 18).

During his last productive interval, Castera wrote *Querens* (1890), another, longer work in the science-fictional genre so ideally suited to expressing his inner dualities. While "Celestial Journey" is an exploration of "outer space" and *Querens* of "the inner cosmos" (Trujillo Muñoz, *Biografías* 52), both texts share the *between* quality of Castera's philosophical limbo. Indeed, *Querens* centers on a collaboration incarnated by two characters, one who espouses a more scientific/materialist view of the world and one who takes a more spiritual/metaphysical approach. Castera almost certainly chose the title *Querens*—never directly referred to in the novel—in homage to Flammarion's seeker, Quaerens, in *Lumen*. The name is also a reference to Saint Augustine's *fides quaerens intellectum* [faith seeking understanding], as Castera, like Flammarion, sought to reconcile faith and reason in his life and in his work.[24]

Querens, like "Celestial Journey," opens with the meditations of an unnamed narrator (all of the novel's characters are unnamed) on the wonders of the night skies: "One's soul was elevated to mingle with those distant radiations [of the stars], and the spirit wanted to break free to bestride creation" (389). His thoughts soon turn from the outer heavens to the inner act of meditation itself and to the relationship between idea and feeling. "The will, through memory, evokes sensations, and these engender ideas," he says to himself, continuing, "Reason serves to compare, choose, and give value to ideas, but these cannot be produced in the brain without first passing, as Aristotle said, through the domain of the senses" (390). The chapter closes with his statement, "God is the radiant will of creation" (391). The narrator, likely a representation of Castera himself (recently released from San Hipólito), gradually reveals the inspiration for his musings. He is sick with "ills that are imaginary like all those I have suffered from in my existence"; his doctor (under duress) prescribes that he take the country air (391). He leaves Mexico City for the "pure air," "tropical sun," and "opulent hues" of the village of Tlalpan, where a portion of the population still consists of the "remnants of that valiant Aztec race" (392). Giving the reader the benefit of his metropolitan viewpoint, he describes life in the village in Cervantine terms. He socializes with the local notables, the judge, the priest, and the apothecary. One evening when card playing has palled, our narrator asks the others what there is of note in the village. Only the apothecary's reply contains anything out of the ordinary: there is a man in the village, one with "something strange, mysterious, fateful about him" (398). The rest of the novel essentially consists of the apothecary's tale of his past interactions with this unnamed "eccentric being" [ser extravagante] (397).

A friend had once introduced the apothecary to the strange man, and they immediately struck up a conversation on matters both scientific and philosophical. The man devotes himself to the study of thought; he wants to determine if thought—like heat, sound, electricity, and magnetism—is a physical force. He compares the electrical forces that transmit thought waves to those of the "magnetic fluids that science today, in the heart of the scientific academies themselves, has not been able to deny" (408). He then cites a few standard authorities in the magnetic sciences such as Mesmer, Puységur, and others,[25] and he defines the divisions within the field of Magnetism:

> Magnetism, as a psychological phenomenon and not as part of the physical sciences, has given rise to the magnetic sciences. The spiritualist and the materialist schools currently find themselves on opposite sides in this type of discussion. (410)

> El magnetismo, como fenómeno psicológico y no como parte de las ciencias físicas, ha dado lugar a las ciencias magnéticas. La escuela espiritualista y la materialista se hallan, en estos momentos, frente por frente en este género de discusión.

Not only does Castera's eccentric accurately sum up the role of the emerging science of psychology in the field of psychical research,[26] but he expresses the tensions between the more clinical, materialist branch of Magnetism, which focused on the use of magnetism in medical practice, and the more metaphysical branch, which was more open to influences of North American Spiritualism and contributed to the development of Kardecist Spiritism. The physical-metaphysical debate had been ongoing in French mesmeric circles since the 1850s, and Monroe has coined the helpful terms "therapeutic Mesmerists" and "spiritualist Mesmerists" to define the opposing sides (66n3, 67–72). Despite the eccentric character's early assertions to the contrary in *Querens*, it becomes clear that he is by nature more of a therapeutic Mesmerist. The apothecary is provided as a foil for the eccentric, as he is persistently if spottily portrayed as supporting tenets more in line with spiritualist Mesmerism such as clairvoyance and divination, and his narration is sprinkled with references to God and faith and mystery.

The worldly narrator of the frame interjects the thought that all of the eccentric's talk of Magnetism is old hat, but the apothecary's tale soon ventures into unexplored waters. The eccentric man states that he himself espouses neither school of Magnetism but studies the effects of magnetic sleep with regard to a specific case. He introduces the apothecary to a young woman, an idiot from birth. When magnetized using the standard methods, the woman becomes able to discourse on sophisticated scientific topics and develop arguments based on books she has never read. The eccentric magnetizer explains, "She is obliged to think with my ideas and to reflect my sentiments. It is the absolute control and power of one will over another" (422). The apothecary had believed such a phenomenon impossible in the case of an utterly blank slate such as this woman. He also waxes poetic on the woman's surpassing beauty when magnetized: "She was the personification of Latin American beauty . . . . Desire taking the form of delirium . . . . Eve but indigenous, such was that vigorous incarnation of love" [Era la belleza criolla americana . . . . El deseo cobrando forma de delirio . . . . Eva

159

pero indiana, tal era aquella vigorosa encarnación de amor] (415). Inevitably, the apothecary falls madly in love with her.

The eccentric explains the history of his project to the apothecary and expands upon his goals for the female subject. He had originally begun to seek a cure for her condition in the treatments sanctioned by the canonical sciences—exercises to develop muscles, alkaloids for the nervous system, applications of electricity—but to no avail. He then appears to have expanded his definition of the limits of science to include Magnetism, an extrapolation in keeping with his (and Castera's) expressed belief that the only limit to science is the ignorance of humanity—"Nothing is impossible for science," the eccentric declares, "The human race marches toward perfection. Science will succeed in destroying diseases, destroying the causes that produce them" (423). Other scientists have been held back by the narrow scope of their exclusive definitions; "No one recommends Magnetism, because no one knows anything about it," he remonstrates (411).

The eccentric man's work with Magnetism has met with partial success; "She thinks and she desires. The main thing is complete" [Ella piensa y quiere. Lo principal está hecho], he explains (454). But this success has already been achieved when he meets the apothecary, outside of the narrative space of the novel. *Querens* is the story of the second goal of his project. As the eccentric magnetizer tells the apothecary over the course of several dialogues, he wants his subject to be capable of original thought and feeling. The woman is presently much like Hoffmann's Olimpia (or the earlier stages of the artificially constructed human doubles discussed in chapter 4). The magnetizer compares her current status to that of an "automaton," a "machine":

> Her nervous system has been given life, but life like that produced by galvanism; she has been given a transfusion of ideas, like a transfusion of blood; a voice, like one copied by a phonograph; movement, like the mechanism of a watch; something of instinct awakening the beast, the flesh, the material being; but what is missing is the drive, the impetus, the dreams, the imagination, the emotions, the natural life of the nervous system, the exaltation in desires, the life of thought, with life's fevers and its deliriums, and more than all of this, the life of the feelings, with the life of the heart. (449)[27]

> Se le ha dado la vida nerviosa, pero como la producida por el galvanismo; se ha practicado la transfusión de las ideas, como la transfusión de la sangre; la voz, como la copiada por el fonógrafo; el movimiento, como a la maquinaria de un reloj; algo del instinto despertando a la bestia, a la carne, a la materia; pero falta el arranque, los ímpetus, los sueños, la imaginación, las emociones, la vida nerviosa natural, la exaltación en los deseos, la vida por el pensamiento, y sus fiebres y sus delirios, y más que todo esto, la vida de los sentimientos, con la vida del corazón.

In essence, he wants to create life without creating it. "We cannot create," he tells the apothecary early on in their discussions, but he has manifest intentions of approaching just that feat, as immediately afterward he explains his desire to "discover the vital principle. To surprise the sources from which existence springs. To wrench the origin of life out of the depths of mystery" (407). He is splitting hairs. He aspires to write life onto the blank slate of his subject—just not to create the slate.

The eccentric recognizes that his science, even with the expanded definition that includes therapeutic Mesmerism, has fallen short. His case study is evidence of this. "She only lives via Magnetism" [Sólo vive con la vida magnética], he laments, "Science has failed" (445). In order to produce independent thought—along with that element he variously refers to as a heart, emotions, or a soul—he must extend the limits of science still further to include a metaphysical level. To this end, he proposes a collaboration with the apothecary. The magnetizer's concentration on developing his own intellectual faculties, it emerges, has been at the expense of his emotional development—"I feel nothing, I have never felt anything, I have never felt a thing!" he confesses (446). Throughout the novel, the eccentric is associated with intellect, materialism, the more physical sciences, and the more clinical side of Mesmerism. The apothecary's spiritualist Mesmerism and his love for the female subject make him the ideal complement—"What that man lacked, I had," the apothecary concludes (444). The eccentric magnetizer outlines the next step in the process for his new colleague: "I will try to apply feeling, as I have applied strychnine and phosphorus; not finding it in myself, I will apply yours" (447).

But even this expansion of the limits of science proves insufficient. "You have told her everything a lover could tell her. You have expressed all that passion can express," the magnetizer tells the apothecary on the penultimate page of the novel, adding, "I believe we are at the same point at which we began and that we have wasted our time" (457). The apothecary has prefigured this for the reader chapters earlier: "I believed in the soul . . . but . . . unfortunately her soul did not exist" (440, second ellipsis in the original). They demagnetize the woman, and when they attempt to magnetize her once more, they fail. She has reverted to her original idiocy; even the magnetizer's earlier success is lost. The eccentric vows to begin anew, still holding out hope that answers lie beyond the known limits: "The magnetic sciences open a vast field of study to human thought. We shall see in the future the fruit and the results of new observations" (458).

The apothecary leaves the magnetizer's home, convinced, he says, "that human arrogance and pride can be measured only by their own smallness" (458). Even now, the apothecary tells his listeners, the magnetizer still seems to be searching for answers in the byways of Tlalpan, especially on stormy nights. He concludes his tale with the questions, "Is he trying to provoke fate as he provokes the lightning? Is he looking for inspiration in electricity?" (458). Perhaps the secrets of the "spiritual force" of electricity will lie within the sphere of science after a further expansion (Castera, "Una palabra de la ciencia: La electricidad" 235). It is unclear how much of the failure of the collaboration between magnetizer and apothecary is ultimately due to divinely imposed limitations—if their display of "human arrogance and pride" is judged in the same manner as the hubris of Lugonian scientists or a Doctor Frankenstein—and how much to the present limitations of science. Castera pushes the limits as far as he can, but is unable to achieve the perfect union of the material and the spiritual, even in his literary imaginings. The bravery of his text is to admit this, to represent the agonies of uncertainty, holding out only vague hopes that science may yet exceed its present bounds, uncover the harmonies of the universe, and reveal to all that we are citizens of the heavens.

RESTORING THE LIMITS: BALANCE IN NERVO'S CAUTIONARY TALES

Like fellow modernist Leopoldo Lugones, Amado Nervo was the essence of ambivalence in the physical-metaphysical debate. He too sought a unified solution in the synthesis of orthodox and heterodox, of scientific and spiritual belief systems (see the biography of Nervo in chapter 2). The two stories by Nervo discussed in this chapter include scientific and quasi-scientific elements, such as cutting-edge surgical procedures and sessions of Magnetism, both of which are used to confer godlike (super?)powers. At the same time, the stories contain features that belong to a more spiritual plane, such as reincarnation and a love that breaks through the barriers of time. *The Soul-Giver* [*El donador de almas*] (1899) is one of Nervo's earliest science-fictional works, while "The Sixth Sense" [*El sexto sentido*] (1918) is one of his latest. Although their settings, narrative premises, and levels of heterodoxy are quite different, they are telling variations on a common theme: a character is given an extraordinary gift, a prize that exceeds the standard limits of everyday reality and canonical science, only to find it a mixed blessing and ultimately intolerable curse. In the end prior limits are reinstated and the balance restored, but only after we have been accorded a glimpse of the wonders that await us.

Carlos Monsiváis has called *Soul-Giver* "one of the most original and least-known texts of nineteenth-century Mexico" (89).[28] The nouvelle is a cautionary tale. It recounts certain events that take place between 1886 and 1892 in the life of Rafael Antiga, a successful young doctor from Mexico City. A rather playful narrator is able to give the reader access to the doctor's diary, "due to the all-seeing privilege of authors" (163; 225). Rafael writes of the complete lack of affection in his life, lamenting, "*My kingdom for a little affection!*" (3; 199). He is overcome by ennui—bored by his cat, his housekeeper's cooking, even his work, which he finds predictable on the one hand and—because of the limits of medical science—discouraging on the other. "What do I want?" he asks himself (3; 200). As he recalls the inevitable disappointment when he has obtained things that he wanted in the past, it becomes clear that he has a long history of being unable to satisfy his desires: at sixteen he wanted a horse, but when he got a horse, "I saw that a horse would not do for flying" [vi que un caballo era muy poca cosa para volar] (5; 200); at twenty he achieved his desire to be loved by a beautiful woman, but soon all other women appeared more beautiful to him than she; at twenty-five he wanted to travel, but his journeying only convinced him that the world was an insignificant place and Mexico one of its meanest corners. Now, at thirty, he wants affection, or as he expresses it in his diary in a prophetic synecdoche: "A soul that would love me. A soul upon which I could place my seal, and with whom I could share the awful weight of my restless self . . . A soul . . . My kingdom for a soul!" (5; 200, ellipses in the original).

The doctor's maundering is interrupted by the arrival of his longtime friend, Andrés Esteves. Esteves is a successful poet who owes his fame to Rafael for publishing his first two books. Having thought long and hard of a gift worthy of expressing his gratitude, Esteves declares, he has finally decided to present Rafael with a soul. The medical doctor is a materialist who defines the soul as "the result of the forces that act within our organism" and views the gift-soul as an opportunity to seek "that cerebral matrimony dreamed of by Auguste Comte" (15, 29; 201, 204). Esteves, who is described as "dedicated to literature and occultism" (81; 212), protests Rafael's characterization roundly: "A soul is a spiritual entity, substantive, indivisible, conscious, and immortal . . . . A soul is a spirit which animates a body, upon which it does not depend except for the vital functions" (15, modified; 201–2). Rafael suspects that his friend will use his knowledge of what Nervo always refers to as the "occult" to bring about the gifting of the soul; he writes of Esteves in his diary:

> For four years he has been claiming to possess a psychic force especially directed toward controlling the will of others. He assures me that before long he will make a puppet, with no more powers of reason or will than he might decide to give it, of any man upon whom he might gaze for five minutes. The penetration of his gaze is astonishing! (21)

> Hace cuatro años que pretende poseer una fuerza psíquica especial para encadenar voluntades. Afirma que dentro de poco tiempo hará un maniquí, sin más cogitaciones y voliciones que las que él tenga a bien comunicarle, de todo hombre a quien mire durante cinco minutos. ¡Es asombrosa la persistencia de su mirada! (202)

However much Esteves may draw from the occult end of the scientific spectrum, he is also clearly drawing from Mesmerism and Spirit(ual)ism, closer to the limits of official science. The Mesmeric roots of Esteves's occultism are also evident in a letter Rafael receives from his friend, in which he describes the gift-soul's "divinatory faculties" [facultades adivinativas] that will help the doctor diagnose illness (204);[29] this ability would seem to be a variation on the ability to perform "autoscopy," or self-diagnosis, claimed by some lucid somnambulists (Monroe 68). Esteves also tells Rafael that the gift-soul can be summoned with only a thought, but he warns his friend not to keep the soul too long away from its body.

When Rafael summons the gift-soul, whose spiritual name is Alda, he learns that she is a nun whose body is lying in a hypnotic sleep in her convent. Alda reveals that Esteves possesses many souls that help him in his studies, in order to "perfect us and to perfect himself by acquiring a deeper knowledge of the universe" (35; 205). She confirms that she will be of great diagnostic aid in his medical practice, though she is unable to help him save those patients whose destiny is to die. Finally, Alda crushes Rafael's hopes that she might provide the affection that is lacking in his life. In her hypnotic state, she has no will of her own, so she cannot love him.

Rafael and Alda spend the next four years building his reputation as a physician, conquering London, Paris, and more. But the doctor keeps Alda with him for longer and longer periods of time, not realizing that her physical body is wasting away from neglect. The narrator now reveals that Alda's physical name is Sister Teresa. She is a girl of unknown origins and very expressive eyes, but in her waking state is "almost an idiot" (53; 207). The body of Sister Teresa eventually dies in the middle of the night, and Alda comes to Rafael, unbidden for the first time. Rafael is now in Russia, not coincidentally the birthplace of Helena Blavatsky, founder of the Theosophical movement. Alda tells him that God is not calling her to him yet, so she must become embodied in a new physical form. No one is around at this late hour, so she uses the only body available to her and takes over the left hemisphere of Rafael's brain, leaving him the right. Now that his dearest wish for someone to "share the awful weight of my restless self" and to achieve Comte's "cerebral matrimony" has unexpectedly been granted in full, Rafael is not certain he likes this "intellectual hermaphroditism" (73; 211). Alda consoles him with the thought that, now she is mistress of her own will, she can love him and that, with his unprecedented two souls, he is "almost a god" (73; 211). Rafael shows himself to be amenable to consolation, but the narrator foreshadows: "Alda was a tremendous gift,— such as should never be received" (81; 212).

The honeymoon period is filled with declarations of love and self-kisses. Alda describes for Rafael the journeys she has made to over six hundred planets in forty systems, as a soul in the service of Esteves.

She tells of primitive Venusians, of a more perfected humanity on Mars which "worships God in spirit and in truth," of the inhabitants of Saturn who have evolved beyond physical form, of Sirius and Aldebaran and beyond. She has heard the music of the spheres, the "great symphony of worlds" with its "divine harmony" (93–97, modified; 214–15). Rafael is deliriously happy, and the narrator takes stock of his gains:

> Riches, that was something.
> Fame, that was something more.
> Love, now that was a great deal.
> Faith . . . that was everything!
> Indeed, the doctor became a believer . . . .
> Now Rafael believed in the individual, conscious, spiritual, and immortal soul. (101, modified, first ellipsis in the original)

> Riquezas, esto ya era algo.
> Fama, esto era algo más.
> Amor, esto ya era mucho.
> Fe . . . , ¡esto era todo!
> En efecto, el doctor se volvía creyente . . . .
> Ahora, Rafael creía en el alma individual, consciente, espiritual e inmortal. (215, first ellipsis in the original)

Rafael's belief system is never labeled, but he has left his materialism behind, and his definition of the soul now coincides with that previously given by Esteves.

Soon little differences between Rafael and Alda begin to surface. Alda monopolizes their mouth and Rafael cannot get a word in. She likes to read "fantastic novels such as those of Hoffman, Poe, and Villiers," while he prefers scientific books (103; 216). She studies piano; he hates the piano. He smokes; she hates smoking. She loves sweets . . . . "In a word, those spiritual Siamese twins ended up making each other's lives insufferable" (105; 216). They decide to search out Esteves to bring about a "divorce." They just miss the occultist poet in Alexandria and Cairo but finally locate him in the Holy Land studying the Kabbalah with the high priest Josefo, descendent of Melchisedec. Esteves urges them to reconsider their decision to dissolve the cerebral matrimony, repeating to Rafael "It makes you a god" (123; 219). The couple insist on the separation in order to recommence their love at a tolerable spiritual distance. They ask Esteves to incarnate Alda's soul in another woman's body.

To separate the souls requires a sacred word that, according to Hebrew tradition, confers upon the person who pronounces it correctly "the key to all divine and human sciences" (127; 219). This is the same word that Esteves used to bind the souls of Sister Teresa and ten others . . . but he has forgotten how to pronounce it. After relearning the pronunciation from high priest Josefo, Esteves suggests Rafael's housekeeper, the aptly named doña Corpus, as Alda's avatar, thinking that a strong soul like Alda's should be able to rejuvenate the fifty-something body. Esteves, "his hands laden with fluid," puts doña Corpus into a hypnotic sleep and pronounces the sacred word (222). All seems to be going well, but the process proves to be too much for doña Corpus's body, and she dies of "spiritual congestion" (143; 222). Alda's soul has been successfully detached from the doctor's brain, and she wants to resume her celestial travels. Rafael, however, does not want to let her go. He is again in love with Alda, "precisely because he no longer possessed her" (147; 223). He begs her to stay and search for another solution, saying he cannot bear to live without her, pleading, "Alda, I need an ideal for my life" (147; 223). Alda tells him that his "ideal" is but the "presentiment of the infinite," and she, like all free souls, is filled with a similar instinct to search for it, explaining, "God puts it into them [the free souls] so that they will seek Him" (149, 151, modified; 223). Rafael remains adamant that she stay. After berating Rafael for his fickle desire, Alda promises him he will not be alone. She will come to him on a breeze, in the smile of a grateful patient, in the poetry that moves him. She will no longer be called Alda, but Lumen, as she will light his way until he dies. When that time comes, she promises, "we will be united forever in the infinite, and together we will continue upward on the ladder of perfection, that perfection which is our destiny" (157, modified; 225). He lets her go. After sharing a poem from Rafael's diary from 1892, which indicates that Alda is keeping her promise to visit him, the narrator closes with a final exhortation to the reader:

> This was the story of *The Soul-Giver*, which I have had the pleasure and the sadness of telling you. Treasure it within your heart, and plead with heaven that when your ideal comes to you, you might caress it with a humble spirit and in deep contemplation, so that

it will not distance itself and you might love it when it departs. (169, modified)

Este es el cuento del *Donador de Almas*, que he tenido el placer y la melancolía de contaros. Guardadlo en vuestro corazón, y plegue al cielo que cuando la Quimera llegue hasta vosotros, la acariciéis con humilde espíritu y en alta contemplación, a fin de que no se aleje y hayáis de amarla cuanto parta. (226)

The role of science in *Soul-Giver* is central but deemphasized. None of Rafael's medical feats are described or enumerated. Though there are ample opportunities for such scenes, we do not witness any of Esteves's soul-binding or unbinding or any manipulating of magnetic fluid except at the very end of the nouvelle. There is no *Querens*-like interest in Sister Teresa's physical body—either in bringing her intellect to full functionality or even in engaging in a romantic relationship with her when she is in a conscious state. Nervo goes beyond the limits of both the canonical sciences and therapeutic Mesmerism in this narrative, moving further out into the spheres of spiritualist Mesmerism, Spiritism, and Theosophy. Binding, gifting, and embodying souls (as carried out by Esteves) are all practices rooted in Magnetism to some degree. Esteves uses his will to dominate/magnetize/hypnotize his somnambulists—or, as he puts it, to bind souls—and demonstrates his familiarity with the handling of magnetic fluid in the final unbinding of Alda from Rafael. Esteves's practice of sending souls on interplanetary journeys to bring back descriptions of life on other worlds, including evidence of evolutionary states beyond our own, is a clear nod to Flammarion and Flammarionian Spiritism, a reference made overt by Alda's assumption of the name Lumen as she sets out on her solo journey.

Nervo also amplifies the practices and claims of the occult sciences. Esteves is represented as having a singularly powerful will, even for a magnetizer, with his project to make a puppet of anyone, his cadre of a dozen-odd souls bound to his service, and his research at the known limits of scientific and religious knowledge, from outer space to sacred words of power. His gifting of Alda's spirit, which contributes to the creation of a godlike double-souled Rafael, as well as his unwedding of the two souls inhabiting the doctor's brain, are further evidence of the extent of Esteves's abilities. It is notable, however, that some limits remain inviolable. In the use of the bound spirit for medical diagnosis, the abilities conveyed to Rafael do not include mastery over life and death. The doctor is able to work apparently miraculous cures, but he cannot change a person's fated lifespan or bring a patient back from the dead. The text's ultimate argument is that science is not enough. Rafael, the materialist man of science, lacks not only affection but faith, a fulfilling ideal, and an understanding of the soul. Through the expansion of his belief system into less orthodox realms, he is granted or promised all of these things.

Despite its behind-the-scenes role, science—particularly at its borders with the occult—is the conduit by which characters and readers access the metaphysical structure of the underlying worldview represented in *Soul-Giver*. Theodore Jensen makes a convincing argument that this worldview is essentially Pythagorean in nature. Jensen explains the basic tenets of Pythagoreanism thusly:

> Pythagoreans believed that each mortal body possessed an immortal soul, a part of the divine cosmos. The soul, for a reason not clearly explained, was deprived of its divine omniscience when imprisoned in a body at birth. It was then obliged to undergo a series of transmigrations (Metempsychosis) through which it could eventually regain purity, omniscience and reunion with the divine monad . . . . Pythagoras taught that men could, by their actions, aid in purifying their souls. (400n24)

In the Pythagorean philosophy, the universe consists of "contesting opposite forces, unified by a divine cosmic harmony"; some of the pairs listed in the table of ten opposites are finite-infinite, right-left, male-female, light-darkness (Jensen 400–401n29).The eventual union of these opposites was only supposed to be, as Jensen puts it, "achieved in the aethereal plane" once original purity was regained through the reincarnation cycle (397). *Soul-Giver* contains a number of instances of Pythagorean opposites, principal among them the male-female duality of Rafael-Alda, with their corresponding right brain–left brain abodes (Jensen 396).[30] "Neither Rafael nor Alda had earned such a union," Jensen points out, elaborating, "Their situation became intolerable because it was unnatural. It was achieved by a manipulation of forces men do not understand. By its existence their joining upset the Pythagorean balance of the cosmos, and accordingly could not and did not endure"

(397). Humans are not supposed to be like gods. This is why Esteves cannot remember the sacred word described as the "key to all divine and human sciences"; he is thus allowed, Jensen argues, to separate the "unnatural state" that is Alda-Rafael, but he is not permitted to bring about another by transmigrating Alda's soul yet again into doña Corpus's body (398).[31]

If in *Soul-Giver* the balance of the universe is upset and reestablished, then the "divorce" of Rafael and Alda constitutes a restoration of the original limits of science, in the broadest sense, as well as a restoration of human capacities. In this cautionary tale of what happens when people attain their ideal too soon, or presume to move toward reunion with the divinity too rapidly, Nervo leaves Rafael and the reader with the consolation of hope of an ultimate reward and with counsel for gaining it. The promise of a reunion between Rafael and Alda is the promise of humanity's gradual perfection. If we cultivate in ourselves the "humble spirit" and "deep contemplation" of the narrator's parting advice, a time will come when we too are ready to hear the "divine harmony" of the "great symphony of worlds."

Toward the end of his life, Nervo wrote a less overtly heterodox variation on the *Soul-Giver* theme. In "Sixth Sense," the narrator volunteers for an experimental surgical procedure that will give him the ability to see the future, a gift that will, according to the surgeon, make the receiver "almost a god" (362). As in *Soul-Giver*, the text downplays the scientific aspects of the procedure, and the gift conveys only limited powers (in this case, the protagonist cannot *change* the future). And again, after a honeymoon period, the gift proves not to satisfy the protagonist's desires. The man initially spends most of his time contemplating his future beloved (here there are some slightly fantastic moments, during which his love seems to break through the barriers of time and to communicate something to the young girl). Soon, however, the benefits of his power are outweighed by the horrors of knowing future evils but being unable to avoid them, of knowing future happy events but being unable either to hasten their arrival or to enjoy the pleasures of anticipation, curiosity, or mystery. Eventually, the narrator refers to "my intolerable new sense," and reveals that his vision of the future is "voluntary"—just as people with five senses can choose not to remember events of the past, he can choose not to see those of the future (370). We do not learn of the protagonist's fate, but the story suggests that he will stop using his gift, restoring the limits he has temporarily transgressed. And yet, the use of his power has not been entirely for naught. It has enabled him to communicate that the future will ultimately be a just one, to offer advice on what should be valued in the present (reform and invention versus pride and materialism), and to assure readers, again, of the inevitable perfection of humanity he has seen: "Once the primordial necessities of the species were resolved, it became more angel-like each day" (369). Once the narrator actually meets his beloved, he refuses to tell what happens next, closing with "This story should not have an ending, believe me . . ." (371, ellipsis in the original).

THE DOUBLE FROM SCIENCE TO TECHNOLOGY

The figure of the artificially generated human double permeates the science fiction genre from proto-science-fictional times to the present. The methods of creation or re-creation, and the forms that the double takes, reflect the technology of the day. They also serve as a gauge of society's reactions to that technology, and as a vehicle for further exploration of the age-old question of what makes us human. The current fascination with the clone, for example, has been incarnated in years past in the cyborg, the android, and the robot. Because the term "robot" was not coined until 1920 (by Karel Čapek in R.U.R.: *Rossum's Universal Robots*), we must look even further back—to figures such as the automaton, the golem, and the homunculus, and to works such as Hoffmann's "The Sandman" [Der Sandmann] (1816) and Shelley's *Frankenstein* (1818)—to locate the literary influences on the texts discussed in this chapter: Holmberg's "Horacio Kalibang or The Automatons" [Horacio Kalibang o Los autómatas] (1879), Alejandro Cuevas's "The Apparatus of Doctor Tolimán" [El aparato del Doctor Tolimán] (c.1911), and Horacio Quiroga's *The Artificial Man* [*El hombre artificial*] (1910), "The Portrait" [El retrato] (1910), and "The Vampire" [El vampiro] (1927).[1] Cultural and technological influences, particularly from the United States, also are important issues in these works. Practical North American engineering and inventions, also seen in *Doctor Benignus*, make multiple appearances, and the exports of Hollywood's popular culture industry begin to gain a foothold in the Latin American imagination. In these texts on the double, we will see the modernization and the Latin Americanization of earlier Northern works as well as the transition of Latin American science fiction from a more elite, science-centered genre to one with a broader, more popular audience garnered through the increasing presence of technology in daily life.

Whereas any doubles appearing in the more fantastical texts discussed in chapter 3 are evoked through the powers of strange forces, the doubles here are produced by less overtly mysterious means. In these works of relatively hard science fiction, there are mechanically and biologically constructed doubles, revivified doubles, and two- and three-dimensional doubles reproduced or incarnated via emerging technologies. All of the scientists and inventors in these texts are men. When their creations are male, the predominant issues are generational: the creator's own father, the creator's self-image, or his descendance ("Horacio Kalibang," "Doctor Tolimán," *The Artificial Man*). Females are created less often; in these cases, frustrated love and subsequently stunted biological reproduction are sometimes at issue ("Horacio Kalibang"), or the story is concerned with the degree of a past or present emotional attachment ("The Portrait," "The Vampire").

All of these texts consider two other topics common to this subgenre: the definition of humanity and the line of separation between life and death. When the power to erase the line of demarcation between life and death is posited as achievable in a text, overtones of technophobia often ensue (though they tend to dissipate under close scrutiny), as do religious questions regarding the morality of usurping the position of God as Creator. The question of what it means to be human was also a central topic in the evolutionary tales of chapter 2, and the Latin American tendency toward Lamarckian interpretations of the laws of heredity revealed in those texts continues to appear in texts of the double. Rather than looking back along the *Scala Naturae* for missing links and racially based vestiges of past barbarity, however, these texts look toward the future, seeking to construct and reconstruct life forms that will imitate and improve upon humanity as we know it. An analysis of this corpus of texts reveals something of an inventor's "to-do list." First, make the created being look human, then make it move/function like a human. Next, in an ever-important mark of humanity, the creation must be able to speak like a human. Beyond this, it must have the capacity to reason like a human and, finally, it must possess that special ingredient, variously defined as a soul, emotion, or the experience of humanity as a species.

As a subgenre, the creation of the double is also useful for illustrating how science fiction went from being a fairly elite genre in Latin America to one more associated with popular/mass culture.[2] The process in Latin America differed from that either in the United States, where a pulp tradition in science fiction developed earlier, or in Great Britain, where the persistence of the scientific romance affected the timing of the arrival of the pulp era.[3] The framework that Beatriz Sarlo lays out for Argentina and the River Plate region in *The Technical Imagination* [*La imaginación técnica*] provides a valuable tool for explaining this sea change in Latin American science fiction. Sarlo describes the process by which the hegemony of the "knowledge" of science in Argentine literature and culture makes room for the "know-how" of technology and engineering (8).[4] The writings of a Holmberg or a Lugones are informed by a science based in universities, libraries, and laboratories; they are associated with a discourse of ultimate but remote authority (27–29). Sarlo locates the beginning of what she calls "a new accent" in the work of Horacio Quiroga (4). Quiroga, she says, differs from writers of earlier generations in the relationship he establishes with his readers and in his relationship with science. While his mentor, Lugones, located himself in a position of authority with respect to readers ("Lugones thought himself superior to his own," says Sarlo), Quiroga put himself on equal footing with them (2). For Quiroga, science did not reside in an ivory tower but functioned, in the form of technology, as a part of the fabric of life and of narrative:

> The masterly, oracular style that Lugones used in *Las fuerzas extrañas* [*Strange Forces*] did not allow the "science" in his stories to be anything but the most superficial kind of plot element; Lugones's poetics, like his life, remained unaffected . . . . Quiroga distinguished himself from Lugones by incorporating technology into his life, both aesthetically and pragmatically. (2)

With Quiroga we begin to have a generation of writers and readers from more diverse walks of life, for whom technology was an integral part of their daily existence. The transition from science to technology in Latin America, and elite to popular in early Latin American science fiction, is particularly clear in these science-and-technology-heavy tales of the double. These stories provide examples of modernization or "technologization" of earlier works, employing emerging and extrapolated advances in knowledge and know-how in their quest to imagine—and to question—the future of technology and of humanity.

THE SENTIMENTAL MATERIALIST AND THE MAD MECHANICAL GENIUS: HOLMBERG'S "HORACIO KALIBANG"

The first Latin American writer to center a narrative on the construction of a human double was none other than Eduardo Ladislao Holmberg, in the short story "Horacio Kalibang or The Automatons." According to Antonio Pagés Larraya, the tale was an immediate success and the original sixteen-page booklet rapidly sold out (76–78). It has remained one of Holmberg's most frequently reprinted works. Although sales of "Horacio Kalibang" were good for the time and place, and although Holmberg wrote in multiple genres considered "popular" today, Sarlo is correct in associating both author and work with remote, elite science rather than with readily accessible popular technology. Besides the fact that Holmberg was a scientist, access to his works was still restricted to a fairly small percentage of the population, based on who could read them and who could buy them. In 1879 literacy rates in Argentina had not yet experienced the increases seen after 1884, when for the first time Law 1420 guaranteed a free education to children six to fourteen in Buenos Aires, or after 1905, when this guarantee was extended to the entire country. Likewise the Argentine middle class had yet to grow to the respectable proportions achieved around the turn of the century, which further limited Holmberg's readership to those with the disposable income to purchase books, booklets, and magazine subscriptions.

At first glance "Horacio Kalibang" seems to be a something of a departure from Holmberg's longer, looser works of science fiction, *Nic-Nac* and *Two Factions*. Rather than scientific debates in Buenos Aires or journeys to occasionally utopian Martian countries, here we have the case of an inventor of automatons in Germany. Despite the difference in setting and subgenre, there are clear narrative and philosophical continuities with the earlier works. If there is no marvelous journey to Mars in "Horacio Kalibang," there is a strong element of estrangement in the work's Germanic setting.[5] If we are not presented with a utopian society in which science is valued equally with religion, we are given a glimpse of the dystopia that would result were technological, materialist tendencies taken to extremes. If there is no open debate between the Darwinists and the creationists, there is an opposition presented between those who profess themselves materialists and those of more faith-based personal philosophies. Holmberg continues to explore the question of what makes us human, though this time no clear answer—or missing link—emerges. If the influences of Verne and Flammarion are less apparent in this text, there are strong echoes of other works of early science fiction such as Shelley's *Frankenstein* and Hoffmann's "The Sandman."

"Horacio Kalibang" is prefaced by a dedication to Dr. José María Ramos Mejía. Holmberg and Ramos Mejía had known one another since adolescence and were classmates in medical school. Holmberg dedicates the tale to his friend as an homage to Ramos Mejía's recently published book, *Cerebral Traumatism* [*Traumatismo cerebral*] (1879). Holmberg calls the book the "delight of materialists" and accuses its detractors of desecrating "your pages of light" ("Horacio Kalibang" 147). When Holmberg acknowledges that "Those of us who write works of this genre cannot keep from giving some of the characters at least a trace of our own character" (147), he also introduces the first of the doubles in the story. There is a great deal of our author in the tale's sentimental materialist, Burgomaster Hipknock. At the same time, there is also something Holmbergian about Hipknock's nemesis, Oscar Baum, the mad mechanical genius. While Holmberg was an avowed supporter of what he terms the "marvelous school" [escuela formidable] of materialism (147), he does not hesitate to reveal the weaknesses of a strict adherence to materialistic tenets, with his usual sense of humor and irony.

The text begins with a dinner party at Hipknock's home on the occasion of his daughter Luisa's fifteenth birthday. The good burgomaster and his nephew, Lieutenant Hermann Blagerdorff, are discussing the talk of the town, one Horacio Kalibang, described as "the man who has lost his center of gravity" (151).[6] Young Hermann is convinced that the existence of such a man is cause for belief in the supernatural ("I have come to understand that there are strange phenomena which human science does not explain, and which perhaps it will never be able to explain"; 148). His uncle denies the possibility of any such superstitious interpretation: "Do you presume to suspect that you are talking with a religious fanatic who is going to accept your biases that are based on convictions or on faith?" (148). He expresses an unwavering materialistic certainty based on "the truths revealed to man by his unceasing work and application to the study of nature" (148). Several puns are made by the company on the word "gravity," so as to remind the reader of the spirit of levity that underlies this "debatable toy" [juguete discutible], as Holmberg describes the story to Ramos Mejía (147). At this point our narrator introduces himself to the reader as Fritz, another of Hipknock's relatives. He announces that he has arrived just in time to witness the above conversation as well as the subsequent arrival of Horacio Kalibang himself.

Kalibang is described in detail. He is 1.443 meters in height, his expressionless face looks like it has come out of a "mold from a mask factory," and his lips make the same unvarying movement no matter what words come out of his mouth (151). He has come, it seems, for no purpose other than to demonstrate his existence. Leaning at a humanly impossible angle, he declares to all present, "Now you see that I am not a myth," then takes his leave (152). Burgomaster Hipknock's materialist logic will not allow him to rest until he finds a rational explanation for Kalibang's feat, so he sets off in pursuit. Fritz follows Hipknock at a suitably narratorial distance. Kalibang is eventually joined by Oscar Baum. Baum takes a small object from his pocket and uses it to wind up his oddly leaning companion, who repeats the same words he has uttered moments before at the dinner party. Hipknock recognizes what he is seeing and says—with the satisfaction of one whose faith in physics has been confirmed—"Horacio Kalibang, now I know that you are no more than an automaton!" (157).[7]

The burgomaster, after the fashion of the true materialist, believes in neither God nor the devil (he and his descendants have been excommunicated unto the fifth generation), and does not have favorable feelings "either toward spiritualists or toward clerics" (159). Still, he is something of a sentimental scientist:

> He is a materialist for inescapable reasons, but he does not believe that an atheist people exists, nor that it should or can exist. "Scientific societies," he says, "have reason on their side; the people have only sentiment on theirs; for sentiment, there is God; for sentiment, there is an immortal soul. (155)
>
> Es materialista por la fatalidad de las razones, pero no cree que exista pueblo alguno ateo, ni que deba o pueda existir. Las sociedades científicas—dice—tienen derecho de ser la razón; el pueblo

no tiene más derecho que el sentimiento; para el sentimiento hay Dios; para el sentimiento, hay un alma inmortal.

Hipknock's attitude toward Christianity (and religion in general) is not that of either the traditional believer or the nonbeliever. Like Nic-Nac (and, likely, Holmberg), he might say he interprets such matters "in my own way" (*Nic-Nac* 97).

Baum invites Hipknock to view his automatons. In his letter of invitation, Baum states that nationalism and a competitive spirit have been motivating factors in his work, declaring that "the latest discoveries of Edison have wounded my national pride" and that these discoveries have also inspired him to design "an independently functioning brain" [un cerebro con funciones propias] (158).[8] The burgomaster expresses no surprise at the news of Baum's daring aspirations. During the visit Baum intimates that he can not only build a brain but also a soul, asking "What is the brain but a great machine, whose exquisite springs move by virtue of impulses transformed thousands and thousands of times? What is the soul but the combination of those mechanical functions?" [¿Qué es el cerebro, sino una gran máquina, cuyos exquisitos resortes se mueven en virtud de impulsos mil y mil veces transformados? ¿Qué es el alma, sino el conjunto de esas funciones mecánicas?] (161). The burgomaster is unfazed, "I am a materialist, and your words are neither frightening nor news to me" (161).

However, Hipknock does value the ability to differentiate between an automaton, or constructed being, and a human, a being "created" in the Judeo-Christian tradition. At Baum's factory, the automatons put on a series of *tableaux mécaniques* for the delectation of Hipknock and the narrator. The *pièce de résistance* is a representation of the previous night's dinner party, with each guest portrayed by a perfect copy. During the visit, Fritz immediately discerns that, in addition to the admittedly mechanical performers, the doorman and two different Oscar Baums also are automatons. The burgomaster, on the other hand, is unable to tell that his hosts are not human beings until the first Oscar Baum's leg falls off (due to technical difficulties) and the second removes his own arm. Fritz attributes this lack of discrimination to the fact that Hipknock is "somewhat shortsighted" (160).

The burgomaster's initial confusion between humans and mechanical doubles only grows worse once the first automatons are revealed:

"If these are automatons, it must be confessed that they do not differ very much from us," said Hipknock.

"If the burgomaster will permit me," observed Baum, "I would invert the proposition." (162)

Two pages later, Hipknock's befuddlement is complete. The burgomaster declares: "Whether it is they who are the automatons or whether it is we who are, I do not know" (164). Another automaton then emerges, offering a more oblique version of the standard Holmbergian warning against mob violence: "I am not only the greatest of the automatons, I am all of humanity, and when humanity speaks with force, reason is the most insignificant of children's toys" (164). The automaton answers some of Hipknock's questions, revealing that Baum has been manufacturing automatons for quite some time, that they have infiltrated human society throughout the world, and that this infiltration, combined with Baum's newest technology, represents a threat to humanity. "When what you call their winding-up and what our leader calls their ability has run out, they will return to receive new power, and then, Burgomaster, then . . . good night" [Cuando se les acabe lo que ustedes llaman la cuerda, y que nuestro conductor llama su habilidad, volverán a recibir nuevas fuerzas y entonces, señor burgomaestre, entonces . . . buenas noches] (164, ellipsis in the original). By the time Hipknock and Fritz leave, confusion is turning to paranoia: "'Could Fritz be an automaton?' the burgomaster asks himself. 'Could the burgomaster be an automaton?' I ask myself" (165).

In the final scene, the wedding banquet of Luisa Hipknock and Herman Blagerdorff, the burgomaster seems to have gone over the edge. He asks the guests if any of them are automatons: "They all looked at each other: some because they did not know what an automaton was; others because they knew all too well" (165). Our narrator's description of the guests' responses gives Hipknock's paranoia a solid foundation, implying that the automatons have infiltrated even to the level of one's own family and friends. Fritz himself is noticeably absent from the banquet, but his means of learning what is happening there are soon revealed—in a letter that Kalibang delivers during dessert. In the letter, Fritz states that he himself is Oscar Baum, the inventor. On two earlier occasions—at Luisa's birthday party and on the visit to view the automatons with Hipknock—Fritz has been represented by an automaton of himself (his sources for what happens in his/its absence must, then, be his other creations among the company). Fritz reveals that he too is in love with Luisa but, thwarted in his intentions by Hermann, has made an automaton of her "that will love me perpetually" instead (165). As a wedding gift, the letter continues, Fritz is sending Kalibang to tutor Luisa and Hermann's future children.

Fritz warns the couple that Kalibang, an early model automaton that looks noticeably machinelike, is the only being they should trust. The later models not only look and move like humans, they possess that most human of characteristics, language. His most advanced models, with their independently functioning brains, will have the ability to reason and to produce original conversation, and may even be endowed with mechanical souls. Holmberg underscores the question of what makes us human by having Fritz add intentionally unhelpful tips to his letter on how to tell his constructed beings from created beings. Mechanical doubles, Fritz implies, give themselves away by their own illogicalities: politicians who lack reason and honor, scientists who base their arguments on the mysteries of faith, doctors who kill, lawyers who lie, patriots who deceive. Fritz's true intentions become clear, however, in his conclusion: "I have the world in my hands, because I control it with my automatons . . . . I have filled the world with the products of my manufacture" (166).

The burgomaster's materialist side seems strangely reassured—even encouraged—by Fritz's letter. He tells his daughter that she will have children if she obeys her "organic automatonism" [automatismo orgánico] (166). But even the shortsighted Hipknock senses at least a blurry outline of what Fritz's inventions mean for the future of humanity. The burgomaster closes with the advice he will pass on to his first grandchild: "My son, before distributing the aromas that gush forth from your heart, examine with care whether the cup that receives them is not an automaton" (167). But our narrator—also an automaton?—has the last word: "The reader will pull the remaining strings" [El lector tocará los demás resortes] (167).

"Horacio Kalibang" and *Frankenstein*

There is a tendency to forget that artificially constructed human doubles did not spring fully formed out of the computer age or the years immediately preceding, as can be seen in Angela Dellepiane's affirmation: "[Holmberg] was many years ahead of Karel Čapek, the inventor of *robots*, creating them in his 'Horacio Kalibang and [*sic*] The Automatons'" ("Narrativa argentina de ciencia ficción" 516). While the automaton was an important precursor of the robot, to retrolabel Holmberg's automatons as early examples of robots is to tell only half the story. Perhaps more impressive than Holmberg's anticipation of things to come is how, in doing so, he reshaped what had come before him.

Probably the most famous tale of the construction of a human being written after the book of Genesis is Mary Shelley's *Frankenstein; or, The Modern Prometheus*, often cited as the first work of science fiction. While there is no specific evidence that "Horacio Kalibang" was influenced by *Frankenstein*, both texts deal with the effects of unprecedented scientific progress on society and tell of brilliant scientists who construct humanlike beings that pose a threat to humanity. A brief comparison sheds light on their very different approaches to this subject matter and on the effects created by the almost diametrically opposite endings. Both the nameless Frankenstein creature and the automatons are brought to life by scientific means, and both function at least somewhat independently of their creators. But while both induce fear in the human members of society, only Frankenstein's creation inspires sympathy as well. In *Frankenstein*, creator and creation are eliminated at the end of the story, leaving the world to rest easy, while in "Horacio Kalibang," characters and readers are left with sleepless nights.

Victor Frankenstein constructs his creature out of bits and pieces of human and animal remains obtained from charnel houses, dissecting rooms, and slaughterhouses. Frankenstein then "infuse[s] a spark of being" into the creature through a scientific technique not revealed in its entirety but which is clearly meant to indicate that he has penetrated the mysteries of electricity further than any scientist to date (Shelley 52). Once the creature is imbued with life, he possesses a will, and indeed a soul, of his own. By the next page Frankenstein is referring to his creation as a "miserable monster," and he abandons it (53). Frankenstein's "monster" eventually becomes a sympathetic figure, however, when he describes how the hatred and scorn of others have caused him to act like the fiend that he resembles physically.

In contrast, Fritz constructs Kalibang and the other automatons out of mechanical parts. His creations have no spark of being, neither the crude wind-up models nor the later versions with the soon-to-be-completed, independently functioning brain. Rather than possessing free will, the automatons have so far been programmed—or the nineteenth-century equivalent thereof—according to the will of their manufacturer. When the models with autonomous brain function are completed, it is implied that Fritz's plans will be included in their design (at least at first), though these plans may merely consist of a chaos-inducing element of illogic. Fritz's automatons inspire no sympathy either in Holmberg's human characters or in the reader. They are represented as the cogs of a spurned inventor's plot for replacing friends, family, a narrator, oneself. Like Hipknock and his circle, the reader begins to wonder where (and if) their infiltration ends.

Frankenstein and Fritz both suffer from something of a God complex. Each tale moves beyond the initial creation to address the possibility that a creation may one day gain independence from its creator. Frankenstein's project stems from a desire to create, to give life, or to reverse death, not unnatural preoccupations for a scientist whose mother has recently died. His error lies in letting this desire to do something good grow beyond his control. He later repents for being one who "aspires to become greater than his nature will allow," admitting that "life and death appeared to me ideal bounds, which I should first break through, and pour a torrent of light into our dark world. A new species would bless me as its creator and source . . . . No father could claim the gratitude of his child so completely as I should deserve their's [sic]" (48, 49). When his creation turns out to be not a child but the monstrous double of his own presumption and neglect, Frankenstein's conscience will not allow him to grant the request for a female partner—an Eve for his Adam—even to save his near and dear from the creature's wrath. The threat to all of humanity was too great, Frankenstein realizes with horror: "One of the first results of those sympathies for which the dæmon thirsted would be children, and a race of devils would be propagated upon the earth, who might make the very existence of the species of man a condition precarious and full of terror. Had I a right, for my own benefit, to inflict this curse upon everlasting generations?" (163). In the end, an epic chase leads to the destruction of both Frankenstein and his creation. The reader is left with Shelley's warning to the presumptuous—Frankenstein has been destroyed not by his scientific creation but as a result of his own ambition. The threat to society has been eliminated, however, and the world has returned to normal.

Fritz also suffers from delusions of deity ("I have the world in my hands"), but shows no sign of possessing Frankenstein's conscience, proceeding to create his own Eve (an automaton Luisa) as well as a mechanical version of Frankenstein's feared "race of devils" ("I have filled the world with the products of my manufacture"; 166). At the story's close, Holmberg does not present us with a dying figure who recognizes the error of his ways; rather we have a scientist at the height of his powers whose imitations grow more and more indistinguishable from their models. Fritz's automatons, while a threat to society, are not self-reproducing and do not, at this point, involve multiple, independent wills that are out of his control. He is the master puppeteer—the "leader/conductor" [conductor] (164)—and his minions work in concert to carry out his diabolical plans. The risk that Fritz's ever-improving human doubles might one day escape his control is, however, implied. The reader, "pulling the remaining strings," may wonder if the automatons have their own agenda, or whether they might develop the ability to procreate (proconstruct?).

For the moment, however, Fritz's declared intention is to control the world through his superstitious scientists, lying lawyers, and so on. He seems to delight in perversity (in Poe's sense of "The Imp of the Perverse"), sowing doubt and mistrust, forcing humans to wonder if those around them have been replaced by his machines. Since there are human lawyers who have been known to stray from the truth and human scientists who rely on faith rather than evidence, the key that Fritz gives us to differentiate the born from the built contains an inherent flaw. The threats that exist at the close of "Horacio Kalibang" arise as much from the inhumanity of humans as from the rapid technological progress that enables megalomaniacal individuals to gain power over others through science. While one side effect of the narrative is a certain sense of technophobia, this is neither the primary impact of the story nor a dominant theme in Holmberg's work. Holmberg is a sentimental materialist who pokes gentle fun at the illogical, "immaterial" nature of his own spiritual beliefs, and a writer who, with his own absence of "gravity," uses humor to invite his readers to consider just what it is that makes them human.

"Horacio Kalibang" and "The Sandman"

According to Pagés Larraya, the author who had the greatest influence on Holmberg's work was E. T. A. Hoffmann, particularly upon texts such as "The Haunted House" [La casa endiablada], "Hoffmann's Pipe" [La pipa de Hoffmann], and "Horacio Kalibang" (43-45). Hoffmann's story "The Sandman" is usually classified as a fantastic or gothic tale, but it is also recognized as an important precursor to robot and android sf stories (Clute and Nichols, "Hoffmann" 576–77). Although Holmberg models his automaton army after Hoffmann's construction, Olimpia, his more perfect doubles represent a far greater threat to society.

"The Sandman" is the story of a young man called Nathanael, whose childhood fears that "a mysterious destiny has hung a dark veil of clouds about my life," are revived with the apparent reappearance of Coppelius, a former business associate of his father's, who has somehow been involved in his father's untimely and violent death (42). Nathanael feels that Coppelius has returned to ruin his life. When his sweetheart, Clara, responds to his premonitions by telling him that they are all in his head, Nathanael calls her a "damned lifeless automaton" (55). He spurns the love of this "intelligent, childlike, large-hearted girl" for the perceived affections of a professor's daughter, Olimpia, whose rhythmical dance steps put his own to shame, and whose cold lips say "Ah! Ah! Ah!" in agreement with his every impassioned declaration (51, 62). To Nathanael's friends, Olimpia seems "singularly statuesque and soulless," her movements "strangely measured . . . as if they were dependent upon some wound-up clockwork" (64). His friends sense that something is not quite right with the object of Nathanael's affection, and tell him frankly, "We felt quite afraid of this Olimpia, and did not like to have anything to do with her; she seemed to us to be only acting like a *living* creature, and as if there was some secret at the bottom of it all" (64).

In Kalibang's case, his apparent ability to defy gravity causes people to believe in the existence of strange phenomena beyond the ken of modern science. Hoffmann's wooden doll and Holmberg's automatons are purely mechanical beings, with no actual human flesh or life-giving spark involved (with the possible exception of Olimpia's eyes, a discussion for another day). Fritz's creations are more high-tech than Olimpia, with physical appearances that can deceive even those who know and love the original human models, and the ability to speak, ranging from the preset lines of the crudest models to the completely original utterances that the soon-to-be produced, independently functioning brains will be able to invent. Nathanael, like Hipknock, only recognizes an automaton for what it is when he sees it disassembled before his eyes; he is blinded by love. His friends and family, however, learn from Nathanael's mistakes and gain at least a chance of discovering whether or not their lovers are human by performing tests for detecting mechanical behavior:

> The history of this automaton had sunk deeply into their souls, and an absurd mistrust of human figures began to prevail. Several lovers, in order to be fully convinced that they were not paying court to a wooden puppet, required that their mistress should sing and dance a little out of time, should embroider or knit or play with her little pug, &c., when being read to, but above all things else that she should do something more than merely listen—that she should frequently speak in such a way as to really show that her words presupposed as a condition some thinking and feeling. (69)

Although the burgomaster is not blind but merely suffers from short-sightedness, he has little chance of distinguishing Fritz's automatons from the humans they have replaced, endowed as they are with the ability to perfectly portray human imperfection.

Hoffman's story is set around 1816, and Nathanael's professor describes Olimpia as "my best automaton—at which I've worked for twenty years—my life work" (67). Over his entire career, therefore, he has managed to produce only one functioning mechanism—and it fools only one man of delicate mental balance. Although this single deception plants seeds of doubt in the town, the "automaton test" will likely serve to improve rather than destroy human relationships. By the latter part of the same century, however, Holmberg is speculating about a fairly young scientist who controls mass-produced automatons that have already infiltrated society, taking the places of humans in influential professions, and insinuating themselves among the protagonist's friends and family. Forewarned by revelations earlier in the story, the reader is still surprised to learn that the narrator himself has been replaced at some (or all?) points by a double. If the reader can be fooled, then these more humanlike, more numerous automatons—this more advanced science—pose a real threat to society. The absence of a reliable test for humanness seems destined to lead to chaos and uncertainty. Or to a new automaton order and another end of the world as we know it.

"Horacio Kalibang" goes beyond the secret life forces and handcrafted wooden dolls (and the apes and the Akkas) of the doubles of its predecessors, giving us gears and springs assembled on a wide scale into facsimiles of ourselves. Here science threatens to change not only a people's way of life, but the very ways in which those people perceive and define themselves. In "Horacio Kalibang," Holmberg satirizes the extremity of two opposing worldviews. He is dismissive of those like Hermann who do not question their faith but content themselves with the answer that there is no logical explanation. But he also issues a warning to extreme or literal materialists who, like Hipknock, believe that humans are utterly explainable, like a machine that acts in accordance with "the destiny of its permutations" [la fatalidad de sus permutaciones] (161). Be careful what you wish for, Holmberg seems to say, because you may not like what you get.

BLOOD WILL TELL: ALEJANDRO CUEVAS'S "THE APPARATUS OF DOCTOR TOLIMÁN"

Alejandro Cuevas (1870–1940) was a practicing lawyer who argued cases at a variety of levels, including the Mexican Supreme Court. He was a well-known composer and playwright, and published one collection of short stories, *Macabre Tales* [*Cuentos macabros*] (1911). Some of the stories had previously been published in the *Illustrated Sunday Supplement* [*Suplemento ilustrado*] of the Mexico City newspaper *El Diario* in 1908 (Larson 129). It is unknown at this time whether "The Apparatus of Doctor Tolimán" appeared in *El Diario*, but it was almost certainly written prior to August 27, 1909, the date with which Juan de Dios Pesa signed his prologue to *Macabre Tales*. In the prologue Pesa cites the great influence of French literature on Cuevas (the best known from this extensive list of writers are Alexandre Dumas, fils, and Zola), and notes commonalities between Cuevas's work and Hoffmann's tales of gothic suspense, specifically the use of "characters from real life" (ii). Pesa compares Cuevas's combination of "the fantastic" [lo fantástico] and "facts" [realidades] to the work of other Mexican writers, among them two writers of early science fiction, Ignacio Altamirano (1834–93) and Pedro Castera (iii). Larson calls Cuevas "Mexico's master of terror" (12). The most science fictional of the *Macabre Tales* is "Doctor Tolimán." This is not a classic tale of a constructed human being, because the doubling in the story is more mental than physical. Still, "Doctor Tolimán" is best discussed in the context of this chapter. The work deals with the fine line between life and death, as well as issues of paternity and descent based on a Lamarckian interpretation of heredity.

In addition, the "apparatus" that Tolimán uses to revivify the dead does not belong purely to the realms of the scientific but incorporates elements of Sarlo's "everyday" technology.

As the story begins, our narrator is visiting a cousin's home in the Mexican capital. The city cousin, Luciano Bernaldez, is a well-known psychiatrist and director of one of the Federal District's principal asylums for the insane. The narrator has a particular interest in visiting the asylum, as he subscribes to a literary magazine that publishes a section of works by the mentally ill. The cousins are received at the asylum by Dr. Tolimán, "a man of around thirty-five, medium height, and a somewhat rickety constitution" with "a vague air of wariness/distrust" [una vaga expresión de desconfianza] (168). Dr. Tolimán gives the narrator a guided tour of the facilities, impressing the visitor with his "vivid imagination and cultivated intelligence" and his technical explanations of the patients' cases (168).

Once the two cousins are alone in the director's office, the narrator is astounded to learn that Dr. Tolimán is not a physician at the asylum but a patient. Beyond the evidence of Tolimán's intellect and urbane manners, the narrator had been convinced of the man's position by his "scientific appraisals and classification," a classic association of science with truth and reason (170). Bernaldez tells his cousin that Tolimán suffers from an incurable case of *speculofobia*; for the most part he appears completely sane, but he goes into an almost epileptic frenzy when he sees his own image in a mirror. The psychiatrist gives his cousin Tolimán's diary, saying it may contain an explanation of the man's strange malady. Our narrator closes his contribution to the text with an affirmation that he is providing a faithful copy of Tolimán's words, edited only to remove entries extraneous to the principal story. To the reader he allots the task of using reason to establish logical links among the diary entries and imagination to fill in "any gaps he may believe he has found" (172).

Tolimán's diary begins with a rather melodramatic declaration of teenage angst:

> I have reached the age of eighteen years . . . Today I begin this book that no one will ever see, impelled by the need to confide my sorrows and my impressions to someone, even if only to a sheet of paper . . . Joys I have none nor have I ever had any: a rickety and sickly boy . . . (172, all ellipses but the last in the original)

> He cumplido dieciocho años . . . Empiezo hoy este libro que jamás conocerá nadie, impulsado por la necesidad de confiar á alguien, siquiera sea á una hoja de papel, mis tristezas y mis impresiones . . . alegrías no tengo ni jamás las he conocido: niño raquítico y enfermizo . . .

He speaks in stirring tones of a childhood filled with poverty and abuse, both at home and at school. In primary school, he writes, "my delicate and sickly appearance, my somber character and my unpleasant physiognomy attracted the taunts, the torments, and the ill will of my schoolmates" (172). At home his godfather don Cástulo abuses him mentally and physically. Tolimán states his hatred for his godfather repeatedly and passionately. He likens don Cástulo's sallow, pockmarked face, his long irregular nose, and his scanty hair to that of Shakespeare's Shylock, and he carries the association with Shylock further, recounting a story he has heard at school that his once-wealthy guardian has not really lost his business to bankruptcy but hides his stolen wealth behind an appearance of penury. He also accuses his godfather of false religious piety and madness. Given this background, Tolimán asks, is it any wonder that his soul is filled with "skepticism and misanthropy" or that he is "pusillanimous and impressionable" of spirit (172–73, 176)? When don Cástulo decides that Tolimán must go to medical school, the boy is incapable of standing up for himself: "I have no strength to rebel, my will is of wax and my godfather's of steel" (176). When don Cástulo refuses to let Tolimán marry the girl that he loves, Tolimán again concedes, but his hatred grows.

Although Tolimán had not wanted to pursue medicine, his professors believe he has a talent for it. While still a medical student, he reads an article that impresses him greatly. A doctor has seemingly brought a deceased patient back to life, at least temporarily, by opening his chest and manually compressing his heart. (At this point, the text's sole footnote seeks to establish a factual basis for this story. Although it is unclear whether the footnote is attributed to the narrator or the author, it affirms that the experiment has been mentioned in a newspaper in the capital.) The article makes such an impression on Tolimán that he devotes an entire diary entry to questioning the significance of the experiment, writing, "Where does life end? . . . . . . Where does death begin? . . . . . . What is the precise instant when day expires and night begins?" (179–80, ellipses in the original).

Descriptions of his growing interest in the topic alternate with evidence of Tolimán's abilities as a doctor and as a scientific inventor.[9] He successfully performs a risky surgery that eminent physicians had refused to attempt. He uses spark-producing electrical circuits, watch works, magnets, and batteries to build the apparatus of the story's title. This device will produce the regular, mechanical compressions lacking in the experiment described in the article. He also discovers a formula that reverses blood clotting and breaks up calcium deposits. After carrying out trials on animals, he injects the formula in a gravely ill human patient, instantly curing him. Tolimán's first impulse to share his marvelous discovery with his medical colleagues rapidly gives way to caution. His decision to wait until he has more data before taking the formula public is a prudent one. However, an equally strong motivation for secrecy stems from the skeptical and misanthropic nature developed in his youth; he suspects his colleagues would conspire against him: "Won't they brand me a charlatan and then steal my invention?" (182). With his medical experience, his apparatus, and his formula, Tolimán possesses everything he needs to erase the line between life and death.

Unlike the scientist-inventors of Hoffmann, Shelley, and Holmberg, Cuevas's protagonist does not seek to construct new life but to reclaim once-living beings from death. When don Cástulo dies of a chronic liver condition, Tolimán has the chance to put his discoveries into practice. After caroling his freedom from his "tormentor" [verdugo], Tolimán realizes that this is a perfect opportunity: another doctor has signed the death certificate, the hour is late, and he is alone with the body (185). He hauls the cadaver to an operating table in the most isolated room in the house. The light from his petroleum lamp is insufficient, so he brings the funeral candles to illuminate the proceedings. The expression on his godfather's face is "serene, gentle, bathed in a tranquility and a sweetness of which I was never able to believe him capable" (186–87). After a few more ghoulish details (the removal of the handkerchief that prevented don Cástulo's jaw from dropping, the first flies laying their eggs on his dead face), Tolimán connects the body to his apparatus, injects his de-clotting liquid, and closes the electrical circuit. He expresses his hopes of producing a "marvelous phenomenon no mortal has ever witnessed," though at the same time he feels "a particular uneasiness" that he associates with stepping into the mysterious and supernatural territory of death (189).

Rather than bestowing the gift of life, however, the apparatus proves to be an instrument of torture. Don Cástulo cries out in horror, suffering worse pain than he has experienced while dying. His demand that Tolimán turn off the apparatus is met with sarcastic laughter and a look that Tolimán himself describes as "diabolical" (191). Cástulo begs for mercy, only to hear Tolimán's taunt, "the science you forced into my brain with blows delivers you today to my justice . . . . . . or to my revenge; it is all the same to me" (192). Tolimán's interest in scientific progress and his commitment to the healer's oath are outweighed by his hatred. The doctor thus reveals himself to be one of those characters who Josefina Ludmer has termed "the men of science 'in crime'" (73). With Frankensteinian disdain, he tells Cástulo that he is indifferent to the fact that his resurrection is "against your will and that of nature itself" (192). Displaying a God complex much like Shelley's Frankenstein and Holmberg's Fritz, he compares Cástulo to a "new Lazarus who rises at my voice," casting himself in the role of Jesus (192). Don Cástulo refutes this characterization, accusing his erstwhile charge of sacrilege, crying out, "You profane the kingdom of death . . . . . . which belongs to God!" (192). Cástulo then declares that it must be God who is punishing him for the sins he committed during his life, for which his efforts at atonement have not been enough. This reminds Tolimán of the rumors of hidden fortune, and he demands to know the location of Cástulo's riches. "Ask your mother about them . . . . . . that is, if you can find her," Cástulo replies (193).

Don Cástulo proceeds to reveal the truth of Tolimán's parentage and the reasons behind his own actions. Cástulo himself is Tolimán's father. Tolimán's mother deserted both her husband and Cástulo for a third lover and ran off with Cástulo's fortune, leaving him penniless and destroying his good name. His harsh treatment of Tolimán has been due partly to an inability to love the product of his own broken relationship, and partly because, as he tells his son, "you have, infiltrated in your blood, the poison of your criminal origin. . . . your rebellious nature had to be punished . . . . . . subdued . . . . . . in order to cleanse your sins and save you" [tienes infiltrado en la sangre el veneno de tu origen criminal . . . . tu naturaleza rebelde debía ser castigada . . . . . . dominada . . . . . . para limpiarte de culpa y salvarte] (194, long ellipses in the original). It is notable that the only maternal figure who appears in all of our tales of creation is mentioned solely in her capacity as the carrier of criminal blood. Cástulo prohibited Tolimán from marrying to prevent him from passing on this trait. This notion of criminal tendencies as acquired characteristics, passed on from generation to generation, reveals the same Lamarckian interpretation of the laws of heredity that underpinned Latin American eugenics movements.[10]

Tolimán's experiment ends with Cástulo cursing his son, using the same term that Tolimán had previously applied to Cástulo: "Patricide! . . . . . . Patricide! . . . . . . Curse you! . . . You are my son. The issue of my offense and you are my *tormentor* . . . . . . ! Curse you!" [¡Parricida! . . . . . . ¡Parricida! . . . . . . ¡Maldito seas! . . . Eres mi hijo. El hijo de mi delito y eres mi *verdugo* . . . . . . ! ¡Maldito seas!] (194, long ellipses in the original, emphasis mine).[11] Upon hearing his father's words, Tolimán faints, disconnecting the apparatus in the process. He awakens the next morning to find Cástulo dead once more, the rictus of the cadaver's open mouth seeming to curse him again. Tolimán hides the evidence of his medical malfeasance, weeping tears of repentance. But his father's curse weighs on him in the days after the funeral. He cannot eat or sleep. Finally, in the last entry of the diary, Tolimán notes a horrifying transformation in himself. The complete entry reads:

> What is happening to me? . . . . . . I'm not me! . . . . . . Am I him? . . . . . . It is impossible for my face to have changed so much in two weeks! . . . . . . It is his; it is my father's . . . . . . his expression . . . . . . his gesture . . . . . . everything! . . . . . . No! It is that his vengeful ghost places itself and will always place itself between me and the mirror! (196)

> ¿Qué es lo que pasa en mí? . . . . . . ¡No soy yo! . . . . . . ¿Soy él? . . . . . . Imposible es que en dos semanas mi rostro haya cambiado de tal manera! . . . . . . Es el suyo; es el de mi padre . . . . . . su mirada . . . . . . su gesto . . . . . . ¡todo! . . . . . . ¡No! ¡Es que su fantasma vengador se interpone y se interpondrá siempre, entre mí y el espejo!

Tolimán's "strange mania" is now explained: he cannot tolerate the reminder that he has become what he most hated (170). The reader is left to determine the causes and extent of doubling in "Doctor Tolimán." While it is possible that Tolimán now notices family resemblances to which he had previously been blind, we know that his appearance has not, in fact, changed to any significant degree. His physical description, as noted in his diary, is easily recognizable in the patient who the narrator meets at the asylum, and this appearance differs markedly from that of Cástulo. These descriptions agree with his own perception of reality, as his last diary entry reveals that he does not believe that he looks like don Cástulo to others, but only to himself. In conjunction with other elements of the gothic macabre in the story, Tolimán's claim that Cástulo's "vengeful ghost" causes his reflection to resemble that of his tormentor/father/victim might appear to push the reader toward a more fantastic interpretation of events, but this explanation is negated by the strong suggestion of psychological trauma in the text. In his diary, Tolimán seems to indicate that mental and emotional chemistry, rather than supernatural causes, are at the root of his speculophobia.

The reader must then determine the relative weights of nature and nurture in the case. Were Cástulo's actions toward Tolimán at all justifiable? Did Castulo's belief in Tolimán's "criminal blood" warrant, if not the abusive treatment of his son, then Castulo's decisions to prevent Tolimán's marriage and force him to follow a lucrative career that would allow the rebuilding of the family fortune? Or was it Cástulo's cruel treatment that corrupted Tolimán's character and ultimately destroyed his life? The first-person narration in the diary prevents an absolute apportionment of fault, either by a neo-Lamarckian or a contemporary reader. Impassioned descriptions of Cástulo's misdeeds are counterbalanced by hints that he may not actually be the ogre that Tolimán portrays. A comparison of "Doctor Tolimán" to texts of other scientist-inventors "in crime"—such as *Frankenstein* and those of our Latin American corpus—suggests that Tolimán bears a significant degree of responsibility for his own destruction, though this is due less to hubris than to the desire for revenge.

One feature unique to the story is that only Tolimán (along with the narrator and reader) knows of his double's existence. It has no physical presence, yet it rules his life and determines his future just as surely as the monster rules Frankenstein. In contrast to Frankenstein's creation, however, Tolimán's electrically regenerated being cannot be discussed in terms of the engendering of a new species. Like Frankenstein, Tolimán suffers from lost love and has no prospect of offspring, but— unlike the scientist-inventors of Shelley, Holmberg, and Quiroga—he is also incapable of generating life through science. While Cástulo was alive, Tolimán could not act independently of his father's will. After

Cástulo's death—and Tolimán's experiment on the cadaver—that influence continues in the particular form taken by Tolimán's madness. Tolimán is unable to literally or figuratively "conceive of" a being that might continue after him, because he cannot escape the destructive relationship with his own progenitor.

DONISSOFF (AND CO.); OR, THE MODERN FRANKENSTEIN: HORACIO QUIROGA'S *THE ARTIFICIAL MAN*

Horacio Quiroga (1878–1937) is frequently discussed in the context of Argentine literature, although he was born and raised across the River Plate, in Uruguay. His father was from Argentina, a descendant of the caudillo Juan Facundo Quiroga, and Quiroga himself lived there for many years. He resided both in cosmopolitan Buenos Aires and on the virgin frontier in the north. He produced some of the country's most celebrated regional literature, based on his years spent as something of a pioneer in Misiones province. Quiroga's compelling biography of personal tragedy is well known. He was a master of the short story, and is one of the most canonical writers discussed in this book. It is his less canonical side, however, that is of particular interest to us here. Quiroga is a key figure in the transition of Latin American science fiction from the elite, scientific form of the nineteenth century to the more popular, technology-driven genre of the twentieth. The text that best exemplifies this transition is *The Artificial Man*.

In a society in which the knowledge and authority of science were accessible only to the relatively small portion of the population that attended university, a familiarity with technology was seen as an alternate route to improving one's financial and social status. In a situation somewhat analogous to that of information technology today, those who understood the design and function of radios or motor vehicles in early twentieth-century Argentina enjoyed unprecedented opportunities for advancement: "Technology made up for the knowledge and skills that one might lack in other areas. It had a dual purpose: cultural modernization, on the one hand, and compensation for cultural differences, on the other" (Sarlo 5). Quiroga had an abiding fascination with technology throughout his life. From the more mechanical sphere of cycling, boat building, and a Model T Ford, his interests expanded to chemistry, photography, galvanoplasty, and beyond (Sarlo 13–18). He launched a variety of experimental ventures over the years, partly out of intellectual curiosity, but also in hopes that technology would give him the financial independence to escape the "burden of poorly paid writing for newspapers and magazines" (Sarlo 14). Paradoxically, his most technological text belonged in this category of obligatory writing and remained unpublished under Quiroga's name during his lifetime. Like several other Quiroga *folletines* [narratives appearing in serial form], *The Artificial Man* was published under the pseudonym S. Fragoso Lima in the popular Argentine magazine *Caras y Caretas*. Noé Jitrik locates *The Artificial Man*, along with five other Lima narratives, on the margins of Quiroga's oeuvre, saying that Quiroga viewed them as "mere instruments for earning money" (7).

The text was written during a transitional period in the life of this transitional writer. Quiroga was pulled between old and new in terms of literature, science, readership, and genre. The influence of Spanish American modernism was starting to wane as Quiroga began to develop the more realistic style that would characterize his Misiones narratives.[12] The influence of the modernists and of Shelley and Poe jostled in his work with narrative innovations suggested by film and by recent advances in science and technology. While he was part of a new technological generation, Quiroga could not escape either the theoretical power or the ultimate authority belonging to more established Science. With *The Artificial Man*, Sarlo explains, "Quiroga, a writer fascinated by knowledge of a practical kind, wrote a work of fiction in which such knowledge was projected onto the 'scientific' backdrop that made it possible" (36).[13]

Although Quiroga aspired to write exclusively under his own name, free from the requirements imposed on his fiction by the market, he was also cognizant of the emerging Argentine middle class, and his technological *folletín* was designed to appeal to this new reading public. As for the nascent science fiction genre, at the same time the Gernsback years were on the horizon in the United States, we find Quiroga at the juncture where the science fictional was becoming science fiction. Both Sarlo and Cano locate Horacio Quiroga, the writer, and *The Artificial Man*, the text, on this cusp. As we have seen, Sarlo distinguishes the part that Quiroga's work plays in the transition from science to technology in Argentine literature and society. In his study of Spanish American science fiction, Cano identifies *The Artificial Man* as the point in Latin American literature when the science fiction tradition is able to break free of the fantastic and stand alone, and when the influence of the canonical sciences predominates over that of the occult (141). We have witnessed this transition to a slightly lesser degree in Cuevas's "Doctor Tolimán," but Quiroga's text is more firmly grounded both in the foundational works and tropes of the genre and in twentieth-century technology. At the same time, Quiroga placed greater emphasis on the Argentine locus of his tale and on the role of geography, economic class, and social status in power relationships. He also showed himself to be in tune with tendencies in genre readership that would solidify during the 1930s and '40s in the United States and during the late 1950s in Latin America. *The Artificial Man* is thus representative of global trends in science fiction and of the alternative perspectives that Latin American writers had been contributing to the genre for over five decades.

The story opens with three scientist-inventors huddled around a rat on a laboratory table. Donissoff, whose "angelic beauty" contrasts with his "hard, implacable tone" and "terrible will," coordinates their activities and is clearly the leader of the group (95). Ortiz mans the electrical switches connecting the rat to some of the "complex apparatuses for chemistry, anatomy, and bacteriology" (96). Sivel injects the motionless animal with a "red liquid" (96). The rat's heart begins to beat. After three years of hard work, they have created a living being: "They, they alone *had made* that which was lying there!" (96). The characters, setting, and terminology make it plain that no magic or inexplicable forces have been employed in the creation process, though the theory and techniques push the limits of science and technology to such an extent that the three associates are described, at the close of the first chapter, as "three warlocks whom three hundred years earlier the Inquisition would have burned without hesitation" (98).

Nicolás Ivanovich Donissoff is the last descendant in a line of Russian nobility. His parents died when he was a child, but he was very close to his guardian, Prince Dolgorouky. During his days as a medical student specializing in bacteriology, Donissoff loses his respect for the czarist regime and becomes an anarchist. A true devotee of the cause, he renounces his noble title and his fortune. He even goes so far as to advocate the assassination of his beloved but elitist guardian, but the prince's death leaves Donissoff "forever wounded" and unable to continue in the revolutionary movement (101). Departing the fatherland, he continues his scientific studies in Vienna, Paris, and London before going to Buenos Aires in late 1905.

FIGURE 4.1. *Donissoff, Sivel, and Ortiz create a rat*. The Artificial Man, *drawing by José Friedrich*. Caras y Caretas *588 (8 January 1910), Buenos Aires, Argentina.*

Long before Luigi (sometimes called Stefano) Marco Sivel synthesized the red liquid for the rat in the laboratory, blood had played a central role in his life. He was born into a poor Italian family of small-time crooks. His mother has died, presumably when he was very young; we hear of her only when Sivel thinks of his "dearest mother" while awaiting a beating from his abusive father (103). Unlike Tolimán, Sivel eventually stands up to his progenitor. In response, Sivel's father truly acknowledges their kinship for the first time, saying "I recognize my blood. You are a worthy son of mine" (103). Unable to tolerate any challenge to his authority, however, he casts his son out of the house. Despite these inauspicious beginnings, the brilliant Sivel manages to attend medical school and become a celebrated doctor. The story of his broken engagement is another matter, requiring its own chapter in the novella. One day a young woman is brought to Sivel's hospital in Rome. She has lost a great deal of blood, but Sivel's fiancée forces him to promise not to donate any of his own blood to the patient. Incapable of watching the woman die, Sivel breaks his promise, and his fiancée ends their relationship. His blood saves the patient's life, but he contracts an infection and is horribly disfigured. When the patient declares both her gratitude and her love for him, Sivel cruelly rejects her, and she throws herself under a bus. Physically and emotionally scarred, Sivel believes his life to be "forever shattered," but eventually replaces his human relationships with his love for science: "His passion for science took hold of him again, this time with great ardor. All of his faculties seemed to have been reborn with an intense orientation toward the study of anatomy" (106). He arrives in Buenos Aires in 1904.

The third member of the trio is Ricardo Ortiz. Born into a wealthy Buenos Aires family, he studies electrical engineering in the United States, that fount of practical know-how. Upon his return to Buenos Aires, Ortiz does not practice his profession or take his place in society. Instead he becomes an inventor, researching and experimenting with electric batteries in search of "a new element of amazing intensity and constancy" (106). With the disdain of the Latin American upper class for anything resembling manual labor, Ortiz's family decries his "hands [that] were often impossibly filthy" and considers his studies of little use, "his science wasted" (106). Ortiz's father declares his son a disgrace and cuts off his allowance, saying "I'm embarrassed!" (107). The young engineer breaks off relations with his family and pursues his work with electricity. A year later, when his father is dying, Ortiz renounces his sizable inheritance.

These three characters are representative of the population of Buenos Aires in the early twentieth century, when a great wave of immigrants poured into Argentina's capital. In addition, all of the young men are outstanding in their various scientific specialties. None is married, nor is there a love interest in the picture. All have rebelled against their respective father figures, and all have tragic personal histories. Each seeks to forget the past and begin anew, and they meet and establish their partnership in Buenos Aires circa 1906. Sivel puts up the money to furnish their laboratory with "the most perfect types of machines and instruments ordered expressly from the United States," and they immediately embark on the rat project, "the highest work of genius of which humanity is capable: *to make* a living organism" (108). They construct the rat beginning at the subcellular level, using carbon, hydrogen, and oxygen as building blocks. Progress is often slow. After one of many setbacks, Ortiz questions their venture saying, "It is impossible! . . . We are tempting God or the devil with this!" (108). On August 23, 1909, the "artificial rat" is finally complete but, only hours after its heart has begun to beat, the rat's bones dissolve and it dies. However, the team soon identifies and solves the problem with its physical composition. On that same day, they decide that their next project will be to construct a man (the possibility of building an artificial woman is expressly rejected by Donissoff).

With the rat, our scientists had completed the first two steps on the inventor's "to-do list" (discussed in the introduction to this chapter); they had constructed an artificial living organism that both looks and moves like the original. Three additional levels are involved in constructing a human being: language, reason, and that final *je ne sais quoi*. They agree that their artificial human must possess an adult's capacity for thought and reason from the beginning. A grown man with the nervous system and abilities of a newborn would be "an eternal embarrassment for us" (110). According to Donissoff, adult-level thought and understanding could only be achieved by endowing the being with the sum of the experiences of the human race as a whole. By writing a sort of genetic memory onto the *tabula rasa* of their creation, they will imbue it with humanity at a stroke. Donissoff clarifies the scientific (not spiritual) nature of this X factor for Ortiz, insisting, "No, electrician; it is not a question of soul, but of heredity"

(111). He elaborates using an electrical analogy evocative of Tolimán's apparatus:

> Vivid though the sensations may be, his brain will lack the *habit* needed in order to perceive, firstly, and in order not to confuse the sensations, later. I think it is the same with your batteries. When they are newly made, they accumulate very little electricity, and they do not release any. All of the current is used to *make* the battery, to tune it. The successive charging and discharging gradually modify it until it becomes capable of storing electricity and releasing it normally. This will happen with the man that we make. (111)

> Por vivas que sean las sensaciones, le faltará *hábito* al cerebro para percibir, primero, y para no confundir las sensaciones, después. Con sus acumuladores pasa lo mismo, creo. Cuando están recién hechos, acumulan muy escasa electricidad, y no devuelven nada. Toda la corriente se emplea en *hacer* el acumulador, en afinarlo. Las cargas y descargas sucesivas lo van modificando, hasta que llega a almacenar electricidad y devolverla normalmente. Esto pasará con el hombre que hagamos.

Technical progress will enable them to accelerate the process of reproducing the neural pathways, developed over millions of years of human evolution, that are inherited by "natural" humans. Ortiz and Sivel are daunted by the task, but Donissoff, whose beauty is now described as that of "a rebellious archangel," urges them to take advantage of the abilities, science, and technology at their disposal (111). He admonishes them, "We are thinking like *created beings* and not like *creators*" (111). Donissoff sets the condition that he alone be responsible for the "tuning" that will allow their artificial man to attain the level of development exclusive to adult humans (112).

The progeny of the three bachelors, then, will be a man; no newborn, but their peer, their double. They name him Biógeno, "Biógeno, that is: *I engender life*. (In truth, they themselves were the ones engendering life; but the name had passed)" (116). The inverted name reflects both the unique confusion of the familial relationship between the inventors and their creation, and also something of the trio's unresolved issues with their own father figures. The construction of Biógeno occupies the standard ten-month gestation period for a human, and he is completed on June 11, 1910.[14] Physically he is a flawless specimen, and the narrator waxes poetic about the "marvelous proportion" of "that marvelous being that lay there naked, breathing harmoniously" (115). Biógeno appears to be around twenty-five years of age. A younger self from happier times? Or another chance, perhaps, for Donissoff, Sivel, and Ortiz to begin anew as sons or as fathers.

Donissoff now attempts to put Biógeno's mental capacity "in tune" with his physical appearance. Sivel and Ortiz surely expect Donissoff to display further scientific and technical brilliance. What they do not expect is that Donissoff's means of accomplishing his self-appointed task, so neatly sanitized in his argument ten months before, will involve torture using a very low-tech pair of pliers. Donissoff brings in a thin, poorly dressed man and explains to his colleagues (in English) that this is the "definitive element" in his plan: "The production of an intense amount of pain, of a high-pitched current of pain, is indispensable for provoking a sensitivity in his nervous system that only years of experience would give it" (117–18). Donissoff continues to use English, then French, to keep the poor man from understanding his orders to Sivel and Ortiz.[15] Despite the repugnance they feel, they tie the victim down with ropes. The narrator remarks that, "The torment of a poor innocent human being could not be an obstacle to the triumph of their scientific ideal. There was nothing purer and simpler than the hearts of those three men" (118). But this defense is contradicted by a single glimpse from the victim's perspective. At a slip of the tongue by Ortiz, who utters the word "torture" in Spanish, the poor man renews his struggle to escape what is now described as "that laboratory with its hellish appearance, and the three demons, devourers of men" (119). The ropes hold. All of the sophisticated electrical connections are made, and Donissoff uses the pliers to pull out the man's fingernails, one by one. Although Sivel and Ortiz do not like the idea of torture and cannot bear to watch after the sixth fingernail, neither moves to stop him. All now fit Ludmer's description of "men of science 'in crime.'"

The transmission of experience from the real man to the artificial one appears to be a success on all levels. The three associates look at the unconscious Biógeno. "His expression was different: the expression of a man who has lived, loved, suffered. Yes, that closed mouth had shouted; those eyes had seen, that forehead, no longer smooth, had thought!" (121). But when they awaken Biógeno his first expression is that of the suffering torture victim, his first sensation is of pain in his

FIGURE 4.2. *The three scientists and the subject to be tortured, at the moment of Ortiz's slip.* The Artificial Man, *drawing by José Friedrich.* Caras y Caretas *591 (29 January 1910), Buenos Aires, Argentina.*

fingertips, and his first utterance is "Oh! My fingernails!" in the poor victim's voice (123). Sivel fears that they have accomplished merely the simple transfer of an existing life rather than the creation of a new one, "That man has no life of his own. He is a puppet [maniquí]; we have transferred the other's soul to him" (123). Donissoff insists that it is only a matter of residual influence that will soon dissipate, "That being has life of its own, or will have" (124).

But the most immediate problem is a physical one. While the torture victim feels nothing at all and will soon die of shattered nerves, Biógeno is now hypersensitive; his five senses are so acute that a drink of water, a glimpse of light, or the touch of a hand would be unutterable agony for him. The three colleagues identify the root of the problem: "We have discharged the source too much . . . . And the battery, on the other hand, has been overloaded" [Hemos descargado demasiado la pila . . . . Y el acumulador, en cambio, se ha sobrecargado] (127). Out of pity, Sivel and Ortiz advocate killing their "monster of pain" (123), but the iron-willed Donissoff proposes to effect a discharge of Biógeno's overloaded senses by torturing Biógeno and using himself, in a hypnotized state, as the receiver. His colleagues entreat him, "For that which you love most in this world, do not do that!" (129). Their words evoke the memory of a secret committee meeting on that bitter day from Donissoff's past, "on which he had sacrificed more than his own life" (130). Although he has allowed his father figure to die, he cannot do the same for his offspring. Sacrificing Biógeno would break the last true emotional tie each of them has left, Donissoff argues, saying "All that still binds us to life we have placed in this miserable machine of suffering" (130).

The initial stages proceed as anticipated; Sivel hypnotizes Donissoff, and Ortiz tortures Biógeno. But Donissoff has misjudged both the level of Biógeno's accumulated suffering and his own ability to tolerate it. The discharge occurs all at once, killing both creator and creation. The narrator laments at length the loss of "the greatest and noblest of all men . . . who had created the greatest thing it is possible to create in this world" (132). As for the fates of Sivel and Ortiz, we know from an earlier reference that, several days after the tragic end of their experiment, they are called before an examining magistrate to provide scientific (and presumably personal) testimony in an investigation of the matter (118). As the tale ends, however, we are told only that the three deaths have destroyed their last hopes and dreams, along with their last pretensions to artificial reproduction. The novella closes:

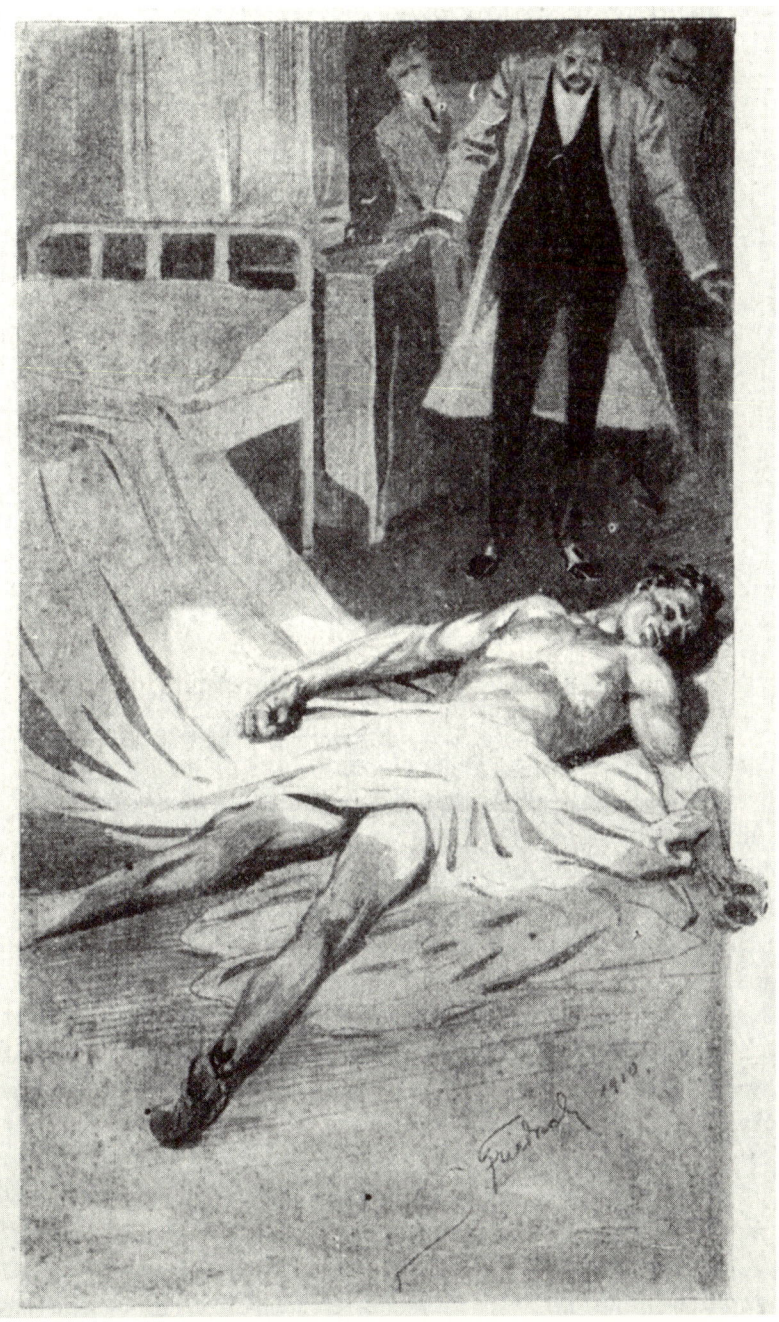

FIGURE 4.3. *Biógeno suffering from sensory overload.* The Artificial Man, *drawing by José Friedrich.* Caras y Caretas *593 (12 February 1910), Buenos Aires, Argentina.*

Everything was over! Never, never would they aspire to anything! Never again would they enter the laboratory! Their entire future was dead now, as the man with the bandaged hands was dead; as their abominable creation was dead; as there lay dead— sublime creature, archangel of genius, will, and beauty—, Donissoff. (132)

¡Todo estaba concluído! ¡Jamás, jamás volverían a aspirar a nada! ¡Nunca más entrarían en el laboratorio! Su porvenir entero estaba muerto ya, como había muerto el hombre de las manos vendadas; como había muerto su creación abominable; como allí–criatura sublime, arcángel de genio, voluntad y belleza–, estaba muerto Donissoff.

In the end, we do not learn whether the ultimate failure of the project was due to a mere miscalculation or to a faulty hypothesis. At the same time, it remains unclear if language, reason, and the final X factor of humanity were only transferred to Biógeno from another, or if the trio actually created these human traits and the appearance of transference was indeed, as Donissoff insisted, due to the persistence of "influence." We do know that their intended ideal version of humanity never becomes more than a stunted double, and that the three inventors themselves never truly escape from their own stunted pasts. Unlike Tolimán, Quiroga's Donissoff, Sivel, and Ortiz are strong-willed "men of character" (108). Though better able than Tolimán to move beyond the immediate domination of their father figures, to recover from the loss of love, to make a fresh start together in the New World, and to attempt to (pro)create a next generation, they too fail in their ambitions. They improve neither upon the human race nor upon the failings of their fathers. Donissoff is guilty of elitism (torturing a poor man and using languages of science and power to dominate him); Sivel of violence (he condones then participates in torture); Ortiz of allowing embarrassment about imperfect offspring to cause him to act inappropriately (he also condones then participates in torture). Like their fathers before them, they all lose a son.

The Artificial Man is a modernization of *Frankenstein*, the paradigmatic double tale published ninety-two years earlier. The most cursory reading of the texts indicates that Shelley's novel must have been a direct model. In both works, initial success is followed by ultimate failure

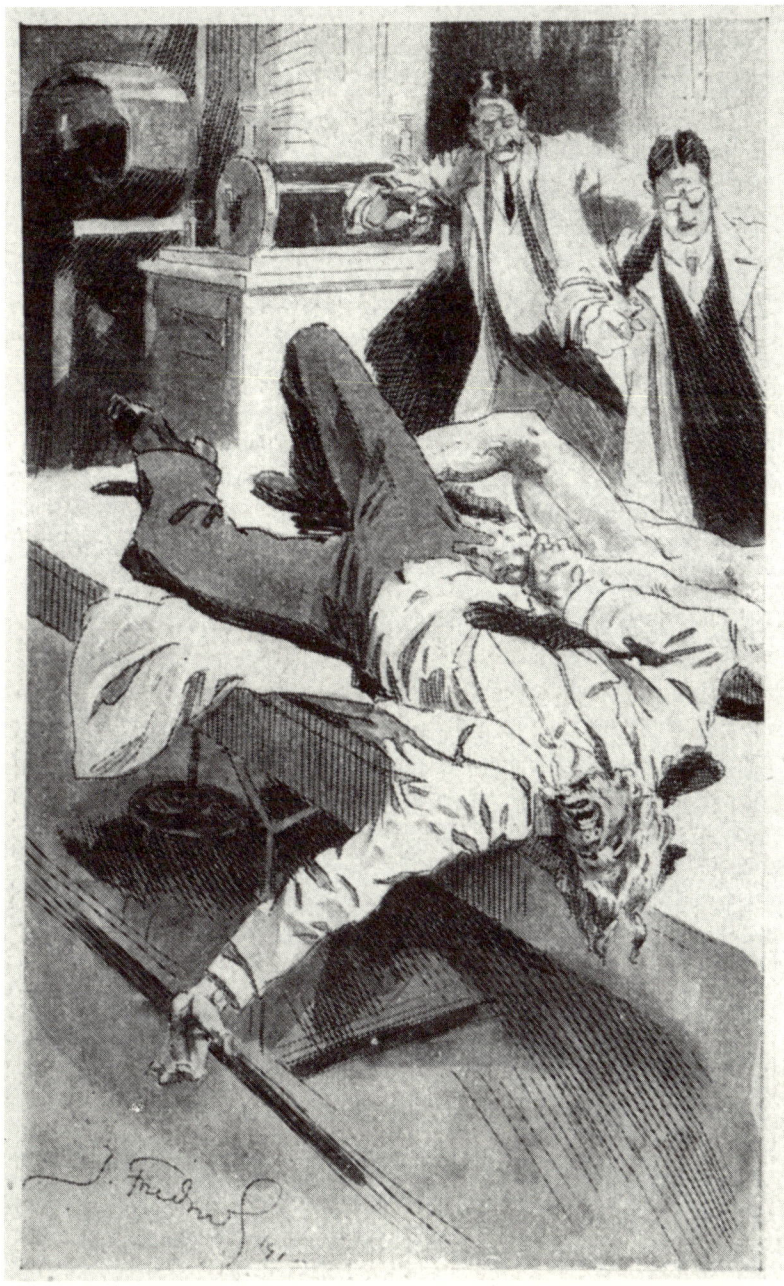

FIGURE 4.4. *Deaths of Donissoff and Biógeno, creator and creation.* The Artificial Man, drawing by José Friedrich. *Caras y Caretas* 593 (12 February 1910), Buenos Aires, Argentina.

in the quest to create a human being. Both Donissoff and Frankenstein push the limits of science. They are compared to God in his capacity as Creator but, as their experiments take terrible turns for the worse, references to them as fallen archangels predominate. Each scientist's hubris eventually leads to his own demise and that of his creation. However, these narratives are knit together by the flesh as well as by the bare bones of the texts. Many elements of *The Artificial Man*, from its sympathetic narration to the role of electricity, are in constant resonance with its predecessor.[16]

The modernity of Quiroga's text appears to have been constructed in deliberate contrast to Shelley's work, from the temporal proximity of the story's events relative to the author's reality, to the characters, their approaches to science, and their resulting creation. *Frankenstein* is set outside Shelley's native England, in the more romantically exotic region of Switzerland, and she brings the story to an end in September of 17—, at least nineteen years prior to the novel's composition. While Shelley's tale is safely tucked away in the past, Quiroga pushes his into the unknown territory of the future. The narrative is set in his readers' hometown of Buenos Aires, and takes place in a Vernian near future (the date given for the completion of the artificial man is four months after the publication of the text's final installment in *Caras y Caretas*).

Although we can observe similarities in ability and temperament among Shelley's Frankenstein and Quiroga's three inventors, the differences between them are generally indicative of the changes in scientists and science that occurred in the intervening decades. These changes are revealed in the scientists' educational background and training, in their work structure and practices, and in the level of sophistication of the scientific procedures performed. Victor Frankenstein's interest in science is first sparked by the works of noncanonical authorities such as Agrippa, Albertus Magnus, and Paracelsus. While he breaks with this past by beginning study of the modern sciences at university, the seeds of his preoccupation with the creation of life, with "immortality and power," are to be found in what he terms the "boundless grandeur" of the aspirations of the ancients (Shelley 41). Without that early interest, he says, "It is even possible, that the train of my ideas would never have received the fatal impulse that led to my ruin" (33). Quiroga's inventors, on the other hand, are firmly grounded in the canonical sciences of their day and, in addition to their scientific knowledge, they employ both practical and technical skills in their endeavor to create an artificial man. Although Donissoff is painted as a Renaissance man of the sciences, even a genius of his stature must work on a team with others, as the increase in the body of scientific knowledge has encouraged specialization. It is also significant that the more modern scientists do not begin their investigations with humans, but first construct that epitome of modern scientific inquiry, a rat. Finally, Quiroga brings Shelley's cut-and-paste techniques up to date. With less gothic gore, his artificial man is created at the molecular level, constructed "element by element, milligram by milligram" (114).

Although Biógeno never attains either the capacity to narrate or the status of narrator achieved by Shelley's monster, Quiroga and his scientists seem to be addressing that creature's shortcomings, seeking to modernize and improve upon him. While Frankenstein designs his creature to be physically stronger and more aesthetically perfect than naturally conceived humans, he is successful only in the former. "I had selected his features as beautiful," he laments, but describes the resulting figure as a "wretch" with "yellowed skin," "watery eyes," "shrivelled complexion," and "un-human features" (52). Throughout Shelley's novel, the creature is repeatedly referred to as a "monster" by one and all, while in Quiroga's narrative the term is used only in the phrase "monster of suffering," to indicate the pain that Biógeno experiences through the torture connection and due to his heightened senses. The social stigma which Frankenstein's creature suffers due to his monstrous exterior, and for which he blames his monstrous nature, would not have been an issue for Donissoff and company's idealized being. And whereas the Frankenstein creature is brought to life with a blank mental slate, Quiroga's scientists attempt to create a being who begins life possessing the abilities and intellect of an adult. Biógeno is never rejected by his creators, perhaps because of his physical perfection (or perhaps because of Sivel's and Ortiz's [sub]conscious determination not to repeat the actions of their fathers). Quiroga endows his inventors with enough forethought to consider the immediate consequences of creating a life (perhaps because they anticipate success due to the triumph of the rat experiment). While Frankenstein does not appear to have thought beyond the moment of vivification, fleeing his "workshop" until his newly animated creation departs (50), Donissoff, Sivel, and Ortiz meticulously plan how their creation will acquire knowledge and envision—if only on a superficial, embarrassment-avoidance level—Biógeno's public debut and the reactions he will inspire.

The Artificial Man is a Latin Americanization as well as a modernization of *Frankenstein*; it is a *Frankenstein*-inspired text representative of 1910 Argentina. We have said that the national origins of the protagonists reflect the changing composition of Argentina at the time, but Latin American characters, settings, and idiomatic expressions are only superficial indicators of a science fiction that is truly Latin American (Capanna in "Coloquio a distancia" 20). In our discussion of Quiroga's text, we have further identified the contexts in which different countries are mentioned as illustrative of Latin American perceptions of their roles in the world: the United States is associated with technology, European countries with science, and Northern languages and cultures with science, technology, dominance, and control. In *The Artificial Man*, an elite international team possesses the potential to conduct cutting-edge research and produce a more perfect man (Argentine?). Although they fail, there is no suggestion that a group from another socioeconomic class, of different national origins, or with varying educational backgrounds will supplant them. *The Artificial Man*, like much Latin American science fiction, is also an intensely political work, in which political ideologies, socioeconomic class structure, and historical paradigms such as "civilization and barbarism" reveal a Latin American perspective on the power dynamics at work at both local and international levels.

Ludmer takes up Sarlo's discussion of ethics and science in *The Artificial Man* (as part of her analysis of "men of science 'in crime'") but goes beyond Sarlo to characterize political aspects of the text. Ludmer writes: "In *El hombre artificial*, in 1910, the relationship between *ethics and science* is posed at the same time as the relation between *ethics and revolutionary politics*" (69). Ludmer locates the nexus of the relationship between ethics and politics in the person of Donissoff, "who as an *anarchist* in Russia hands over a fellow noble ('for the sake of the revolution') and as a *scientist* in Argentina tortures a poor man ('for the sake of life')" (69). So Donissoff, defender of the people against the oppression of nobles, himself becomes an oppressor of the poor, although he shows no sign of recognizing that he has transplanted the hated power structure of his past. His self-deception is aided, perhaps, by the different labels in his new setting. He does not seem to equate the injustices perpetrated by the despised Russian nobility with the inequalities perpetuated by the wealthy, "civilized," scientifically literate Argentine elite. Somehow the peasant classes that he was willing to make sacrifices for in his homeland become expendable in the New World; he flashes back to his revolutionary days when it comes to inflicting pain on Biógeno, but not when torturing the poor man.

The Argentine class structure is further represented in the lives of Ortiz and Sivel. Quiroga's portrayal of Ortiz's upper class *porteño* family reveals a society that still privileges wealth, social standing, and old money, though an education from the United States, when put to appropriate use, is also valued. Sivel is an example of the social mobility possible in the Argentina of the day. The son of a "barbaric" and poor rogue of a father, he becomes "civilized" (educated, wealthy, cultured, sensitive) through education and through science. Sivel is never considered the inferior of the three because of his humble origins; rather he is second in command to Donissoff, and nearer to being their leader's equal than Ortiz, who is a distant third. Ortiz's inferior position is explained in part by the fact that his past has been less traumatic ("Ortiz has not yet suffered," as Donissoff puts it [130]), and in part because his work is with technology rather than with the more authoritative—even for the technology-mad Quiroga—science.[17] It also cannot be coincidence that Ortiz is of Argentine rather than European origin like the others.

The text does not contain a clear program of advocacy for either Argentine nationalism or social justice. Nor does Quiroga demonstrate a strong inclination to sit in judgment of the role of science in modern society (the motivation of individual hubris clearly trumps any technophobic interpretations). In the reality portrayed in *The Artificial Man*, the team members view the torture of an unscientific and uncivilized character as acceptable in the service of science and in the creation of a being who is designed to be his creators' equal or better. Quiroga portrays the inventors' willingness to sacrifice Argentina's "barbaric" past for the purpose of constructing a more "civilized" future as a repetition of the sins of their fathers. There is no indication as to how the case will be judged in court.

LOOKING FORWARD

The Artificial Man is not as marginal a part of Quiroga's corpus as its pseudonymous and virtually orphaned state might infer. Quiroga also deals with the technology of the double in two short stories that he signed with his own name: "The Portrait" appeared in *Caras y Caretas* in 1910 and "The Vampire" in the newspaper *La Nación* in 1927.[18] "The Vampire" is a modernization and refocusing of the earlier "Portrait" and also, to a lesser degree, of *The Artificial Man*.[19] A closer look at the choices that Quiroga makes in his rewritings further clarifies both the old constants and the new trends at the end of Latin American science fiction's first wave.

Horacio Quiroga, "The Portrait"

"The Portrait" is the story of a young British scientist, Rudyard Kelvin, who has lost his fiancée, Edith, to injuries sustained in a car accident. Kelvin has been living in Buenos Aires for the past ten months and tells his story to our narrator, a South American, on a ferry crossing between Buenos Aires and Montevideo. The two men find that they share an interest in a work by Gustave Le Bon, *The Evolution of Matter* [*L'évolution de la matière*] (1905). Kelvin, a photography buff, is particularly fascinated by an experiment in which Le Bon demonstrates that "an object exposed to the sun for a moment, and placed in complete darkness on a sensitive plate, makes an impression upon it" (361). The Englishman tells the narrator that he carried this experiment one step further in his own laboratory, using his eye instead of some other physical object to produce an impression on the plate, but read soon afterward that this had already been done in the United States.

Beginning with this extra step, Kelvin's story grows increasingly fantastic. The narrator uses a less-than-objective description to refer to Kelvin's area of expertise as "what we would call the black magic of light: cathodic rays, X rays, ultraviolet rays and more" (361–62). The time that Kelvin spends recounting the last days of his fiancée's life, the emphasis he places on the way in which her eyes gazed fixedly upon him as she lay "dying and watching me ceaselessly" [muriéndose y mirándome sin cesar], and the fact that she sends her family away, preferring to die alone with him, prepare the reader for a bond-beyond-death scenario (362). And in the first months after Edith's death, Kelvin believes that this is happening. He uses his scientific knowledge to reproduce the image of the one he sees most in his mind's eye by staring at his photographic plate, "thinking of Edith with the desperate love that overflowed my soul. I saw her there, she looked at me with the look of love that one remembers above all things" (363). When the plate is developed, it reveals Edith as she once was, looking out at her lover with the special smile she reserved for him. Initially Kelvin repeats the process on a daily basis, then every few days. When he leaves a two-week interval between portraits, Edith's face appears clouded over, especially around her eyes. When he waits a month before reproducing her portrait, the image that appears is of Edith dead, and Kelvin then understands he has stopped loving her.

At this point the narrator realizes the extent to which he has been wrapped up in the story and how much credence he has given to the relationship between the couple's love and the ability to reproduce an image of one who can no longer be physically seen, admitting, "For my part, I confess that I had forgotten the scientific aspect of the phenomenon" (364). Kelvin then recounts his final repetition of the process. He performs the experiment in the presence of a reliable witness, a lab assistant who had seen Edith only a few times. Her image appears on the plate, smiling as radiantly as ever. But she is looking in the direction of the assistant, imprinted by his gaze and not Kelvin's. "The miniscule amount of affection that he might have had for her was enough to evoke her" [El ínfimo cariño que pudiera haberle tenido a ella la revivía], Kelvin laments, "What do you want me to do after that?" [¿Qué quiere usted que yo haga después de eso?] (364). It had not been the greatness of his love that reproduced Edith's image, but science.[20]

Horacio Quiroga, "The Vampire"

Guillermo Grant, the Spanish American narrator (country undefined) of "The Vampire," has written an article in which he extrapolates from work done by scientists such as Le Bon (and also from the scientific extrapolations Quiroga had already carried out in "The Portrait"). Considering the way in which a radio circuit can turn invisible signals into the sound of a human voice, Grant suggests that it may be possible to "corporealize" images, or "visual emanations" (170).

> If the retina, after being exposed in ardent contemplation to a portrait, can impress a sensitive plate to the point of obtaining a "double" of that portrait, in the same way the living forces of the soul are able, when excited by these emotional rays, not to produce, but rather to "create" an image in a visual and tangible circuit. (171)
>
> Si la retina impresionada por la ardiente contemplación de un retrato puede influir sobre una placa sensible al punto de obtener

un "doble" de ese retrato, del mismo modo las fuerzas vivas del alma pueden, bajo la excitación de tales rayos emocionales, no producir, sino "crear" una imagen en un circuito visual y tangible.

Grant's ideas interest one don Guillén de Orzúa y Rosales—"or so he said he was called"—a fellow scientific dabbler with old money and a mysteriously non-Hispanic accent (170). Rosales sets out to apply these principles to his own hypotheses on cinematography. He posits that the projected rays of films must carry with them to the screen more than a mere "frozen electrical enlargement" of an image, that they must contain something beyond "a galvanic copy of life" in order to be capable of moving entire rooms full of people to intense emotion (173).

In this story, Quiroga deliberately modernizes "The Portrait" and *The Artificial Man,* as well as Poe's "The Oval Portrait" (1845). A two-dimensional reproduction such as Rudyard Kelvin's is no longer of interest to Rosales. He has already carried out an identical process and, he tells Grant, it is a "poor experiment that I will not repeat again" (173). Rosales compares his goal to that of the painter in Poe's tale; he wants to reproduce "'life itself'" (173). The being he has chosen to corporealize is a famous Hollywood actress he has "met" only in the cinema.

Quiroga upgrades the technology from photography to cinematography, from two dimensions to three. He also moves beyond the X rays and ultraviolet rays with which Kelvin experimented to so-called N^1 rays.[21] In Rosales's experiments, film projectors and other laboratory equipment are combined with a number of more fantastic elements, including some extremely subjective, undocumentable forces. The first of these is a vivid imagination, which Grant calls the only "stimulant of the strange forces capable of causing a soul to explode" (171). There is also the great force of Rosales's will, described in very similar terms to that of Donissoff and to that of a *magnétiseur* (see chapter 3), and which likewise will lead him to make extreme decisions. Grant, the harbinger of doom, warns the reader early on: "For those who live on the frontier of what is beyond the rational, the will is the only sesame that can open the doors of the eternally prohibited" (172).

Rosales invites Grant to dinner at his home, where he demonstrates the partial success of his initial experiments. Grant is amazed to find that Rosales has managed to evoke a semitransparent, three-dimensional version of his favorite Hollywood star. Rosales's hypotheses about reproducing "life itself" appear to be confirmed by the ghost-actress's ability to walk and talk: she even professes to recognize Grant, having seen him in the audience from the screen. Rosales explains the process by which he has expanded the recreation of the single instant captured in a photograph to the flow of time captured in the multiple frames of a film clip: "From the moment when the film begins to run past the excitation of the light, the voltage, and the N^1 rays, it is completely transformed into a vibrant sketch of life" (177). But Rosales is not satisfied with producing a "ghost" of the actress, saying that he must find a way to endue her with "the life to which every creation has the right, if it is not a monster" (175, 179). He insists, however, that even this ghostly version of life is superior to any life engendered "by the mere routine force of subsistence," because she is the "work of a conscience" (179).

The rest of the tale describes the lengths to which Rosales is willing to go to fully realize his goal. In the process, he reveals himself to be a forerunner of the overly enthusiastic fan—the stalker of the stars—as well as another "man of science 'in crime.'" In order to complete his life-giving process, Rosales paradoxically decides to kill the actress herself. More extreme than Donissoff, he incorporates the death into his calculations, hoping to concentrate all of her life into his copy. He makes the long trip to Hollywood and succeeds in murdering the woman, but his own recreation disappears as well. When he tries to evoke his creation again, only her skeleton appears. He then decides that the lesson to be drawn from this experiment is the opposite of that learned by Rudyard Kelvin. Whereas Kelvin realizes that love had never been part of the process that produced the image, Rosales believes that it is precisely the element of love that had been missing when he eliminated the original actress, that the equation should read: science + imagination or strange forces + will + *love* = life. As Rosales tells Grant: "I created sterilely, and therein lies my error . . . . Love is not necessary in life; but it is indispensable for knocking at the doors of death. If I had killed for love, my creature would palpitate with life today on the divan" (182–83).

Rosales re-evokes the actress, this time including love in the process. She returns, but her corporealization is not complete and her appearance is still spectral. Although her disposition is apparently unchanged, Grant notices that she is now consumed with passion for Rosales, while he no longer feels anything for her. He urges Rosales to destroy this "monster of feeling," not for her own good—as in the case of Biógeno, the "monster of pain"—but for her creator's (184). "She is a vampire, and you have nothing to give to her!" Grant warns (184).²² Rosales does not follow his friend's advice. He is found dead, his camera and film in flames, the evocation of the actress gone. Although "his dead face retained its habitual warm tone," Grant concludes, "I am certain that in the furthest reaches of his veins there remained not a single drop of blood" (185). Whereas Donissoff is destroyed when input from his artificial man overloads his senses, Rosales meets his end when his creation drains him of emotion. Rosales's downfall is brought about by the same tragic flaws displayed in *The Artificial Man*: the inhumanity of those who seek to create humanity, and their fatal presumptions regarding both their own abilities and the superiority of their creations.

Despite the pivotal role of *The Artificial Man* in the trajectory of Latin American science fiction, its publication neither signaled a definitive separation between science fiction and the fantastic nor triggered a new and larger wave of science fiction in Latin America. It remains, however, an important marker in science fiction's transition from a more elite narrative form in Latin America to a more popular genre that appealed to a broader readership. Together, Quiroga's *The Artificial Man* (1910), "The Portrait" (also 1910), and "The Vampire" (1927, the year after Gernsback's landmark editorial), indicate the trajectory of the nascent genre. The three texts illustrate the wide range of genre hybridity present in Latin America, even within the corpus of a single author. They also reflect the changes taking place in the dynamics of influence in Latin America. Finally, these texts mark the status of science-fictional writing in Latin America during the years when more formal genre codification was getting underway in the North, and provide important precedents for the golden age of Latin American science fiction in the 1950s and '60s.

But if *The Artificial Man* can be said to represent the trend toward genre independence for science fiction in Latin America, then "The Vampire" provides an interesting contrast. In that story, Quiroga takes earlier science fictional material and moves it toward the fantastic. Whereas Donissoff's strong will is represented as an individual's drive to succeed, Rosales summons a less intangible, more manipulable power in performing his laboratory experiment. Similarly, Kelvin uses techniques of visualization in "The Portrait" to evoke an *image*, but Quiroga prefers the fuzzier term "*imag*ination" in "The Vampire" and links it with the evocation of Lugonian "strange forces." And whereas love is deliberately removed from the reproduction of the double in "The Portrait," emphasizing the scientific nature of the process, Rosales adds love to his formula in order to cross "the frontier of what is beyond the rational."[23] Even the poetic justice of "Vampire" is fantastic in nature, as Rosales is killed by a being who seeks the very love that had been missing in the creation process. Quiroga's 1927 rewriting of his own earlier works serves as a useful reminder of the strong tradition of hybridity among the genres, and of the particular proximity of the fantastic and science fiction which would continue to exist in Latin America.

Quiroga's three texts exemplify the continuities as well as the shifts in the tensions between influence and originality in Latin America. Establishing national identity and a national/regional role in the world preoccupies Latin American writers long after independence is achieved, and their science fiction continues to reflect international political, cultural, and scientific power dynamics, though these elements are not always as clearly denoted as they were in nineteenth-century Latin American utopian fiction. As we can see in Quiroga's works, Europe remains the central source for theoretical science. The two leading scientists in *The Artificial Man* are European by nationality and by training; Rudyard Kelvin in "The Portrait" is British; and the work of Gustave Le Bon forms the theoretical basis for both "Portrait" and "Vampire." As in earlier texts, such as *Doctor Benignus*, the United States is associated with applied science, though there is some expansion into more theoretical territory. Ortiz has been trained as an engineer in New York, and the instruments in the team's ultramodern laboratory are imported from the United States. Kelvin discovers that his experiment based on Le Bon's theory has already been carried out in the United States while, in "Vampire," the U.S. film industry is the main source of new technology. Northern literary influence continues in Quiroga's science fictional works, with Mary Shelley and Poe predominating, though regional literary antecedents, such as Lugones, also persist. Quiroga's "Vampire" registers the advent of the influence of U.S. mass culture in Latin America, with its incorporation of a Hollywood icon. Latin American contributions are still portrayed as secondary, but Latin American participation is on the rise. Quiroga sets the construction of the first artificial animal and human in Argentina, with an Argentine on the team, even if he is the least of its members. The characters in "Portrait" follow the pattern of the European, traveling in Latin America, who finds a Latin

American confidant knowledgeable of the latest European scientific advances. In "Vampire," a foreigner of unknown national origin also finds himself in a Latin American country, but an essential addition to a Frenchman's scientific ideas is provided by the theoretical work of the Argentine narrator.

The golden age of Latin American science fiction does not arrive until the 1950s, with early genre magazines such as *Beyond* [*Más Allá*] (Argentina, 1953–57), *Fantastic* (Brazil, 1955–60), and *Fantastic Stories* [*Los Cuentos Fantásticos*] (Mexico, 1948–53), and seminal works such as *The Superior Ones* [*Los altísimos*] (Chile, 1959) and the comic *The Eternaut* [*El Eternauta*] (Argentina, 1957–59+). Until relatively recently, the emergence of Latin American science fiction was typically identified as occurring within this golden age. This was possible as long as works by Jorge Luis Borges, Adolfo Bioy Casares, and other canonical authors from the first half of the twentieth century were categorized as above the genre's reach, and as long as the earliest works of Latin American science fiction remained unclaimed. Retrolabeling, bibliographical projects, and scholarly studies in the field have reached a quantitative and qualitative critical mass. The contributions of Latin American writers to this global genre have become evident, as has the place of science fiction in the Latin American literary landscape.

CONCLUSION
A GLOBAL GENRE IN THE PERIPHERY

In the preface to his excellent book on the early science fiction of England, France, and the United States, *Science Fiction before 1900*, Paul Alkon observes that "science fiction has from its outset been an international phenomenon transcending political boundaries while nevertheless taking on distinctive features that reflect different national preoccupations" (xiii).[1] Let us then consider the features that have distinguished Latin American science fiction from the outset. A recurring theme of science fiction in Latin America and in other areas of the periphery is the definition of national identity, along with its corollary, the relationship between the post-colonial self and the Northern other. This sf also has a strong tendency toward political content; the nationality, race, and social class of characters are given more weight than in Northern sf. Further, works that may be discussed as sf are more likely to be hybrids, also claimed by other genres.[2] The following examination of the characteristics of Latin American sf encompasses the full time span of the genre there, but focuses on the defining elements of nineteenth-century works.

From the beginning, Latin Americans themselves have been the most persistent questioners as to whether there can be a Latin American science fiction and, if so, what makes it Latin American. "We will only admit the necessity for and the validity of a Latin American sf to the degree that we recognize in it something that could not have been written in other latitudes," declares critic Pablo Capanna (in "Coloquio a Distancia" 20). The debate as to the acceptable degrees of imitation, borrowing, or influence of Northern sf versus the desired percentages and characteristics of local, national, or Latin American contributions is ongoing in the Latin American sf community.

In recent decades, this debate has perhaps been clearest in the Brazilian arena, due to the competing volleys of manifestos. In his "Cannibalistic Manifesto of Brazilian Science Fiction—Supernova Movement" [Manifesto Antropofágico da Ficção Científica Brasileira—Movimento Supernova] (1988), inspired by Oswald de Andrade's "Cannibal Manifesto" [Manifesto antropófago] (1928), Ivan Carlos Regina protests against the Brazilian tendency to produce derivative sf: "Copying the foreign model creates ... mental poverty among intellectuals who seek, in grotesque imitation, to recreate the *modus vivendi* of technologically developed countries."[3] While as recently as 2004, the "Anti-Brazilitis Manifesto" [Manifesto Antibrasilitite] attacked—with particular emphasis on sf and other genre media—"the necessity of a mask or veneer of Brazilianness for a work of fiction written/produced by a Brazilian to be taken seriously by critics and by potential financial backers" (Reis).[4]

Prior to 1920, there were no genre-based literary circles or fandoms in which this debate could take place. Nevertheless, tensions between originality and influence (or nationally produced versus imported, or independent versus colonial identity) formed part of the cultural fabric in the relatively young Latin American nations. The frontispiece of Luis Holmberg's biography of his father, Eduardo Ladislao Holmberg, includes a quotation dated 1876, in his father's own handwriting, reflecting upon precisely this issue: "I am Argentine, and I love my country, my country which is so beautiful and so prosperous but which has until now gone begging to Europe when she had in her bosom models of her own, sufficient for all the world." Although, as we have argued, the perils of imitating the North were more often perceived in the nineteenth century as mitigated by the benefits of gaining Northern scientific knowledge and by the historical influence of Northern culture, the issue of influence was of supreme importance to writers of science fictional texts at that time. Along with their literary roles, many of these writers participated in the construction of their nations' identities in political, legal, educational, or scientific capacities. When writing science-fictional works, they were highly cognizant of actively importing literary tools and tropes from Northern science fictional texts, even as they adapted them for their own purposes.

Considering González Echevarría's pertinent reminder that, in Latin America, "the outside is also always inside" (41), it is clear that there is room for more than two positions in this self/other debate. Braulio Tavares, a contemporary Brazilian writer-critic, takes a more universalist view:

> It does not seem to me that there exists a "Brazilian," "European," or "American" science . . . : there exists a science which, viewed as a system of ideas, belongs to humanity as a whole. . . .
>
> As for the importation of themes and images of foreign sf, this seems an interesting question, but secondary. . . . Certain literary conventions, by being used outside their place of origin so frequently, end up becoming universal. (*O que é* 81–82)

The positions of the majority of Latin Americans—including many whose statements in this debate we have just noted—consist of some mixture of acknowledging the inevitability of a degree of Northern influence in the genre, while at the same time seeking to find their own voices. They reject not so much the influence of Northern sf, but its idealization by Latin American writers who thereby reveal themselves to be incapable of imagination. Sergio Gaut vel Hartman states that, for Latin Americans who write science fiction, "Lost purity (or forced hybridization [*mestización*]) has dictated the norms of our way of writing without deliberation or reflection" (11). What Gaut vel Hartman seems to object to most is the blind imitation of Anglo-Saxon sf. The *mestización* he accepts as part of the apprenticeship of the sf writer, stating: "Those of us who grew up reading Anglo-Saxon science fiction had already lost our purity the day we sat down to write science fiction for the first time" (11). His use of the term *mestización* indicates, however, that he is also aware that Latin American writers do not come to science fiction empty-handed, a fact he makes more explicit with examples: "Borges plus Sturgeon, Macedonio [Fernández] by way of Bester produce explosive, unpredictable results" (11).

In his *Biographies of the Future: Mexican Science Fiction and Its Authors* [*Biografías del futuro: La ciencia ficción mexicana y sus autores*], Gabriel Trujillo Muñoz reflects on how far science fiction has come as a genre in Latin America: "Now we have a historical consciousness of belonging to a global movement and, at the same time, we respond to this world science fiction movement with our own characteristics, with notable antecedents and with distinctive, complementary aspirations" (355). With the exception of Trujillo Muñoz's nod to recent progress in retrolabeling, this assertion is not so far from what might have been said of Latin American sf in the nineteenth century, for science fiction has been a truly global genre from the earliest times of genre formation. As we have seen, there is both direct and indirect evidence that nineteenth-century Latin American writers were reading Verne, Wells, Poe, Shelley, and other Northern writers and were seeking to write science-fictional texts that described their own realities. The difference, perhaps, is that these writers might have thought of themselves as *joining* a global movement rather than *belonging* to one as a fully integrated participant. I. F. Clarke has described authors of early Northern sf as writing "for the nation and for the world" and as having "an international audience for their stories" (xiii). Their nineteenth-century Latin American counterparts, however, did not feel described by such narratives, and so they produced their own. A closer look at the early texts being retrolabeled in Latin American science fiction genealogies reveals the "notable antecedents" in a tradition of works engaged in dialogue with global literature and making original contributions to that dialogue.

Latin American science fiction is frequently characterized as more political than that written in the North. This is a particularly apt distinction in the nineteenth century, when Latin American sf tends to reflect a more concrete and detailed political agenda than science fiction written in nations with longer histories of political independence and stability. Writers of early Latin American sf were often intimately involved in the process of deciding the future course of their nations, and they used the nascent genre not just to circulate their ideas in the public arena, but to show their countrymen and women their view of the present reality and their vision of a better, more modern one to come. This is not to say that the science fiction of Northern writers such as Bellamy or Wells did not promote specific political agendas, but that their agendas were not as dependent, for example, on a ceasefire this month so that the new president could take office, or a vote for the right candidate in the next elections to prevent the worst sort of military rule, or the expansion of transportation and communication networks so that the nation could function as a unified whole.

Even in subgenres with less overt political content than the relatively popular utopias and dystopias, Latin Americans gave greater emphasis in their texts to reflections on politically charged issues of national identity and national composition. This is most consistently demonstrated in representations of nationality, race, and social class or profession in Latin American works. Many character types that have since become stock players in the global science fiction megatext—such as the scientist, the scientist's assistant, or the cicerone to an alien environment—first appeared in nineteenth-century sf. In early Latin American science fiction, however, a prominent role also is played by the anti-scientific character, inevitably a figure inimical to the social, scientific, or political progress of the nation, who must be opposed or educated by the hero of the piece. Foreign characters have long been used to represent the other, the exotic, the strange, but in Latin American sf the figure of the foreigner is accompanied by more political baggage, as characters' nationalities reflect an author's views on international power dynamics and on the ideal makeup of the national population. In the nineteenth century, the European (though rarely an Iberian) or North American character is often employed to represent authority, either the authority who can recognize and legitimize the position of Latin American nations in the world or the authority from whom power must be wrested. Characters from the United States tend to represent the applied sciences, whereas Northern Europeans typically represent the theoretical sciences or the pinnacle of culture and the arts. Finally, there are "less desirable" foreign or minority characters that represent countries and races perceived to be less developed or less "evolved" than the nineteenth-century Latin American ideal. The national origins of this lower-tier component—usually recent immigrants—vary depending on the Latin American nation and the time period. As in Northern nations, the genetic and cultural contributions of those of African or indigenous descent were, with notable exceptions, rarely valued in nineteenth-century Latin America or in its science fiction, but the question of what to do about these groups was more pressing in relatively unpopulated Latin American nations whose national composition was considered "uneugenic" by Northerners. These character dynamics have changed markedly in more recent Latin American sf, though distinctions between those from central nations and those from the periphery usually still hold.

The most common characterizations of Latin American science fiction have long been that it is "soft" rather than "hard," and that it is more dependent than Northern sf on strategies of the fantastic and magic realism. While strong cases can be made for these generalizations, it is important to qualify them with a comparison to trends in Northern sf, with insights from contemporary critics, and in light of the extended perspective afforded by a consideration of nineteenth-century texts. The thorny issue of genre delimitations has been discussed in the introduction to this volume. The "softness" of Latin American sf is perhaps best described as "less true than might be assumed" (Bell and Molina-Gavilán 14). There have been periods in U.S. and European science fiction in which content/plot or the social sciences were emphasized over the traditional hard science approach, most notably during the Campbell years in the 1940s and the New Wave movement in the mid-1960s. An examination of the complete panorama of the genre in Latin America reveals that, like Northern sf, Latin American sf also varies according to local and global literary trends, scientific and technological developments, and the national and international mood of the time. Much of the science fiction produced in Latin America in the nineteenth century falls distinctly toward the hard end of the spectrum. Most of the writers in question had either a professional scientific background or a strong working knowledge of the sciences. Scientific didacticism is if anything more prominent in nineteenth-century Latin American sf than in Northern sf, because Latin American writers felt it was their duty to educate and inform their compatriots, in order to encourage the sort of scientific mindset that would spur sluggish national progress. At the turn of the twenty-first century, the personal computer and the Internet are somewhat diminishing the "multitemporal heterogeneity" of Latin America by providing increased access to cutting-edge science (García Canclini 47). This has undoubtedly contributed to the inclusion of "harder" elements in the works of some contemporary Latin American writers.

With the possible exceptions of Argentina and the River Plate region, the texts from the time period discussed in this book were not foundation stones for national sf traditions in their respective countries. Eighteenth, nineteenth, and even early twentieth-century works of Latin American sf had little if any influence on Latin American sf writers of subsequent generations because the earlier works had virtually disappeared. This occurred for various reasons: the condemnation of such works by the Inquisition, their limited distribution in periodicals or monographs, and the extremely local nature of some texts. Lately, however, these retrolabeled early works of Latin American sf seem to be coming into their own. They are now becoming valued as reflections of Latin American attitudes toward science, literature, national identity, and other sociocultural issues of their times. And they are, at long last, becoming appreciated as evidence of the roots of Latin American participation in the sf genre.

At last count there are over ninety works of Latin American science fiction, from eleven different countries, published before 1920. I do not claim that this clustering of texts constitutes a wave of Latin American science fiction in and of itself, but suggest that these works are evidence of Latin American participation in the global wave of early science fiction. Bell and Molina-Gavilán are right to characterize our authors as having "no particular commitment to the genre," and they are equally correct in saying that there is "no cohesive science fiction tradition" in Latin America in these years ("Introduction" 4). Most of these authors wrote in many genres, literary and otherwise, and did not identify themselves primarily as writers in the science-fictional vein. They were all at least cognizant of the sf tradition, however, and some were actively engaged with the works and mores of the sf tradition. These writers may not have been aware of each other's works, or of the fact that together they were establishing a pattern of Latin American participation in the genre, but they were most certainly aware of the "bonds of kinship" between their texts and those of writers in the North (Stableford, *Scientific Romance* 4). Taking these early authors and texts into account, it becomes clear that science fiction is more firmly anchored in Latin American literary and cultural history than has previously been recognized. The genre should be seen not as just a space-age or computer-age phenomenon in Latin America, but as literature that has evolved over time, literature that has been adapted by Latin Americans to reflect their perspectives, to say what "could not, perhaps, have been expressed in any other way" (Holmberg, *Nic-Nac* 186).

CHRONOLOGY LATIN AMERICAN SCIENCE FICTION THROUGH 1920

The following chronology covers the science fiction published between the years 1775 through c. 1920 in all Latin American countries. If a country is not represented, I do not know of works of proto- or early science fiction published there. As discussed in the introduction, I have chosen to err on the side of inclusivity in establishing selection criteria.

This chronology is intended for use in conjunction with the bibliography of primary texts, which provides more complete reference information. Multiple bibliographical entries are provided for texts that can be more difficult to locate due to age, rarity, or length (i.e., shorter works published in periodicals and anthologies). Whenever possible, bibliographical information has been taken directly from the first or best recent edition of the text itself. Other sources are listed below. I would welcome notice of pertinent additions or corrections.

The point of departure for this chronology is the excellent "Chronology of Latin American Science Fiction, 1775–2005" by Yolanda Molina-Gavilán, Andrea Bell, Miguel Ángel Fernández-Delgado, M. Elizabeth Ginway, Luis Pestarini, and Juan Carlos Toledano Redondo published in *Science Fiction Studies* (No. 103, Vol. 34.3, November 2007). I am not only indebted to this and other publications by these six scholars, but to the generous aid of many of them, in particular Andrea Bell (Chilean sf), Miguel Ángel Fernández-Delgado (Mexican sf), M. Elizabeth Ginway (Brazilian sf), and Luis Pestarini (Argentine sf). Personal communication with the following scholars also has been invaluable: Roberto de Sousa Causo, Josefina Ludmer, Iván Molina Jiménez, Braulio Tavares, and Omar Vega. Additional written sources include: Abraham's "Las utopías argentinas en el período 1850–1950," Cano's *Intermitente recurrencia*, Causo's *Ficção científica, fantasia e horror no Brasil 1875–1950*, the digital database *Memoria Chilena* of the National Library of Chile,[1] Larson's *Fantasy and Imagination in the Mexican Narrative*, Ludmer's *The Corpus Delicti*, Molina Jiménez's "La polémica de *El problema* (1899), de Máximo Soto Hall," Tavares's *Fantastic, Fantasy and Science Fiction Literature Catalog*, Trujillo Muñoz's *Biografías del futuro* and *El futuro en llamas*. For my own part, archival work, WorldCat, and web searches have contributed additional titles and data.

ARGENTINA

1816	Valdés, Antonio José (originally anon.). "Delirio"
1850	Sarmiento, Domingo Faustino. *Argirópolis*
1865	Gorriti, Juana Manuela. "Quien escucha, su mal oye: Confidencia de una confidencia"
1875	Holmberg, Eduardo Ladislao. *Dos partidos en lucha: Fantasía científica*
	———. *Viaje maravilloso del señor Nic-Nac*
1876	Alcántara, J.M. de. "Buenos Aires en el año 4000"
	Gorriti, Juana Manuela. "Yerbas y alfileres"
1877	Cané, Miguel. "Las armonías de la luz"
1879	Holmberg, Eduardo Ladislao. "Horacio Kalibang o Los autómatas"
	Sioen, Achilles. *Buenos Aires en el año 2080: Historia verosímil*
1880	Olivera, Carlos. "El hombre de la levita gris"
1881	Monsalve, Carlos. "De un mundo á otro"
	———. "Historia de un paraguas"
	Waleis, Raúl. (pseud. of Luis V. Varela). *El doctor Whuntz: Fantasía*
1883	Olivera, Carlos. "Los muertos a hora fija (Revelaciones de un médico)"
	———. "Fantasmas"
1884	Holmberg, Eduardo Ladislao (orig. publ. under the pseud. Ladislao Kaillitz). "Filigranas de cera"
	Monsalve, Carlos. "El hombre de piedra"
1891	Ezcurra, Eduardo de. *Buenos Aires en el siglo XXX*
1893	Popper, Julio. *Atlanta: Proyecto para la fundación de un pueblo marítimo en Tierra del Fuego*
1901	Cione, Otto Miguel. "La atrevida operación del doctor Orts"
1904	Vera y González, Enrique. *La estrella del sur (a través del porvenir)*
1906	Lugones, Leopoldo. *Las fuerzas extrañas* (anth.; significant rev. 1926)
1907	Bunge, Carlos Octavio. *Thespis (novelas cortas y cuentos)*
	Chiappori, Atilio. *Borderland* (anth.)
	Lynch, Benito. *1932*
1908	Dittrich, Julio O. *Buenos Aires en el 1950: Bajo el regimen socialista*
1909	Quiroule, Pierre (pseud. of Joaquín Alejo Falconnet). *Sobre la ruta de la anarquía. (Novela libertaria)*
1910	[Anon]. "La ciudad del porvenir"

1914	Quiroule, Pierre (pseud. of Joaquín Alejo Falconnet). *La ciudad anarquista americana; obra de construccion revolucionaria con el plano de la ciudad libertaria*
	Soiza Reilly, Juan José de. *La ciudad de los locos*
1915	Holmberg, Eduardo Ladislao. *Olimpio Pitango de Monalia*
1917	Rojas, Ricardo. *La psiquina*
1918	Angelici, Pedro. *Homúculus*

BOLIVIA

c. 1920	Zamudio, Adela. "El vértigo"

BRAZIL

1857	Macedo, Joaquim Manuel de. "O fim do mundo"
1862	Santos, Joaquim Felício dos. "A história do Brasil escrita pelo Dr. Jeremias no ano de 2862"
1868–72	Santos, Joaquim Felício dos. *Páginas da história do Brasil escripta no anno de 2000*
1869	Macedo, Joaquim Manuel de. *A luneta mágica*
1875	Zaluar, Augusto Emílio. *O Doutor Benignus*
1882	Assis, Joaquim Maria Machado de. "O Imortal"
1893	Azevedo, Aluísio. "Demônios"
1899	Freitas, Emília. *A rainha do ignoto: Romance psicológico*
1909	Barnsley, Godofredo Emerson. *São Paulo no Anno 2000, ou, Regeneração Nacional (Chronica da sociedade brasileira futura)*

CHILE

1829	Egaña, Juan. *Ocios filosoficos y poéticos, en la quinta de las delicias*
1875	Tallman, Benjamín. *¡Una vision del porvenir!, o, El espejo del mundo en el año de 1975*
1877	Miralles, Francisco (orig. publ. under the pseud. Saint Paul). *Desde Júpiter: Curioso viaje de un santiaguino magnetizado*

COLOMBIA

1896	Silva, José Asunción. "Futura" (poem)
1905	Acosta de Samper, Soledad. "Bogotá en el año 2000"

COSTA RICA

1920	Gagini, Carlos. *La caída del águila: (novela)*

CUBA

1875	Calcagno, Francisco. *Historia de un muerto y noticias del otro mundo* [2nd ed. titled *Historia de un muerto: Meditación sobre las ruinas de un hombre*]
1888	Calcagno, Francisco. *En busca del eslabón; historia de monos*
1920	Planas y Saínz, Juan Manuel. *La corriente del golfo*

GUATEMALA

1899	Soto Hall, Máximo. *El problema*

MÉXICO

1775	Rivas, Fray Manuel Antonio de. "Sizigias y cuadraturas lunares ajustadas al meridiano de Mérida de Yucatán por un anctítona o habitador de la luna, y dirigidas al bachiller don Ambrosio de Echeverría, entonador de kyries funerales en la parroquia del Jesús de dicha ciudad, y al presente profesor de logarítmica en el pueblo de Mama de la península de Yucatán, para el año del Señor de 1775"[2]
1810	[Anon]. "Cuento" [also republished as "Narración interplanetaria"][3]
1844	Fósforos-Cerillos (may be pseud. of Sebastián Camacho Zulueta or José Joaquín Mora). "México en el año 1970"
1849	Del Castillo Lenard, Gerónimo. "Gacetín de Mérida, Capital del Bajo Yucatán. (Año I, Dia 30, Hora II.) Enero 30 de 1949"[4]
1861	Pizarro, Nicolás. *El monedero*
1862	Nepomuceno Adorno, Juan. "El remoto porvenir"
1870	Altamirano, Ignacio Manuel. *La Navidad en las montañas*
1872	Castera, Pedro. "Un viaje celeste"
1890	Castera, Pedro. *Querens*
	———. "Rosas y fresas"
1895	Nervo, Amado. "La diablesa"
1898	Natalis (possible pseud. of Amado Nervo). "Cuentos de los siglos futuros: Las guerras y los ejércitos," "Cuentos del porvenir: El periodismo en la antiguedad," "Cuentos del porvenir: El interés en el dinero"[5]
	Nervo, Amado. "La última guerra" [exact date uncertain, 1906 at latest]
1899	Nervo, Amado. *El donador de almas*

1900	Barrios de los Ríos, José María. "El buque negro" [exact date uncertain, 1908 at latest]
1904	Nervo, Amado. "La literatura lunar y la habitabilidad de los satélites" (lecture)
1905	Nervo, Amado. "Astros" and "Yo estaba en el espacio" (poems)
1906	Nervo, Amado. "Dentro de cincuenta años: Diálogos hipotéticos"
	———. "La última diosa (cuento absurdo)"
1909	Nervo, Amado. *Ellos* [including "Las varitas de virtud," "Las nubes," "La última diosa (cuento absurdo)," "Cien años de sueño"]
1910	Toro, Carlos. "El dieciocho de mayo"[6]
1911	Cuevas, Alejandro. "El aparato del Doctor Tolimán"
1912	Nervo, Amado. "El resucitador y el resucitado"
	———. "La serpiente que se muerde la cola"
1917	Guzmán, Martín Luis. "Cómo acabó la guerra [en 1917]"
	Torri, Julio. "La conquista de la Luna" and "Era un país pobre"
	Nervo, Amado. "El diamante de la inquietud"
	———. "El gran viaje" (poem)
1918	Nervo, Amado. "El sexto sentido"
	———. "Amnesia" [between 1916–18]
1919	Urzaiz (Rodríguez), Eduardo. *Eugenia: Esbozo novelesco de costumbres futuras*
1921	Nervo, Amado. *Cuentos misteriosos* [including "Diana y Eros (cuento astronómico)," "Los congelados," "El país en que la lluvia era luminosa"]

PERÚ

1843	Portillo, Julián M. del. "Lima de aquí a cien años"
1904	Palma, Clemente. "La última rubia: Cuento futuro"
1910	Palma, Clemente. *Crónicas del Halley: El día trágico*

URUGUAY

1898	Piria, Francisco. *El socialismo triunfante: Lo que será mi país dentro de 200 años*
1907	Quiroga, Horacio. "El mono ahorcado"
	———. "El almohadón de plumas"
1909	Fragoso Lima, S. (pseud. of Horacio Quiroga). "El mono que asesinó" [sometimes "El mono que asesinaba"]

1910	Fragoso Lima, S. (pseud. of Horacio Quiroga). *El hombre artificial*
	Quiroga, Horacio. "El retrato"
1920	Quiroga, Horacio. "El salvaje"
1927	Quiroga, Horacio. "El vampiro"
1935	Quiroga, Horacio. *Más allá* (anth.)

NOTES

The original Spanish or Portuguese has been provided for all titles of works, for passages including key terms (particularly scientific or technical ones), whenever translation issues arise, and for a number of longer passages. All translations are my own unless otherwise indicated. The orthography in primary sources may vary from modern usage, as citations are taken from the earliest available edition of each work (editions used are indicated in the bibliography). Emphases in citations are present in the original unless otherwise indicated.

INTRODUCTION

1. As Brian Stableford writes in the entry on "Proto Science Fiction" in *The Encyclopedia of Science Fiction*, "Hugo Gernsback clearly believed that he was merely attaching a name to a genre which already existed" (965). Gernsback's "scientifiction" genre label had become "science fiction" by 1929. Like Stableford, I reserve the term "proto science fiction" for pre-nineteenth-century works. For texts written in the nineteenth century through 1926 I employ terms such as "early science fiction," "science-fictional," and "belonging to the science fiction tradition."

2. Gernsback was not the first to recognize the existence of an sf tradition; nineteenth- and early twentieth-century writers and readers of science-fictional texts were well aware of the "loose bonds of kinship" of these texts to others. What Stableford has written of scientific romance in Britain holds true as well for science fiction written in other Northern countries and in Latin America prior to 1926:

> What entitles us to think of scientific romances as a kind is not a set of classificatory characteristics which demarcate them as members of a set, but loose bonds of kinship which are only partly inherent in the imaginative exercises themselves and partly in the minds of authors and readers who recognise in them some degree of common cause. What binds together the authors and books to be discussed here is mainly that they were perceived by the contemporary audience as similar to one another and different from others. (*Scientific Romance* 4)

3. Geographical distinctions commonly used among Latin American(ist)s may require some explanation. The term "periphery" (as opposed to the "center") is a virtual substitute for denominations such as "third-world" or

"developing" regions; note, for example, the title of a recent anthology of sf from Mexico: *Visions from the Periphery: Anthology of Mexican Science Fiction* [*Visiones periféricas: Antología de la ciencia ficción mexicana*] (ed. Fernández-Delgado). Additionally, my capitalization of "North" and "Northern" throughout this book is a deliberate effort to designate the region that has historically exercised the greatest political, cultural, and sf genre influence on Latin America. Most often this region includes the United States, Great Britain, France, Germany, and perhaps Russia and excludes Spain, Portugal, and usually Italy.

4. I am referring to the local reader base. Little science fiction from Latin America has been translated or reaches an international audience. A notable exception to this rule is the 2003 anthology *Cosmos Latinos*, edited by Andrea Bell and Yolanda Molina-Gavilán. Internet magazines and fanzines such as the Argentina-based *Axxón* also make Latin American sf available to national and international readers of Spanish or Portuguese.

5. Although the situation has improved in recent years, in his 2001 introduction to *Visiones periféricas*, the Mexican writer and critic Miguel Ángel Fernández-Delgado is still defending Mexican sf against the expectation of charges of "the *malinchismo* that could be assumed in the cultivators of a literary movement that came from outside" (14). *Malinchismo* is a phenomenon described most famously by Octavio Paz in his essay, "The Sons of La Malinche" [Los hijos de la Malinche]; one aspect of *malinchismo* is the use of the "contemptuous adjective *malinchista* . . . to denounce all those who have been corrupted by foreign influences" (86).

6. Gabriel Trujillo Muñoz dates the change of fortune in the reception and the writing of Mexican science fiction from the 1968 publication of Carlos Olvera's *Mexicans in Space* [*Mejicanos en el espacio*], and he sees a similar trend in the rest of Latin America at around the same time:

> [With *Mexicans in Space*] for the first time in this genre, the future is not a superior stage of human evolution, but rather an avalanche of prejudices and complexes shared by all with humor and without shame.
>
> Since the 1970s, national [Mexican] science fiction, like Latin American sf, is taking new paths. Social criticism, a libertarian spirit, stylistic experimentation, and the search for less obvious themes are transforming the paradigms of the future visualized by the youngest creators. (*Biografías* 346)

The more recent phenomenon of retrolabeling the earliest works of Latin American sf is another sign of the increasing acceptance of the legitimacy of the genre there. For more on retrolabeling and on recent developments in the field, see my "Back to the Future."

7. González Echevarría defines hegemonic discourse as "one backed by a discipline, or embodying a system, that offers the most commonly accepted description of humanity and accounts for the most widely held beliefs of the intelligentsia" (41).

8. Ginway has also described elsewhere the unique perspective that science fiction written in the periphery provides on the genre and the cultures of both the first and the third worlds:

> The production of a genre like science fiction in the Third World narrates a 'displacement,' or a shuttling between center and periphery. Thus, instead of condemning Brazilian science fiction as a simulacrum or cultural borrowing, it could be seen as uncentered and contingent, a useful tool for deconstructing literary and historical narratives and re-shaping the boundaries between national and international literatures. (*Brazilian* 34–35)

9. My discussion of Ryman's ideas is based on my own notes taken at his talk, "In Praise of Science Fiction." The *Journal of the Fantastic in the Arts* has since published a revised version of this speech, titled "The Science Fiction Dream."

10. Fernández-Delgado states that this mis-characterization of science fiction as magic realism and magic realism as science fiction in Latin American texts by Gunn is part of a larger phenomenon, calling it a result of widely held "prejudices . . . rooted in the mindset of the societies of the developed countries, and from which a considerable portion of their researchers are not exempt" ("Discurso").

11. Ortiz subsequently cites Verne, Flammarion, Poe, and Hoffmann as important influences on Holmberg's work, though he identifies these writers only with the fantastic ("Transition" 84).

12. See my "First Wave." In Latin American science fiction, as in Northern science fiction, it is common practice to talk of "waves," "golden ages," and "booms" when discussing the trajectory of the genre, although these terms are usually applied to time periods such as the late 1950s or the turn of the millennium. Considering Latin American science fiction as part of a larger phenomenon, we can locate our texts of early Latin American sf within the leading edge of what Suvin has termed the Euro-Mediterranean sf tradition's "fin-de-siècle cluster (ca. 1870–1910)" (87).

1. DISPLACEMENT IN SPACE AND TIME

1. While some of these texts were claimed for the genre earlier (*Nic-Nac* by Goligorsky in 1968, "Mexico 1970" by Staples in 1987), they have been consistently cited as foundational Latin American sf texts only in more recent years.

The bibliography in the entry on "Latin America" by Mauricio-José Schwarz and Braulio Tavares in the second edition of *The Encyclopedia of Science Fiction* lists *Brazil 2000* and *Nic-Nac*. All three texts are included in the important chronology compiled by Yolanda Molina-Gavilán et al. in *Chasqui* in 2000 and in their revised and updated chronology published in English in *Science Fiction Studies*. See my "Back to the Future" for more on the vagaries of the textual histories of these and other works of early Latin American sf.

2. A number of other works that have been retrolabeled as early Latin American sf are utopian in nature and/or involve displacement in space or time. *Syzygies and Lunar Quadratures* [*Sizigias y cuadraturas lunares*] (New Spain/Mexico, 1775) by Manuel Antonio de Rivas (dates unknown) contains a fantastic voyage to the moon; this text has been discussed by González Casanova, Larson, Fernández-Delgado and Dziubinskyj. Another work that centers around displacement in space is Francisco Miralles's (1837–date unknown) *From Jupiter: The Curious Voyage of a Magnetized Man from Santiago* [*Desde Júpiter: Curioso viaje de un santiaguino magnetizado*] (Chile, 1877), which has been studied by Andrea Bell. Juan Nepomuceno Adorno's (1807–80) "The Distant Future" [El remoto porvenir] (Mexico, 1862/1882) describes a utopian future for humanity; excerpts translated into English are in the *Cosmos Latinos* anthology (ed. Andrea Bell and Yolanda Molina-Gavilán). The anonymous text "Delirium" [Delirio] (Argentina, 1816), since attributed to Antonio José Valdés (Pestarini, "Delirio"), is the tale of his contemporary Buenos Aires magically modernized by the giant Tremebundo. *Argirópolis* (Argentina, 1850) is something of a long political pamphlet in which Domingo Faustino Sarmiento (1811–88) outlines his plan for creating a more utopian society in Argentina's near future. Perhaps the best-known Latin American work that discusses displacement in space and foregrounds Latin America as a historically privileged setting for "first contact" with an alien species is Amado Nervo's poem "The Great Journey" [El gran viaje] (Mexico, 1917), in which he asks:

> Who, in a not too distant future, will be
> the Christopher Columbus of another planet?
> Who, with mighty machine, will succeed in
> exploring the ocean
> of ether . . . (lines 1–5)
>
> ¿Quién será, en un futuro no lejano,
> el Cristóbal Colón de algún planeta?
> ¿Quién logrará, con máquina potente,
> sondar el oceano
> del éter . . .

3. The capabilities of the science-fictional utopia for complex temporal negotiations between past, present, and future are elucidated by Moylan (25–26).

4. The identity of Fósforos-Cerillos has been variously posited as either Sebastián Camacho y Zulueta (Fernández-Delgado in the *Chasqui* and *SFS* chronologies) or José Joaquín Mora (Trujillo Muñoz, "El futuro en llamas" 12). Lacking definitive proof, I base my characterization of the writer on the content of "Mexico 1970" and on the fact that a number of other articles in the same issue of *El Liceo Mexicano* on sociocultural and scientific themes are signed "Fósforos," "Fósforos-Cerillos," or "F.C." I take this to indicate a certain degree of involvement on the part of this writer in the journal and in the publication mission proclaimed in its introduction. "Mexico 1970" is signed "Fósforos" at the end of the article in *El Liceo Mexicano*, and its author is listed as "Fósforos-Cerillos" in the index to the issue.

5. I am indebted to Paul Alkon's discussions of the interplay of metafictional, realistic, and fantastic elements in his *Origins of Futuristic Fiction* (124–25, 193–206).

6. Here Alkon is summarizing and building upon ideas from Bronislaw Baczko's analysis of Mercier's *L'An 2440* [translated in the United States as *Memoirs of the Year Two Thousand Five Hundred*] in *Lumières de l'utopie* (165n22).

7. There is some vacillation in the utopian portrayal of the estranged society in the case of *Nic-Nac*. My characterization of Holmberg's representation of the relationship between Europe and Argentina is based on another of his texts in addition to *Nic-Nac*: the 1875 science-fictional work *Two Factions Struggle for Life*, discussed in chapter 2.

8. See Burns (*History* chapter 4, particularly 158–61 and 168–71, from which information for the overview in this paragraph is taken) for a more detailed description of the revolution in Brazilian transportation and communication in this period as well as for discussions of progress versus modernization and development versus growth in Brazil.

9. I am indebted to Braulio Tavares and to the staff of the Biblioteca Nacional in Rio de Janeiro for their help in acquiring copies of over a hundred pages of the manuscript.

10. This passage was chosen from a number of possibilities because it provides fairly clear evidence of the influence of Mercier on Felício dos Santos. A footnote in chapter 1 of Mercier's *Memoirs of the Year Two Thousand Five Hundred* [*L'An Deux Mille Quatre Cent Quarante*] reads: "The whole kingdom is in Paris. France resembles a ricketty child, whose juices seem only to encrease [*sic*] and nourish the head, while the body remains weak and emaciated" [Tout le royaume est dans Paris. Le royaume ressemble à un enfant rachitique. Tous

les sucs montent à sa tête et la grossissent . . . mais le reste du corps est diaphane et exténué] (4; 82).

11. Pedro II was one of the few rulers in his time, and the only Brazilian, elected to one of the eight places reserved for foreigners in the Academy of Sciences of Paris. The French astronomer and geographer Emmanuel Liais (1826–1900), who carried out extensive research in Brazil and was director of the Astronomical Observatory of Rio de Janeiro in 1871, writes of the emperor's "vast scientific knowledge," and used data from astronomical observations carried out by Dom Pedro at São Cristóvão in order to complete his own work (Liais 142). Felício dos Santos portrays Liais as praising Pedro II's scientific acumen in exchange for monetary support (*Brazil 2000* Feb. 21, 1869).

12. Phase two of *Brazil 2000* continues to employ the mediated history text brought back from the year 2000. The text now includes an account of Pedro II's visit to the Brazil of the future, but is filtered, as usual, through the nineteenth-century editor and others.

13. I have changed this quotation from the plural to the singular. Originally it referred to both Joaquim Felício dos Santos and his *Brazil 2000* and to another text by Justiniano José da Rocha that cannot at present be located.

14. The diversity of Holmberg's publications and his work as a scientific generalist at a time when specialization was increasingly valued is explained by Luis Holmberg as a necessary sacrifice during that generation in a country of "little scientific culture" (140–41). His reasoning shares a number of similarities with Nancy Stepan's arguments against attempts by modern Latin American nations to reproduce the structures of Northern scientific research systems in the final chapter of her *Beginnings of Brazilian Science*.

15. In *Nic-Nac* the inhabitants of Mars are referred to as "Marcialitas" [Martialites], a nod to the warlike tendencies of some of the inhabitants. As these inhabitants appear only in a few chapters of the tale, we will use the more standard "Martians" to avoid confusion.

16. The two authorities mentioned, Mr. Gould and Dr. Uriarte, were public figures in Argentina at the time. Benjamin Gould (1824–96) was an American astronomer and the first director of the National Observatory, established at Córdoba in 1871. Dr. José María Uriarte was the first director (1863–76) of San Buenaventura, a mental institution in Buenos Aires (subsequently renamed "José T. Borda National Hospital" [Hospital Nacional José T. Borda]; this asylum is featured in the award-winning Argentine sf film *Man Facing Southeast* [*Hombre mirando al sudeste*] [1986]).

17. Camille Flammarion (1842–1925) was a French scientist, popularizer of science, and sometime Spiritist. *Lumen* was a dramatization of ideas he had first expounded in several nonfictional books (Stableford, "Introduction" xiv).

In the tale, Lumen is the spirit of a recently deceased Frenchman who describes the edifying interplanetary travels of his spirit to his former student, Quaerens. But while Flammarion uses Spiritism to give his title character greater authority, Holmberg uses it both to claim greater authority for Nic-Nac and simultaneously to call Nic-Nac's authority into question. Lumen speaks to his student from a higher plane of existence, but Holmberg brings Nic-Nac back to Earth to tell his tale from our terrestrial, material plane, where Nic-Nac faces charges that his tale is the product of hallucination or of a deranged mind. While Flammarion's belief in and defense of Spiritism eventually damaged his reputation in scientific circles, Holmberg continued his work as a respected scientist throughout his career. Pagés Larraya writes of Holmberg's attitude toward Spiritism: "Although [Holmberg] may not have been a militant adept of these practices and even satirizes them . . . it is common knowledge that they interested him greatly" (42). Holmberg's treatment of Spiritism is less satirical in other works of fiction, but he uses Spiritism as a literary device in *Nic-Nac*.

18. In 1878 in *The Argentine Naturalist*, Holmberg compared certain scientists unfavorably to Verne: "Those men of science, who keep themselves completely isolated from the world that surrounds them without reaching them, are certainly not those who pour the heat and the light of the truth onto the populace" (qtd. in Luis Holmberg 136). Luis Holmberg identifies both Burmeister and "the German professors Sarmiento brought to form the Academy of Sciences in Córdoba" as being guilty of sundry acts of inaccessibility in the eyes of his father (139).

19. New discoveries and retrolabeling of works of utopian/dystopian science fiction from these "generations" in Latin America preclude detailed discussion of all of them here. Tales of utopias displaced in space are now much less common, but see particularly Emília Freitas's *The Queen of Incognito* [*A rainha do Ignoto*] (Brazil, 1899) and Eduardo Ladislao Holmberg's *Olimpio Pitango of Monalia* [*Olimpio Pitango de Monalia*] (Argentina, 1915).

20. Lamarckian hereditarian thought was not discredited for decades after our texts were written. As Stepan says, "The centrality of Mendelism to our modern genetics has made it easy to overlook the continued vitality of non-Mendelian ideas in medicine and science until well into the 1940s" (*Hour* 65).

21. A major flaw in such thinking (reflected in these early Latin American utopias, which depended heavily on eugenic solutions) was that it diverted attention from far more pressing problems. As Stepan says, in Latin America "the hereditary aspects of poverty and disease were minor in comparison with the economic and political ones" (*Hour* 101).

22. This saying was coined by the Argentine statesman Juan Bautista Alberdi (1810–84) in his influential work *Bases and Points of Departure for the*

Political Organization of the Argentine Republic [*Bases y puntos de partida para la organización política de la República Argentina*] (1852).

23. Darío mentions Ezcurra briefly in his autobiography (Rubén Darío, *La vida de Rubén Darío escrita por él mismo* [Alicante, Spain: Biblioteca Virtual Miguel de Cervantes, 2000] XLIII), and a fragment of a letter from Ezcurra to Darío exists in the National Library of Chile. Lucio V. López (1848–94) is best known as the author of *The Great Village* [*La gran aldea*] (1884).

24. See Rock 157–61 for an overview of the Argentine situation in this period, including the statistics that follow. The cumulative effects of the financial crises were rising unemployment and falling wages in Buenos Aires; the impact this had on immigration to Argentina is staggering. A net gain of 220,000 immigrants in 1889 shrank to only 30,000 in 1890 and became a net loss of 30,000 in 1891.

25. Ezcurra was not alone in his literary reflections on the national situation, though he was the only writer to do so in science-fictional mode. The year 1891 also saw the publication of the first three works of the aptly named "Stock Exchange Series" [ciclo de La Bolsa] (Oviedo 160).

26. Such juxtapositions of the nineteenth and thirtieth centuries outside the literary project of Andros and Filos are constant throughout the text. This technique is somewhat reminiscent of *Brazil 2000*, though without the presence of a time traveler they are rather more forced. Other metafictional techniques employed in *Brazil 2000* such as the footnote and the citation of invented authorities are also present in *Century XXX* (see 34, 106 for examples).

27. Stepan's study of eugenics in Latin America centers around the years in which eugenics societies first appeared there (1918), but she also cites evidence of the circulation of eugenics-related ideas much earlier. Eugenics was discussed in Argentina as early as the 1880s (Stepan, *Hour* 35n2); the three science-fictional texts examined in this section support this assertion.

28. The population of Buenos Aires doubled during the 1880s to reach half a million inhabitants. The foreign-born made up 19.8 percent of the population of Buenos Aires province when the 1869 census was taken; this percentage had increased to 30.8 percent in the 1895 census (Rock 153, 141).

29. This is not to say that there was no racism in Argentina. The country has a long national history of privileging Anglo-Saxon immigrants and avoiding mixing with nonwhite races. Stepan calls Argentina (versus Brazil and Mexico) "the most conventionally racist in its eugenic ideology" (*Hour* 139), and she states that, unlike Mexicans, "Argentinians condemned racial and cultural intermixture as threats to the unity of an Argentine nationality" (106). The only reference to racial or ethnic difference in *Century XXX* is in the name of the women's charitable association, "The Daughters of Mandinga" [Las Hijas de

Mandinga]. Members of the association are characterized as the antithesis of Parelia, that paragon of womanhood, and a footnote pretends to give the etymology of the term Mandinga as "From *man*, man, and *dinga*, boat" [De *man*, hombre, y *dinga*, embarcación] (206n1). Thus we have literally "man just off the boat," or newcomer/immigrant/upstart, but the evocation of West Africa is also clearly present.

30. Moylan traces the "sibling" relationship between the eutopia/positive utopia and the dystopia/negative utopia; both imagine a "coherent whole" and drive the reader either toward or away from the reality depicted (see especially xiii, 127, 129, 133).

It should also be noted that the use of the term "perfection" throughout this chapter reflects its use by the authors themselves. I am not defining a utopian society as one that "must be perfect and *therefore* unrealizable" (see Sargent, "Three Faces" 6).

31. As part of this discussion on education and work, Ezcurra calls the middle classes those who "best preserved the type of the species" [conservaban mejor el tipo de su especie], as long as they avoided the inappropriate temptation of "envy and imitation of the upper classes" (279).

32. Little information is available about Barnsley's life. I am grateful to Godfrey Barnsley, his grandson, for virtually all biographical data, and I am indebted to M. Elizabeth Ginway for providing contact with Mr. Barnsley.

33. Alberto Santos Dumont (1873–1932) is widely cited by Brazilians as the first to solve the problem of heavier-than-air, unassisted flight, disputing the claim of the Wright brothers.

34. This description contains a clear reference to the ending of H. G. Wells's *When the Sleeper Wakes* (1899). At the end of Wells's novel the Sleeper is engaged in an airplane battle and finds himself falling out of the sky, though the reader never learns when and where he lands.

35. *Century XXX* is not a true tale of the far distant future. Like the texts set in the year 2000, it can be viewed as containing the seeds of change, as Ezcurra used the wide gap between the years 3000 and 1891 as a satirical disconnect between two time periods that he was equating allegorically.

36. Dr. Oswaldo Cruz had had great success at eradicating yellow fever in the Rio de Janeiro area by 1906 (Burns, *History* 272). Unfortunately for Barnsley, who later contracted an ultimately fatal case of yellow fever while fishing in Mato Grosso, the disease was virtually unheard of in the cooler climate of São Paulo, and he was misdiagnosed (Godfrey Barnsley, message to the author).

37. For more on the treatment of Afro-Brazilians and Brazilian Indians in *São Paulo 2000*, see Haywood Ferreira, "Emergence" 269–70. At the crux of Barnsley's differentiation between Brazilian and Northern views on race and

racism was Brazil's use of miscegenation rather than segregation to resolve its race issues. Racism and social flexibility among the races have always functioned differently in Brazil than in the North; Barnsley's views on this topic were eminently Brazilian. Stepan's discussion of these issues is useful for understanding these differences more clearly: "'Constructive miscegenation,' it could be said, was thus as much a product of racism as its reverse," she writes (*Hour* 170).

38. As Stepan explains, in 1933–34 Italians and Latin Americans from multiple nations worked within the Latin International Federation of Eugenics Societies [Federación Internacional Latina de Sociedades de Eugenesia] to explore "commonalities" among the nations (*Hour* 189–92). "'Latinity,'" writes Stepan, "was constructed as an oppositional identity to 'Anglo-Saxonism'" (189).

39. Much of the republication of Urzaiz's works has been carried out by the press of the Universidad Autónoma de Yucatán (UADY), including several editions of *Eugenia* (of the novel's seven editions—1919, 1947, 1955, 1976, 1982, 2002, and 2006—at least three [1947, 1976, and 2002] were published by or in concert with the UADY).

40. Eugenic ideas and writings on eugenics were present in Mexico prior to World War I (Stepan, *Hour* 56, 58). However, Urzaiz was still breaking very new ground in his use of eugenic methodology in his novel. Historian Beatriz Urías Horcasitas has called *Eugenia* "one of the first manifestations of eugenics [in Mexico] during the twentieth century" (59). In contrast Amado Nervo, Urzaiz's compatriot and fellow writer of early science fiction, wrote against eugenics during this same time period, see Nervo, "Eugenesia."

41. The usual word for "eugenics" in Spanish is "eugenesia." Urzaiz's use of the term "eugenética" [eugenetics] is clearly meant to emphasize the scientific, genetic foundation of the Bureau and of his utopia.

42. Terminology and regulations surrounding the Bureau of Eugenetics suggest that Urzaiz modeled his system of obligatory, government-run reproductive service after Bellamy's system of required service in his industrial army.

43. Dziubinskyj tells us that Urzaiz was "an advocate of birth control and of access to post-secondary education for women at a time when these issues were taboo" ("Eduardo Urzaiz's *Eugenia*" 463); Urzaiz's advocacy of women's rights and women's education are also described in Urzaiz Jiménez (40), Souza de Fernández (12), and López Cortes (33–34). At the same time, Urzaiz's equality of the sexes has its limits. Women in Villautopía were scholars and doctors, but they also tended to occupy the more traditional occupations of childcare worker and waitress (working "amid pinches and flirtatious remarks"; Urzaiz

34). While all men in Villautopía have long been able to easily discern and separate carnal from romantic love, "only some superior women have been capable of this" (106).

44. Urzaiz is also conscious of Malthusian population projections, and he posits that government control of reproduction will eventually be useful in cases of overpopulation (59, 62, 148).

45. A "sanitary dictatorship" had been declared in Mexico in 1918 to promote hygiene and fight disease by Dr. José María Rodríguez, director of the national Superior Council of Health [Consejo Superior de Salubridad] (Urías Horcasitas 60).

46. Mexico is the only country in Latin America where sterilization was ever legalized, though it was legal in only one state (Veracruz), and it is unlikely any ever took place. Stepan credits the legislation to the fact that Mexican eugenicists had closer connections to U.S. scientists than did their counterparts in other Latin American countries (*Hour* 131–32). There are also two Brazilian science-fictional texts from the 1920s that advocate eugenic sterilization: *The Kingdom of Kiato* [*O Reino do Kiato*] (1922) by Rodolfo Teófilo and *The Clash of the Races; or, The Black President; An American Novel of the Year 2228* [*O choque das raças; ou, O presidente negro; romance americano do anno de 2228*] (1926) by José Bento Monteiro Lobato.

47. Later in the novel, the United States is criticized for enslaving and then segregating blacks rather than, it is to be supposed, seeking to mix them with other, superior races in the population (Urzaiz 124–25).

2. THE IMPACT OF DARWINISM

1. Not all of the concepts mentioned are purely Lamarckian, though they are often associated with him. Darwin and Lamarck did not diverge so widely in their ideas as is generally supposed, see Eiseley 199–204.

2. I would argue that there are geographic locations in Europe with strong temporal connotations, especially to the past, yet I agree that this is not so in the historically distinctive pattern of the United States.

3. *Doctor Benignus* is neither the first nor the last literary text to locate earlier stages of evolved animal and human life in the Brazilian interior. One Northern example that was well known in Latin America is Sir Arthur Conan Doyle's novel, *The Lost World* (1912). The expedition of Conan Doyle's Professor Challenger also finds the trappings of the "civilised world" on the Brazilian coast, at Pará in the north (196). But it is in the heart of the Brazilian Amazon—amid areas that are labeled on the crude, hand-drawn map included in the novel as "unexplored," "morass," and "many snakes and tarantulas"—that Challenger locates living evidence of the past: both dinosaurs and Darwin's missing link,

the ape-men (82). (This text was translated into Spanish by Eduardo Ladislao Holmberg.)

4. Although Zaluar favored the abolition of slavery, he includes virtually no mention of the influence of Africa on the formation of Brazil in this text. The location of blacks in Zaluar's racial hierarchy is based on the following passage: "There is proof today that less difference exists between a chimpanzee and a negro from Lake Albert than between the latter and Newton or Kepler" (36). Whereas Indians were seen as a symbol of Brazilianness, of what differentiated Brazil from Europe and made it unique, and were thus to be integrated into Brazilian society, African slaves were considered foreigners. They were often left out of nineteenth-century Brazilian attempts at constructing a national history (Bertol Domingues and Romero Sá 84).

5. In his book *Science Fiction, Fantasy, and Horror in Brazil 1875–1950* [*Ficção científica, fantasia e horror no Brasil*] Roberto de Sousa Causo describes *Doctor Benignus* as a tale in which science and technology are accessible only to the Brazilian elite, play only "passive" roles, and do not have a significant impact on Brazilian society (131–32, 142). Causo extends this characterization to the Brazilian sf of the nineteenth century through the 1920s and 30s, citing the absence of actual time travelers in early Brazilian science-fictional works as further evidence of this phenomenon (145). A more active role for science and technology than that posited by Causo is suggested in Zaluar's work, both by the charge to Dr. Benignus from the more advanced Sun Being to spread scientific knowledge as a route to progress, and by the culmination of the novel in the foundation of a utopian colony, the success of which depends upon scientific and technological advances. The addition of *Brazil 2000* and *São Paulo 2000* to the corpus of early Brazilian sf reveals that the genre does indeed possess time travelers and that science and technology—with regard to transportation, communication, hygiene, and more—are represented multiple times as key components in the creation of Brazilian utopias.

6. Marún quotes Domingo F. Sarmiento's diary entry of 12 August 1868 (originally quoted in Alberto Palcos, "Darwin, Sarmiento y Holmberg," *La Prensa* 25 Feb. 1945).

7. Burmeister (1807–92) did not become a supporter of Darwin's ideas on evolution until 1889, shortly before his death (Montserrat 23).

8. This narrative frame occurs on the page prior to 1, in a section titled "Dos Palabras" [Two Words].

9. Holmberg took part in his first scientific expedition at the age of twenty, under the aegis of the Argentine Scientific Society [Sociedad Científica Argentina]. At that time Río Negro (in Patagonia) was part of a relatively unknown

area of the southern lands. The region was still Indian territory and would not be claimed for the Argentine state until seven years later, as a result of Roca's Conquest of the Wilderness. Among Holmberg's other expeditions, sponsored by the Argentine government and by various scientific societies, were journeys to the northern provinces (1877); the Curá-Malal mountains (1883); Paraná, Santa Fe, and Misiones (1884–86); Chaco (1885); and Uruguay (1890).

10. These debates are surely modeled after the 1860 debate between the Darwinist T. H. Huxley and the creationist Samuel Wilberforce.

11. Holmberg uses his characters' names to typify the characters themselves and/or to allude to the contemporaries they represented in whole or in part (see Montserrat 27n18). Holmberg multiplies his own scientific authority and authorial voice via the creation of multiple semiautobiographical characters in a number of his literary texts. For a discussion of the Kaillitz-Griffritz example in *Two Factions*, see Dellepiane, "Ciencia" 474. For an expansion of this discussion to include the Holmberg-narrator, see Haywood Ferreira, "Emergence" 40–45, 58–59.

12. The political content of *Two Factions* attracted attention from Holmberg's contemporaries. Just after its publication, the author and critic Miguel Cané (1851–1905) criticized Holmberg's choice of temporal setting as too close for comfort to "the vivid memories of the violent upheaval which has agitated the republic" (Cané, "*Dos partidos*" 174). Note that the political context for *Two Factions* is the same as that for *Nic-Nac*.

13. The process of locating and confirming the status of the missing link in *Two Factions* involves a third geographical-temporal journey, that of an Argentine expedition to Africa, the place of humanity's origins, and their return with an Akka to Buenos Aires.

14. Holmberg's use of the Akka as proof of Darwin's theory of evolution should not be misinterpreted as evidence that the Argentine author and scientist espoused a teleology-driven evolutionism that rejected natural selection. Rather, this shows that Holmberg was not immune to repeating the errors of other overzealous Darwinists, who placed existing peoples "on the time scale of the fossil past" (Eiseley 277). Darwin himself used a "living taxonomic ladder" to a certain extent in formulating his hypotheses (Eiseley 288).

15. This epigraph is signed "Holmberg." Thus the fictional Kaillitz (presented by a fictionalized Holmberg) is linked to Holmberg's real-and-now-fictionalized translation.

16. The tradition extends from Holmberg and Lugones on to Horacio Quiroga (1878–1937), Jorge Luis Borges (1899–1986), and Adolfo Bioy Casares (1914–99). Although all of these authors knew (or knew of) one another, not all science-

fictional influences carried forward. Borges, clearly unaware of the contributions of Holmberg and others to the genre, called Lugones's "Yzur" the first work of science fiction in Spanish ("Prólogo" to *La estatua de sal* 12).

17. Even classifying the stories according to the categories constructed for this book is not always a clear-cut process. "An Inexplicable Phenomenon" [Un fenómeno inexplicable], for example, is an evolutionary tale, involves strange forces, and includes a double (it is discussed in chapter 3).

18. For more on the relationship between literature and science in Lugones, see Cano 110–11.

19. Poe's essay, "Eureka," is commonly acknowledged to be the model for "Cosmogony."

20. An earlier Argentine science-fictional work containing explanations of Biblical tales of origins is Carlos Monsalve's "From One World to Another" [De un mundo á otro] (1881), in which Adam and Eve are discovered to be immigrants from an overpopulated planet.

21. These concepts do not originate with Lugones but are, in the words of Conil Paz, "mere recreation—with modern scientific additions—of principles enunciated by the beloved Helena Petrovna Blavatsky in her *Secret Doctrine*, which appeared in 1888" (116).

22. Lugones specifies his divergence from the canonical sciences in "Cosmogony" (255).

23. All of the texts in *Strange Forces* have been translated by Alter-Gilbert, with the exception of "Cosmogony." Alter-Gilbert's translations tend to err on the side of the literal, and at times they are incorrect. I have used Woodruff's superior translation of "Yzur," but upon occasion he is overly figurative. Parenthetical citations in this book include the corresponding page number of the Spanish edition of *Las fuerzas extrañas*, even when the original Spanish has been omitted. Where two page numbers are given, separated by a semicolon, the first indicates the translation by Alter-Gilbert or Woodruff, respectively, and the second indicates the Spanish original. Where only one page number is given, it pertains to the Spanish edition; this indicates that I have provided my own translation. Where I have made very minor modifications to the translation, the page number of the translation is given followed by the word "modified."

24. *Sirena* is the word for "siren" and also for "mermaid" in Spanish, as "siren" once was in English. The mermaid has symbolic meanings associated with mythology but also with the New World. In the accounts of his voyages Christopher Columbus famously described seeing mermaids in the waters off the coast of the Americas.

25. This is a further example of the symbiotic relationship between Lugones's "Cosmogony" and his "Origin of the Flood." Only in "Origin of the Flood" do

we hear from such a creature, and only in "Cosmogony" is its provenance explained in detail: "The vehicle that those lunar spirits used to come to the Earth was the cone of shadow that the Earth projects on the moon, and which, during eclipses, brings us evil exhalations from that heavenly body; as the moon is a cadaver, it must not emanate life naturally" (278).

26. In his book on science fiction and the Hispanic American canon, Luis C. Cano provides an excellent discussion of the ape stories of both Lugones and Quiroga (111–25).

27. Lugones frequently employs a first-person narrator who addresses the reader directly. As Borges has written, Lugones never achieved the type of "close, intimate confidence" [confidencia íntima] with the reader of a Darío; indeed, "Lugones customarily disdained the conversion of the reader, preferring rather to intimidate him" (*Leopoldo Lugones* 20, 82). "Yzur" is an exception to this tendency toward intimidation.

28. Lugones took this concept of the ape as a devolved human directly from Blavatsky's *Key to Theosophy* (1889; Barcia 34).

29. As has been discussed earlier in this chapter with regard to *Doctor Benignus,* the African was commonly cited in the nineteenth century as an example of a less-evolved human, an unfortunate use of new scientific precepts to support older racist attitudes. In apparent acts of political correctness, both Alter-Gilbert's and Woodruff's English translations of "Yzur" omit this last comparison between Yzur and people of African descent, thus denying the reader a more complete picture of the prevalence and depth of racist attitudes at the time.

30. There are a number of commonalities between the narrators of "Yzur" and "The Tell-Tale Heart." Each man's grip on reality appears to loosen as his tale proceeds (this is admittedly more extreme in the case of Poe's narrator), and both are very desirous of convincing the reader that this is not so. Compare the overdone protestations of Lugones's narrator at the end of "Yzur" (discussed later in this section), to Poe's opening lines: "True!—nervous—very, very dreadfully nervous I had been and am; but why *will* you say that I am mad? . . . Hearken! and observe how healthily—how calmly I can tell you the whole story" (92).

31. Scari identifies Lugones's models of perversity in other works of Poe, such as "The Imp of the Perverse" and "The Black Cat" (182–83n38).

32. Due to the double meaning of *amo* as either "master" or "I love," more than one translation is possible for Yzur's final utterance. If we discard the option of "I love water" for the first sentence, the alternate translation is: "Water, master. I love my master." This would, perhaps, be the version preferred by the narrator, as it not only provides a successful scientific experiment, but also conveys Yzur's respect and forgiveness.

245

33. The publication date of 1898 is taken from the Molina-Gavilán et al. "Chronology." "The Last War" was first collected in the 1906 anthology *Souls that Pass* [*Almas que pasan*]. I have been unable to locate an earlier edition of the story. Nervo's works in general are difficult to date precisely. The data on his works listed in this book's chronology have been compiled from information given in his *Complete Works* [*Obras completas*] of 1962, as well as in Larson, the Molina-Gavilán et al. "Chronology," the catalogs of various national libraries in Latin America, and WorldCat.

34. A publication date of 1856 has traditionally been listed for "The End of the World" because this date is given by Macedo himself in the anthology *The Novels of the Weekly Paper* [*Os Romances da Semana*] (1861). The date 1856 is repeated no fewer than four times on pages 47–49 (1873 edition) of Macedo's introduction to the story, but the date 1857 is given twice on page 51, which lists the subtitle as "The End of the World in 1857." Historical information in Yeomans confirms 1857 as the correct date. (My thanks to Kris Stacy-Bates, science and technology librarian at Iowa State University, for locating this information.)

35. The expression used is "encontrei todos os bancos *rotos*" (67), playing on a double meaning: "I found all of the banks had gone into bankruptcy" ("bancarrota" and "bancos rotos" both mean "bankruptcy") and "I found all of the banks broken" ("rotos" also means "broken"). The discussion of banks in the story reflects the impact of the newly established banking sector, dominated for most of the 1850s by the Bank of Brazil, as well as the brief financial crisis of 1857.

36. The cooperation between the parties during the Period of Conciliation (1853–57) was so effective that Burns describes these years as "apolitical" (*History* 176). Macedo casts some aspersions on the spirit of this cooperation by having Martinho spy a newspaper bulletin stating, "The political parties reconciled definitively" [Conciliárão-se definitivamente os partidos politicos] at 11:00 A.M. on June 13, 1857—an hour before the comet struck (76; see also 73).

37. For more on the romantic and naturalist currents present in "Demons," see Toledo (though I disagree with a number of her genre-related statements).

38. The imaginary reverse-evolution in "Demons" may well have been inspired by Axel's dream in chapter 32 of Verne's *Journey to the Centre of the Earth*. My thanks to Arthur Evans for bringing the similarities to my attention.

39. If the original publication date of 1898 is correct, the Spanish American War (April–August 1898) may have had some influence on the composition of "The Last War." For a discussion of the impact of the war on Spanish American modernists, see Durán 77–78.

40. "The Last War" is not the only text in which Nervo adopts a Danilevsky-type vision of cyclical history. In the 1898 text "Tales from Future Centuries: Wars and Armies" [Cuentos de los siglos futuros: Las guerras y los ejércitos], written under the pseudonym "Natalis," Nervo states that the past (i.e., present) habit of marrying within one's own "tribe" leads to a process in which "races formed thusly remained so for centuries, degenerating in the end and giving way to other new races" (481). In the short piece "The 'Monkey-Man'" [El 'mono-hombre'], Nervo extrapolates what might happen if such beings did exist: "Only that if one day one of those anthropoids happened to be a little more intelligent than the others, rebellion was certain. . . . We would return to the eternal story of revolutions. The underdogs would take the throne . . . and back to the beginning!" (718, second ellipsis in the original).

41. The title of this work in its original version, as published in *Revista Universal*, is "How the War Ended" [Cómo acabó la guerra]. All subsequent editions, including the edition published by Guzmán scholar Emmanuel Carballo in Guzmán's lifetime, carry the title "How the War Ended in 1917" [Cómo acabó la guerra en 1917]. It is not known if this change was made by Guzmán himself, but I have retained it because of the aforementioned conditions and because the inclusion of the year serves as a useful (and likely intentional) contextualization for readers who encounter the work elsewhere than in the original periodical.

42. At the outset of Charlie Chaplin's *Modern Times* (1936), the Little Tramp's life also is controlled by a machine, leading to a mental breakdown.

3. STRANGE FORCES

1. See chapter 2 for a discussion of the complete text of *Two Factions*.

2. Clarke's statement or "law" is quoted by numerous writers, including Nicholls and Shippey in their *ESF* entry on "Magic" (765).

3. Stepan explicitly notes the appeal of Lamarckian interpretations of evolution to those she terms "religiously inclined" (*Hour* 74).

4. I have found Paul Alkon's discussion of the influence of "the non-occult wing of mesmerism" on Félix Bodin's formulation of the first poetics of futuristic fiction (*Le Roman de l'avenir*, 1834) particularly helpful in developing the framework for this chapter (*Origins* 277–89; quotation on 288).

5. Some notable members of the SPR were Alfred Russell Wallace, Oliver Lodge, Carl Jung, Sigmund Freud, and Alfred, Lord Tennyson; members or associate members of the ASPR included William James and Edward Pickering of Harvard, G. Stanley Hall of Johns Hopkins, and Theodore Roosevelt (Monroe 206–7; Moore 142–43).

6. As Monroe states, "Throughout the 1890s . . . many considered psychical research to be a legitimate branch of psychology" (209).

7. These assertions by Moore about North American Spiritualism are also generally applicable to European Mesmerism, Spiritualism, and Spiritism and also to these alternative sciences in Latin America. American Spiritualism had a significant impact on the European movements, and the alternative sciences tended to arrive in Latin America via France (see Monroe 15–18 and 72–75, Machado 42–45).

8. The other three main principles of Spiritualism listed by Moore are: "a firm belief in the inviolability of natural law, a reliance on external facts rather than on an inward state of mind, and a faith in the progressive development of knowledge" (19).

9. It is notable that greater opposition to Spiritualism came from Christianity than from science (Moore 31). The liberties taken with orthodox beliefs by French Spiritists, for example, led to considerable conflict with the Catholic Church, including the placement of work by Kardec and other Spiritists on the church's list of forbidden books (see Monroe 142–46).

10. The original source is D. Alverico Peron, *A Fórmula do Espiritsmo*, trans. from Spanish (Bahia: Tip. de Francisco Queirolo, 1874), 46.

11. Stableford subsequently links this phenomenon of literary hybridization with the emergence of alternative belief systems such as Theosophy and Spiritualism (*Scientific Romance* 35–43).

12. Several Brazilian works discussed elsewhere in the book would fit quite well into this chapter, for example, *Brazil 2000* and *Doctor Benignus*. Two other texts included in the chronology that could conceivably be discussed in chapter 3 are: *The Magic Spectacles* [*A luneta mágica*] (1869) by Joaquim Manuel de Macedo, and "The Immortal" [O Imortal] (1882) by Joaquim Maria Machado de Assis (1839–1908).

13. Some of the stories in *Strange Forces* appeared in magazines prior to being anthologized in 1906. The following information is taken from Arturo García Ramos's introductory material to the Cátedra edition (page 85): *El Diario* published "La fuerza Omega" (January 1, 1906); "Un fenómeno inexplicable" originally appeared with the title "La Licantropía" in the theosophical magazine *Philadelfia* in 1898; and *Caras y Caretas* published "El Psychon" (January 1, 1898), "Viola acherontia" (January 1, 1899, under the title "Acherontia Antropos"), and "La metamúsica" (June 29, 1898).

14. See chapter 2, note 23, for citation format used for stories with published translations.

15. Lugones describes Paulin as a "Spiritualist" [espiritualista], but it is clear that he is not narrowly identifying the character with a specific strain of Anglo-

American Spiritualism. Paulin also practices some form of Mesmerism with a somnambulist and is compared to the French occultist Déodat Roché (1877–1978) and the British Spiritualist scientist William Crookes (1832–1919) in the same line (118–19; 221–22).

16. This ending is reminiscent of Amado Nervo's short story "The Frozen Ones" (discussed briefly in chapter 2). In that tale, a scientist experimenting in cryogenics invites the narrator to his laboratory to view the people he has frozen. Doubting the "slyly aggressive mystery" in the doctor's smile and fearing for his own safety, the narrator does not keep the appointment (402).

17. Masiello links the causes of this fragmentation to Gorriti's internationalism and the vagaries of exile (47).

18. Only three women are known to have written science-fictional works during the time period covered in this study (see the chronology in this book).

19. Sayers Peden's translation deviates from the structure of the original at several points. It does not contain the dedication, the short introductory section is transposed and included in section I, and section I is given the subtitle "Confidence of a Confidence" (the original has no subtitle for section I, only for section II, for which the translation does match). See chapter 2, note 23, for citation format used for texts with published translations.

20. The translations of the first two phrases are mine, the third is by Sayers Peden (81). I give more literal translations of passages for the purpose of subsequent analysis of the Magnetism/Mesmerism practiced by the woman in the tale. Sayers Peden renders *fascinados* as "mesmerized" (81); this is an excellent translation, but I have used the cognate "fascinated" in order to support the argument that Gorriti does not employ the rhetoric of Mesmerism in the text (an argument also made by Cano 76, 85).

21. Soriano provides approximate dates for each of the subplots in "He Who Listens" (277–78). The amorous adventures of the grandfather took place in early nineteenth-century colonial Peru, the male narrator-conspirator's tale in the 1850s or early 1860s, his subsequent political adventures between 1860 and 1862, and the female narrator's recounting of his incomplete confession shortly afterwards.

22. With some original additions (particularly of terminology related to the alternative sciences), this sentence is a summary of Soriano's discussion of the generational changes in "He Who Listens" (249–52, 272–73).

23. See Schneider (7–8, 18–22, 25) and Trujillo Muñoz (*Biografías* 50–53) for more on Castera's dualism.

24. Fernández Delgado makes the connection to Saint Augustine's words in his entry on Castera in *Latin American Science Fiction Writers* (52), though our interpretations of the reference differ somewhat. It is also possible that the

249

intended spelling was indeed "Querens," meaning "The Lamenter," which would be in keeping with the end of the apothecary's tale. The Flammarion reference would still stand by association. My thanks to my colleague Madeleine Henry, professor of classical studies, for consultation on this title.

25. The majority of the scientists listed are also mentioned in Olaguíbel's article, discussed above. All of the many scientific, philosophical, and literary authorities cited throughout *Querens* are European, with the exception of the odd reference to India as the source of the origins of Magnetism. Mexico is associated with India via climactic comparisons. As in *Doctor Benignus*, the New World is touted for its untouched natural wonders and its vigor, though this is a less central theme for Castera than for Zaluar.

26. The First International Congress of Psychology had just been held in Paris in 1889. For more on the relationship and eventual separation of psychology from psychical research, see Monroe 199–219.

27. Arthur Evans has noted similarities between this description of Castera's "indigenous Eve" and Hadaly in Villiers de l'Isle-Adam's *Tomorrow's Eve* [*L'Ève future*] (1886). Villiers's meditation on Cartesian dualism also may well have exercised some degree of influence on texts such as Nervo's *The Soul-Giver* (discussed in this chapter) and Quiroga's *The Artificial Man* and "The Vampire" (discussed in chapter 4). Magnetism is a central element of many of these works, as is the location of the animating spark for a woman in her male lover (the electrification of Adam's rib). Edison tells Ewald that Hadaly will be given life by "a single one of those still-divine sparks, drawn from your own soul" (67), and Ewald, not Edison, is called "her creator" in the end (204). In several of the Latin American texts a man's love is the activating influence.

28. *The Soul-Giver* has been translated into English by Michael Capobianco and Gloria Schaffer Meléndez, making it one of a very few prose works by Nervo available in translation. Capobianco and Schaffer Meléndez's edition is bilingual, but there is some variation between the Spanish original they work from and the edition I am using. I cite in Spanish from the 1962 *Obras completas*, and the translations given are faithful to that version. When Capobianco and Schaffer Meléndez's original (and thus translation) diverge from the *Obras completas* or, occasionally, from my preferred wording, I modify their translation accordingly. Where only very minor modifications have been made, the page number of the translation is given followed by the word "modified." See chapter 2, note 23, for citation format used for texts with published translations.

29. I have preferred the broader term "divinatory" to describe the gift-soul's abilities rather than the translators' "prophetic" (33). No ability to know the future is mentioned in the text, while the ability to diagnose illness is both prac-

ticed and described by the gift-soul, Alda, who tells the doctor: "With me at your side, there will be no illness you cannot diagnose correctly" (35; 205).

30. A further example of male-female duality given in the nouvelle is Alda's propensity for fantastic literature versus Rafael's preference for scientific treatises. Jensen also discusses the Rafael-Andrés duality (396).

31. I agree with the great majority of Jensen's arguments, including his assertion that Nervo's belief system was—with the exception of the element of metempsychosis—essentially Christian in nature (393). I do not concur entirely with his argument that the ultimate goal of the nouvelle is Rafael's "Christian conversion" (398). While Rafael is converted *from* his former materialistic beliefs, he is not explicitly or necessarily converted *to* Christianity, as can be seen in my discussion of the changes in Rafael's definition of the soul.

4. THE DOUBLE

1. While no Brazilian texts are discussed in chapter 4, it cannot be categorically confirmed that there are no Brazilian science-fictional texts involving the creation of a double or artificial being. Because there has been so much recent retrolabeling of early Latin American science-fictional works (and because this process is ongoing), we do not yet have a firm idea of the extent of the corpus or the types of subgenres, themes, and narrative tendencies represented in it.

2. See my "*Más Allá*" for more on the expansion of the science fiction readership in Latin America in the 1950s.

3. See Stableford's *Scientific Romance* for a comparison of the development of the North American and British speculative fiction traditions.

4. Sarlo's translator, Xavier Callahan, points out the difficulties of translating apparent Spanish-English cognates such as *sector*, *popular*, and *técnico/a* (see "Translator's Note" xi–xiii). Callahan translates the adjective *técnico/a* as "both 'technical' and 'technological,' according to the specific context" (xiii). The noun *técnica* also has multiple translations, "'technology' or 'technique' when those nouns serve both meaning and voice, and otherwise as 'the technical' and 'the technological' or, occasionally, as 'engineering'—the very field to which so many puttering dreamers in Buenos Aires once aspired" (xiii).

5. Upon the publication of "Horacio Kalibang," Holmberg was criticized in a magazine by someone writing under the pseudonym Anastasio for "this eagerness to distance himself from his country and constantly present foreign characters in remote lands" (*El Álbum del Hogar* 16 Feb. 1879). Pagés Larraya rebuts this accusation with an argument, almost science-fictional in nature, regarding the uses of displacement: "But, for those who know how to get to the meat of the story, the allusions to the people and customs of his own country are quite clear. In that way he could dissect them with greater impiety" (79).

6. Allusions are drawn by the company between the name Horacio Kalibang and that of a character from Shakespeare's *The Tempest*, clearly Caliban. Although another member of the party quickly dismisses this reference, saying "That is going off on a tangent," Holmberg certainly intended to imply connections between the two figures (151). Both Caliban and Kalibang are slaves of powerful masters; they are subhuman figures (Horacio Kalibang was the most imperfect of all of his master's creations). Perhaps Holmberg was interested in including the indirect connection with the New World in Shakespeare's work; perhaps he was influenced by Ernest Renan's *Caliban, suite de "La tempête"* (1878; see Frederick 60n4).

7. The complete record of Oscar Baum's actions here indicates that Horacio Kalibang is a mechanical golem. See my "Emergence" 318n70.

8. The "national pride" to which Baum refers can be read as Argentine as well as German. Holmberg's reference to Thomas Edison (1847–1931) uses the figure of the American inventor in a somewhat similar way as Villiers de l'Isle-Adam seven years later in *Tomorrow's Eve*. In the "Advice to the Reader" with which he prefaced his novel, Villiers stated that the character of Thomas Edison in his work was not a representation of the real man but of "a LEGEND [that] has thus sprung up in the popular mind regarding this great citizen of the United States" (3).

9. The "scientific inventor" is Sarlo's term, which she connects with the laboratory rather than with the doctor's office or surgeon's operating room, which would have been more familiar to readers of the day. The scientific inventor is, Sarlo writes, a more "exotic" and "intensified" version of the "technological innovator," though without "the social and economic goals that motivated the technologically oriented, pragmatic inventor" (*Technical Imagination* 36).

10. Another work of early Latin American science fiction that deals with the transmission of criminal tendencies through inheritance, specifically through the blood, is "Doctor Orts's Daring Operation" [La atrevida operación del doctor Orts] (Argentina, 1901) by Otto Miguel Cione (1875–1945). Orts is a physician who tries to combat the degeneracy, insanity, and criminality that occur in his family in every other generation. While he is normal, even brilliant, his son demonstrates physiognomical, phrenological, and behavioral characteristics of "a *born criminal*" (*Caras y Caretas* has no pagination). Orts performs a daring surgery, transplanting lobes from a healthy brain to replace the diseased portions in his son's brain (Ludmer calls Orts "an *Argentine Frankenstein*" [*Corpus* 228]). The son changes both physically and mentally for the better, but within a year shows signs of reverting to his former self. "It was the blood that contained the germ of crime," Dr. Orts realizes. His son's own blood has changed the new cerebral lobes "molecule by molecule" until they become identical to

the originals. The doctor extends this medical revelation to all of society: "The blood was what had to be changed, purified, fortified, so that the boy, what am I saying, so that all of humanity would not be so degenerate, so insane, so criminal" [La sangre era la que había que transformar, purificar, fortalecer, para que el niño, qué digo, toda la humanidad, no fuera tan degenerada, tan loca, tan criminal]. Orts dies of rage at his own impotence in the face of such a "terrible/inevitable law of inheritance" [fatal ley de herencia].

11. Note that *verdugo* can also be translated as "executioner." I have preferred "tormentor" here to maintain the parallel with Tolimán's previously cited use of the term (Cuevas 185). "Executioner" is not an appropriate rendering in the earlier instance, which means that the foreshadowing provided by the use of the word "verdugo" on page 185 will be lost somewhat in translation.

12. Despite the generational and individual contrasts between Quiroga and Lugones discussed in the introduction to this chapter, Lugones's influence on Quiroga should not be underestimated. Lugones introduced him both to modernism and to Misiones. When Lugones traveled to Misiones in 1903 to study the Jesuit ruins—as research for his *The Jesuit Empire* [*El imperio jesuítico*] (1904)—Quiroga went as the expedition's photographer. As Jitrik summarizes the relationship between the two, "[Quiroga] has in Lugones a protector, a friend, a mentor, and a guide" (12).

13. Sarlo elaborates on the authority of science versus technology: "Science is remote; technology, proximate. For this very reason, science has an authority to which technology must finally defer" (*Technical Imagination* 28).

14. The date given is June 11, 1909 (see page 114), but the text also indicates that this date fell ten months after the completion of the rat on August 23, 1909 (115, 109). Numbers and dates are specified throughout *El hombre artificial*, but on more than one occasion they are inconsistent (for example, five years of study in Europe are described for Donissoff, yet somehow this time period begins in 1903 and ends with his move to Buenos Aires in 1905 [100–101]). Pages given here are from the 1967 edition for ease of reference; the inconsistencies originate with the 1910 serialized version of the text in *Caras y Caretas*.

15. As in evolutionary tales such as "Yzur," power dynamics can be traced through language. In *The Artificial Man* the languages of the North, of science and technology, and of wealth and power are used to subjugate a lower-class, monolingual speaker of Spanish. For more on the role of language and social class in the representation of power dynamics in the text, see Ludmer (*Corpus* 67–69).

16. Although the structure of Quiroga's shorter nouvelle is less complex than that of Shelley's text with its multiple narrators and multiple frames, the narrator's sympathy for Donissoff and for the greatness of his endeavor is

reminiscent of Walton's attitude toward Victor Frankenstein and his work. Alkon has called Walton "the first misreader of Frankenstein's story," and the same can be said of Quiroga's narrator (*Science Fiction before 1900* 31). The charisma of electricity as a fantastic yet scientific force spans the century between the two works.

17. Ortiz is frequently a step behind Donissoff and Sivel. "If you were not so intelligent," Donissoff tells him at one point, "you would seem like a child sometimes" (110).

18. "The Vampire" [El vampiro] of 1927 should not be confused with the short story with the same title published by Quiroga in 1911.

19. Rodríguez Barilari notes the repetition in "Vampire" of some characters and a scientific principle that had originally appeared in "Portrait" (7).

20. The successful use of optography, the process of "tak[ing] a picture with the living eye"—enabling others to view the last image seen by a person who has died—was thought to be imminent at this time, both in scientific circles and in popular belief (Evans, "Optograms and Fiction" 342). While "Portrait" locates the production of the image using the mind/eye of the beholder rather than that of the dead person, Quiroga, a photographer, was almost certainly aware of optography and of literary treatments of it by writers such as Villiers de l'Isle-Adam, Verne, and Kipling (see article by Evans, quoted above). Note in particular that the Kelvin character's given name is Rudyard. The contemporary scientific credentials of optography, in addition to the extrapolations in the story on the work of Le Bon, support a more scientific—in the broader sense of science, discussed in chapter 3—interpretation of the text.

21. The index of Le Bon's *The Evolution of Matter* (the source cited in "Portrait") contains only three subheadings under "Rays," these are cathode, Röntgen, and X (435). Quiroga's N^1 rays are almost certainly extrapolated from the "N rays" the French physicist René-Prosper Blondlot (1849–1930) claimed to have discovered in 1903. Le Bon, as well as several other scientists and at least one Spiritualist, also claimed to have discovered these rays (Klotz 169–70).

22. It is clear that this new evocation of the actress is not a vampire in the traditional sense. No identifying factors for vampires (lack of image in mirrors, pronounced canine teeth, avoidance of sunlight) or methods of combating them (garlic, crosses, wooden stakes) are mentioned in the text.

23. Sarlo discusses "Portrait" and "Vampire" in *Technical Imagination* (18–22), describing Quiroga's literary and technical innovations in "Vampire" at the same time as she points out how he connects the "sinister aspect of technological extrapolation" to older literary forms and to more fantastic images, the "archaic phantasms of hysteria and vampirism" and the "archaic laws of guilt and vengeance" (21).

CONCLUSION

1. I use the term "global" rather than "international" in order to underline the inclusive scope of the genre. Alkon also calls science fiction "the genre best suited to speak for and attract the marginalized" (37–38), referring to the feminist subtext of Shelley's *Frankenstein*, but his statement is equally as applicable to the Latin American as to the female "other."

2. See, for example, Morosetti's work on science fiction in West Africa for a discussion of similar tendencies toward genre hybridity elsewhere in the periphery.

3. Regina's call to arms is answered by Roberto de Sousa Causo, who criticizes the values expressed in Anglo-Saxon sf as "alien" to Brazilians, in particular the representation of "the future populated only by citizens of the first world, the techno-scientific idyll, an ideology of the bipolarization of conflicts" ("Introdução" 8). Although Causo himself declared Regina's manifesto defunct in the mid-1990s, because it "never found market support or a solid discourse, and it was easily dismissed" ("Brazilian Science Fiction" 125), the debate continued.

4. For more on this debate in Brazil, see Ginway, *Brazilian* 139–43, and Ginway in Molina-Gavilán et al., "Chronology" 384.

CHRONOLOGY

1. As kindly pointed out by Omar Vega, the database includes scans of several works of early Chilean sf (database information given in bibliography of secondary sources under "Literatura de ciencia ficción en Chile").

2. Bibliographical information for the original manuscript varies in scholarship on the work. Because I have not consulted the original manuscript, I refer the reader to the following sources: González Casanova 104–18; Larson 55 and bibliography; Morales 556–57; Fernández-Delgado's 2001 edition of the text.

3. See entries under both titles in the bibliography of primary texts; note that the "Narración interplanetaria" in the *Guía de Forasteros* edition is missing the frame story. My thanks to Miguel Ángel Fernández-Delgado for providing copies of the text and bibliographical information as this book was going to press.

4. This short story by Gerónimo del Castillo Lenard (1804–1866) was retrolabeled as science fiction by Fernández-Delgado after reading about the text in Ruz Menéndez (Molina-Gavilán, Fernández-Delgado et al., "Chronology" 407; message to the author, 5 Aug. 2008).

5. The connection between Natalis and Amado Nervo was made by Fernández-Delgado.

6. My thanks to Miguel Ángel Fernández-Delgado for providing bibliographical information as this book was going to press and to Pepe Rojo for bringing this text to my attention with the *Minibúks* series.

BIBLIOGRAPHY

PRIMARY TEXTS OF LATIN AMERICAN SCIENCE FICTION THROUGH 1920

This bibliography provides more complete bibliographical information for all works listed in the chronology († indicates editions cited in the text).

Acosta de Samper, Soledad. "Bogotá en el año 2000." [Colombia?]: n.p., 1905.

Alcántara, J. M. de. "Buenos Aires en el año 4000." *Almanaque Ilustrado Sudamericano*. [Arg.]: n.p., 1876.

Altamirano, Ignacio Manuel. *La Navidad. (En las montañas)*. Folletín of *La Iberia* Dec. 1870: n.p.

———. *La Navidad. (En las montañas)*. In *Álbum de Navidad: Páginas dedicadas al bello sexo*. Mexico City: Imprenta de Ignacio Escalante, 1871. 199–296.

———. *Noche de navidad en las montañas*. Paris: Casa editorial Franco-Ibero-Americana, 1890.

———. *La Navidad en las montañas: Reproducción facsímile del manuscrito y de la primera edición*. 1870. Intro. and notes Harvey L. Johnson. Mexico City: Librería de Manuel Porrúa, 1972.

Angelici, Pedro. *Homúculus*. [Buenos Aires?]: n.p., 1918.

Assis, Joaquim Maria Machado de. "O Imortal." *A Estação* [Rio de Janeiro] 15 July–15 Sept. 1882.

———. "O Imortal." 1882. *Obra completa*. Ed. Afrânio Coutinho. Vol. 2. Rio de Janeiro: José Aguilar, 1959. 855–69.

Azevedo, Aluizio [*sic*; older spelling]. "Demônios." *Demônios*. São Paulo: Teixeira & Irmão, 1893. 9–81. (†)

Azevedo, Aluísio. "Demônios." *Demônios*. São Paulo: Livraria Martins Editôra, 1961. 37–80.

Barnsley, Godofredo Emerson. *São Paulo no Anno 2000, ou, Regeneração Nacional. (Chronica da sociedade brasileira futura)*. São Paulo: Typographia Brazi de Rothschild, 1909.

Barrios de los Ríos, José María. "El buque negro." *El país de las perlas y Cuentos californios*. [written c. 1900]. Mexico City: Biblioteca Estarsiana, 1908. 87–100.

Bunge, Carlos Octavio. *Thespis (novelas cortas y cuentos)*. Buenos Aires: Imp. de la Nación, 1907.

Calcagno, Francisco. *En busca del eslabón; historia de monos.* Barcelona: S. Manero, 1888.

———. *Historia de un muerto y noticias del otro mundo.* Habana, Cuba: Imp. del Directorio, 1875.

———. *Historia de un muerto: Meditación sobre las ruinas de un hombre.* 1875. 2nd ed. of *Historia de un muerto y noticias del otro mundo.* Barcelona: Casa editorial Maucci [etc., etc.], 1898.

Cané, Miguel. "Las armonías de la luz." *Ensayos.* Buenos Aires: Imprenta de la Tribuna, 1877. 233–58. (†)

———. "Las armonías de la luz." *Ensayos.* 1877. Buenos Aires: Sopena, 1940. 133–46.

Castera, Pedro. *Querens.* In collection *Impresiones y recuerdos; Las minas y los mineros; Los maduros dramas; Dramas en un corazon; Querens.* 1890. Ed. Luis Mario Schneider. Mexico City: Editorial Patria, 1987. 387–458. (†)

———. *Querens. El Universal* [Mexico City] begun 8 Jan. 1890.

———. *Querens.* Mexico City: Tipografía de E. Dublán y comp., 1890.

———. *Querens; novela original.* Mexico City: Imp. Escalerillas, 1890.

———. "Rosas y fresas." *Dramas en un córazon.* Mexico City: Tipografía de E. Dublán y comp., 1890. 69–207.

———. "Un viaje celeste." *El Domingo: Semanario de Literatura, Ciencias y Mejoras Materiales* [Mexico City] 1 Dec. 1872: 430–32. (†)

———. "Un viaje celeste." *Impresiones y recuerdos.* 1872. Mexico City: Imp. del "Socialista" de S. López, 1882. 111–19.

———. "Un viaje celeste." *Impresiones y recuerdos; Las minas y los mineros; Los maduros dramas; Dramas en un corazon; Querens.* 1872. Ed. Luis Mario Schneider. Mexico City: Editorial Patria, 1987. 96–101.

Chiappori, Atilio. *Borderland.* Buenos Aires: A. Moen y hermano, 1907.

———. *Borderland. La eterna angustia.* Buenos Aires: G. Kraft, 1954.

Cione, Otto Miguel. "La atrevida operación del doctor Orts." *Caras y Caretas* IV.133, 20 Apr. 1901: n.p.

"La ciudad del porvenir." *Caras y Caretas* XIII.601, 9 Apr. 1910: n.p.

"Cuento." *Diario de México*, 9 Feb. 1810: 157–58; 24 Feb. 1810: 217–18.

Cuevas, Alejandro. "El aparato del Doctor Tolimán." *Cuentos macabros.* Mexico City: J. R. Garrido y Hermano, 1911. 165–96.

Del Castillo Lenard, Gerónimo [under the heading "Ocios de G.C."]. "Gacetín de Mérida, Capital del Bajo Yucatán. (Año I, Dia 30, Hora II.) Enero 30 de 1949. (Las siete de la mañana." *Miscelánea instructiva y amena. Colección escogida de escritos sobre todas materias, en prosa y en verso, originales, copiados y traducidos.* Tomo I. Mérida, Yucatán, Mexico: Oficina Tipográfica de Rafael Pedrera, 1849. 129–37.

Dittrich, Julio O. *Buenos Aires en el 1950: Bajo el regimen socialista*. Buenos Aires: Ventas por Mayor, 1908.

Egaña, Juan. *Ocios filosoficos y poéticos, en la quinta de las delicias*. London: D. Manuel Calero, 1829.

Ezcurra, Eduardo de. *En el siglo XXX*. Buenos Aires: Juan A. Alsina, 1891.

Fósforos-Cerillos. "México en el año 1970." *El Liceo Mexicano* 1 (1844): 347–48. (†)

———. "México en el año 1970." Ed. Anne Staples. *Ciencia y desarrollo* 12.73 (1987): 149–52.

———. "México en el año de 1970" [sic]. *El futuro en llamas: Cuentos clásicos de la ciencia ficción mexicana*. 1844. Ed. Gabriel Trujillo Muñoz. Mexico City: Grupo Editorial Vid, 1997. 37–44.

Fragoso Lima, S. [see Quiroga, Horacio]

Freitas, Emília. *A rainha do ignoto: Romance psicológico*. 1899. Ed. and intro. Constância Lima Duarte. Florianópolis, Brazil: Mulheres, 2003.

Gagini, Carlos. *La caída del águila: (novela)*. San José, Costa Rica: Trejos Hnos, 1920.

Gorriti, Juana Manuela. "He Who Listens May Hear—To His Regret: Confidence of a Confidence." *The Oxford Book of Latin American Short Stories*. Trans. Margaret Sayers Peden. Ed. Roberto González Echevarría. New York: Oxford University Press, 1997. 76–84.

———. "Quien escucha, su mal oye: Confidencia de una confidencia." *Sueños y realidades. Obras completas de la señora doña Juana Manuela Gorriti*. Vol. 2. Buenos Aires: Impr. de Mayo de C. Casavalle, 1865. 135–51. (†)

———. "Quien escucha, su mal oye." *Sueños y realidades*. 1865. *Obras completas*. Vol. 4. Salta, Argentina: Fundación Banco del Noroeste, 1995. 217–23.

———. "Yerbas y alfileres." *Panoramas de la vida*. Vol. 2. Buenos Aires: Impr. y Librerías de Mayo, 1876. 265–75.

Guzmán, Martín Luis. "Cómo acabó la guerra." *Revista Universal* [New York] Dec. 1917: 18, 22.

———. "Cómo acabó la guerra en 1917." *El cuento mexicano del siglo XX*. Ed. and prol. Emmanuel Carballo. Mexico City: Empresas Editoriales, 1964. 191–99. (†)

Holmberg, Eduardo Ladislao. *Cuentos fantásticos*. Ed. and comp. Antonio Pagés Larraya. Buenos Aires: Librería Hachette, 1957.

———. *Dos partidos en lucha: Fantasía científica*. Buenos Aires: Imprenta de *El Arjentino*, 1875. (†)

———. *Dos partidos en lucha: Fantasía científica*. Ed. and intro. Sandra Gasparini. Buenos Aires: Corregidor, 2005.

———— [under pseud. Ladislao Kaillitz]. "Filigranas de cera." *La Crónica* [Buenos Aires] 7–10 Apr. 1884.

————. "Filigranas de cera." *Filigranas de cera y otros textos*, ed. Enriqueta Morillas Ventura, 2000. 65–102.

————. *Horacio Kalibang ó Los autómatas*. Buenos Aires: Imprenta de "Álbum del Hogar," 1879.

————. "Horacio Kalibang o Los autómatas." *Cuentos fantásticos*. 1879. Ed. Antonio Pagés Larraya. Buenos Aires: Libreria Hachette, 1957. 147–67. (†)

————. "Horacio Kalibang o Los autómatas." *Historias futuras: Antología de la ciencia ficción argentina*. 1879. Ed. Adriana Fernández and Edgardo Pígoli. Buenos Aires: Emecé, 2000. 15–38.

————. *Olimpio Pitango de Monalia*. Written 1915. Edición principe. Ed. Gioconda Marun. Dimensión Argentina. Buenos Aires: Solar, 1994.

————. "Viaje maravilloso del señor Nic-Nac" [selections]. *Los argentinos en la luna*. 1875–76. Ed. Eduardo Goligorsky. Buenos Aires: Ediciones de la Flor, 1968. 15–31.

————. *Viaje maravilloso del señor Nic-Nac al planeta Marte*. 1875–76. Colección Los Raros. Ed. Pablo Crash Solomonoff. Buenos Aires: Biblioteca Nacional; Ediciones Colihue, 2006.

————. *Viaje maravilloso del señor Nic-Nac en el que se refieren las prodijiosas aventuras de este señor y se dan á conocer las instituciones, costumbres y preocupaciones de un mundo desconocido: Fantasía espiritista*. Buenos Aires: El Nacional, 1875. (†)

————. "Viaje maravilloso del señor Nic-Nac en el que se refieren las prodijiosas aventuras de este señor y se dan á conocer las instituciones, costumbres y preocupaciones de un mundo desconocido: Fantasía espiritista." *El Nacional* 29 Nov. 1875–13 Mar.1876, sec. Folletín del Lunes.

Lugones, Leopoldo. "Ensayo de una cosmogonía en diez lecciones. *Las fuerzas extrañas*. 1906. Revised 1926. Madrid: Cátedra, 1996. 233–83.

————. "Un fenómeno inexplicable." *Las fuerzas extrañas*. 1898 (as "La Licantropía" in *Philadelphia*). Madrid: Cátedra, 1996. 125–35.

————. "La fuerza Omega." *Las fuerzas extrañas*. 1906 (in *El Diario*). Madrid: Cátedra, 1996. 97–110.

————. *Las fuerzas extrañas*. Buenos Aires: Arnaldo Moen y Hermano, 1906.

————. *Las fuerzas extrañas*. 1906. Revised 1926. Madrid: Cátedra, 1996. (†)

————. "La metamúsica." *Las fuerzas extrañas*. 1906. Revised 1926. Madrid: Cátedra, 1996. 155–71.

————. "El origen del diluvio." *Las fuerzas extrañas*. 1906. Revised 1926. Madrid: Cátedra, 1996. 173–80.

———. "El Psychon." *Las fuerzas extrañas*. 1898 (in *Tribuna*). Madrid: Cátedra, 1996. 219–31.
———. *Strange Forces*. Trans. Gilbert Alter-Gilbert. Discoveries. Pittsburgh, PA: Latin America Literary Review, 2001.
———. "Viola Acherontia." *Las fuerzas extrañas*. 1899 (as "Acherontia Antropos" in *Tribuna*). Madrid: Cátedra, 1996. 191–98.
———. "Yzur." *Las fuerzas extrañas*. 1906. Revised 1926. Madrid: Cátedra, 1996. 199–209.
———. "Yzur." *The Oxford Book of Latin American Short Stories*. Trans. Gregory Woodruff. Ed. Roberto González Echevarría. New York: Oxford University Press, 1997. 111–17.
Lynch, Benito. "1932." *El Día de La Plata*. n.d. 1907: n.p.
———. *1932*. 1907 [*El Día de La Plata*]. [La Plata, Argentina]: Universidad Nacional de La Plata, Biblioteca Pública, 1994.
Macedo, Joaquim Manuel [or Manoel] de. "O fim do mundo." *Jornal do Commercio* [Rio de Janeiro] 13 June 1856 [probably 1857]: folhetim.
———. "O fim do mundo." *Os Romances da Semana*. [1857]. Rio de Janeiro: B.L. Garnier, 1873. 46–86. (†)
———. *A luneta magica*. Rio de Janeiro: B.L. Garnier, 1869.
———. *A luneta mágica*. 1869. São Paulo: Ática, 1981.
Miralles, Francisco [orig. publ. under pseud. Saint Paul]. *Desde Júpiter: Curioso viaje de un santiaguino magnetizado*. Santiago, Chile: Imprenta i Litografía de El País, 1877.
Monsalve, Carlos. "De un mundo á otro." *Páginas literarias*. Buenos Aires: Ostwald y Martinez, 1881. 41–64.
———. "Historia de un paraguas." *Páginas literarias*. Buenos Aires: Ostwald y Martinez, 1881. 92–137.
———. "El hombre de piedra." *Juvenilia*. Buenos Aires: El Diario, 1884. 107–14.
"Narración interplanetaria." 1810. *Guía de Forasteros*, Instituto Nacional de Bellas Artes, México D.F. 15 Oct. 1984: 1+.
———. 1810. *Minibúks: Temporada 1*. Taller (e)Media. Dir. Pepe Rojo. Tijuana: Universidad Autónoma de Baja California, 2009. N.p.
Nepomuceno Adorno, Juan. "El remoto porvenir." *La armonía del universo o la ciencia en la teodisea*. Mexico City: n.p., 1862.
———. "El remoto porvenir." *La armonía del universo: Ensayo filosófico en busca de la verdad, la unidad y la felicidad*. Mexico City: Tipografía de Juan Abadino, 1862 (and on same cover page) Mexico City: Tipografía de Gonzalo A. Esteva, 1882. 98–114.

Nervo, Amado. "Amnesia." *Obras completas*. [Between 1916 and 1918.] Ed. Francisco González Guerrero and Alfonso Méndez Plancarte. Vol. 1. Madrid: Aguilar, 1962. 344–60.

———. "Astros." *Obras completas*. 1905 (in *Boletín de la Sociedad Astronómica de México*; collected in *En voz baja*). Ed. Francisco González Guerrero and Alfonso Méndez Plancarte. Vol. 2. Madrid: Aguilar, 1962. 1587–89.

———. "Cien años de sueño." *Obras completas*. 1909 (in *Ellos*). Ed. Francisco González Guerrero and Alfonso Méndez Plancarte. Vol. 2. Madrid: Aguilar, 1962. 625–27.

———. "Los congelados." *Obras completas*. (collected in 1921 in *Cuentos misteriosos*). Ed. Francisco González Guerrero and Alfonso Méndez Plancarte. Vol. 1. Madrid: Aguilar, 1962. 400–402.

———. "La diablesa." *Obras completas*. 1895 (in *Cuentos de juventud*). Ed. Francisco González Guerrero and Alfonso Méndez Plancarte. Vol. 1. Madrid: Aguilar, 1962. 129–35.

———. "Dentro de cincuenta años: Diálogos hipotéticos." *Obras completas*. 1906 (in *La Semana*; collected in *Crónicas de Europa*). Ed. Francisco González Guerrero and Alfonso Méndez Plancarte. Vol. 1. Madrid: Aguilar, 1962. 1251–52.

———. "El diamante de la inquietud." *Obras completas*. 1917 (in *La novela corta* [Madrid], Núm. 62). Ed. Francisco González Guerrero and Alfonso Méndez Plancarte. Vol. 1. Madrid: Aguilar, 1962. 275–93.

———. "Diana y Eros (cuento astronómico)." *Obras completas*. (collected in 1921 in *Cuentos misteriosos*). Ed. Francisco González Guerrero and Alfonso Méndez Plancarte. Vol. 1. Madrid: Aguilar, 1962. 382–83.

———. *El donador de almas. Obras completas*. 1899 (in installments in *Cómico* beginning with III.15 of 9 Apr.). Ed. Francisco González Guerrero and Alfonso Méndez Plancarte. Vol. 1. Madrid: Aguilar, 1962. 199–226.

———. "El gran viaje." *Obras completas*. 1917 (in *El estanque de los lotos*). Ed. Francisco González Guerrero and Alfonso Méndez Plancarte. Vol. 2. Madrid: Aguilar, 1962. 1787–88.

———. "La literatura lunar y la habitabilidad de los satélites." *Obras completas*. 1904 (lectures read at the Sociedad Astronómica de México on 7 Sept. and 8 Oct.). Ed. Francisco González Guerrero and Alfonso Méndez Plancarte. Vol. 2. Madrid: Aguilar, 1962. 498–518.

———. "Las nubes." *Obras completas*. 1909 (in *Ellos*). Ed. Francisco González Guerrero and Alfonso Méndez Plancarte. Vol. 2. Madrid: Aguilar, 1962. 602–3.

———. "El país en que la lluvia era luminosa." *Obras completas*. (collected in 1921 in *Cuentos misteriosos*). Ed. Francisco González Guerrero and Alfonso Méndez Plancarte. Vol. 1. Madrid: Aguilar, 1962. 407–9.

———. "El resucitador y el resucitado." *Obras completas*. 1912 (in *Mis filosofías*). Ed. Francisco González Guerrero and Alfonso Méndez Plancarte. Vol. 2. Madrid: Aguilar, 1962. 584–86.

———. "La serpiente que se muerde la cola." *Obras completas*. 1912 (in *El Imparcial*; collected in 1921 in *Cuentos misteriosos*). Ed. Francisco González Guerrero and Alfonso Méndez Plancarte. Vol. 1. Madrid: Aguilar, 1962. 394–95.

———. "El sexto sentido." *Obras completas*. 1918 (in "La Novela Semanal" of *El Universal Ilustrado*). Ed. Francisco González Guerrero and Alfonso Méndez Plancarte. Vol. 1. Madrid: Aguilar, 1962. 360–71.

———. *The Soul-Giver = El donador de almas*. Trans. Michael F. Capobianco, and Gloria Schaffer Meléndez. Lewiston, NY: Edwin Mellen Press, 1999.

———. "La última diosa (cuento absurdo)." *Obras completas*. 1906 (in *Revista Moderna de México* 2a Ser., 7, pages 118–20; collected in 1909 in *Ellos*). Ed. Francisco González Guerrero and Alfonso Méndez Plancarte. Vol. 2. Madrid: Aguilar, 1962. 615–17.

———. "La última guerra." [1898?] *Almas que pasan*. Madrid: Tipografía de la Revista de Archivos, 1906. 27–43.

———. "La última guerra." *Obras completas*. [1898?] (in *El Mundo*; collected in 1906 in *Almas que pasan*). Ed. Francisco González Guerrero and Alfonso Méndez Plancarte. Vol. 1. Madrid: Aguilar, 1962. 239–45. (†)

———. "Las varitas de virtud." *Obras completas*. 1909 (in *Ellos*). Ed. Francisco González Guerrero and Alfonso Méndez Plancarte. Vol. 2. Madrid: Aguilar, 1962. 597–99.

———. "Yo estaba en el espacio." *Obras completas*. 1905 (in *Boletín de la Sociedad Astronómica de México*; collected in *En voz baja*). Ed. Francisco González Guerrero and Alfonso Méndez Plancarte. Vol. 2. Madrid: Aguilar, 1962. 1569–71.

[Nervo, Amado?]. Publ. under pseud. Natalis. "Cuentos de los siglos futuros: Las guerras y los ejércitos." *El Mundo* [Mexico City]. Tomo I.25. 19 June 1898: 481.

[Nervo, Amado?]. Publ. under pseud. Natalis. "Cuentos del porvenir: El periodismo en la antiguedad." *El Mundo* [Mexico City]. Tomo I.8. 20 Feb. 1898: 141–42.

[Nervo, Amado?]. Anon. "Cuentos del porvenir: El interés en el dinero." *El Mundo* [Mexico City]. Tomo I.6. 6 Feb. 1898: 101–2.

Olivera, Carlos. "Fantasmas." *En la brecha. 1880–1886*. 1883 (in newspaper *El Diario*). Buenos Aires: Lajouane, 1887. 190–95.

———. "El hombre de la levita gris." *En la brecha. 1880–1886*. 1880 (in newspaper *El Diario*). Buenos Aires: Lajouane, 1887. 32–41.

———. "Los muertos a hora fija (Revelaciones de un médico)." *En la brecha. 1880–1886*. 1883 (in newspaper *El Diario*). Buenos Aires: Lajouane, 1887. 141–50.

Palma, Clemente. *Crónicas del Halley: El día trágico*. 1910 [1989 is first edition]. Ed. María Tellería Solari. Lima: CONCYTEC, 1989.

———. "La última rubia: Cuento futuro." *Cuentos malévolos*. Barcelona: Imp. Salvat, 1904. 91–103.

Piria, Francisco. *El socialismo triunfante: Lo que será mi país dentro de 200 años*. Montevideo: Dornaleche y Reyes, 1898.

———. *El socialismo triunfante: Lo que será mi país dentro de 200 años*. Buenos Aires: Dornaleche Rutrin, 2002.

Pizarro, Nicolás. *El monedero*. Mexico City: Imprenta de Nicolás Pizarro, 1861.

Planas y Saínz, Juan Manuel. *La corriente del golfo*. Habana, Cuba: El Fígaro, 1920.

Popper, Julio. *Atlanta: Proyecto para la fundación de un pueblo marítimo en Tierra del Fuego*. [Buenos Aires]: [author's edition, 6 copies], 1893.

———. *Atlanta: Proyecto para la fundación de un pueblo marítimo en Tierra del Fuego y otros escritos*. 1893. Colección reservada del Museo del Fin del Mundo. Buenos Aires: Eudeba, 2003.

Portillo, Julián M. del. "Lima de aquí a cien años." 1843. *Ajos y zafiros* 7 (2005): 172–93.

———. "Lima de aquí a cien años." *El Comercio*. 30 June–2 Aug. 1843, folletín.

Quiroga, Horacio. "El almohadón de plumas." *Caras y Caretas* X.458, 13 July 1907: n.p.

———. "El almohadón de plumas." *Cuentos de amor de locura y de muerte*. Buenos Aires: "Buenos Aires" Socieded Cooperativa Editorial Limitada, 1917. 93–98.

——— [under pseud. S. Fragoso Lima]. "El hombre artificial." *Caras y Caretas* XIII.588–93, 8 Jan.–12 Feb. 1910: n.p.

——— [orig. publ. under pseud. S. Fragoso Lima]. *El hombre artificial*. 1910. *Obras inéditas y desconocidas*. Ed. Angel Rama. Novelas Cortas. Vol. 1. Montevídeo: Arca, 1967. 95–132. (†)

———. *Mas allá*. Buenos Aires and Montevideo: Sociedad Amigos del Libro Rioplatense, 1935.

———. "El mono ahorcado." *Caras y Caretas* X.472, 19 Oct. 1907: n.p.

——— [under pseud. S. Fragoso Lima]. "El mono que asesinó." *Caras y Caretas* XII.552, 553, 555, 556, 557; 1 May–5 June 1909: n.p.

———. "El retrato." *Caras y Caretas* XII.639, 31 Dec. 1910: n.p.

———. "El retrato." *Cuentos completos*. 1910. Ed. Carlos Dámaso Martínez. Vol. 2. Buenos Aires: Seix Barral, 1997. 360–64. (†)

———. "El salvaje." *El salvaje*. Buenos Aires: "Buenos Aires" Cooperativa Editorial Limitada, 1920. 5–38.

———. "El vampiro." *La Nación* [Buenos Aires] 11 Sept. 1927.

———. "El vampiro." *Cuentos completos*. 1927. Ed. Carlos Dámaso Martínez. Vol. 2. Buenos Aires: Seix Barral, 1997. 168–85. (†)

Quiroule, Pierre. *La ciudad anarquista americana; obra de construccion revolucionaria con el plano de la ciudad libertaria*. Buenos Aires: "La Protesta," 1914.

———. *La ciudad anarquista americana*. 1914. Madrid: Ed. Tuero, 1991.

———. *Sobre la ruta de la anarquía. (Novela libertaria)*. Buenos Aires: Fueyo, 1909.

Rivas, Fray Manuel Antonio de. *Sizigias y cuadraturas lunares ajustadas al meridiano de Mérida de Yucatán por un anctítona o habitador de la luna, y dirigidas al bachiller don Ambrosio de Echeverría, entonador de kyries funerales en la parroquia del Jesús de dicha ciudad, y al presente profesor de logarítmica en el pueblo de Mama de la península de Yucatán, para el año del señor de 1775*. Ed. and Paleographic reconstruction Miguel Ángel Fernández-Delgado. Mexico City: Goliardos, 2001.

———. *Syzigias y quadraturas lunares ajustadas al meridiano de Mérida de Yucatán por un anctítona o havitador de la luna, y dirigidas al Bachiller Don Ambrosio de Echeverría, entonador que had sido de kyries funerales en la Parroquia de el Jesús de dicha ciudad, y al presente profesor de logaríthmica en el pueblo de Mama de la península de Yucatán; para el año del Señor de 1775*. Ed. and notes Ana María Morales. Text included within article by Morales "Un viaje novohispano a la luna (*ca.* 1772), de fray Manuel Antonio de Rivas, franciscano" [see Morales entry].

Rojas, Ricardo. *La psiquina*. Buenos Aires: La novela semanal, 1917.

Santos, Joaquim Felício dos. "A história do Brasil escrita pelo Dr. Jeremias no ano de 2862." *O Jequitinhonha* [Diamantina] Dec. 1862.

———. "A história do Brasil escrita pelo Dr. Jeremias no ano de 2862." 1862. *Revista do Livro* 2.6 (1957): 111–13.

———. *Páginas da história do Brasil escripta no anno de 2000*. *O Jequitinhonha* [Diamantina] 23 Aug. 1868–[date unknown] 1872: [pages vary]. (†)

———. *Páginas da história do Brasil escrita no ano de 2000* [Excerpts]. Comp. and ed. Alexandre Eulálio *Revista do Livro* 2.6 (1957): 103–60. (†)

Sarmiento, Domingo Faustino. *Argirópolis*. Intro. and ed. Ernesto Quesada. 1850. Buenos Aires: La Cultura Argentina, 1916.

Silva, José Asunción. "Futura." *Poesía completa; De sobremesa* [in *Gotas amargas*.] 1896. Santafé de Bogotá, Colombia: Casa de Poesía Silva, 1996. 132–33.

Sioen, Achilles. *Buenos Aires en el año 2080: Historia verosímil.* Buenos Aires: Igon Hermanos, 1879.

Soiza Reilly, Juan José de. *La ciudad de los locos (aventuras de Tartarín Moreira): Novela sudamericana.* Illus. by José Friedrich. Barcelona: Casa editorial Maucci [etc., etc], 1914.

———. *La ciudad de los locos y otros textos.* Buenos Aires: Adriana Hidalgo, 2007.

Soto Hall, Máximo. *El problema.* San José, Costa Rica: Lines, 1899.

Tallman, Benjamín. *¡Una vision del porvenir!, o, El espejo del mundo en el año de 1975.* Santiago, Chile: Impr. Nacional, 1875.

Toro, Carlos. "El dieciocho de mayo." *El miedo: Algunos cuentos.* 1910. Mexico: S.E.P., 1947. 121–25.

———. "El dieciocho de mayo." 1910. *Minibúks: Temporada 1.* Taller (e)Media. Dir. Pepe Rojo. Tijuana: Universidad Autónoma de Baja California, 2009. N.p.

Torri, Julio. "La conquista de la luna." *Ensayos y poemas.* Mexico City: Porrúa Hermanos, 1917. 29–34.

———. "Era un país pobre." *Ensayos y poemas.* Mexico City: Porrúa Hermanos, 1917. 127–40.

Urzaiz (Rodríguez), Eduardo. *Eugenia. (Esbozo novelesco de costumbres futuras).* Mérida, Yucatán, México: [Talleres gráficos A. Manzanilla], 1919. (†)

———. *Eugenia: Esbozo novelesco de costumbres futuras.* 1919. Mérida, Yucatán, México: Universidad Autónoma de Yucatán, 2002.

Valdés, Antonio José. "Delirio," *La Prensa Argentina* [Buenos Aires] 11 and 18 June 1816: 6137–41 and 6143–47.

Varela, Luis V. [under pseud. Raúl Waleis]. *El doctor Whuntz: Fantasía.* Buenos Aires: C. Casavalle, 1881.

Vera y González, Enrique. *La estrella del sur.* Buenos Aires: La sin bombo, 1904.

———. *La estrella del sur: A través del porvenir.* 1904. Buenos Aires: Instituto Histórico de la Ciudad de Buenos Aires, 2000.

Zaluar, Augusto Emílio. *O Doutor Benignus.* 2 vols. Rio de Janeiro: Typographia do Globo, 1875.

———. *O Doutor Benignus.* 1875. 2nd ed. Rio de Janeiro: UFRJ, 1994. (†)

Zamudio, Adela. "El vértigo." *Cuentos breves.* [c. 1920]. Cochabamba, Bolivia: Los Tiempos–Los Amigos del Libro, 1988. 63–72.

SECONDARY SOURCES

Abraham, Carlos. "El género utópico en la Argentina: La obra de Eduardo de Ezcurra." *Axxón* 113 (2002). Web. 2 Aug. 2007.

———. "Las utopías literarias argentinas en el período 1850–1950." *The International Association for the Fantastic in the Arts*. 2007. Web. 1 Dec. 2007.

Abreu Gómez, Ermilo. *Martín Luis Guzmán*. Mexico City: Empresas Editoriales, 1968.

Alkon, Paul K. *Origins of Futuristic Fiction*. Athens: University of Georgia Press, 1987.

———. *Science Fiction before 1900: Imagination Discovers Technology*. 1994. Twayne. Genres in Context. Ed. Ron Gottesman. New York: Routledge, 2002.

Alter-Gilbert, Gilbert. "Foreword." *Strange Forces*. By Leopoldo Lugones. Discoveries. Pittsburgh, PA: Latin America Literary Review Press, 2001. 11–20.

Anastasio [pseud.]. "Horacio Kalibang" [commentary on the text]. *El tipo más original y otras páginas*. 1879. By Eduardo Ladislao Holmberg. Eds. Sandra Gasparini and Claudia Roman. Buenos Aires: Simurg, 2001. 159–64.

Babini, José. "Los 'Tres Grandes': Ameghino, Moreno, Holmberg." *La Argentina del ochenta al centenario*. Eds. Gustavo Ferrari and Ezequiel Gallo. Buenos Aires: Sudamericana, 1980. 819–27.

Bajarlía, Juan-Jacobo, ed. *Cuentos argentinos de ciencia-ficción*. Buenos Aires: Merlín, 1967.

Barcia, Pedro Luis. "Introducción biográfica y crítica." *Cuentos fantásticos*. By Leopoldo Lugones. Ed. Pedro Luis Barcia. Madrid: Castalia, 1987. 9–54.

Barnsley, Godfrey. Message to the author. 21 May 2008. E-mail.

———. Message to M. Elizabeth Ginway. 26 Feb. 2004. E-mail.

Beaver, Harold. "Introduction." *The Science Fiction of Edgar Allan Poe*. Ed. Harold Beaver. New York: Penguin, 1976. vii–xxii.

Bell, Andrea. "*Desde Júpiter*: Chile's Earliest Science-Fiction Novel." *Science Fiction Studies* 22.2 (1995): 187–97.

Bell, Andrea, Roger Bozzetto, and Elana Gomel. "Current Trends in Global Sf." *Science Fiction Studies* 26.3 (1999): 431–46.

Bell, Andrea L., and Yolanda Molina-Gavilán. "Introduction: Science Fiction in Latin America and Spain." *Cosmos Latinos: An Anthology of Science Fiction from Latin America and Spain*. Eds. Andrea L. Bell and Yolanda Molina-Gavilán. The Wesleyan Early Classics of Science Fiction. Ed. Arthur B. Evans. Middletown, CT: Wesleyan University Press, 2003. 1–19.

Bellamy, Edward. "How I Came to Write *Looking Backward*." *The Nationalist*. May 1889. Science Fiction Studies, n.d. Web. 19 July 2006.

———. *Looking Backward from 2000 to 1887*. *Project Gutenberg*. NetLibrary, n.d. Web. 25 July 2003.

Bertol Domingues, Heloisa Maria, and Magali Romero Sá. "La introducción del Darwinismo en Brasil: Las controversias de su introducción." *El Darwinismo en España e Iberoamérica*. Eds. Thomas F. Glick, Rosaura Ruiz and Miguel Angel Puig-Samper. Mexico: Universidad Nacional Autónoma de México, 1999. 83–102.

Blanco-Fombona, Rufino. *El modernismo y los poetas modernistas*. Madrid: Editorial Mundo Latino, 1929.

Borges, Jorge Luis. *Leopoldo Lugones*. Buenos Aires: Editorial Troquel, 1955.

———. "Prólogo." *La estatua de sal*. By Leopoldo Lugones. Sel. Jorge Luis Borges. Madrid: Ediciones Siruela, 1985. 9–14.

———. "Prólogo." *La invención de Morel*. 1940. By Adolfo Bioy Casares. Buenos Aires and Madrid: Emecé and Alianza, 1989.

Brescia, Pablo A. J. "La sintaxis del secreto en Juana Manuela Gorriti." *Signos Literarios y Lingüísticos* 2.2 (2000): 63–73.

Brown, J. Andrew. *Test Tube Envy: Science and Power in Argentine Narrative*. Lewisburg, PA: Bucknell University Press, 2005.

Burns, E. Bradford. "Cultures in Conflict: The Implication of Modernization in Nineteenth-Century Latin America." *Elites, Masses, and Modernization in Latin America, 1850–1930*. Ed. Virginia Bernhard. Austin: University of Texas Press, 1979. 11–77.

———. *A History of Brazil*. 3rd ed. New York: Columbia University Press, 1993.

Cândido, Antônio. "O honrado e facundo Joaquim Manuel de Macedo." *Formação da literatura brasileira (momentos decisivos)*. Vol. 2. São Paulo: Editora da Universidade de São Paulo, Editora Itatiaia, 1975. 136–45.

Cané, Miguel. "*Dos partidos en lucha (Fantasía científica)* por Eduardo L. Holmberg." *Ensayos*. 1875. Buenos Aires: Imprenta de la Tribuna, 1877. 173–79.

———. "Positivismo." *Ensayos*. 1872. Buenos Aires: Imprenta de la Tribuna, 1877. 9–13.

Cano, Luis C. *Intermitente recurrencia: La ciencia ficción y el canon literario hispanoamericano*. Buenos Aires: Corregidor, 2006.

Capanna, Pablo. "La ciencia ficción y los argentinos." *Minotauro* 10 (1985): 42–56.

———. "Entrevista con Pablo Capanna (Interviewed by Eduardo Carletti)." *Axxón* 106 (2000): 162–70. Web. 15 Nov. 2004.

———. *El mundo de la ciencia ficción: Sentido e historia*. Buenos Aires: Letra Buena, 1992.

———. "Prólogo." *El cuento argentino de ciencia ficción*. Ed. Pablo Capanna. Buenos Aires: Nuevo Siglo, 1995. 5–15.

———. *El sentido de la ciencia ficción*. Buenos Aires: Columba, 1966.

Carballo, Emmanuel. "Prólogo." *El cuento mexicano del siglo XX*. Mexico City: Empresas Editoriales, 1964. 9–103.

———. "Dos textos poco conocidos de Martín Luis Guzmán." *El realismo y lo fantástico en la obra de Martín Luis Guzmán (Dos textos poco conocidos)*. Ed. Emmanuel Carballo. Spec. supplement of *Tiempo: Semanario de la Vida y la Verdad* 80.2068 (21 Dec. 1981): 5–6.

Carneiro, André. *Introdução ao estudo da "science-fiction."* São Paulo: Conselho Estadual de Cultura, 1967.

Castagnino, Raúl Héctor. *Miguel Cané: Cronista del ochenta porteño*. Buenos Aires: Oeste, 1952.

Carvalho, José Murilo de. "Prefácio: Benigna ciência." *O Doutor Benignus*. 1875. By Augusto Emílio Zaluar. 2nd ed. Rio de Janeiro: UFRJ, 1994. 7–11.

Castera, Pedro. "Una palabra de la ciencia: El vapor." *El Domingo: Semanario de Literatura, Ciencias y Mejoras Materiales* [Mexico City] 23 Feb. 1873: 147–49.

———. "Una palabra de la ciencia: La electricidad." *El Domingo: Semanario de Literatura, Ciencias y Mejoras Materiales* [Mexico City] 6 Apr. 1873: 234–37.

Causo, Roberto de Sousa. "A antropofagia modernista e o movimento antropofágico da ficção científica brasileira." Unpublished essay. São Paulo, June 1998. 1–7.

———. "Brazilian Science Fiction: The Anxiety of Influence." *Altair V: Journal of Speculative Fiction* (1998): 121–25.

———. *Ficção científica, fantasia e horror no Brasil 1875–1950*. Belo Horizonte, Brazil: UFMG, 2003.

———. "Introdução." *D.O. Leitura* 12.138 (1993): 8.

Cervantes Saavedra, Miguel de. *The History and Adventures of the Renowned Don Quixote*. Trans. Tobias Smollett. Athens: University of Georgia Press, 2003.

———. *El ingenioso hidalgo don Quijote de la Mancha*. Clásicos Castalia. Ed. Luis Andrés Murillo. Madrid: Editorial Castalia, 1984.

Chamberlin, J. Edward, and Sander L. Gilman, eds. *Degeneration: The Dark Side of Progress*. New York: Columbia University Press, 1985.

Clarke, I. F. *Tale of the Future: From the Beginning to the Present Day*. 3d ed. London: Library Association, 1978.

Clute, John, and Peter Nicholls. "Apes and Cavemen (in the Human World)." *The Encyclopedia of Science Fiction*. Ed. John Clute and Peter Nicholls. New York: St. Martin's Griffin, 1995. 46–48.

———. "Hoffmann, E. T. A." *The Encyclopedia of Science Fiction*. Ed. John Clute and Peter Nicholls. New York: St. Martin's Griffin, 1995. 576–77.

"Coloquio a Distancia." *Plural: Revista Cultural de Excelsior* Apr. 1985: 14–21.

Conan Doyle, Arthur. *The Lost World*. 1912. Chicago: Academy, 1990.
Conil Paz, Alberto A. *Leopoldo Lugones*. Buenos Aires: Librería Huemul, 1985.
Damazio, Sylvia F. *Da elite ao povo: Advento e expansão do espiritismo no Rio de Janeiro*. Rio de Janeiro: Bertrand Brasil, 1994.
Darío, Rubén. "Cuento de Pascuas." *Cuentos fantásticos*. Obras completas. Vol. 4. Madrid: A. Aguado, 1950. 373–81.
———. *Los raros*. La Plata: Calomino, 1945.
Del Mar, Emanuel. *A Guide to Spanish and English Conversation* [also titled *Guia para la conversacion en español é inglés*]. 4th ed. London: Dulau, 1853.
Del Fiorentino, Teresinha Aparecida. *Utopia e realidade: o Brasil no começo do século XX*. São Paulo: Cultrix, 1979.
Dellepiane, Angela B. "Ciencia y literatura en un texto de Eduardo L. Holmberg." *Homenaje a Alfredo A. Roggiano: En este aire de América*. Eds. Keith McDuffie and Rose S. Minc. Pittsburgh.: Instituto Internacional de Literatura Iberoamericana, 1990. 457–76.
———. "Narrativa argentina de ciencia ficción: Tentativas liminares y desarrollo posterior." *Actas del IX congreso de la Asociación Internacional de Hispanistas: 18–23 agosto 1986, Berlin*. Ed. Sebastian Neumeister. Frankfurt am Main: Vervuert, 1989. 515–25.
Duffey, J. Patrick. "Amado Nervo." *Latin American Science Fiction Writers: An A-to-Z Guide*. Ed. Darrell B. Lockhart. Westport, CT: Greenwood, 2004. 135–39.
Durán, Manuel. *Genio y figura de Amado Nervo*. Buenos Aires: Editorial Universitaria de Buenos Aires, 1968.
Dziubinskyj, Aaron. "The Birth of Science Fiction in Spanish America." *Science Fiction Studies* 30.1 (2003): 21–32.
———. "Eduardo Urzaiz's *Eugenia*: Eugenics, Gender, and Dystopian Society in Twenty-Third-Century Mexico." *Science Fiction Studies* 34.3 (2007): 463–72.
Eiseley, Loren. *Darwin's Century: Evolution and the Men Who Discovered It*. Garden City, NJ: Doubleday, 1958.
Englekirk, John Eugene. *Edgar Allan Poe in Hispanic Literature*. New York: Russell & Russell, 1972.
Eulálio, Alexandre. "Apêndices." *Memórias do Distrito Diamantino da Comarca do Sêrro Frio, Província de Minas Gerais*. By Joaquim Felício dos Santos. 3rd ed. Rio de Janeiro: O Cruzeiro, 1956. 425–62.
———. *Joaquim Felício dos Santos: Cronista romântico*. São Paulo: Jacaremirim, 1976.

———. "A obra menor de Joaquim Felício dos Santos: Notícia literária." *Memórias do Distrito Diamantino da Comarca do Sêrro Frio, Província de Minas Gerais*. By Joaquim Felício dos Santos. 3rd ed. Rio de Janeiro: O Cruzeiro, 1956. 31–45.

———. "As páginas do ano de 2000: Joaquim Felício dos Santos." *Revista do Livro* 2.6 (1957): 103–8.

Evans, Arthur B. *Jules Verne Rediscovered: Didacticism and the Scientific Novel*. Contributions to the Study of World Literature. 27. New York: Greenwood, 1988.

———. "Optograms and Fiction: Photo in a Dead Man's Eye." *Science Fiction Studies* 20.3(1993): 341–61.

Fernández-Delgado, Miguel Ángel. "Discurso sobre un nuevo método para el estudio de la ciencia ficción latinoamericana." *Ciencia Ficción Mexicana*. N.p., n.d. Web. 5 Oct. 2006.

———. "Introducción." *Visiones periféricas: Antología de la ciencia ficción mexicana*. Ed. Miguel Ángel Fernández-Delgado. Mexico D.F.: Lumen, 2001. 7–17.

———. "Pedro Castera." *Latin American Science Fiction Writers: An A-to-Z Guide*. Ed. Darrell B. Lockhart. Westport, CT: Greenwood, 2004. 50–51.

———. "Ciencia ficción mexicana (primeras respuestas: Nervo y Natalis)." Message to the author. 26 July 2008. E-mail.

———. "Re: Más respuestas." Message to the author. 5 Aug. 2008. E-mail.

Flammarion, Camille. *Lumen*. Trans. Brian Stableford. The Wesleyan Early Classics of Science Fiction Series. Ed. Arthur B. Evans. Middletown, CT: Wesleyan University Press, 2002.

Foote, Bud. *The Connecticut Yankee in the Twentieth Century: Travel to the Past in Science Fiction*. New York: Greenwood, 1991.

Foster, David William. "Prólogo (Preface)." *Ciencia ficción en español: Una mitología moderna ante el cambio*. By Yolanda Molina-Gavilán. Lewiston, NY: Edwin Mellen Press, 2002. v–vii.

Franklin, H. Bruce. *Future Perfect: American Science Fiction of the Nineteenth Century: An Anthology*. Rev. and expanded. New Brunswick, NJ: Rutgers University Press, 1995.

Fraser, Howard M. "Apes and Ape Lore in Turn-of-the-Century Buenos Aires." *Studies in Latin American Popular Culture* 8 (1989): 61–79.

———. "Apocalyptic Vision and Modernism's Dismantling of Scientific Discourse: Lugones's 'Yzur.'" *Hispania* 79.1 (1996): 8–19.

———. *Magazines & Masks: Caras y Caretas as a Reflection of Buenos Aires, 1898–1908*. Tempe: Center for Latin American Studies, Arizona State University, 1987.

Frederick, Bonnie. "A State of Conviction, a State of Feeling: Scientific and Literary Discourses in the Works of Three Argentine Writers, 1879–1908." *Latin American Literary Review* July–December (1991): 48–61.

Frye, Northrop. "Varieties of Literary Utopias." *Utopias and Utopian Thought*. Ed. Frank Edward Manuel. Boston: Houghton Mifflin, 1966. 25–49.

Gandolfo, Elvio E. "La ciencia-ficción argentina." Prologue. *Los universos vislumbrados: Antología de ciencia-ficción argentina*. Ed. Jorge A. Sánchez. Buenos Aires: Andrómeda, 1995. 13–50.

García, Guillermo. "El otro lado de la ficción: Ciencia ficción." *Historia crítica de la literatura argentina*. Eds. Noé Jitrik and Susana Cella. Vol. 10. Buenos Aires: Emecé, 1999. 313–40.

García Canclini, Néstor. *Hybrid Cultures: Strategies for Entering and Leaving Modernity*. Trans. Christopher L. Chiappari and Silvia L. López. Minneapolis: University of Minnesota Press, 1995.

García Mérou, Martín. *Recuerdos literarios*. Buenos Aires: La Cultura Argentina, 1915.

García Ramos, Arturo. "Introducción." *Las fuerzas extrañas*. By Leopoldo Lugones. Letras Hispánicas. Madrid: Cátedra, 1996. 9–91.

Gaut vel Hartman, Sergio. "Prólogo." *Latinoamérica fantástica*. Ed. Augusto Uribe. Barcelona: Ultramar, 1985. 11–13.

Gernsback, Hugo. "A New Sort of Magazine." *Amazing Stories* 1.1 (1926): 3.

Ginway, M. Elizabeth. *Brazilian Science Fiction: Cultural Myths and Nationhood in the Land of the Future*. Lewisburg, PA: Bucknell University Press, 2004.

———. "A Working Model for Analyzing Third World Science Fiction: The Case of Brazil." *Science Fiction Studies* 32.3 (2005): 467–94.

"Godfrey Barnsley and Barnsley Gardens." *Barnsley Gardens Resort*. Cartersville-Bartow County Visitor Information Center, n.d. Web. 15 May 2008.

Goligorsky, Eduardo, ed. and comp. *Los argentinos en la luna*. Buenos Aires: De la Flor, 1968.

Goligorsky, Eduardo. "Prólogo." *Los argentinos en la luna*. Buenos Aires: Ediciones de la Flor, 1968. 9–13.

González, Santiago. *Miguel Cané*. Buenos Aires: Centro Editor de América Latina, 1968.

González Casanova, Pablo. *La literatura perseguida en la crisis de la colonia*. México: Colegio de México, 1958.

González Echevarría, Roberto. *Myth and Archive: A Theory of Latin American Narrative*. 1990. Durham, NC: Duke University Press, 1998.

Gunn, James E. "Spain and Latin America." *The Road to Science Fiction Volume 6: Around the World*. Ed. James E. Gunn. Vol. 6. Clarkston, GA: White Wolf, 1998. 480–83.

Gutiérrez Girardot, Rafael. *Modernismo*. Barcelona: Montesinos, 1983.
Hahn, Óscar. "Estudio." *El cuento fantástico hispanoamericano en el siglo XIX*. Mexico City: Premia Editora, 1982. 11–98.
Haywood Ferreira, Rachel. "Back to the Future: The Expanding Field of Latin-American Science Fiction." *Hispania* 91.2 (2008): 352–62.
———. "By Burro and by *Beagle*: Geographical Journeys through Time in Latin American Science Fiction." *Journal of the Fantastic in the Arts* 18.2 (2007): 166–86.
———. "The Emergence of Latin American Science Fiction: A Global Genre in the Periphery." Diss. Yale University, 2003.
———. "The First Wave: Latin American Science Fiction Discovers Its Roots." *Science Fiction Studies* 34.3 (2007): 432–62.
———. "*Más Allá*, *El Eternauta*, and the Dawn of the Golden Age of Latin American Science Fiction: (1953–59)." *Extrapolation* 51.2 (2010): 281–303.
Hicken, Cristóbal M. *Bibliografía del Dr. Eduardo Ladislao Holmberg*. Buenos Aires: Coni, 1922.
Hoffmann, E. T. A. "The Sandman." 1816. *Fantastic Tales: Visionary and Everyday*. Ed. Italo Calvino. New York: Vintage, 1997. 33–72.
Holmberg, Eduardo Ladislao. *Carlos Roberto Darwin*. Buenos Aires: El Nacional, 1882.
———. *Lin-Calél*. Buenos Aires: L.J. Rosso, 1910.
Holmberg, Luis. *Holmberg el último enciclopedista*. Buenos Aires: Colombo, 1952.
"Introducción." *El Liceo Mexicano* 1.1 (1844): 3–4.
Jackson, Rosemary. *Fantasy: The Literature of Subversion*. 1981. New Accents. New York: Routledge, 1998.
Jameson, Fredric. "Progress Versus Utopia; or, Can We Imagine the Future?" *Science Fiction Studies* 9.2 (1982): 147–58.
———. "Third-World Literature in the Era of Multinational Capitalism." *Social Text* 15 (1986): 65–88.
Jensen, Theodore W. "Christian-Pythagorean Dualism in Nervo's *El donador de almas*." *Kentucky Romance Quarterly* 28.4 (1981): 391–401.
Jitrik, Noé. "Prólogo." *Obras inéditas y desconocidas*. By Horacio Quiroga. Ed. Angel Rama. Novelas Cortas. Vol. 1. Montevideo: Arca, 1967. 7–22.
Jrade, Cathy L. "Modernist Poetry." *The Cambridge History of Latin American Literature*. Eds. Roberto González Echevarría and Enrique Pupo-Walker. Vol. 2. Cambridge: Cambridge University Press, 1996. 7–68.
Klotz, Irving M. "The N-Ray Affair." *Scientific American* May 1980: 168–75.

Kopp, James J. "The Other Y2K Crisis." *Eclectica Magazine* 3.2. (1999): n.p. Web. 6 Feb. 2002.

Kumar, Krishan. *Utopia and Anti-Utopia in Modern Times*. Oxford: Blackwell, 1987.

Landon, Brooks. *Science Fiction after 1900: From the Steam Man to the Stars*. Genres in Context. New York: Routledge, 2002.

Larson, Ross. *Fantasy and Imagination in the Mexican Narrative*. Tempe: Arizona State University Press, 1977.

Le Bon, Gustave. *The Evolution of Matter*. Trans. F. Legge. New York: Walter Scott Publishing Co., 1907.

Le Guin, Ursula K. "Introduction." *The Norton Book of Science Fiction: North American Science Fiction, 1960–1990*. Eds. Ursula K. Le Guin and Brian Attebery. New York: W.W. Norton, 1993. 15–42.

Liais, Emmanuel. *L'Espace Céleste et la Nature Tropicale. Description Physique de L'Univers D'après des Observations Personnelles Faites dans les Deux Hémispheres*. Paris: Garnier Frères, 1865.

"Literatura de ciencia ficción en Chile." *Memoria Chilena*. Biblioteca Nacional de Chile y otras instituciones de la Dirección de Bibliotecas, Archivos y Museos (DIBAM), n.d. Web. 30 Apr. 2007.

Lobo Carneiro, Fernando. "Comentários ao romance *O Doutor Benignus*." *O Doutor Benignus*. By Augusto Emílio Zaluar. 1875. Rio de Janeiro: UFRJ, 1994. 13–17.

Lojo, María Rosa. "Prólogo." *Juanamanuela, mucho papel: Algunas lecturas críticas de textos de Juana Manuela Gorriti*. Comp. Amelia Royo. Salta, Argentina: Ediciones del Robledal, 1999. 11–14.

López Castro, Ramón. *Expedición a la ciencia ficción mexicana*. Mexico City: Lectorum, 2001.

López Cortes, Br. Silvia. Essay on Eduardo Urzaiz Rodríguez. *Dr. Eduardo Urzáiz Rodríguez*. Certamen de biografías de yucatecos ilustres, 1. Mérida, Mexico: Ediciones de la Universidad de Yucatán, 1977. 23–48.

Ludmer, Josefina. *The Corpus Delicti: A Manual of Argentine Fictions*. Trans. Glen S. Close. Pittsburgh: University of Pittsburgh Press, 2004.

———. *El cuerpo del delito: Un manual*. Buenos Aires: Perfil Libros, 1999.

Machado, Ubiratan. *Os intelectuais e o espiritismo: De Castro Alves a Machado de Assis*. Rio de Janeiro: Edições Antares; Instituto Nacional do Livro, 1983.

Magalhães, Basílio de. *Estudos da história do Brasil*. São Paulo: Companhia Editora Nacional, 1940.

Marini Palmieri, Enrique. *El modernismo literario hispanoamericano: Caracteres esotéricos en las obras de Darío y Lugones*. Colección Estudios Latinoamericanos. Buenos Aires: Fernando García Cambeiro, 1989.

Martins, Wilson. *História da inteligência brasileira*. 7 vols. São Paulo: Cultrix, 1976.

Marún, Gioconda. "Introducción." *Olimpio Pitango de Monalia*. Ed. Gioconda Marún. Ed. príncipe. Buenos Aires: Ediciones Solar, 1994. 7–69.

———. "Obra literaria de Holmberg." *Eduardo L. Holmberg: Cuarenta y tres años de obras manuscritas e inéditas (1872–1915)*. Madrid: Iberoamericana; Vervuert, 2002. 51–52.

Más allá: Revista mensual de fantasía científica [Buenos Aires] 1.1–4.48 (1953–1957).

Masiello, Francine. *Between Civilization & Barbarism: Women, Nation, and Literary Culture in Modern Argentina*. Engendering Latin America, v. 2. Lincoln: University of Nebraska Press, 1992.

McLemee, Scott. "Back to the Future." *New York Times Book Review*, 24 Dec. 2000, 23.

Meehan, Thomas C. "Una olvidada precursora de la literatura fantástica argentina: Juana Manuela Gorriti." *Chasqui* 10.2–3 (1981): 3–19.

Menéndez Díaz, Conrado. Preface to the 1947 edition. *Eugenia. (Esbozo novelesco de costumbres futuras)*. By Eduardo Urzaiz (Rodríguez). Mérida, Yucatán, México: Universidad Autónoma de Yucatán, 2002. 13–17.

Mercier, Louis-Sébastien. *L'An Deux Mille Quatre Cent Quarant*. 1771. Bordeaux, France: Ducros, 1971.

———. *Memoirs of the Year Two Thousand Five Hundred*. 1771. Trans. W. Hooper. Philadelphia: Thomas Dobson, 1795. New York: Sentry, 1973.

Meyer, Michael C., William L. Sherman, and Susan M. Deeds. *The Course of Mexican History*. 6th ed. New York: Oxford University Press, 1999.

Molina-Gavilán, Yolanda. *Ciencia ficción en español: Una mitología moderna ante el cambio*. Lewiston, NY: Edwin Mellen, 2002.

Molina-Gavilán, Yolanda, Andrea Bell, Miguel Ángel Fernández-Delgado, M. Elizabeth Ginway, Luis Pestarini, and Juan Carlos Toledano Redondo. "A Chronology of Latin American Science Fiction, 1775–2005." *Science Fiction Studies* 34.3 (2007): 369–431.

Molina-Gavilán, Yolanda, Miguel Ángel Fernández-Delgado, Andrea Bell, Luis Pestarini, and Juan Carlos Toledano "Cronología de cf latinoamericana: 1775–1999." *Chasqui* 29.2 (2000): 43–72.

Molina Jiménez, Iván. "La polémica de *El problema* (1899), de Máximo Soto Hall." *Revista Mexicana del Caribe* 12 (2001): 147–87.

Monroe, John Warne. *Laboratories of Faith: Mesmerism, Spiritism, and Occultism in Modern France*. Ithaca: Cornell University Press, 2008.

Monsiváis, Carlos. *Yo te bendigo, vida: Amado Nervo, crónica de vida y obra*. [Nayarit, Mexico]: Gobierno del Estado [de] Nayarit, 2002.

Montserrat, Marcelo. "La mentalidad evolucionista en la Argentina: Una ideología del progreso." *El Darwinismo en España e Iberoamérica*. Ed. Thomas F. Glick, Rosaura Ruiz and Miguel Angel Puig-Samper. Mexico City: Universidad Nacional Autónoma de México, 1999. 19–46.

Moore, R. Laurence. *In Search of White Crows: Spiritualism, Parapsychology, and American Culture*. New York: Oxford University Press, 1977.

Morales, Ana María. "Un viaje novohispano a la luna (*ca.* 1772), de fray Manuel Antonio de Rivas, franciscano." *Literatura Mexicana* 5.2 (1994): 555–68.

Morosetti, Tiziana. "A Fence against the Other: Utopian and Science Fiction in West Africa." MLA Convention. Sheraton Hotel, Chicago. 29 Dec. 2007.

Moylan, Tom. *Scraps of the Untainted Sky: Science Fiction, Utopia, Dystopia*. Boulder, CO: Westview Press, 2000.

Needell, Jeffrey D. *A Tropical Belle Epoque: Elite Culture and Society in Turn-of-the-Century Rio de Janeiro*. Cambridge Latin American Studies 62. New York: Cambridge University Press, 1987.

Nervo, Amado. "Los aeroplanos: Esto matará a aquello.—el automóvil vivirá poco." *Obras completas*. 1911 (collected in *Crónicas de Europa*). Ed. Francisco González Guerrero and Alfonso Méndez Plancarte. Vol. 1. Madrid: Aguilar, 1962. 1273–74.

———. "Eugenesia." *Obras completas*. 1916. Ed. Francisco González Guerrero and Alfonso Méndez Plancarte. Vol. 2. Madrid: Aguilar, 1962. 821–26.

———. "La literatura maravillosa." *Obras completas*. [1908]. Ed. Francisco González Guerrero and Alfonso Méndez Plancarte. Vol. 2. Madrid: Aguilar, 1962. 706–7.

———. "El 'mono-hombre.'" *Obras completas*. 1908. Ed. Francisco González Guerrero and Alfonso Méndez Plancarte. Vol. 2. Madrid: Aguilar, 1962. 717–18.

Nicholls, Peter. "Devolution." *The Encyclopedia of Science Fiction*. Ed. John Clute and Peter Nicholls. New York: St. Martin's Griffin, 1995. 325–26.

Nicholls, Peter, and Tom Shippey. "Magic." *The Encyclopedia of Science Fiction*. Ed. John Clute and Peter Nicholls. New York: St. Martin's Griffin, 1995. 765–67.

Nicolson, Marjorie Hope. *Voyages to the Moon*. New York: Macmillan Co., 1948.

Oesterheld, Héctor G., and Francisco Solano López. *El Eternauta: 1957–2007, 50 años*. 1957–1959. Buenos Aires: Doedytores, 2007.

Olaguíbel, Manuel de. "El magnetismo." *El Domingo: Semanario Político y Literario* [later subtitled *Semanario de Literatura, Ciencias y Mejoras Materiales*] [Mexico City] 15 Oct. 1871: 38–39.

Ortiz, Eduardo L. "On the Transition from Realism to the Fantastic in the Argentine Literature of the 1870s: Holmberg and the Córdoba Six." *Science and the Creative Imagination in Latin America*. Eds. Evelyn Fishburn and Eduardo L. Ortiz. London: Institute for the Study of the Americas, 2005. 59–85.

———. "The Transmission of Science from Europe to Argentina and Its Impact on Literature: From Lugones to Borges." *Borges and Europe Revisited*. Ed. Evelyn Fishburn. London: University of London, 1998. 108–23.

Oviedo, José Miguel. *Historia de la literatura hispanoamericana*. Vol. 2. Madrid: Alianza, 2003.

Pagés Larraya, Antonio. "Estudio preliminar." *Cuentos fantásticos*. By Eduardo Ladislao Holmberg. Buenos Aires: Librería Hachette, 1957. 7–98.

Paz, Octavio. "The Sons of La Malinche." Trans. Lysander Kemp, Yara Milos and Rachel Phillips Belash. *The Labyrinth of Solitude*. New York: Grove, 1985. 65–88.

Peniche Vallado, Leopoldo. "El mensaje de *Eugenia*." Preface to the 1955 edition. *Eugenia. (Esbozo novelesco de costumbres futuras)*. By Eduardo Urzaiz (Rodríguez). Mérida, Yucatán, México: Universidad Autónoma de Yucatán, 2002. 19–30.

Pesa, Juan de Dios. "Prólogo." *Cuentos macabros*. By Alejandro Cuevas. Mexico City: J. R. Garrido y Hermano, 1911. i–iv.

Pessina, Héctor R., and Jorge A. Sánchez. "Esbozo para una cronología comentada de la ciencia-ficción argentina." Supplement. *Los universos vislumbrados: Antología de ciencia-ficción argentina*. 1978. Ed. Jorge A. Sánchez. 2nd ed. Buenos Aires: Andrómeda, 1995. 275–86.

Pestarini, Luis. "'Delirio': El primer cuento de ciencia ficción en Argentina." *Cuasar*. 13 May [2005?]. Web. 2 June 2008.

Poe, Edgar Allan. "The Tell-Tale Heart." *The Oxford Book of American Short Stories*. Ed. Joyce Carol Oates. New York: Oxford University Press, 1992. 92–96.

Rabkin, Eric S. "Introduction: Why Destroy the World?" *The End of the World*. Ed. Martin H. Greenberg, Eric S. Rabkin, Joseph D. Olander. Carbondale, IL: Southern Illinois University Press, 1983. vii–xv.

Regina, Ivan Carlos. "Manifesto Antropofágico da Ficção Científica Brasileira—Movimento Supernova." 1988. *D.O. Leitura* 12.138 (1993): 8.

Reis, Osíris. "Manifesto Antibrasilitite." *Movimento Antibrasilitite*. N.p., Sept. 2004. Web. 4 May 2007.

———. "Pergunta sobre Manifesto." Message to the author. 23 June 2009. E-mail.

Rejón Osorio, María Cristina. "Chinaco Rosas." *Dr. Eduardo Urzáiz Rodríguez.* Certamen de biografías de yucatecos ilustres, 1. Mérida, Mexico: Ediciones de la Universidad de Yucatán, 1977. 7–21.

Rela, Walter. *Horacio Quiroga: Repertorio bibliográfico anotado, 1897–1971.* Buenos Aires: Casa Pardo, 1973.

Rock, David. *Argentina 1516–1987: From Spanish Colonization to Alfonsín.* Rev. and expanded. Berkeley: University of California Press, 1987.

Rodríguez, Julia. *Civilizing Argentina: Science, Medicine, and the Modern State.* Chapel Hill: University of North Carolina Press, 2006.

Rodríguez Barilari, Elbio. "El otro Quiroga." *Los perseguidos: Cuentos.* By Horacio Quiroga. Montevideo: Banda Oriental, 1989. 5–8.

Rose, Mark. *Alien Encounters: Anatomy of Science Fiction.* Cambridge: Harvard University Press, 1981.

Ruz Menéndez, Rodolfo. "Visión del futuro proveniente del pasado: Yucatán, en 1949, entrevisto, con un siglo de antelación, por notable escritor vernáculo." *Ensayos Yucatanenses.* Mérida de Yucatán: Universidad de Yucatán, 1976. 273–78.

Ryman, Geoff. "In Praise of Science Fiction." *28th International Conference on the Fantastic in the Arts.* Hilton Fort Lauderdale Airport Hotel, Fort Lauderdale, FL, 15 Mar. 2007.

———. "The Science Fiction Dream." ICFA 2007 Guest of Honor Address. *Journal of the Fantastic in the Arts* 18.2 (2007): 232–46.

Sargent, Lyman Tower. "The Three Faces of Utopianism Revisited." *Utopian Studies: Journal of the Society for Utopian Studies* 5.1 (1994): 1–37.

———. "Utopia: The Problem of Definition." *Extrapolation: A Journal of Science Fiction and Fantasy* 16.2 (1975): 137–48.

Sarlo, Beatriz. *La imaginación técnica: Sueños modernos de la cultura argentina.* Buenos Aires: Ediciones Nueva Visión, 1992.

———. *The Technical Imagination: Argentine Culture's Modern Dreams.* Trans. Xavier Callahan. Stanford, CA: Stanford University Press, 2008.

Sarmiento, Domingo Faustino. *Facundo: Civilización y barbarie: Vida de Juan Facundo Quiroga.* Mexico: Porrua, 1989.

Scari, Robert M. "Ciencia y ficción en los cuentos de Leopoldo Lugones." *Revista Iberoamericana* enero-junio (1964): 163–87.

Schneider, Luis Mario. "Pedro Castera: Un delirante del XIX." *Impresiones y recuerdos; Las minas y los mineros; Los maduros dramas; Dramas en un corazon; Querens.* By Pedro Castera. México: Editorial Patria, 1987. 7–30.

Schwarz, Mauricio-José and Braulio Tavares. "Latin America." *The Encyclopedia of Science Fiction.* Ed. John Clute and Peter Nicholls. New York: St. Martin's Griffin, 1995. 693–97.

Schwarz, Roberto. "Nacional por subtração." *Que horas são? Ensaios.* São Paulo: Cia. das Letras, 1987. 29–48.

"Scientific method." *Shorter Oxford English Dictionary.* 5th ed. 2002.

Shelley, Mary Wollstonecraft. *Frankenstein; or, the Modern Prometheus (the 1818 Text).* Chicago: University of Chicago Press, 1982.

Silva, Cesar and Marcello Simão Branco. *Anuário brasileiro de literatura fantástica: Ficção científica, fantasia e horror no Brasil em 2005.* São Bernardo do Campo, São Paulo, Brazil: Hiperespaço / Sociedade Brasileira de Arte Fantástica, 2006.

Skidmore, Thomas E. *Brazil: Five Centuries of Change.* Latin American Histories. New York: Oxford University Press, 1999.

Sommer, Doris. *Foundational Fictions: The National Romances of Latin America.* Berkeley: University of California Press, 1991.

Soriano, Michèle. "El saber de la ficción en 'Quien escucha su mal oye': Estudio sociocrítico de los inicios del género fantástico." *Juanamanuela, mucho papel: Algunas lecturas críticas de textos de Juana Manuela Gorriti.* Comp. Amelia Royo. Salta, Argentina: Ediciones del Robledal, 1999. 241–84.

Souto, Marcial. *La ciencia ficción en la argentina : Antología crítica.* Colección Literatura Actual. Buenos Aires: Eudeba, 1985.

Souza de Fernández, Candelaria. "Prólogo." *Oficio de mentor: Biografía del Dr. Eduardo Urzaiz Rodríguez.* By Carlos Urzaiz Jiménez. Mérida, Yucatán, Mexico: Ediciones de la Universidad Autónoma de Yucatán, 1995. 9–13.

Stableford, Brian M. "Far Future." *The Encyclopedia of Science Fiction.* Ed. John Clute and Peter Nicholls. New York: St. Martin's Griffin, 1995. 415–16.

———. "Frankenstein and the Origins of Science Fiction." *Anticipations : Essays on Early Science Fiction and Its Precursors.* Ed. David Seed. Syracuse, NY: Syracuse University Press, 1995. 46–57.

———. "Introduction." *Lumen.* Trans. Brian M. Stableford. The Wesleyan Early Classics of Science Fiction Series. Ed. Arthur B. Evans. Middletown, CT: Wesleyan University Press, 2002. ix–xxxv.

———. "Man-Made Catastrophes." *The End of the World.* Ed. Martin H. Greenberg, Eric S. Rabkin, Joseph D. Olander. Carbondale, IL: Southern Illinois University Press, 1983. 97–138.

———. "Near Future." *The Encyclopedia of Science Fiction.* Ed. John Clute and Peter Nicholls. New York: St. Martin's Griffin, 1995. 856–58.

———. "Proto Science Fiction." *The Encyclopedia of Science Fiction.* Ed. John Clute and Peter Nicholls. New York: St. Martin's Griffin, 1995. 965–67.

———. *Scientific Romance in Britain, 1890–1950.* New York: St. Martin's, 1985.

Standage, Tom. *The Victorian Internet: The Remarkable Story of the Telegraph and the Nineteenth Century's On-Line Pioneers*. New York: Walker, 1998.

Staples, Anne. "Una primitiva ciencia ficción en México." *Ciencia y Desarrollo* 12.73 (1987): 145–48.

Stepan, Nancy. *Beginnings of Brazilian Science: Oswaldo Cruz, Medical Research and Policy, 1890–1920*. New York: Science History Publications, 1976.

———. *The Hour of Eugenics: Race, Gender, and Nation in Latin America*. Ithaca: Cornell University Press, 1991.

Stern, Irwin. *Dictionary of Brazilian Literature*. New York: Greenwood, 1988.

Suárez de la Torre, Laura. "Los intereses de las principales casas editoriales de la Ciudad de México entre 1840 y 1855." *Literatura mexicana del otro fin de siglo*. Ed. Rafael Olea Franco. Mexico City: Colegio de México, 2001. 577–93.

Suvin, Darko. *Metamorphoses of Science Fiction: On the Poetics and History of a Literary Genre*. New Haven: Yale University Press, 1979.

Tavares, Braulio. "Como era o ano 2000 na imaginação dos artistas enquanto ele não chegava." *Estado de São Paulo: Jornal da Tarde*. 29 July 2000, Saturday Supplement. Web. 6 Feb. 2002.

———. *Fantastic, Fantasy and Science Fiction Literature Catalog*. International Publications Series. 2. Rio de Janeiro: Biblioteca Nacional, [1991].

———. "As origens da ficção científica no Brasil." *D.O. Leitura* 12.138 (1993): 2–3.

———. Personal interview. Rio de Janeiro, 4 July 2000.

———. *O que é ficção científica*. 1986. Primeiros Passos. São Paulo: Brasiliense, 1992.

Tavares, Braulio and Mauricio-José Schwarz. "Latin America." *The Encyclopedia of Science Fiction*. Ed. John Clute and Peter Nicholls. New York: St. Martin's Griffin, 1995. 693–97.

Teixeira Neves, José. "Joaquim Felício dos Santos: Estudo biográfico." *Memórias do Distrito Diamantino da Comarca do Sêrro Frio, Província de Minas Gerais*. By Joaquim Felício dos Santos. 3rd ed. Rio de Janeiro: Edições O Cruzeiro, 1956. 19–30.

Todorov, Tzvetan. *The Fantastic: A Structural Approach to a Literary Genre*. Trans. Richard Howard. Ithaca: Cornell University Press, 1973.

Toledo, Marleine Paula Marcondes e Ferreira de. "Demônios." *D.O. Leitura* 12.138 (1993): 16.

Trujillo Muñoz, Gabriel. *Biografías del futuro: La ciencia ficción mexicana y sus autores*. Mexicali, Mexico: Universidad Autónoma de Baja California, 2000.

———. *La ciencia ficción: Literatura y conocimiento*. Libros de Baja California. Mexicali, Mexico: Instituto de Cultura de Baja California, 1991.

———. "El futuro en llamas: Breve crónica de la ciencia ficción mexicana." *El futuro en llamas: Cuentos clásicos de la ciencia ficción mexicana*. Ed. Gabriel Trujillo Muñoz. Mexico DF: Vid, 1997. 7–29.

———. "Prólogo." *Más allá de lo imaginado: Antología de ciencia ficción mexicana*. Ed. Federico Schaffler González. México, D.F.: Tierra Adentro and Consejo Nacional para la Cultura y las Artes, 1991. 7–15.

Urías Horcasitas, Beatriz. "El 'Hombre nuevo' de la posrevolución." *Letras Libres* May (2007): 58–61.

Urzaiz Jiménez, Carlos. *Oficio de mentor: Biografía del Dr. Eduardo Urzaiz Rodríguez*. Mérida, Yucatán, Mexico: Ediciones de la Universidad Autónoma de Yucatán, 1995.

Vega, Omar. "Ciencia ficción chilena." Message to the author. 20 Nov. 2006. E-mail.

———. "En la luna: Un bosquejo de la ciencia-ficción chilena." *Memoria Chilena*. Biblioteca Nacional de Chile y otras instituciones de la Dirección de Bibliotecas, Archivos y Museos (DIBAM), n.d. Web. 20 Nov, 2006.

Verne, Jules. *Journey to the Centre of the Earth*. Trans., introd. and notes by William Butcher. Oxford: Oxford University Press, 2008.

Villiers de L'Isle-Adam, Auguste. *Tomorrow's Eve*. 1886. Urbana: University of Illinois Press, 1982.

Wagar, W. Warren. "The Rebellion of Nature." *The End of the World*. Ed. Martin H. Greenberg, Eric S. Rabkin, Joseph D. Olander. Carbondale, IL: Southern Illinois University Press, 1983. 139–72.

———. "Round Trips to Doomsday" *The End of the World*. Ed. Martin H. Greenberg, Eric S. Rabkin, Joseph D. Olander. Carbondale, IL: Southern Illinois University Press, 1983. 73–96.

———. *Good Tidings: The Belief in Progress from Darwin to Marcuse*. Bloomington: Indiana University Press, 1972.

Weinberg, Félix. *Dos utopías argentinas de principios de siglo*. Dimensión Argentina. Buenos Aires: Solar/Hachette, 1976.

Wells, H.G. *Anticipations of the Reaction of Mechanical and Scientific Progress upon Human Life and Thought*. New York: Harper, 1902.

———. *The Time Machine*. In *The Works of H. G. Wells*. Atlantic edition. Vol. 1. New York: Charles Scribner's Sons, 1924. 3–118.

———. *A Critical Edition of the War of the Worlds: H.G. Wells's Scientific Romance*. Intro. and notes David Y. Hughes and Harry M. Geduld. Bloomington: Indiana University Press, 1993.

———. *When the Sleeper Wakes*. Project Gutenberg. NetLibrary, n.d. Web. 31 July 2003.

Westfahl, Gary. "Fantastic." *The Encyclopedia of Fantasy*. Ed. John Clute and John Grant. New York: St. Martin's Griffin, 1999. 335.

Wolfe, Gary K. *Critical Terms for Science Fiction and Fantasy: A Glossary and Guide to Scholarship*. Westport, CT: Greenwood, 1986.

———. *The Known and the Unknown: The Iconography of Science Fiction*. Kent, OH: Kent State University Press, 1979.

———. "The Remaking of Zero: Beginning at the End." *The End of the World*. Ed. Martin H. Greenberg, Eric S. Rabkin, Joseph D. Olander. Carbondale, IL: Southern Illinois University Press, 1983. 1–19.

Yeomans, Donald K. *Comets: A Chronological History of Observation, Science, Myth, and Folklore*. Wiley science editions. New York: Wiley, 1991.

Zaluar, Alba. "América redescoberta: O civilizado cientista e seus outros." *O Doutor Benignus*. By Augusto Emílio Zaluar. 1875. Rio de Janeiro: UFRJ, 1994. 371–76.

INDEX

Page numbers in bold refer to overview sections for principal works. Page numbers in italics refer to figures.

Abraham, Carlos, 48, 50
Acayaca (Santos), 23
Adam and Eve theme, 112–13, 122–23, 129, 182, 244n20, 250n27
"aeroplanos, Los" (Nervo). *See* "Airplanes"
Agrippa, Heinrich Cornelius, 206
águila y la serpiente, El (Guzmán). *See Eagle and the Serpent, The*
"Airplanes" (Nervo), 118
Akka people, 98–99, 243n14
Alberdi, Juan Bautista, 45, 237n22
Alencar, José de, 28
Alkon, Paul K., 17, 27, 217, 235nn5–6, 247n4, 253n16
allegory, 47, 239n35
Altamirano, Ignacio Manuel, 157, 186
Alter-Gilbert, Gilbert, 244n23, 245n29
American Society for Psychical Research, 135, 247n5
Anastasio (pseud.), 251n4
Andrade, Oswald de, 218
Andral, Gabriel, 150
androids, 172, 184–85
"aparato del Doctor Tolimán, El" (Cuevas). *See* "Apparatus of Doctor Tolimán, The"
apocalyptic themes: overview, 109–16; apocalyptic comet in "The End of the World," 110–13; apocalyptic modernism, 117; end-of-wars in *Eugenia*, 76; last-man-alive themes, 110, 125; natural catastrophe in "Demons," 113; spiralform pattern in "The Last War," 123; technological catastrophe themes, 128–29, 181–83
"Apparatus of Doctor Tolimán, The" (Cuevas), **186–93**; human double theme in, 172–73; plot structure of, 187–92, 253n11; resurrection theme in, 189–92; scientific discourse in, 189, 252n9
Argentina: eugenics movement in, 238n27; fictional representation in *Nic-Nac*, 40–42; Generation of 1880, 35, 46, 50, 146; *pampa* as primitive region, 82–83; political unrest of the 1870s, 34–35, 96–97; population discourse and, 45; Quiroga representation of Buenos Aires, 195–98; representations of race in, 238n29; republican government, 93; Revolution of 1890, 46, 238n24; Rosas political ascendancy, 147; scientific discourse in, 14, 40, 237n18; sf as nationalist discourse, 100, 222
Argentine Naturalist, The (Holmberg), 35–36, 237n18
Argirópolis (Sarmiento), 234n2
Ariosto, Ludovico, 118

283

"armonías de la luz, Las" (Cané). *See* "Harmonies of Light, The"

Artificial Man, The (Quiroga), **194–209**; Biógeno (created being) in, 199–204, *201, 203, 205,* 207, 214, 253n16; *Frankenstein* compared with, 204, 206–8; limits of humanity in, 214; national identity in, 215; as pivotal sf work, 194–95; plot structure of, 195–99, 253n14, 253n17; power dynamics in, 253n15; social issues in, 208–9; Villiers influence on, 250n27; writing of, 193–94

"atrevida operación del doctor Orts, La" (Cione). *See* "Doctor Orts's Daring Operation"

Augustine of Hippo (St. Augustine), 157, 249n24

automatons, 172–73, 178–80, 183–86

automobiles, 57, 65–66, 118–19

autoscopy, 164–65

Avellaneda, Nicolás, 96–97

Azevedo, Aluísio: apocalyptic themes in, 110; political and religious views, 113. Works: *The Brazilian Tenement*, 113; "Demons," 110, **113–16**, 246nn37–38; *The Mulatto*, 113

Baczko, Bronislaw, 235n6

balloons, 19–20, 22, 91

Barbosa, Rui, 55–57, 64

Barnsley, Godofredo Emerson: biographical sketch, 42–43, 53–54, 239n36; on national regeneration, 59–60, 64–66; on race, 63–65; on women, 60–61, *62*. See also *São Paulo in the Year 2000 or National Regeneration*

Bell, Andrea, 222–23, 232n4, 234n2

Bellamy, Edward: Ezcurra references to, 49; influence on Barnsley, 54, 64–66; influence on Latin American sf, 43; influence on Urzaiz, 240n42; political agendas in, 220; time-travel as history in, 33, 58–59. Works: *Looking Backward from 2000 to 1887*, 33, 49, 54, 64–66

Belzú, Manuel Isidoro, 147

Bergsonian Vitalism, 117

Bester, Alfred, 219

biological doubles. *See* human doubles

Bioy Casares, Adolfo, 10, 216, 243n16

Blanco-Fombona, Rufino, 117

blanqueamiento, 45

Blavatsky, Helena, 165, 244n21, 245n28

Blondlot, René-Prosper, 254n21

Bodin, Félix, 247n4

Bolivia, 147

Bonpland, Aimé, 130

Borges, Jorge Luis: Latin American sf and, 10, 216; literary influences on, 243n16; on Lugones, 100, 244n16, 245n27; *pampa* depiction in, 83. Works: "The South," 83

branqueamento, 45, 91–92

Brave New World (Huxley), 66

Brazil: Anglo-Saxon sf and, 255n3; Barbosa presidential campaign, 55–57; derivative sf in, 218; fantastic tradition in, 139; human double theme in, 251n1; magic realism in, 9; modernization of the 1890s, 34; Period of Conciliation, 112, 246n36; political unrest of the 1860s, 24–25, 27–30; population discourse and, 45; Portuguese colonization, 23–24; racial discourse in, 32, 61, 63,

239n37; republican government, 31–32, 59, 65; social and intellectual overview, 54–55; Spiritism in, 30, 136; technology in Brazilian sf, 242n5; transportation/communication revolution in, 235n8

Brazil 2000. See *Pages from the History of Brazil Written in the Year 2000*

Brazilian Tenement, The (Azevedo), 113

Brescia, Pablo A. J., 149

Broca, Paul, 98–99

Buddhism, 117

Burmeister, Karl Hermann, 40, 95–96, 237n18, 242n7

Burns, E. Bradford, 246n36

Burroughs, Edgar Rice, 105

Callahan, Xavier, 251n4

Camacho y Zulueta, Sebastián, 235n4. *See also* Fósforos-Cerillos

Campbell, John W., Jr., 222

Cândido, Antônio, 111

Cané, Miguel, 133, 243n12. *Works*: "The Harmonies of Light," **143–46**

Cano, Luis C., 102, 139, 153

Capanna, Pablo, 6–7, 217–18

Čapek, Karel, 172, 180–81

Capobianco, Michael, 250n28

Carajá Indians, 91

Carballo, Emmanuel, 124, 247n41

Carmen (Castera), 157

Carvalho, José Murilo de, 84

Castera, Pedro: biographical sketch, 157–58; Cuevas compared with, 186; non-canonical science and, 155–62, 250n25. Works: *Carmen*, 157; *Querens*, 138, **157–58**, 168, 249nn24–25; "A Word on Science," 156. *See also* "Celestial Journey, A"

cathodic rays, 210, 254n21

Causo, Roberto de Sousa, 242n5, 255n3

"Celestial Journey, A" (Castera), **154–62**; Magnetism in, 156–62; Mesmerism in, 158–59, 161; plot structure of, 154–55; Spiritism/Spiritualism in, 155–57, 159

Century XXX. See *In the Thirtieth Century*

Cervantes Saavedra, Miguel de, 17, 30, 38–39, 68, 79

Chaplain, Charlie, 247n42

"Cien años de sueño" (Nervo). *See* "One Hundred Years of Sleep"

cinematographic technology, 211–12

Cione, Otto Miguel, 252n10

Civilización y barbarie o vida de Juan Facundo Quiroga (Sarmiento). See *Civilization and Barbarism or the Life of Juan Facundo Quiroga*

Civilization and Barbarism or the Life of Juan Facundo Quiroga (Sarmiento), 82–83

Clarke, Arthur C., 132

Clarke, I. F., 220, 247n2

class: access to technology in *Doctor Benignus*, 242n5; class advocacy in sf, 255n1; class ideology in *Artificial Man*, 197–98, 208–9; class mobility in *Century XXX*, 51–52, 239n31; eugenics and, 44–45; European aristocratic identity, 51, 56; language as articulation of power, 108, 253n15; manual labor stigma, 197–98; nineteenth-century upper class readers, 5; Northern literary genres and, 9; popularization of Latin American sf, 14, 174–75, 193; "social automo-

class (*continued*)
bile" image in Barnsley, 65–66; social revolution in "The Last War," 119–21; transportation technology in Brazil and, 24. *See also* hegemony
Clemens, Samuel, 81–82
cloning, 172
cognitive estrangement, 12–13, 16–17, 43
colonialism: colonialism as post-colonial "other," 5–6; European "light and civilization" in *Brazil 2000*, 34; Europe as source of scientific knowledge, 35, 40, 97–98; Latin America as repository of raw materials, 93; in North vs. South America, 82; perception of sf as imperialist medium, 3; political autonomy in Holmberg, 96–97; Portuguese colonization of Brazil, 23–24; post-colonial identity in sf, 217; space travel similarity to, 36. *See also* Europe
Columbus, Christopher, 244n24
communication themes: animal communication in "The Last War," 121; clairvoyant gaze in "He Who Listens," 150–51; communication technology in *Brazil 2000*, 30; language as a defining component of humanity, 173; surgical clairvoyance in "Sixth Sense," 170–71; telegraph, 22, 24, 31, 50; telepathy in "Demons," 114; thought-reading devices, 141
"Cómo acabó la guerra en 1917" (Guzmán). *See* "How the War Ended in 1917"
Comte, Auguste, 164–65
"congelados, Los" (Nervo). *See* "Frozen Ones, The"

Conil Paz, Alberto A., 244n21
Córdoba Six (European scientists in Argentina), 40, 95, 237n18
Corelli, Marie, 118
Corrêa Vasques, Martinho, 111
cortiço, O (Azevedo). *See Brazilian Tenement, The*
cosmogony, 102–5
Cosmos Latinos (Bell and Molina-Gavilán), 232n4
Crookes, William, 248n15
Cruz, Oswaldo, 239n36
"Cuentos de los siglos futuros" (Nervo). *See* "Tales from Future Centuries"
Cuentos macabros (Cuevas). *See Macabre Tales*
Cuevas, Alejandro, 14, 186. *See also* "Apparatus of Doctor Tolimán, The"
Cunha, Euclides da, 83
Customs Legislation: Concordances, Jurisprudence and Commentaries (Ezcurra), 46
cyborgs, 172
Cyrano de Bergerac, Savinien de, 118

daguerreotypes, 22
Danilevsky, Nicolai, 81
Darío, Rubén, 46, 116, 138, 245n27
Darwinian evolution: civilization vs. barbarism debate and, 13; Darwin as *Two Factions* character, 96–99; extraterrestrial life and, 85, 86; in Holmberg, 36, 94–99, 130, 138, 243n14; Lamarckian evolution similarity to, 241n1; Latin American influence of, 83; social Darwinism in *Doctor Benignus*, 90; Zaluar influenced by, 84. *See also* evolution theory

degeneration, 50–51
Del Fiorentino, Teresinha Aparecida, 66
Dellepiane, Angela B., 180–81
"Demônios" (Azevedo). *See* "Demons"
"Demons" (Azevedo), 110, **113–16**, 246nn37–38
devolution: devolutionary metamorphosis in "Demons," 114–16, 246n38; Earth formation as cyclical in Lugones, 103; millennial Apocalypse in Lugones, 109; modernism and, 13; speaking-animals theory in Lugones, 105, 109. *See also* evolution theory
Diccionario del lenguaje argentino (Holmberg). *See Dictionary of the Argentine Language*
Dictionary of the Argentine Language (Holmberg), 36
Dios Pesa, Juan de, 186
disintegration devices (science fiction weapons), 140
Doctor Benignus (Zaluar), **84–99**; devolved/evolved life in, 90–91, 116; as naturalist travel narrative, 83, 87–92, *89*, 250n25; plot structure of, 84–87; racial hierarchy in, 90, 242n4; role of technology in, 172, 242n5
"Doctor Orts's Daring Operation" (Cione), 252n10
"Doctor Tolimán". *See* "Apparatus of Doctor Tolimán, The"
donador de almas, El (Nervo). *See Soul-Giver, The*
Don Quijote of la Mancha (Cervantes), 17, 30, 38–39
Dos partidos en lucha: Fantasía científica (Holmberg). *See Two Factions Struggle for Life: A Scientific Fantasy*

doubles (biological doubles). *See* human doubles
double temporal perspective, 17, 20–21
Doutor Benignus, O (Zaluar). *See Doctor Benignus*
Doyle, Arthur Conan, 118, 241n3
Dumas, Alexandre, fils, 186
Durán, Manuel, 116–17
Dziubinskyj, Aaron, 234n2, 240n43

Eagle and the Serpent, The (Guzmán), 124
Edison, Thomas, 178, 252n8
Einstein, Albert, 100
Eiseley, Loren, 243n14
"End of the World, The" (Macedo), **110–13**, 246nn34–36
En el siglo XXX (Ezcurra). *See In the Thirtieth Century*
"Ensayo de una cosmogonía en diez lecciones" (Lugones). *See* "Essay on a Cosmogony in Ten Lessons"
"Essay on a Cosmogony in Ten Lessons" (Lugones), 13, **102–5**, 244n19, 244n22, 244n25
"Eugenesia" (Nervo). *See* "Eugenics"
Eugenia (Urzaiz): overview, 42–43, 67–79; eugenics/sterilization in, 67, 69–70, 72, 76, 79, 239nn40–41; futuristic setting of, 69–70; historical context of, 69; plot structure of, 69–74, 79; printings of, 239n39; utopian/dystopian themes in, 66–67, 78–79
eugenics: "eugenesia" vs. "eugenética" as Spanish term, 240n41; eugenics/sterilization in *Eugenia*, 67, 69–70, 72, 76, 79, 239nn40–41; genetic theory and, 44–45; Latin

287

eugenics (*continued*)
American scientific modernism and, 6; "Latin race" term and, 63; Mexican Revolution and, 69; national consciousness and, 13, 43–44; national degeneration and, 50–51; Northern views of Latin America and, 221; population discourse and, 45–46; sterilization initiatives, 45, 241n46. *See also* population discourse
"Eugenics" (Nervo), 240n40
Eulálio, Alexandre, 25–26, 34
Europe: aristocratic identity and, 51, 56; Donissoff as European in *Artificial Man*, 196; eugenics movement in, 45–46; European ascendancy as sf theme, 23–24; Germany as "Horacio Kalibang" setting, 175; models of civil law in *Century XXX*, 52; models of racial classification, 5; as modernist ideal, 87; non-canonical science in, 135–36, 248n7; Northern nations in, 232n3; Parisian literary modernism, 116; scientific romance in Great Britain, 174; as source of scientific knowledge, 35, 40, 97–98, 215, 237n18; uncontrollable powers theme and, 139–40; U.S. views on, 82. *See also* colonialism; North, the
Evans, Arthur B., 250n27
evolution theory: Africans in human evolution, 98–99, 106, 243n14, 245n29; civilization vs. barbarism debate and, 13, 208; conceptions of time and, 80–81; creationism vs. evolutionism in Argentina, 96–99, 243n10; Hegelian natural progression, 98; in Latin America vs. the U.S., 80; national degeneration and, 50; nature as originary/primitive component of, 86–92, 96. *See also* Darwinian evolution; devolution; genetic theory; Lamarckian genetics; Mendelian genetics; Spencerian Social Darwinism
extraterrestrial beings: historical witnessing in Lugones, 104–5; Lamarckian evolution and, 85, 86; Martians in *Nic-Nac*, 36–37, 39–41, 236n15; Nervo views on, 117–18, 234n2. *See also* human-like beings
extraterrestrial travel, 36–37, 39–41, 234n2
Ezcurra, Eduardo de, 42–43, 46–47, 61, 238n25. See also *In the Thirtieth Century*

fantastic, the: defined, 148; as alternative genre for sf, 7; *Artificial Man* as departure from, 194–95, 214; avoidance of fantasy in *Brazil 2000*, 27; body of work in, 10; in Brazil, 139; Cuevas as proponent of, 186; fantastic voyage theme, 17–18; as feminine genre, 251n30; Gorriti as formative writer, 148; Holmberg treatment of, 130–33; human doubles and, 173; as interpretive frame in *Nic-Nac*, 37, 42; Northern writers associated with, 233n11; "The Sandman" as, 184; "The Vampire" as evocative of, 214–15
"fenómeno inexplicable, Un" (Lugones). *See* "Inexplicable Phenomenon, An"
Fernández, Macedonio, 219
Fernández-Delgado, Miguel Ángel, 232n5, 233n10, 234n2, 249n24

288

fiction/literature (as genre), 9
Figuier, Louis, 36
"fim do mundo, O" (Macedo). *See* "End of the World, The"
Flammarion, Camille: biographical sketch, 236n17; association with North, 40; in Castera, 154, 157, 250n24; devolved/evolved beings in, 116; on extraterrestrial life, 117–18; Holmberg and, 36, 176, 233n11; Latin American influence of, 13, 83; mentioned in *Nic-Nac*, 17, 38, 42; mentioned in *Two Factions*, 36; science-religion synthesis in, 137; Spiritism of, 168; in — Zaluar, 85, 86. Works: *Lumen*, 38, 116, 154, 157, 236n17; *The Plurality of Inhabited Worlds*, 85; *Stories of Infinity*, 85
folletines (serialized narratives), 194
Fonseca, Marechal Hermes da, 56
Foote, Bud, 81–82, 87
Fortuny, Francisco, 7
Fósforos-Cerillos, 19, 21–22, 235n4. Works: "Mexico in the Year 1970," 15–16, **18–23**, 25, 233n1
Foster, David William, 8–9
Frankenstein (Shelley): Biógeno compared with, 204, 206–8, 253n16; in Cione, 252n10; "Doctor Tolimán" compared with, 192–93; as formative sf work, 12, 181; as human double, 172, 180–83, 204, 206–7; influence on Holmberg, 176, 181–83; narration compared to *The Artificial Man*, 253n16. *See also* Shelley, Mary
Fraser, Howard M., 105, 109
Freitas, Emília, 237n19
Freud, Sigmund, 247n5
Freyre, Gilberto, 45

"Frozen Ones, The" (Nervo), 118, 249n16
Frye, Northrop, 16, 39–40, 64
"fuerza Omega, La" (Lugones). *See* "Omega Force, The"
fuerzas extrañas, Las (Lugones). *See Strange Forces*

García Canclini, Néstor, 3
García Ramos, Arturo, 101, 141
Gaut vel Hartman, Sergio, 10, 219
Generation of 1880 (Argentina), 35, 46, 50, 146
genetic theory: in Barnsley, 56; in *Eugenia*, 68; eugenics and, 44; Mendelian vs. Lamarckian genetics, 44, 76; utopian childbearing in *Eugenia*, 70–79. *See also* evolution theory; Lamarckian genetics; Mendelian genetics
genre: gendered literary genres, 251n30; genre hybridity in Latin America, 8, 139, 214, 219; joining vs. belonging in literary movements, 220; retrolabeling, 1–7, 11, 111, 219–20, 222–23, 232n6, 234n2; science-religion synthesis and, 137, 248n11; time periods in genre development, 233n12
geographic-temporal travel. *See* spatial/geographic travel themes; time-travel themes; transportation technology
Gernsback, Hugo, 1, 214, 231nn1–2
Giménez, Aurelio, 1, 2
Ginway, M. Elizabeth, 7, 233n8
Godwin, Francis, 118
golems, 172, 252n7
Goligorsky, Eduardo, 233n1
Gómez de Avellaneda, Gertrudis, 148
González Casanova, Pablo, 234n2

289

González Echevarría, Roberto: on hegemonic scientific discourse, 5–6, 233n7; on Latin America as part of the Western tradition, 6, 219; on naturalist-explorers, 92; on travel to Latin America, 86

Gorriti, Juana Manuela, 146–47, 249n17. *Works*: "Herbs and Pins," 148; "He Who Listens May Hear—To His Regret," **148–54**, 249nn19–22

gothic, the, 10, 184

Gould, Benjamin, 40, 236n16

"gran viaje, El" (Nervo). *See* "Great Journey, The"

"Great Journey, The" (Nervo), 118, 234n2

Gunn, James E, 8, 233n10

Guzmán, Martín Luis, 124–25. Works: *The Eagle and the Serpent*, 124; "How the War Ended in 1917," **124–29**, 247n41; *The Shadow of the Tyrant*, 124

Haeckel, Ernst, 84

Hall, G. Stanley, 247n5

"Harmonies of Light, The" (Cané), **143–46**

Hegelian natural progression, 98

hegemony: defined, 233n7; science as hegemonic discourse, 5–6, 12, 35, 40; of scientific knowledge, 174; subaltern/outsider perspective, 7. *See also* class

"Herbs and Pins" (Gorriti), 148

Hernández, José, 83

"He Who Listens May Hear—To His Regret" (Gorriti), **148–54**, 249nn19–22

Hinduism, 117

"História do Brasil escrita pelo Dr. Jeremias no Ano de 2862, A" (Santos). *See* "History of Brazil Written by Dr. Jeremias in the Year 2862, A"

"History of Brazil Written by Dr. Jeremias in the Year 2862, A" (Santos), 26

Hitchhiker's Guide to the Galaxy, The, 36–37

Hoffmann, E. T. A.: Cuevas compared with, 186, 189; influence on Ezcurra, 49; influence on Holmberg, 14, 176, 233n11; influence on Latin American sf, 43, 172; in Nervo's *Soul-Giver*, 166; Olimpia as model for human doubles, 160. *Works*: "The Sandman," 172, 176, 183–86

Holberg, Ludvig, 118

Holmberg, Eduardo Ladislao: approach to the fantastic, 130–33; biographical sketch, 35–36, 92–93, 242n9; Cuevas compared with, 189–90, 192–93; on dependency on Europe, 218; on evolution, 36, 94–99, 130; as Latin American literary influence, 99–100; on Latin American sf, 223; literary influences on, 233n11, 237n17, 242n3; on materialism, 175–78, 180; nationalism and, 35–36, 251n5, 252n8; naturalist travel narratives of, 83, 93; political views, 93; religious views, 101, 175–76; scientific writings, 14, *94,* 175, 236n14. Works: *The Argentine Naturalist*, 35–36, 237n18; *Dictionary of the Argentine Language*, 36; *Lin-Calél*, 36; *Nelly*, 100; *Olimpio Pitango of Monalia*, 237n19. See also "Horacio Kalibang or The Automatons"; *Marvelous Journey of Mr. Nic-Nac to the Planet Mars, The*; *Two Fac-*

290

tions Struggle for Life: A Scientific Fantasy
Holmberg, Luis, 36, 93, 218, 236n14, 237n18
Holmberg y Abalbastro, Eduardo, 93
hombre artificial, El. See *Artificial Man, The*
homeopathy, 142
homunculus, 172
Honduras, 56
"Horacio Kalibang o Los autómatas" (Holmberg). See "Horacio Kalibang or The Automatons"
"Horacio Kalibang or The Automatons" (Holmberg), **174–80**; automaton figure in, 172–73, 178–80, 252n7; *Frankenstein* and, 180–83; nationalist motivation in, 178, 252n8; plot structure of, 176–80; popularization of sf and, 14; rational vs. spiritual worldview in, 139, 175–76; "The Sandman" and, 183–86; *The Tempest* and, 252n6
"How the War Ended in 1917" (Guzmán), **124–29**, 247n41
Huffeland (or Hufeland), Christoph Wilhelm, 150
human doubles: overview, 14, 172–73, 175–76, 251n1; cinematographic copying in "The Vampire," 212–13; Hoffman's Olimpia, 184–85; Holmberg's automaton, 178–80, 183–86; photographic copying in "The Portrait," 210–11; Quiroga's Biógeno, *201, 203, 205,* 207, 214; resurrection of the dead in "Doctor Tolimán," 189–92; Shelley's Frankenstein creature, 181–83, 192–93. See also human-like beings

human-like beings: animal metamorphosis in "Demons," 114–16; anthropoid rebels in "Monkey-Man," 247n40; anthropomorphic apes in "Yzur," 105–9, 245n28, 245n32; beastly doubles in "An Inexplicable Phenomenon," 142–43; early life forms in "Cosmogony," 103, 244n24; non-corporeal existence as utopian end, 123; rebellion of the animals in "The Last War," 120–23; reincarnation themes, 163; spiritual powers in Nervo, 163, 165–68. See also extraterrestrial beings; human doubles
Humboldt, Alexander von, 130
Huxley, Aldous, 66, 84
Huxley, T. H., 243n10
hybridity (of genres), 8, 214, 219
hypnotism: autosomnambulism in "An Inexplicable Phenomenon," 142–43; of Dom Pedro in *Brazil 2000,* 31, 133; of Donissoff in *The Artificial Man,* 202; hypnotism in "He Who Listens," 152–53; in *The Soul-Giver,* 165, 167–68. See also Magnetism; Mesmerism

immigration: in Argentina, 51, 238n28; Italian immigration in Brazil and Argentina, 63; national degeneration in *Century XXX* and, 50–51; national identity and, 45
indigenous peoples: absence in *Eugenia*, 76; in *Barnsley*, 63, 239n37; Brazilian racial categories and, 239n37, 242n4; in Zaluar, 90–92
"Inexplicable Phenomenon, An" (Lugones), 139, **142–43**, 244n17

invención de Morel, La (Bioy Casares). See *Invention of Morel, The*
Invention of Morel, The (Bioy Casares), 10

Jackson, Rosemary, 148, 154
James, William, 247n5
Jameson, Fredric, 32
Jensen, Theodore W., 169, 251n31
Jequitinhonha, O (Santos), 23, 24, 26
Jitrik, Noé, 194, 253n12
Jrade, Cathy L., 101
Juárez Celman, Miguel, 46
Jung, Carl, 247n5

Kannitz, Eduardo, Baron of Holmberg, 93
Kardecist Spiritism, 159
Kepler, Johannes, 17, 118, 144
Kipling, Rudyard, 254n20
Kirchen (likely Athanasius Kircher), 118
Kopp, James J., 59–60

Lamarckian genetics: in Barnsley, 56; civilization vs. barbarism debate and, 13, 80; Darwinian evolution similarity to, 241n1; eugenics and, 44; extraterrestrial life and, 85, 86; human doubles and, 186–87; impact in Latin America, 80; inherited criminal tendencies, 191, 252n10; modern disdain for, 237n20; utopian childbearing in *Eugenia*, 70–72, 76; Zaluar influenced by, 84. *See also* evolution theory
Larson, Ross, 66, 124, 234n2
"Last Goddess, The" (Nervo), 118
"Last War, The" (Nervo), 110, **116–24**, 246n33, 246–247nn39–40

Latin American science fiction: defining characteristics of, 217–23; alternatives to canonical science and, 14; anti-scientific characters in, 221; "Chronology of Latin American Science Fiction through 1920," 10–11, 225–30; continental vs. global roots, 1–3, 220; "first wave," 11; formative works of, 10, 13, 15–16; golden age of, 216; labeling/mislabeling of, 7–9; literary influences in, 243n16; political agendas in, 220; popularization of, 14, 174–75; as "soft" sf, 30, 221–22; *Strange Forces* considered as, 102; time periods in genre development, 233n12
Le Bon, Gustave, 210, 211, 215, 254nn20–21
Legislación aduanera; concordancias, jurisprudencia y comentarios (Ezcurra). See *Customs Legislation: Concordances, Jurisprudence and Commentaries*
Le Guin, Ursula K., 9
Liais, Emmanuel, 236n11
Liceo Mexicano, El, 18–19
light waves, 143–46
Lima, S. Fragoso (pseudonym). See Quiroga, Horacio
Lin-Calél (Holmberg), 36
Lippmann, Gabriel, 144
literatura fantástica. See fantastic, the
"literatura lunar y la habitabilidad de los satélites, La" (Nervo). See "Lunar Literature and the Habitability of the Satellites"
"literatura maravillosa, La" (Nervo). See "Marvelous Literature"
Little Dark-Complexioned Girl, The (Macedo), 111

Lobato, José Bento Monteiro, 241n46
Lodge, Oliver, 247n5
Lojo, María Rosa, 147–48
Longfellow, Henry Wadsworth, 68
López, Lucio V., 46
López de Santa Anna, Antonio, 19
Lucian of Samosata, 118
Ludmer, Josefina, 35–36, 190, 208
Lugones, Leopoldo: biographical sketch, 99–100; devolution portrayed in, 13, 106, 245n28; historical witnessing technique of, 104–5; influence on Quiroga, 253n12; on limitations of canonical science, 103, 244n22; literary influences on, 105; as modernist, 100–101, 139, 162–63; narrative style of, 105–6, 245n27, 245n30; popularization of scientific discourse and, 14, 174; Spiritist characters in, 139, 141, 248n15; Theosophy involvement in, 101–2, 139; uncontrollable powers theme in, 139–43. *Works*: "Essay on a Cosmogony in Ten Lessons," 13, **102–5**, 244n19, 244n22, 244n25; "An Inexplicable Phenomenon," 139, **142–43**, 244n17; "Metamusic," 139, **143–46**; "The Omega Force," 139, **140**; "The Origin of the Flood," 13, **102–5**, 139–40, 244n25; "Psychon," 139, **141–42**, 248n15; "Viola Acherontia," 139, **142**, 249n16; "Yzur," 13, **105–9**, 245nn27–30. See also *Strange Forces*
"Lunar Literature and the Habitability of the Satellites" (Nervo), 117–18

Macabre Tales (Cuevas), 186
Macedo, Joaquim Manuel [or Manoel] de, 111. *Works*: "The End of the World," **110–13**, 246nn34–36; *The Little Dark-Complexioned Girl*, 111
Machado, Ubiratan, 136
Magalhães, Basílio de, 25
magic realism, 7, 8–9, 233n10
Magnetism: overview, 153; in *Brazil 2000*, 133, *134*; Cartesian dualism and, 250n27; Castera on, 156–62, 250n25; disillusionment with empirical science and, 13–14; in Gorriti, 148, 152–53; in "He Who Listens," 249n20; mainstream acceptance of, 135; in Nervo's *Soul-Giver*, 163, 168. See also hypnotism; Mesmerism
"Magnetism" (Olaguíbel), 157
"magnetismo, El" (Olaguíbel). See "Magnetism"
Magnus, Albertus, 206
malinchismo, 232n5
Malthus, Thomas Robert, 241n44
Martí, José, 157
Marvelous Journey of Mr. Nic-Nac to the Planet Mars, The (Holmberg), **34–42**; overview, 15; devolved/evolved life in, 116; as a fantastic text, 10; "Horacio Kalibang" compared with, 175; as Latin American sf, 233n1; plot structure of, 36–37; Spiritism role in, 236n17; *Two Factions* compared with, 243n12; utopian theme in, 37–41, 175, 235n7
"Marvelous Literature" (Nervo), 118
Marxism, 65
Masiello, Francine, 147, 249n17
materialism, 175–78, 180
Matto de Turner, Clorinda, 147–48
McLemee, Scott, 33
Meehan, Thomas C., 147

Memoirs of the Diamantino District (Santos), 23, 27

Memórias do Distrito Diamantino (Santos). See *Memoirs of the Diamantino District*

men: as creators of human doubles, 173; gestators in *Eugenia*, 70, 73, 74; scientific treatises as masculine, 251n30; as utopian procreators in *Eugenia*, 241n43

Mendelian genetics, 44, 68, 76, 237n20

Menéndez Díaz, Conrado, 68

Mercier, Louis-Sébastien, 17, 235n10

Mesmerism: in "He Who Listens," 152–53, 249n20; in Lugones, 248n15; mainstream acceptance of, 248n7; in Nervo's *Soul-Giver*, 164, 168; non-occult Mesmerism, 247n4; therapeutic vs. spiritual Mesmerism, 158–59, 161, 168. See also hypnotism; Magnetism

mestiçagem, 45

mestización (hybridity), 219

mestizo, 45, 76–78, 219

"Metamusic" (Lugones), 139, **143–46**

"metamúsica, La" (Lugones). See "Metamusic"

Mexico: description in "Mexico 1970," 20–23; historical context for *Eugenia*, 69, 74–76; literary magazines, 18–19; Mexican Revolution, 69, 76, 124; *Mexicans in Space* as pivotal work, 232n6; mid-nineteenth-century social unrest, 19; population discourse and, 45; public health initiatives in, 241n45; sterilization initiatives in, 241n46

"México en el año 1970" (Fósforos-Cerillos). See "Mexico in the Year 1970"

"Mexico in the Year 1970" (Fósforos-Cerillos), 15–16, **18–23**, 25, 233n1

Meyer, Michael C., 19

Miralles, Francisco, 234n2

Mitre, Bartolomé, 96–97

modernism: apocalyptic modernism, 117; evolution and, 13; influence on Quiroga, 194; Lamarckian evolution and, 80; Lugones as modernist, 100–101, 139, 146, 162–63, 253n12; Nervo as modernist, 116–17, 162–63; principles of, 101; science as foundation for progress, 35–36

Molina-Gavilán, Yolanda, 8, 222–23, 232n4, 234n1, 246n33

"Monkey-Man, The" (Nervo), 247n40

"mono-hombre, El" (Nervo). See "Monkey-Man, The"

Monroe, John Warne, 136–37, 153, 159, 247n6

Monsalve, Carlos, 244n20

Monsiváis, Carlos, 163

Montserrat, Marcelo, 95

Moore, R. Laurence, 101–2, 248nn7–8

Mora, José Joaquín, 21–22, 235n4. See also Fósforos-Cerillos

moreninha, A (Macedo). See *Little Dark-Complexioned Girl, The*

Moreno, Francisco Pascasio, 96

Moylan, Tom, 67, 235n3, 239n30

mulato, O (Azevedo). See *Mulatto, The*

Mulatto, The (Azevedo), 113

multitemporal heterogeneity, 3

Münchhausen, Baron Karl, 55

musical instruments, 143–46

mysticism, 117

N rays and N¹ rays, 254n21

Napoleon I, 23, 56

narrative: diary as narrative device, 163, 187–88; don Prospero as metafictional narrator, 20–22; first-person narrators in Lugones, 245n27, 245n30; *folletines* (serialized narratives), 194; framed narrative in early sf, 17; futuristic metanarrative in *Brazil 2000*, 27–30; narrative framing in *Century XXX*, 47–48; narrative framing in *Nic-Nac*, 38–39, 42; scientists as narrators, 106

nationalism: diminished nationalism in *Eugenia*, 69, 74, 76; foreigners as sf characters, 221; Generation of 1880 (Argentine scientific nationalism), 35, 46, 50, 146; in Holmberg, 35–36, 251n5, 252n8; imitation of foreign models, 217–19, 233n8; Latin American nation building, 6; literary utopia and, 13; *malinchista* as term contemptuous of foreigners, 232n5; *mestización* (hybridity) and, 219; modern technology as symbol for, 19–20, 22; national degeneration in *Century XXX*, 46–47, 50–53, 238n25; national identity as literary concern, 214–17; national origin in *Artificial Man*, 196–98, 208; national regeneration in *São Paulo 2000*, 57–60, 64; national status of African slaves, 242n4; population discourse and, 45; republicanism vs. monarchy in *Brazil 2000*, 28, 33; sf as medium for identity, 3, 217; utopian nationalism in *Nic-Nac*, 41–42, 235n7; utopian sf and, 16–17

native peoples. *See* indigenous peoples

Naturalista Argentino, El (Holmberg). See *Argentine Naturalist, The*

nature: Holmberg as naturalist, 93; natural catastrophe in "Demons," 113; naturalist travel narratives, 83, 87–92, *89*; New World as natural repository, 86, 250n25

nebular hypothesis, 39

Nelly (Holmberg), 100

Nepomuceno Adorno, Juan, 234n2

Nervo, Amado: apocalyptic themes in, 110, 116–24; biographical sketch, 116–19; critique of science fiction by, 118; as modernist, 162–63. Works: "Airplanes," 118; "Eugenics," 240n40; "The Frozen Ones," 118, 249n16; "The Great Journey," 118, 234n2; "The Last Goddess," 118; "The Last War," **116–24**, 246n33, 246–247nn39–40; "Lunar Literature and the Habitability of the Satellites," 117–18; "Marvelous Literature," 118; "The 'Monkey-Man'," 247n40; "One Hundred Years of Sleep," 118; "The Sixth Sense," 163, **170–71**; "Tales from Future Centuries," 247n40. See also *Soul-Giver, The*

Nicaragua, 56

Nicholson, Marjorie Hope, 17

Nic-Nac. See *Marvelous Journey of Mr. Nic-Nac to the Planet Mars, The*

non-canonical science: anti-scientific characters, 221; disillusionment with empirical science and, 14; influence on human double themes, 206; mainstream acceptance of, 135–37, 247–48nn4–7;

non-canonical science (*continued*) plant revivification incident and, 130–33; Pythagorean dualism and, 169–70; rationalization as framing device for, 153; rational vs. spiritual worldview and, 138–39, 155–62, 162–63, 214–15; Spanish American modernists and, 117; speculative fiction and, 248n11. *See also* fantastic, the; Magnetism; scientific discourse; Spiritism/Spiritualism; Theosophy

North, the: characteristics of early sf, 15–16; definition and scope of, 232n3; eugenic perspective of Latin America, 221; first-world utopias and, 255n3; Latin Americanization of Northern sf, 64–66, 172–73; literary influences on Ezcurra, 49; "magic realism" as Northern label, 8–9; North American engineering/applied science, 172, 215, 221; North American spiritualism, 135–36; Northern-influenced characters in Quiroga, 197–98, 215; scientific hegemony and, 40; sf as international movement in, 1–3, 220; sf literary influence of, 218; temporal differences in perceptions of, 3; uncontrollable powers theme and, 139–40. *See also* Europe; United States

occult, the. *See* fantastic, the; magic realism; non-canonical science; *particular sciences*
Olaguíbel, Manuel de, 157, 250n25
Olimpio Pitango de Monalia (Holmberg). See *Olimpio Pitango of Monalia*
Olimpio Pitango of Monalia (Holmberg), 237n19
Olivera, Carlos ("Death at a Fixed Hour"), 137–38
Olvera, Carlos (*Mexicans in Space*), 232n6
"Omega Force, The" (Lugones), 139, **140**
"One Hundred Years of Sleep" (Nervo), 118
optography, 254n20
"origen del diluvio, El" (Lugones). *See* "Origin of the Flood, The"
"Origin of the Flood, The" (Lugones), 13, **102–5**, 139–40, 244n25
Ortiz, Eduardo, 10, 40, 100, 233n11

Pages from the History of Brazil Written in the Year 2000 (Santos), **23–34**; overview, 15–16; as Latin American sf, 234n1; publication of, 23–26; structure of, 26–30; time-travel theme in, 26–29, 31, 37–38, 133, 236n12, 238n26, 242n5
Pagés Larraya, Antonio, 93, 175, 183–86, 237n17, 251n5
Páginas da história do Brasil escripta no anno de 2000 (Santos). See *Pages from the History of Brazil Written in the Year 2000*
"palabra de la ciencia, Una" (Castera). *See* "Word on Science, A"
Palma, Ricardo, 147
pantheism, 117
Paracelsus, 206
Paraguay, 25, 27
Paz, Octavio, 232n5
Pedro I, 24, 31, 57–58
Pedro II, 24–25, 27–34, 37–38, 59–60, 84, 92, 236nn11–12

Peniche Vallado, Leopoldo, 67, 68, 74
Peregrinação pela Província de S. Paulo (Zaluar). See *Peregrination through the Province of São Paulo*
Peregrination through the Province of São Paulo (Zaluar), 83
Peru, 147, 249n21
photographic technology, 210–12, 254n20
Pickering, Edward, 247n5
Planet of the Apes film series, 105
pluralité des mondes habitées, La (Flammarion). See *Plurality of Inhabited Worlds, The*
Plurality of Inhabited Worlds, The (Flammarion), 85
Poe, Edgar Allan: influence on Ezcurra, 49; influence on Holmberg, 233n11; influence on Latin American sf, 1, 13, 17, 43, 220; influence on Lugones, 13, 105, 107; influence on Quiroga, 194, 215; influence on the Latin American fantastic, 10; Nervo fondness for, 118; in Nervo's *Soul-Giver*, 166. Works: "The Black Cat," 245n31; "Eureka," 13, 244n19; "The Imp of the Perverse," 183, 245n31; "The Murders in the Rue Morgue," 105; "The Oval Portrait," 212; "The Tell-Tale Heart," 107, 245n30
population discourse, 45, 50–51, 69, 76, 241n44. *See also* eugenics
"Portrait, The" (Quiroga), **210–11**; human double theme and, 172–73; optographic technology in, 254n20; publication of, 209–10; Sarlo on, 254n23; as "Vampire" precursor, 212, 215, 254n19
psychology: alternatives to canonical science and, 135; cerebral matrimony in Nervo's *Soul-Giver*, 165–68; madness in "Doctor Tolimán," 187–93; music and emotions relationship, 145–46; psychical research and, 159, 250n26; spiritual powers in Nervo, 163, 165–68, 170–71; therapeutic vs. spiritual Mesmerism, 158–59, 161, 168; thought-reading devices, 141; torture of Biógeno in *Artificial Man*, 199–204, *201, 203, 205,* 208–9, 213
"Psychon" (Lugones), 139, **141–42**, 248n15
Puységur, Marquis de, 135, 158–59
Pythagoras, 144, 169–70

Querens (Castera), 138, **157–58**, 168, 249nn24–25
"Quien escucha, su mal oye" (Gorriti). *See* "He Who Listens May Hear—To His Regret"
Quiroga, Horacio: biographical sketch, 193–94; canonical science influence on, 206–7; Cuevas compared with, 192–93; literary influences on, 243n16, 253n12; national identity as concern of, 215–16; popular appeal of, 14, 174, 193; Shelley influence on, 14, 194, 204, 206–8. *See also Artificial Man, The*; "Portrait, The"; "Vampire, The"
Quiroga, Juan Facundo, 193

Rabelais, François, 49, 118
Rabkin, Eric S., 109–10
race: *branqueamento*, 45, 91–92; Brazilian racial homogeneity, 61, 63, 239n37; eugenics and, 44–45, 51; European models in Latin America, 5; Felício dos Santos predic-

race (*continued*)
tion of Brazilian mixed-race president, 32; "Latin race" term, 63, 239n38; Mexican racial heterogeneity, 76–78; national race in Argentina, 51, 238n29; racial degeneration in "Tales from Future Centuries," 247n40; racial hierarchy in *Doctor Benignus*, 90, 242n4; racial hybridization, 45; racial poisons, 45, 51; sf depiction of minorities, 22

radio waves, 140, 211

railroads, 24

Ramos Mejía, José María, 176

Raspail, François-Vincent, 150

realism, 27, 155

Rebellion in the Backlands (Cunha), 83

Regina, Ivan Carlos, 218, 255n3

reincarnation themes, 163

religion: Adam and Eve theme, 112–13, 122–23, 129, 182, 244n20; apocalyptic themes and, 109; creationism vs. evolutionism in Argentina, 96–99, 243n10; Cuevas's Tolimán as Jesus figure, 190; Eastern religion influence on scientific belief, 117; Holmberg religious views, 101; human doubles and, 173, 175–78; Lugones's "Cosmogony," 103; Mendelian vs. Lamarckian genetics and, 247n3; non-canonical science and, 136–37, 155–62, 162–63, 248n9; pantheism, 117; religious conversion in *The Soul-Giver*, 251n31

Renan, Ernest, 252n6

"retrato, El" (Quiroga). *See* "Portrait, The"

retrolabeling: overview, 1–7, 234n2; acceptance of, 222–23, 232n6; bibliographic work and, 11, 216; "End of the World" as retrolabeled work, 111; Holmberg robots and, 181; Trujillo Muñoz on, 219–20; of utopian/dystopian science fiction, 237n19

Riva Palacio, Vicente, 157

Rivas, Fray Manuel Antonio de, 234n2

robots, 172, 184

Roché, Déodat, 248n15

"rocket-launched" future images, 3, *4*

Rodríguez, José María, 241n45

Rodríguez, Julia, 35, 93

Rodríguez Barilari, Elbio, 254n19

Röntgen rays, 254n21

Roosevelt, Theodore, 247n5

Rosas, Juan Manuel de, 147

Ryman, Geoff, 7, 233n9

Santos, Joaquim Felício dos: biographical sketch, 23–25, 34; Mercier influence on, 235n10; nationalistic visions of, 54, 59, 236n11; on Spiritism, 30, 133. Works: *Acayaca*, 23; Brazilian civil code (revision), 23, 25; "A History of Brazil Written by Dr. Jeremias in the Year 2862," 26; *Memoirs of the Diamantino District*, 23, 27; *O Jequitinhonha*, 23, 24, 26. See also *Pages from the History of Brazil Written in the Year 2000*

Santos Dumont, Alberto, 57, 239n33

São Paulo in the Year 2000 or National Regeneration (Barnsley): overview, 42–43, **53–66**; Bellamy influence of, 54, 64–66; historical context of, 54–55; Latin Americanization of

Northern sf in, 64–66; national regeneration in, 57–60, 64–66; racial themes in, 63–65; time-travel in, 56–57, 59–60, 66, 242n5

São Paulo no Anno 2000 (Barnsley). See *São Paulo in the Year 2000 or National Regeneration*

Sargent, Lyman Tower, 16

Sarlo, Beatriz, 14, 174–75, 193–94, 208, 251n4, 253n13, 254n23

Sarmiento, Domingo Faustino, 35, 82–83, 95, 237n18. Works: *Argirópolis*, 234n2; *Civilization and Barbarism or the Life of Juan Facundo Quiroga*, 82–83

satire: botanical classification as, 96; *Century XXX* as, 49–50, 239n35; *Eugenia* as satire, 79; Felício dos Santos's projected history as, 27; humorous satire in *Brazil 2000*, 27; Macedo's "The End of the World" as satire, 111–12; satirical treatment of technological naivety, 29; satirical utopias, 16–17

Sayers Peden, Margaret, 249n19

Scari, Robert M., 245n31

Schaffer Meléndez, Gloria, 250n28

Schneider, Luis Mario, 155–57

Schwarz, Mauricio-José, 233n1

science fiction: characteristics of early sf, 15–16; the fantastic and, 10–11; *Frankenstein* as chronological marker, 12, 181; as global genre, 1–3, 220, 255n1; hard vs. soft sf, 30, 221–22; magic realism and, 8–9, 233n10; as medium for social change, 16–17; science-religion synthesis in, 137, 162–63; "scientifiction" term as precursor, 1, 231n1

science fiction of the center, 7

scientific discourse: canonical science in *Artificial Man*, 194–95, 214; Cartesian dualism and, 250n27; classification as satire, 96; disillusionment with empirical science, 13–14; fiction as partner to science, 36; influence on human double themes, 206; limits of science in Nervo's *Soul-Giver*, 168–69; practical education in *São Paulo 2000*, 64; as pretense in "Doctor Tolimán," 187; science as hegemonic discourse, 5–6, 12, 35, 40; science vs. technology distinction, 174, 253n13; scientific didacticism in sf, 17–18, 222; scientific footnotes in Lugones, 104; scientific treatises as masculine, 251n30; subversion of scientific discourse in "Yzur," 105–6. *See also* non-canonical science; technology

scientific romance, 137, 174, 231n2

scientifiction, 1, 231n1

Sertões, Os (Cunha). See *Rebellion in the Backlands*

"sexto sentido, El" (Nervo). *See* "Sixth Sense, The"

Shadow of the Tyrant, The (Guzmán), 124

Shakespeare, William, 252n6

Shelley, Mary: Cuevas compared with, 189–90, 192–93; influence on Holmberg, 176, 181–83; influence on Latin American sf, 13, 172, 220; influence on Quiroga, 14, 194, 204, 206–8, 215; non-canonical science influence on, 206–7. See also *Frankenstein*

"Sixth Sense, The" (Nervo), 163, **170–71**

Skidmore, Thomas E., 23–24

299

slavery, 32, 34, 90, 241n47, 242n4
social change: anarchism in *Artificial Man*, 195, 208–9; anthropoid rebels in "Monkey-Man," 247n40; *Century XXX* as roadmap to utopia, 51–52, 58; class advocacy in sf, 255n1; cognitive estrangement as vehicle of, 12–13; communal living in *Eugenia*, 70, 72–74; Lamarckian logic and, 237n21; national regeneration in *São Paulo 2000*, 57–60; prophetic predictions in *Brazil 2000*, 26; social agenda in *Looking Backward*, 59; social revolution in "The Last War," 119–21; social satire in *Brazil 2000*, 23; utopian themes as vehicle for, 16–17, 19. *See also* class; utopian/dystopian themes
Society for Psychical Research, 135, 247n5
sombra del caudillo, La (Guzmán). See *Shadow of the Tyrant, The*
somnambulism, 153, 154–55, 164–65
Soriano, Michèle, 152, 249nn21–22
Soul-Giver, The (Nervo), **163–71**; Alda-Rafael duality in, 251n30; cerebral matrimony theme in, 165–68; plot structure of, 163–64, 250n29; rational vs. spiritual worldview in, 138; religious conversion in, 251n31; scientific discourse and, 168–70; translations of, 250n28; Villiers influence on, 250n27
sound waves, 143–46
"South, The" (Borges), 83
space travel (extraterrestrial and outer space), 36–37, 39–41, 234n2
spatial/geographic travel themes: civilization vs. barbarism and, 13, 208, 241n3; naturalist journeys in *Two Factions*, 83, 96–99, 243nn13–14; New World travel narratives, 244n24; Northern influences on, 17–18; time-space correlation, 81–82, 87–90, *89,* 241n2; transportation technology as national symbol, 19–20; utopian themes and, 237n19. *See also* time-travel themes; transportation technoloSpencerian Social Darwinism, 13, 84
Spengler, Oswald, 81
Spiritism/Spiritualism: arrival in Brazil, 30; Castera on, 155–57; disillusionment with empirical science and, 13–14; in Flammarion, 237n17; Gorriti involvement in, 147; in Holmberg, 237n17; Kardecist Spiritism, 159; Lamarckian evolution and, 80; in Lugones, 139, 141, 248n15; mainstream acceptance of, 135–36, 248nn7–8; in Nervo, 117, 164, 168; in Santos, 133; speculative fiction and, 248n11; Spiritism vs. Spiritualism, 135, 248n7
Stableford, Brian M., 80, 136–37, 231nn1–2, 248n11
Star Trek, 36–37
steamboats, 24
Stepan, Nancy: on degeneration as literary theme, 50–51; on eugenics in Latin America, 43–45, 69, 238n27, 239n38; on Latin American science, 6, 236n14; on Mendelian vs. Lamarckian genetics, 44, 237nn20–21, 247n3; on miscegenation, 239n37; on race in Argentina, 238n29; on regeneration in Latin America, 60; on social stratification in Brazil, 54–55

Stevenson, Robert Louis, 105
Strange Forces (Lugones): apocalyptic themes in, 109; contents of, 139; as Latin American sf, 102; narrators in, 106, 108; publication sources for stories, 248n13; role of science in, 174; translations of, 244n23
strange forces theme, 14, 139–43, 173, 212, 213, 214–15
Sturgeon, Theodore, 219
Suárez de la Torre, Laura, 18
supernatural, the. *See* fantastic, the; magic realism; non-canonical science
"Sur, El" (Borges). *See* "South, The"
Suvin, Darko, 16, 233n12
Swedenborg, Emanuel, 118
Swift, Jonathan, 105

"Tales from Future Centuries" (Nervo), 247n40
Tarzan series, 105
Tavares, Braulio, 26, 219, 234n1
technology: anti-utopian technophobia, 81; big-brother technology in Guzmán, 125–26; human doubles and, 172–73; Nervo technophilia in "The Last War," 123; photographic/cinematographic technology in Quiroga, 210–12, 254n20; relationship with magic, 132; role in Brazilian sf, 242n5; satirical treatment of technological naivety, 29; science vs. technology distinction, 174, 253n13; technological catastrophe themes, 128–29, 181–83; technology as national symbol, 19–20, 22; uncontrollable powers theme and, 140–42, 254n23. *See also* communication themes; scientific discourse; transportation technology; *particular technologies*
telegraph, 22, 24, 31, 50
temporal doubling. *See* double temporal perspective
Tennyson, Alfred, Lord, 247n5
Teófilo, Rodolfo, 241n46
Theosophy: disillusionment with empirical science and, 13–14; Lamarckian evolution and, 80; Lugones involvement with, 101–2; Nervo involvement with, 117; in Nervo's *Soul-Giver*, 165, 168; speculative fiction and, 248n11
third-world discourse, 30, 231n3, 233n8
In the Thirtieth Century (Ezcurra), **46–53**; overview, 42–43; narrative framing in, 47–49, 238n26, 239n35; nationalistic themes in, 46–47, 50–53, 238n25; political and social context, 46–47, 49–50; racial categories in, 51, 238n29
time-travel themes: in Brazilian sf, 242n5; *Century XXX* as roadmap to utopia, 58, 239n35; date span effect on political content, 59–60; as device of history, 32–33; double temporal perspective, 17, 20–21; evolution theory and, 80–81; historical witnessing in Lugones, 104–5; Northern influences on, 17–18; spiralform pattern in "The Last War," 123; temporal framing in *Century XXX*, 47–49, 238n26; time-space correlation, 81–82, 87–90, *89*, 241n2; time-travel in *Brazil 2000*, 26–29, 31, 37–38, 133, 238n26; time-travel in *São Paulo 2000*, 56–57, 59–60, 66. *See also*

time-travel themes (*continued*) spatial/geographic travel themes; transportation technology

Todorov, Tzvetan, 10, 130

transportation technology: "aerostatic packet" transportation, 31; as evolutionary outcome in Zaluar, 91; futuristic transportation in *Eugenia*, 75; heavier-than-air flight, 57–58, 239n33; as national symbol, 19–20; Nervo on future transportation, 118–19; "social automobile" image in Barnsley, 65–66; social class and, 24; Spiritism and, 30. *See also* spatial/geographic travel themes; time-travel themes; *particular modes of transportation*

Trujillo Muñoz, Gabriel, 20, 219–20, 232n6

Twain, Mark, 81–82

Two Factions Struggle for Life: A Scientific Fantasy (Holmberg), **92–99**; creationism vs. evolutionism debate in, 96–99, 243n10; Darwinian evolution in, 36, 95, 130, 138, 243n14; fantastic elements in, 130–33; "Horacio Kalibang" compared with, 175; nationalistic themes in, 235n7, 243n12; as naturalist travel narrative, 83, 96–99, 243nn13–14; plot structure of, 96, 243n13; representation of public figures in, 96, 243n11, 243n15; triumph of rationality in, 138

"última diosa, La" (Nervo). *See* "Last Goddess, The"; "Last War, The"

ultraviolet rays, 210

uncontrollable powers theme, 139–43

United States: Barnsley and, 53–54, 64–65; criticism of slavery in, 241n47; Edison as scientific symbol, 252n8; engineering/applied science association with, 172, 215, 221; eugenics movement in, 45–46; evolution theory in, 80; film industry, 172, 212–13, 215; Latin American literary genres in, 9; as model of democracy, 28, 31, 119; as model of republican nationalism in *Brazil 2000*, 28–29; as modernist ideal, 87; non-canonical science in, 135–36, 248n7; popularization of sf and, 174; space-time relationship in, 81–82, 88; Spanish American War, 246n39. *See also* North, the

Uriarte, José María, 236n16

Urzaiz, Eduardo: biographical sketch, 42–43, 68, 239n39; utopian beliefs of, 69; utopian genetic theories of, 70–79, 240–41nn41–43. *See also Eugenia*

Urzaiz Jiménez, Carlos, 67–68

utopian/dystopian themes: Anglo-Saxon first-world utopias, 255n3; anti-utopian technophobia, 81; apocalyptic utopias, 110; Brazilian future in *Brazil 2000*, 26; date span in time-travel and, 59–60; descent-into-dystopia theme, 66–67, 78–79, 175–76, 232n6; international wars in *Eugenia*, 69–70, 76, *77*; Lamarckian logic in, 237n21; Martian utopia in *Nic-Nac*, 37–41, 175, 235n7; Northern influences on, 17–18; political issues and, 16–17, 19, 220–21; retrolabeling of works with, 237n19; social revolution in "The Last War," 119–21; utopia/

dystopia sibling relationship, 239n30; utopian childbearing in *Eugenia*, 70–79; utopian colony in *Doctor Benignus*, 242n5; utopian communalism in *Eugenia*, 69, 72–74; works associated with, 16, 234n2. *See also* social change

Valdés, Antonio José, 234n2
"Vampire, The" (Quiroga, 1927), **211–16**; classic vampire characteristics and, 254n22; human double theme and, 172–73; literary and technical innovations, 254n23; "Portrait" as precursor, 212, 215, 254n19; publication of, 209–10, 254n18; Sarlo on, 254n23; Villiers influence on, 250n27
vampires, 254n22
Vasconcelos, José, 45
Verne, Jules: in Barnsley, 55; Felício dos Santos compared with, 26; Holmberg and, 37, 95, 176, 233n11, 237n18; influence on Latin American sf, 1, 15–16, 17, 43, 83, 220; Nervo fondness for, 118; optographic technology in, 254n20; in Zaluar, 84–85. Works: *From the Earth to the Moon*, 85; *Journey to the Centre of the Earth*, 246n38
"viaje celeste, Un". *See* "Celestial Journey, A"
Viaje maravilloso del Señor Nic-Nac al planeta Marte (Holmberg). *See Marvelous Journey of Mr. Nic-Nac to the Planet Mars, The*
Villiers de l'Isle-Adam, Auguste, comte de, 166, 250n27, 252n8, 254n20
"Viola Acherontia" (Lugones), 139, **142**, 249n16

Vitalism, 117
Voltaire, 32, 49, 118

Wagar, W. Warren, 119, 123
Wallace, Alfred Russel, 84, 247n5
war themes: end-of-wars in *Eugenia*, 76; man-made vs. natural catastrophes and, 109; social revolution in "The Last War," 119–21; World War I as backdrop for "How the War Ended in 1917," 124–25
weapons (science fiction), 140
Wells, H. G.: influence on Latin American sf, 1, 43, 220; influence on Nervo, 118; nebular hypothesis, 39; political agendas in, 220; time-travel in, 30. Works: *The First Men in the Moon*, 118; *The Island of Dr. Moreau*, 68; *The Time Machine*, 30; *The War of the Worlds*, 118; *When the Sleeper Wakes*, 57
Westfahl, Gary, 10
Wilberforce, Samuel, 243n10
Wilkins, John, 118
women: Barnsley prescriptions for Brazilian women, 60–61, *62*; fantastic literature as feminine, 251n30; feminist subtext in *Frankenstein*, 255n1; Gorriti as feminist, 147–48; human doubles and, 173; nationalistic femininity in *Century XXX*, 52–53; sf depiction of women, 22; as sf writers, 249n18; Urzaiz women's rights advocacy, 240n43; women as reproducers in *Eugenia*, 70–74, *71*
Woodruff, Gregory, 244n23, 245n29
"Word on Science, A" (Castera), 156

303

X-rays, 140, 210, 254n21

Yeomans, Donald, 111
"Yerbas y alfileres" (Gorriti). *See* "Herbs and Pins"
"Yzur" (Lugones), 13, **105–9**, 245nn27–30, 253n15

Zaluar, Augusto Emílio: biographical sketch, 84; naturalist travel narratives of, 83, 250n25; political views, 84, 242n4. Works: *Peregrination through the Province of São Paulo*, 83. See also *Doctor Benignus*
Zola, Émile, 186

**THE WESLEYAN
EARLY CLASSICS OF
SCIENCE FICTION
SERIES**

General Editor ARTHUR B. EVANS

The Centenarian
    Honoré de Balzac
*Cosmos Latinos: An Anthology of Science
    Fiction from Latin America and Spain*
    Andrea L. Bell and Yolanda Molina-
    Gavilán, eds.
Imagining Mars: A Literary History
    Robert Crossley
*Caesar's Column:
    A Story of the Twentieth Century*
    Ignatius Donnelly
*Subterranean Worlds:
    A Critical Anthology*
    Peter Fitting, ed.
Lumen
    Camille Flammarion
The Last Man
    Jean-Baptiste Cousin de Grainville
The Battle of the Sexes in Science Fiction
    Justine Larbalestier
*The Yellow Wave: A Romance of the
    Asiatic Invasion of Australia*
    Kenneth Mackay
The Moon Pool
    A. Merritt

*The Black Mirror and Other Stories:
    An Anthology of Science Fiction
    from Germany and Austria*
    Mike Mitchell, tr., and Franz
    Rottensteiner, ed.
*Colonialism and the
    Emergence of Science Fiction*
    John Rieder
The Twentieth Century
    Albert Robida
*Three Science Fiction Novellas: From
    Prehistory to the End of Mankind*
    J.-H. Rosny aîné
*The Fire in the Stone:
    Prehistoric Fiction from
    Charles Darwin to Jean M. Auel*
    Nicholas Ruddick
The World as It Shall Be
    Emile Souvestre
Star Maker
    Olaf Stapledon
The Begum's Millions
    Jules Verne
Invasion of the Sea
    Jules Verne
The Kip Brothers
    Jules Verne
The Mighty Orinoco
    Jules Verne
The Mysterious Island
    Jules Verne
H. G. Wells: Traversing Time
    W. Warren Wagar
Star Begotten
    H. G. Wells
Deluge
    Sydney Fowler Wright

ABOUT THE AUTHOR

Rachel Haywood Ferreira is an associate professor of Spanish and Portuguese at Iowa State University. Her articles on early and golden age Latin American science fiction have appeared in *Science Fiction Studies*, *Journal of the Fantastic in the Arts*, *Hispania*, and *Extrapolation*.